Anr L.T. P.F.

Two Complete Con
By Bestselling Auth
In One Spe

"Heather Graham writes shining love stories that entrance readers with their hypnotic power!"
—*Romantic Times*

A SEASON FOR LOVE

Ronnie tilted her head back, her eyes shining. Her fingers caressed the rich thickness of Drake's black hair, touching it with devouring reverence. His eyes began to smolder once more as they bored into hers, still carrying that infinite tenderness. His lips touched hers softly. These things she savored sweetly for a cherishable moment, her mouth pliant, her lips moistly parted. Then a brushfire began—a longing, a yearning, a needing of such intensity, it stole her breath away. It took her from the confines of the cabin to a haven where sight, sound, and reality were all lost in abandon to one overwhelming sensation—*him*.

QUIET WALKS THE TIGER

Wes's voice was low, his tone silky. "I must say, darling, that when you sell out, you do go all the way with gusto."

"What?" she whispered incredulously.

"The act is charming, Sloan, but not good. It's time for a little honesty."

Lord, she wondered desperately, what *had* happened? He couldn't have any suspicions regarding her original motives for marriage. "Really, darling, you should have warned me that you wake up like a growling bear!"

"Should I have?" he inquired politely, sauntering slowly toward her. Her instinct was to run, but she stubbornly believed that nothing was wrong. Willpower alone kept her still, presenting a facade of guileless calm.

Other *Love Spell* books by Heather Graham:
TENDER TAMING/WHEN NEXT WE LOVE

HEATHER GRAHAM

A SEASON FOR LOVE <u>AND</u> QUIET WALKS THE TIGER

LOVE SPELL ✦ NEW YORK CITY

For Dennis

LOVE SPELL®

June 1994

Published by

Dorchester Publishing Co., Inc.
276 Fifth Avenue
New York, NY 10001

A SEASON FOR LOVE

PROLOGUE

Tears filled her eyes as she left the house.

She had contained and concealed them through the preceding argument, but now, as she faced the wind, she could allow them to form.

Now that she was alone.

Which was funny really, because she was always alone.

Always calm, always staid, always perfect . . .

Always alone, even among others, even with the man for whom she shed her tears. They spoke, but they never talked. Circumstances barred intimacy, bitterness barred friendship. All she received was harshness.

But she understood, and it was terrible to understand. It meant becoming the marble she lived with, never really showing emotion, choosing a course and following it, humoring him. . . .

She was humoring him now by leaving the house and taking to the sea, a vision of his limpid blue eyes in her mind. Eyes she understood, and fought against.

Standing on deck surrounded by people, her tears left her own sapphire gaze, and it became frosty, assessing. Completely confident, she entered the world she had no wish to join. Humoring. . . .

Suddenly, like the closing of one's eyes after a camera flash, a new vision replaced that of the pale blue eyes—a pair of eyes so darkly, vividly brown that they burned with a coal fire.

She blinked, realizing that she had just seen such a pair of eyes.

And to her dismay that quickly flashed image stayed with her, haunting her. She focused on pale, powdery blue, but the lighter color became continually obliterated by the darker hue.

Extraordinary, really.

And very, very foolish.

Because she would also leave the sea and return to the house.

CHAPTER ONE

Statuesque.

It was the only word to adequately describe the sleek beauty of the tall brunette. Although a multitude of attractive young women frolicked around the poolside, displaying varying amounts of curvaceous flesh, she alone had the power to rivet the eye. She wasn't as voluptuous as some, nor was the teal-blue bikini she wore as bare as many others.

What attracted the eye went further than the perfectly proportioned build and smooth, golden-tanned skin. It was in the grace of her slightest movement, in the fluidity of her composed walk, in the very poise and serenity with which she surveyed the scene she had come upon.

She was as stunning and lithe as a panther, mused one of the men who watched her, and the thought struck him that, like the discreetly moving panther, she was seeking prey with slow, confident deliberation.

He almost laughed aloud at his own thought. With the flick of a finger, this one could draw the male of the species to her without ever needing to seek anything. He could easily imagine half the men around him swarming to her feet on their knees, as if she were a queen bee.

He sat back comfortably in the lounge chair, unaware that he was her male counterpart, and that the majority of the females taking the three-day cruise—from the giggling teenagers to the graying, plump matrons—had already created romantic fantasies in their minds with him in the starring role.

Drake O'Hara was the perfect picture of man at his very best. Black Irish, they would have called him in the land of his forebears, and like the Spaniards of the lost Armada who had been wrecked upon the Emerald Isle, he was dark, his hair a shade deeper than india ink, his eyes a deep, arresting brown. His complexion tanned easily to a golden copper, and when he smiled—an act that could be charming or chilling, depending on his motive—his straight white teeth were almost startling against the backdrop of his skin and the neat black mustache that framed lips that could either be full and sensuous or grim and tight. He had inherited his coloring from the Spaniards, his fiery temper from the Irish. Fortunately, he was also capable of learned control and diplomacy, traits he liked to think he inherited from his American mother.

Drake was giving no thoughts to his own ancestry at the moment. Beneath the shadow of misty glasses, his dark eyes were fixed contemplatively on the brunette. Her poise, he decided, was helped along by her bone structure. Her face was an exquisite oval, the cheekbones high, the hollows classic, the eyes—set beneath slender arched brows—large, thick-lashed, and almost shockingly blue. Her classic nose fit her classic face—small and aquiline. Only her lips offset the marble coolness of her untouchable beauty; they were too full for severity, too sensuously shaped for innocence.

Yet the chin beneath them was determined, and on second speculation, those magnificent blue eyes were hard crystal gems. Hmmm . . . hard, but something else. If she didn't seem such a bastion of icy reserve, Drake mused, he would think of that something else as—tragic.

It was with a bit of surprise that Drake realized she was returning his assessing surveillance. Well aware that she knew he watched her, he made no attempt to avert his eyes. Nor did she. He knew too that she studied him with the same thoroughness to which he had subjected her.

What he didn't know was that she watched him with a wrenching pain. Long ago, in a different lifetime, she had loved

12

a man as magnificent as he. A man of indomitable strength, of pride and arrogance that were uniquely gifts of birth. Broad in the shoulders and chest, ruggedly trim in the hips and legs; tightly sinewed, muscle-coiled rather than muscle-bound . . .

Long, long, ago, so agonizingly long ago, such a man had been hers by right. Now nothing could be right again.

But she knew the message in his eyes, and although the inadvertent action was imperceptible, she swallowed convulsively. Far from seeking prey as he had whimsically envisioned, she was staunchly set on not becoming prey. She didn't want to form any associations, not even the most innocently casual ones. She didn't even want to be on this three-day cruise. For the briefest second she blinked, and caught the mist of tears that threatened to obscure her vision.

If only . . .

God, she wondered fleetingly, why had she seen him? Her resolve had been fixed, her soul could bear no more scars.

But she had seen him, and he was touching her, with his eyes only, as no other man had or could, no, not even Jamie, all those years before. . . .

He lifted a hand to remove his sunglasses. Dimly she noted that hand, shivering within. It was long and broad, and flecked with a smattering of crisp black curls. His fingers were long, the nails short and clipped neatly. She could almost feel the rugged touch of his hands, and a moment of dizziness and fear overwhelmed her. Fear of him, fear of herself. She so desperately longed to just talk to him that she was beginning to rationalize, her mind and senses in a devastating tug of war. She couldn't, she couldn't. . . . But, dear God, why not? She would never see him again . . . this was a ship, and it would dock, and the passengers would go their separate ways. She closed her eyes tightly for the flicker of an instant, waging a fierce battle with the conscience that ruled her. Talk, perhaps share a drink. Was it so very wrong of her, just this once, to envision the simple pleasure of a man's conversation . . . his masculine touch?

13

Oh, God. . . .

She couldn't help herself thinking. Her poise, her manner, her appearance . . . all these she could control. But dreams swept heedlessly into her mind, there was no blocking them. They could tear down the defenses of the strongest willpower.

His black eyes were piercingly upon her as he rose from the lounge chair. She was tall, but she could see immediately that he would tower above her. His legs—adorned with the same masculine curls as his hands and chest—were very long. Added to the impressive length of his tapered torso, they made him very tall indeed, imposingly tall. . . .

He watched her as he walked, his strides long, assured—natural. The easy walk of a confident man. It was not her he approached, but the crystal water that separated them.

He would never need to impose himself; his invitation was out. Acceptance was up to her.

He plunged into the ship's small saltwater pool in a manner she should have anticipated—a perfect, clear-cut dive.

This was it. The messages they had been sending through eye contact were now being tested. He had taken the first move—a relief to her. But now she had to take the second.

Now or never.

Not a muscle in her face twitched. Intense immersion into the drama of life had given her the composure that went far beyond her years.

But inside, it seemed as if her very blood froze. Yearning tinged by guilt waged a war with fear.

And the guilt was ridiculous. She was trying to fulfill a dying man's plea.

But still it was there, because of the yearning. Because she wanted to feel again . . . because she wanted so desperately to know happiness, if only for stolen moments, if only superficially.

The seconds were ticking by. . . .

Drake emerged at the shallow end of the small pool just in time to see her exquisitely sculpted, alabaster-sleek body cut into the water as cleanly as his had. And again he was reminded of

14

the sultry beauty of a feline. But, he wondered, in a quick flight of Gaelic fancy, what was the nature of this cat he counter-stalked. Was she a tigress with claws, or a domesticated, purring Persian?

It didn't really matter. She had completely intrigued him. He had always been fond of and had a way with the fairer sex; he knew their games and played them confidently by the rules. A certain gallantry stayed with him from a bygone age—he only played with those who also knew the rules.

What was her game, he wondered idly. Did she want to be wined and dined and danced? Flattered and cajoled?

There was of course the possibility that she knew who he was and that money or prestige had been the draw. He was self-confident, assured, and, admittedly, arrogant at times, but he had never deluded himself that he had always been sought for his charm alone. Many a fair damsel who had come his way had actually worn the tarnished glitter of gold in her eye . . . and a hope that a band of the same color upon her finger would be the reward.

Drake wasn't really a cynic—he was realistic. Nor did motives bother him, as long as they were honest. He was never anything but honest himself, and it would surprise him very much to know that those who filtered through his sometimes aloof existence respected that honesty and also found that it brought a boundless compassion. He liked life; he lived it vigorously and straightforwardly. When aroused, he was a formidable enemy. When dealt with on a level of his own integrity, he was capable of great chivalry, kindness, and generosity.

Her head bobbed up in the water near his, and he smiled with a lazy charisma. With that lustrous mane of shoulder-length chestnut hair wet and slicked back from her face, one thing was obvious: she had no interest in his finances. Her ears were studded with small but flawless emeralds, and as she rose in the waist-high water, he saw that a slender link gold chain held a matching emerald oval in the deep shadowed cleavage of her breasts.

15

Why she was seeking him, he couldn't imagine. But it would have taken a far more monastic man than he to question such good fortune.

Their eyes met, and for a moment he again sensed that hint of tragedy. But her stare was direct. She wasn't playing cat and mouse.

"Hello," he said, his appreciation unabashed as he watched her at this closer angle. She was perfection. Her skin was lightly golden, as smooth as silk, from the enticing angles of her collarbone to the line of slightly visible ribs to the curve of her hips and tight, concave structure of her waist, navel, and upper abdomen. Someone, he thought idly, some great artist, should paint her image in oil one day, or preserve it forever in the marble she resembled.

"Hello," she returned, and the voice fit the woman. It was low, husky, and melodious, carrying just a hint of well-bred southern culture. Her single word was not aggressive, nor was it coy. That direct stare of hers had not once wavered, and yet he could sense a certain nervousness; he could see it now in the fine pulsation of a light blue vein in the swanlike structure of her neck.

Without his really realizing it, or exactly knowing why, Drake's smile became very gentle, his emotions turned to protection. "My name is Drake O'Hara," he told her, offering her a hand while longing to bring it around her shoulders and cradle her to him with a combination of overwhelming lust and tender care. Strange, that she could affect him so intensely.

She took his hand in her graceful, slender one. "I'm Ronnie."

She didn't offer a last name, and he didn't demand one. His grin broadened. "I think I say I'd like to buy you a drink now."

"I'd like that," she said. A bewitching impishness suddenly replaced that tragic look in her beautiful eyes. "Then I can say I'd like to buy you one."

"I'd like that," he told her huskily, shaken by the violence of the savage desire that ripped through him. He'd barely touched the woman. "I'll hop out and buy my round poolside," he added.

Ronnie couldn't quite manage to look into his face, but she

16

wanted her position clear from the beginning. They could share drinks; he could purchase a round, she could purchase a round. No debts, no commitment. "That's fine," she said softly. "I'll also buy mine poolside."

"Will you?"

His well-modulated voice had fallen a notch, and a chilling quiver of apprehension rippled through Ronnie, seeming to come from the coolness of the water. His two-word question had been a curious musing. He wanted to get to know her.

She couldn't get to know him; it was bad enough that she was coveting this experience so far . . . losing herself in the sight of him, in the sound of his voice. . . .

"I think I'd like you to buy me a drink before dinner." He raised a hand in amused proclamation of honor as she started to speak. "Just dinner," he said sincerely. "Will you?"

Dinner. Just dinner. "Yes," she said, her voice still soft but firm, with no guile. Her blue eyes raised from the water to meet his, yet they seemed an extension of the water they had left. They were like dazzling prisms, as myriad and brilliant as a star-studded night. It was hard to tell if they were as icy as a blizzard, or as warm and torrid as the blazing sun that crested high over the Atlantic.

Drake's eyes flicked only briefly. He had known from the moment he saw her that she was a cool woman of determined purpose. Still, the cloak she wore was an enigma, as mysterious as her stately beauty.

"What shall I bring you to drink?" he asked, his voice carrying that husky timbre he couldn't quite control.

It wasn't the type of question to cause confusion in such an independent lady, but it did. She frowned. "Oh, ah, I don't know. . . ."

"Piña coladas," he decided quickly, again surprised by the surge of protection that assailed him.

She visibly relaxed, making him realize just how overwrought she had been.

"A piña colada sounds lovely," she told him.

17

Drake wasn't fond of the rum and coconut drink himself, but to keep her company, he ordered two. It was, after all, a cruise.

The four-hundred-passenger cruise ship left Charleston Harbor Friday afternoon and would return to its berth early the following Monday morning. Three days of relaxation, with the majority of passengers being businessmen or professionals with little time to spare from hectic schedules. Drake had taken the time himself simply to unwind. He had imagined nothing more than a few hours of sun, fine food when the mood took him, and three peaceful nights rest upon the lull of the Atlantic. He hadn't come for companionship, but rather to avoid it.

And now this. But he was already thoroughly enchanted; he could have refused her no more than he could have asked the sun not to shine. They had spoken so little, but he was dimly aware that her soft, husky, southern-cultured voice would later seep into his dreams.

"A piña colada," he said, sitting poolside, his long, tanned legs dangling in the water. She smiled lightly at his return and hopped lithely from the water to join him. Her arm brushed his as she sat alongside him, their naked thighs touching. The contact was jolting, almost shattering, as if a jagged bolt of lightning had struck from a clear sky to sear through them both.

Ronnie inhaled a sharp breath, meeting Drake's dark gaze, perpetuating no pretense at the intensity of the purely physical pleasure she was experiencing. That which had been hidden away so long it had almost been forgotten, rose to the surface with a crippling poignancy. Just to be beside this man was excitement enough to send waves of heat washing through her—a heat that felt so damn good. She was, after all, a mature woman, so long denied. And even though the reason for her denial was a part of her heart, she couldn't fight this intrinsic beauty that had been granted her.

"Thank you," she said, taking the drink he offered her, once more aware of the beauty of the power of masculine hands. "To the cruise," she offered, tipping her glass to his.

"To the cruise," he repeated solemnly, his black eyes smoldering into pits of raven coal. A saint would be shaking on a pedestal with her so near. "And to you, Ronnie."

"Thank you," she murmured again, and he thought he perceived a soft blush. "Drake . . ." she said, in afterthought, seeming to twirl his name on her tongue as if she savored it. Averting her eyes for a moment, she took a sip of her drink. "Where are you from, Drake?" she queried.

He could have sworn she was somewhat anxious, which was peculiar, because conversation didn't really seem to interest her.

"The Midwest," he replied, sure that his answer pleased her. "Chicago. How about you?"

She smiled again, and this time the curl of her lips lit a true warmth into her eyes. "That's obvious, isn't it?" Her chuckle was as low and melodious as her voice.

"Yes, it is," he answered, his grin deepening to disclose a cleft in his chin she'd yet to discover. "But from where in the South?"

"Oh, ah—Georgia."

She was lying, but why? At this point he had no desire to challenge her. Sitting together, talking, was taking away the initial edge. She had tensed when she lied—a dead giveaway. But other than that, she had begun to truly relax in his presence, as if she had made a decision to trust him completely. Despite her cool sophistication, that trust drew out all his male instincts. Somewhere on a level beneath conscious thought, it was registering with him that she was all he had ever wanted in a woman. Assured yet reserved, aloof yet incredibly warm. He had the feeling that he had touched upon the tip of an iceberg—and that a wealth awaited him beneath the surface. That wealth would be a host of wonders—intelligence, loyalty, and wit to match her rare beauty and poise.

When she spoke, the mystical blue of her eyes was enchantment; when she laughed, it became a shimmering pool of the deepest enticement.

And yet she held that reserve, so he agreeably tread slowly. She shied from personal conversation; they discussed the world and society at large. Time, space, land. He wanted her more than he had ever wanted a woman, but he had never wanted more to woo a woman, to cajole and to please, to care for and to protect.

That evening it was dinner. Just dinner. When he left her at the door to her cabin, he barely brushed her lips.

His rewards were great—breakfast, lunch, and dinner, and delightful times in between, the next day. She hesitated each time she gave him a yes, as if she struggled inwardly. But he asked nothing of her. He was willing to wait for her, for whatever time she needed. He was planning on a long-range assault, and the stakes he slowly realized he was seeking were infinitely high.

Another night passed with his softly brushing her lips at her cabin door; a night that ended a day in which they had both veered from personal queries.

Talk and questions that delved could come later. They simply savored one another's company.

On Sunday afternoon they sat together by the pool again, uniquely comfortable in a companionable silence.

Ronnie's eyes were only half open as she regarded the water, dazzling as it rippled beneath the sun. She was being foolish, and she knew it. But she hadn't been able to refuse Drake, because she didn't want to. She closed her eyes tightly for a minute, against pain, against remorse, against guilt. It might be wrong to want to feel, to cherish this being alive and young and vibrant near this extraordinary man, but in the end, what difference did it make? She would never see him again; who could she hurt but herself?

And how much worse could she possibly hurt?

For years now she had learned to tolerate pain, withdrawing from it into an inner shell. She had learned to be strong; she had learned to turn her cheek. She had done it, because underneath it all she knew she was desperately needed . . . and despite all, still loved. And though her love had changed as the love given to her had, it was still there, along with the memories she could not betray.

This wasn't betrayal, her heart suddenly raged with a surge of rebellion that brought tears to her eyes. She deserved this little happiness she had found. Everyone needed something . . . or else they cracked. And she couldn't crack. No matter what, she couldn't crack. . . .

She was the wall that was leaned upon.

Except now, with Drake. It still made her slightly nervous to have his undivided masculine attention after having been denied such attention for so long. He held her arm, he took her hand, he guided. It was wonderful. It would be so easy to become accustomed to having his strength . . . to his taking any weight from her own shoulders. . . .

"What's wrong?" he suddenly asked, his perceptive dark gaze upon her with instant concern.

She blinked, marveling at how quickly he could read her slightest change of mood. She couldn't allow him to read her so well.

"The sun," she told him with a quick smile. "I left my glasses below."

He insisted they go and get them. She laughed and said she would go herself, but he was determined to accompany her, and he was a very difficult man to dissuade. Impossible, actually, to dissuade.

He followed her into her cabin, and she made a hasty show of searching for her sunglasses.

But suddenly she froze as she delved through a dresser. She could feel his eyes; she could feel his heat. He made no movement, he didn't touch her, but the very air of the cabin seemed charged with an electrical current that was naturally sensual, irrefutably real.

God, how she wanted him, needed him.

It was wrong. . . . It was a dream, yet she so desperately needed that dream.

She straightened, dropping all pretense. Their eyes met. And then, with no further thought, she shortened the space between them and flew into his arms.

They engulfed her, with love, with need, with security, with tenderness.

"Oh, Ronnie," he groaned hoarsely from his chest, "what do you want?"

"I want you to make love to me," she told him honestly, tilting her chin up at him with pride.

She was blatantly honest, beautifully honest, and as her gaze remained amazingly steady there was a tremulous hint of yearning in her tone. A sweet, sweet poignancy.

"Lady," he murmured, his whisper brushing over the top of her hair, "you have got me."

With standing impudence and warmth, her arms clung tighter, relishing in the feel of taut bronze muscles. They constricted and rippled at her touch, drawing a barely perceptible groan from him. Abashed at her brazen impetuousness, Ronnie slipped away for a moment, shaking her wet head in an effort to cover the crimson coloring that was sneaking up her cheeks. What must he think? That she was starved?

She was.

But though her honesty didn't bother her—she could never have played the scene with hypocritical coyness—the urgency that was building within her did. They had the rest of the day, the night. That was it—the dream would be over. It shouldn't matter what he thought of her, but it did.

"Ronnie."

His voice rang with a gentle command, and as she turned back to him, she saw that there was a tenderness in his coal-dark eyes. "You're wonderful," he told her gravely, his look emphasizing his sincerity. "Like a beautiful breath of fresh air. Please don't be ashamed. Not with me. I love it that you want me . . . that you come to me."

He extended his arms to her, and she rushed back to them, choking a sob as she buried her head into the crisp black hair of his chest, finding that sense of comfort in his powerful hold that she craved emotionally as her body craved his physically.

No, she would deny herself nothing today. She would take until she was satiated; she would give for all that she was worth. And then keep giving.

22

She tilted her head back with all this in the iridescence of her eyes. She brought her fingers to lock into the rich thickness of his black hair, touching it with devouring reverence. His eyes began to smolder once more as they bored into hers, still carrying that infinite tenderness. His lips touched upon hers softly, the touch of his mustache tickling delightfully. These things she savored sweetly for a cherishable moment, her own mouth pliant, her lips moistly parted. Then a brushfire began, a longing, a yearning, a needing, of such intensity that it stole her breath away. It took her from the confines of the cabin to a haven where sight, sound, and reality were all lost in abandon to one overwhelming sensation—him.

Drake too had obliterated all conscious thought that didn't have to do with the splendor in his arms. He had meant to be nothing but completely gentle, but the thirst of her response to his first soft touch inflamed his blood to boiling in heedless seconds. Her body molded to his as he kissed her, his tongue probing, plundering, and then ravishing. Never had he come across a woman of a more beautiful, natural sensuality. The satin of her skin was alive and warm, vibrant against him. Her breasts were pressed to his chest firmly, only the scanty bikini top separating the flesh that demanded to touch flesh. He fumbled for the tie as they locked together in that first devastating kiss. Slipping the offensive material away, he allowed it to fall haphazardly to the floor. A groan rumbled from deep within his throat as he felt her hardened nipples now press into his chest with exotic demand. His hands had to experience the pleasure. Fingers that had developed an extra sensitivity crept between the melded bodies to fondle and caress, circling, grazing, finding a firm fullness that swelled beneath his mastery.

He broke the kiss because he had to see her. He had to stare into the beautiful blue eyes that were dilated with passion, had to watch the rapid rise and fall of those perfect proud breasts, had to view with insatiable hunger the exoticism of still hardening, rose-tipped nipples beneath the play of his callused, foraging thumbs.

23

Funny that he had ever thought of her as marble. Marble was cool, cold to the touch. There was nothing cold about her. She was alive with titillating warmth, vibrant, vital, beautiful, breathing flesh and blood. . . .

"Exquisite," he gasped aloud, bringing forth from her a radiating sigh of sweet gratitude that was the most potent intoxication he could imagine. He lifted her into his arms, aware that his desire was raging out of control, but also aware that she needed that savage demand from him. And there was nothing that could ignite a man more than the sure knowledge that *he was* wanted as badly as he wanted. . . .

Although his body decried him, he had to pause as he slipped the bikini briefs from her undulating hips. Again, he had to see her. Against the starched white of the sheets, she was a golden goddess. Her waist, as he had known, was minuscule, her hips flared in a perfect curve, her breasts magnificent mounds of divinity. Her legs were uncanny, long, slender, majestically shapely. . . . His assessment was a slow, self-induced torture, but he couldn't tear his eyes away, not even with the anticipation of touching her again, of taking her as his own completely.

"Drake!" She called his name imploringly, arms outstretched, to break his hypnotic state. And she watched him with awe as he cast aside his own swim trunks to lower himself beside her.

She touched him without hesitancy, free of inhibition, weaving a spell upon him that would never be broken. He had never known a woman to offer so much, to elicit, to respond with such sweetly delicious abandon and unwavering passion. Their hands simultaneously explored what their eyes had discovered, and warmth was soon the blue-gold fire of a blazing inferno.

The forces that catapulted them into the spiraling whirlpool of heedless desire were brought to a primeval level. Man and woman, locked together in the oldest, most beautiful gift of the gods. And as in those times of old, it was man who had to conquer. Conquer with giving and taking the ultimate surrender.

Drake couldn't have recognized the feeling at the time, but his protective attitude had been joined by possessiveness. She had

24

become his, and as if she could be in truth a prize sent from heaven for him alone, he sought to know her completely before establishing the claim that was bursting within him. His kisses, soft and explorative, greedy and demanding, rained down upon her. They circled her breasts, tasting the sweet nectar of chlorine mingled with that of her sweet self; they grazed over her hips, savoring the undulation, and over tender thighs that quivered in delight.

Ronnie thought she would soon go mad from the ecstasy he had created. He was so beautifully, magnificently male. So strong, so powerful, so overwhelming. She had forgotten these wonderful sensations that now engulfed her like the waves of the ocean. Her fingers dug into the breadth of his back, marveling at the shudders that convulsed his shoulders, heedlessly basking in their masterful command. She allowed herself the irresistible wonder of falling into the awesome spell of his compelling domination, almost fainting with sheer glory when he finally took her to himself as one.

But she was relentlessly taken from the moment of near oblivion, caught in a rhythm of stroking satin that demanded reciprocation. Cries tore from her throat as her body responded of its own volition, arching to his, writhing madly. His hands held her hips, guiding them to his will—held her still when they reached a simultaneous, ardent shattering, and she again seemed to lose consciousness for a few seconds, unable to assimilate completely the quivering wonder and beauty of their coming together in pure, delicious ecstasy.

Drake couldn't leave her, couldn't break the physical tie that bound them. Knowing that his weight crushed her, he still covered her body, his hands raking her hair as he whispered feverishly of how he adored her. His thumbs traced the exquisite sculpture of her face until he found the moistness of tears, and then, only then, did he finally pull away to look at her with tender curiosity, his heart wrenched apart.

"My God, Ronnie," he murmured heatedly, "have I hurt you?"

"Oh, no!" she cried vehemently, encircling him with slender arms and drawing their bodies back together. "You are the most wonderful thing I have ever known. Please, keep holding me. . . ." She smiled through that mist of tears, and he obligingly held her, comforting her now with security, smoothing back her tousled hair, soothing her with fingers that lightly stroked the contours of her back.

"I think I'm in love," he mused gently, aloud, amazed at the emotions she could create in his bewildered heart and mind.

She stiffened in his arms for a moment and relaxed. "Is that possible?" she asked softly. "If it is, then I too am in a kind of love." Abruptly she pulled from him, only to set herself above him on his chest, her huge blue eyes looking beseechingly into his. "May I have the night, Drake? Will you be mine until the sun rises in the morning?" Her tone was wistful and almost whimsical.

"I think I may be yours for eternity," he told her, bewitched by her loveliness and the honest poignancy of her sad plea.

Ronnie buried her face into the black mat of his chest, inhaling his scent deeply to ingrain it forever in her memory. The hair tickled her skin, and she rubbed her cheek against it. The moment was a dream, pure illusion, but she couldn't stop herself from cherishing that dream, from perpetuating it.

"Will you be strong and tender and gentle forever?" she inquired impishly, leaning to kiss his lips and delightedly feel the tingle of his mustache.

"I can't promise gentle forever," he told her gravely in return. "There is something about you that makes me feel very fierce. But whatever strength and tenderness I have are yours."

Ronnie smiled again and sighed contentedly, nestling back into his chest. Tomorrow would bring despair, but she would welcome that despair to have this day . . . and this night to sleep beside this man. It was much more than she had bargained for, much more than she could have possibly imagined. And she would let nothing break this spell of enchantment. Not the torture of ifs, not the tremor of conscience.

They spent hours in her cabin, sometimes quietly lying beside one another, sometimes making love. They were slow and teasing and gentle, they were insatiably wild. And inevitably they talked, and in her dream world Ronnie answered questions without really answering. He knew a lot about her, but he really knew nothing. And it wasn't important. Facts could come later. He knew the things a lover should know—her smile, her touch, her mind, her heart.

They left the cabin as evening fell, hunger driving them to an intimate dinner with neither aware of other passengers around them. Dressed impeccably, they were the envy of all eyes that alighted upon them, eyes that believed in the illusion. They were an incredibly handsome couple, he unerringly masculine, she the epitome of feminine beauty and sophistication.

They were regal, their devotion charming. To anyone, they appeared as honeymooners, lost in the star-swept skies of their love, and in the Atlantic night. In mutual silence they toured the deck of the ship, basking in the lulling romance of the ocean breezes that leant enchantment to the illusion, and then returned to Ronnie's cabin, to delight in the pleasure of removing impeccable clothing.

And to make love into the night.

Drake slept well, satiated as he had never been in his life. His first statement had been playful—he had never really been in love. But now he was convinced—with a definite shade of bemusement—that he was. And the feeling was wonderful. As he held her to him, he wondered for the first time in his life how it would be to sleep and to awaken with this exquisite creature at his side every day of his life. He had thought he could never endure such monotony—but with Ronnie there would never be monotony. Only increasing wonder and discovery; increasing commitment and devotion.

He had no doubts that they had only begun something beautiful. She was still a marble beauty, reserved and—statuesque— when she walked and talked and moved. But in his arms she was radiant, a warm and sensuous woman. Only for him; the type he

27

hadn't believed existed—a creature utterly lovely, utterly bright, and utterly worthy of trust. Cynicism that had bordered on the edge of any previous relationships had nothing to do with this one.

He actually wanted to marry her. Now. Not even having known her for more than the past three days. Not even having learned her last name. He didn't want to contemplate the idea of her ever being touched again by another man.

Drake O'Hara—playboy, cynic, hardened rogue of midwestern society—had fallen in love. It had come like a thunderbolt, but it was as sure as the moon in the night sky. And he did not deny the emotion, instead he reveled in it . . . mulling it over and over in his mind with awe.

That the beauty who had captured his heart with a single winning smile could be indulging in only a brief affair never occurred to him. She was too giving, too open, too willing. Too honestly passionate and caring.

And too often she had whispered and cried in the throes of passion that she too loved him. And so he slept well.

Ronnie didn't sleep through the night.

Not because she reflected on the misery of daybreak, but because she didn't want to lose one precious moment of having him beside her, of looking at him, of feeling the vibrancy of his rugged flesh touching hers. She memorized the planes of his face, with her eyes, with her fingers. She would never forget the depth of his dark-brown eyes; the twitch of his mustache when he half-smiled, and its grazing over her skin, sending shivers racing through her.

She had been starved; she was now sated. Still she would take more, even when that taking was lying awake through the night to absorb him—his scent, his feel, his breathing, his face in sleep. A tender smile lit her lips. Sound asleep, he was still imposing. The lines that were etched faintly around his eyes were relaxed, but he still looked formidable, as if his dark eyes could fly open at any minute and challenge with ferocity, as if his muscled length could spring instantly to action. She knew the strength of

28

those muscles, but to her they were nothing but powerfully gentle.

Inevitably, morning came. Still she watched him, and when he did open his eyes, she made no effort to hide her surveillance.

She wanted to have him love her one last time.

The message was in her eyes, and he did love her, taking her into his arms naturally without words. The words came later as he caressed her; they were endearments. Then they were groaned commands; groans from the exotic pleasure that she gave him, and then fervent whispers that were returned with breathless moans.

Waking up was all that he had dreamed it would be. And holding her close after their tumultuous sharing was nothing but sheer, ultimate wonder, and the intimacy of helping her shower and dress, nothing but the contentment of a lifetime.

They would breakfast, and then the ship would dock.

Over coffee and toast, it was time for the facts. But before he could begin to ask she gave him her steady gaze and placed her slender hand over his. "Thank you, Drake. Thank you for this piece of heaven," she told him in her soft, melodious voice.

"Thank you?" He chuckled low in inquiry. "Babe, thank you for being! But our piece of heaven is just beginning."

She frowned and lowered her murky lashes, but not before he sensed the tragedy again in the depths of her crystal-blue eyes. When she looked up again, all warmth was gone from them. He was staring into ice.

"This was just a cruise, Drake. It's over," she told him firmly.

"Over?" His demand was harsh and guttural. He could feel his infamous temper rising in an uncontrollable flash. What was her game? His hand came over hers to grasp it ruthlessly. "What are you talking about?"

Ronnie didn't flinch, nor did she allow her gaze to waver, although she felt as if her insides were melting beneath the burning fury of coal that bored into her. She had never thought she could be afraid of him, of anyone for that matter, and yet she was frightened. It occurred to her belatedly that she had trifled with a man one didn't trifle with. But she couldn't have wanted any other, she couldn't have had her night of magic. She couldn't have fallen in love.

And she was in love, but she knew the tangles and variants of love. She was in love, and in love with being in love. It was precious, to be locked away in her mind and heart to sustain her.

But love was also something else; something else that was mutable, but irrevocable nonetheless. It was—oddly enough—loyalty and devotion even when the stars had long ceased to shine. It was enduring. It was emotional stamina.

"It's over," she repeated numbly.

"No." Drake denied her roughly. "You gave yourself to me completely last night. And I want you. I have no intention of letting you go."

Ronnie's chuckle was brittle, dry, and very bitter. "I'm sorry. I can't be your permanent mistress."

His grip upon her intensified until she was sure her bones would crack. In a moment the dark flames of his eyes would combust into hot red flames, and she would be staring directly at the devil.

"Mistress, woman! Be damned. I want to marry you!"

Her eyes fell. She could no longer face him. When she spoke, it was tonelessly, as if she were very far away.

"I can't marry you, Drake."

For a moment he eased, sensing pain beneath the jagged-glass hardness of her eyes and voice. There was something in her past that had created the glacial reserve that she could hide behind. But he didn't care what it was. He wanted to protect her, to nurture her, to guide her into a world of comfort and happiness.

"I'm rushing you," he said smoothly, and when she glanced at him again, she felt her heart catch in her throat. He was so handsome and virile before her in his perfectly tailored tan suit, the sleek darkness of his hair and eyes and the healthy glow of his tanned ruddy skin emphasized by its cool lightness. The arch of his brows was high as his lips twitched the corners of his mustache in a half-smile. The cooling arrogance of his temper

30

was still discernible, but it was mellowed now to a sure command.

"Ronnie," he continued, rubbing a finger over the veins of her hand, "there are no can'ts, except that I can't let you go. You have to trust me, as you did when we met. I know you're fighting something, but I'll help you. I don't care about your past. I don't care about your present. I'll work mine into it. I don't believe that you don't care about me—as much as I care about you, no matter how ludicrous it is after only three days. I'll go as slow as you like. But you have to keep seeing me. I'll never convince you of my sincerity otherwise."

A torrent of sobs welled in her rib cage, threatening to spill forth. She had to build the wall, retreat, and then get away surely and quickly. The angle of his jawline was square and determined; nothing but the cold truth would keep him away, and she would have to risk his contempt whether it devastated her or not.

She withdrew her hand from his and picked up her coffee cup with cool dismissal. "Drake, I can't—repeat, can't—continue to see you. It's out of the question."

"Really?" An imperious brow arched even higher, and his lips tightened into a caustic line. "And why not? What happened to I love you and forever?"

I do love you, Ronnie whispered to herself sadly, *but you'd never understand, and even if you did, I could never explain.* . . .

She took a sip of coffee and set the cup down briskly. "Oh, come, Drake," she said, "surely a man such as yourself has had his share of flings! Love is just a word. So is forever."

"We didn't spend a day and night exchanging words," he told her sardonically, drawing the hint of a hoped-for blush. No one could make love as she had without feeling!

But his angel of the night had turned back to marble by day. "We played the game to make something pretty of a physical attraction," she said cuttingly. With a wry and glacial smile she added, "To spend a night making love sounds much nicer than spending a night having sex!"

She hadn't anticipated what happened next. He set his iron-clad fingers around her wrist and drew her to her feet in an undeniable gesture that was barely civilized despite the crowd in the dining room. He didn't stop for a second as he led, or rather dragged, her down the corridor and back to her cabin, ignoring her comments, whether they were demanding, angry, or scornful.

He stopped inside the cabin, after he had slammed the door and pinned her to it, claiming her lips, plundering her mouth savagely. His hands moved over territory he knew by heart, aggressively taunting, cradling breasts that were his, searching beneath material to find the answer he expected—flesh that heated to his touch, nipples that grew taut on contact.

Ronnie furiously pummeled against him and twisted her head to avoid his kiss. But his lips were clamped on hers. Her comparatively feeble struggles had no effect on his steellike determination to have his way. Her protests were muffled as his teeth grazed hers, pitted against them, and his tongue found the access to probe her mouth with heady command. Ronnie's attempt at words died, her mouth gave sweetly to his. She would never be able to deny him. A moment later she was arched against his chest, moaning as his fingers worked their spell upon her, twisting at the peak of her breast to send chills of pleasure racing down her spine as he held her in that relentless embrace.

Then he pulled away from her, using his hands and arms as inescapable bars around her. Eyes that were as dark as night seared into hers with ruthless demand.

"Now tell me again that this all means nothing to you," he grated harshly, his breathing as strained as hers.

She was shaking, panting, unnerved. God help her, she couldn't cry. But a lie would not suffice.

"All right!" she flashed in answer to his challenge. "It means something. It means something very wonderful. But it can't be!"

"Why not?" He would not soften now. He wanted answers. The ship was docked in Charleston Harbor. Time was running out. "Ronnie, I want to marry you."

A sob did tear from her throat. "I can't marry you!" she cried, the ice finally melting from her eyes as they stared tremulously into his. "I can't marry anyone. I'm already married."

But she wasn't! her heart cried out.

She was, for all intents and purposes. Discovering the false validity of a piece of paper didn't change anything. And yet she knew in the back of her mind, no matter how irrevocable the future, that the discovery had allowed her this wonderful day. She had used it to rationalize her actions. . . .

Legally, she was free.

But her freedom was empty; the ties that bound her had never had anything to do with legalities.

And none of it could ever be explained to Drake, who stared at her now with deep, piercing fury. . . .

"I am married," she repeated aloud, wrenched from the pain of longing by the staunch reminder to herself of what must be.

Drake emitted a single, explosive oath. If he had been burned to cinders by the roaring heat of lava, he couldn't have been more shocked or wounded. He had been duped in the worst way possible; he had given everything to someone else's *restless* wife. Trust, he thought cynically, as his arms dropped to his sides. What a fool. He had thought he had found the one woman he could love, cherish, and trust eternally.

He stepped away from her, still looking into her eyes, now seeing nothing but traitorous blue; magnificent, treacherous, radiant blue.

He had been used by a conniving witch he had deemed the soul of honesty.

The look alone that he gave her could have shattered a shell of lighter stuff. But even as she felt herself agonizingly ripped asunder inside, as if her heart had been torn from her body, Ronnie stood still.

Composed as marble.

If he touched her again, she would break. But he didn't touch her. She had the feeling that he controlled his temper because he feared what he might do if he let it loose. His hands were balled into fists at his sides, his broad shoulders appeared imposingly massive. But it was his dark face that set her blood racing. His glowering eyes were daggers; his mouth a white line of condemnation. His teeth were clenched together; she could see the twisted angle of his jaw as he ground them against each other.

She wanted to throw herself into his arms and explain. It was unbearable that he hate her so. But for all the rogue she had assessed him to be, she learned swiftly now that he was a man of certain morals. Affairs were fine. Extramarital affairs were unthinkable.

If she could explain, if there was any way—which there wasn't —it would be senseless to fly to him anyway. He would cast her aside as tarnished goods. Her situation was too incredulous to believe or to understand.

Her hands were behind her on the door. She braced them now, for support. "I think you should leave now, Drake."

"As you wish," he replied glacially. "Mrs. uh . . . ?"

"It doesn't matter," Ronnie said blandly, praying he would leave.

"It does matter, Ronnie," he told her gravely. But he didn't press the point. Instead he reached for her arm and pulled her from the door, dropping her arm again quickly after he had moved her out of his way. His touch had been as red-hot as a branding iron.

He stopped for only a second to gaze back at her. "Oh—thank you for a most interesting cruise."

Then he was gone. His piercing gaze, his towering disdain, were all that remained imprinted on her mind. Her knees buckled beneath her and she slid to the floor, gripping her stomach as if he had dealt her a blow with a two-by-four.

But still she didn't cry. She sat rocking, biting her lip. They were calling the passengers ashore. She pulled herself back to her feet by grasping the bedpost. After walking into the cabin's small bathroom, she splashed her face with cool water and made a few makeup repairs, her hands moving mechanically. She curled her hair into a tight bun at the back of her neck and donned sunglasses and a chic, wide-brimmed beige felt hat that matched her smart heels and small sling handbag.

Gathering her things, she left the cabin. But not without looking back at the still-rumpled bed.

She had never intended to; it had been foolish. But she had fallen in love. The precious memories were the ones she would learn to recall, not those of his dark ferocity at her deception. She would learn to remember his eyes as they blazed the tender fire of passion, not the charred embers of scorn.

And in the loneliness of her austere existence, she would sort out the misery of the different types of love. Her tears would come later. Upon the remote windswept island that was her home, she would find ample time for solace. And she would be plunged back into grueling reality.

The woman the world knew as Mrs. Pieter von Hurst walked away from her breakaway cruise, her heels clicking briskly upon the deck.

The immaculate sophisticated lady.

Beautiful, poised, reserved, genteel—yes, the perfect, seldom-seen wife of the world's most brilliant contemporary sculptor.

And one of the most unhappy women alive.

CHAPTER TWO

It was amazing that the sea could change so quickly. It had been calm, glassy, and cobalt-blue for the cruise, serene beneath powdery skies.

Now it matched Ronnie's mind. Foam-flecked waves were pulsating in wild whipped peaks, rising with the whistling of the wind. The sky was losing its early-morning glow, growing gray with a vengeance.

"Storm's blowin' in," Dave Quimby announced unnecessarily, pulling his yellow slicker cap lower over his forehead. He scratched his grizzled beard and gave Ronnie a gap-toothed smile. "Maybe ye'd best head on in to the cabin, Miss Veronica."

Ronnie shook her head and smiled back with affection. Dave, her husband's fulltime captain—a necessity when one lived on one's own island miles off the the shore of Charleston—was her one true friend in her home of five years. He was a man unintimidated by Pieter von Hurst; if he feared and respected anything, it was only the sea. To his credit, Pieter respected and admired Dave.

And if Dave cared for any human being with a degree of his softer nature, it was Pieter's young wife. She might be the courteous Mrs. von Hurst to the rest of the world, but to Dave she was Miss Veronica, as she had been on that day long ago when Von Hurst had returned to the island to stay as a recluse forever.

Dave sensed more than most people. He had known from the beginning that there was something very wrong with his employer's marriage. Brides were supposed to be happy, radiant young things. Miss Veronica had never been happy—not since the day she stepped ashore and looked over the barren island with a deep sigh of resignation. Only he had seen the dejection in her eyes. When Von Hurst had snapped something at her, she had turned to him with a gentle, tolerant smile.

Of course, Von Hurst was sick. Much sicker than most folks knew. If Dave's intuitions were right, Von Hurst was dying. *And God forgive me,* Dave thought, *the sooner the man dies the better.*

Better for the gentle mistress he loved.

Ronnie shook her head at Dave. "I don't want to go below!" she called above the roar of the Boston Whaler's engines and the wind. "I love the sea like this!"

He grinned knowingly. Maybe he loved her because she loved the sea as he did—and because she was like a storm at sea. Her true nature always hidden, unless she was out with him, Miss Veronica had depths as fathomless as the Atlantic, as tumultuous as any gale that blew. Only with him was she like a nymph of Neptune, her feet scampering over planks with excitement when they sailed, her head lifted to the wind. She was always willing to fight the roughest weather.

The sea was her escape.

Too soon they reached the jagged shore of Von Hurst's island. "Go on up to the house, Miss Veronica," Dave yelled over the encroaching wind. "You look too pretty to get a drenching! I'll get your things up right away."

"Thanks, Dave," Ronnie said, slipping her bare feet back into her heels. The pathway to the gray brick manor loomed before her, and she had no choice but to follow it. Resecuring strands of hair as she walked, she made her way along the gravel, her footsteps sure and determined. At the double oak doors she rang the bell; the house was always locked, although their nearest neighbor was islands away. Curiosity seekers sometimes motored too near.

"Good morning, Henri," Ronnie greeted the elderly butler and companion to her husband. "Where is Mr. von Hurst?"

Removing her hat and gloves, Ronnie queried him with the formal propriety that was expected of her. "Is he in his studio?"·

"No, Mrs. von Hurst," Henri replied, equally formal. "Mr. von Hurst had a poor night. He is in his sitting room. He did, however, request that you come to him immediately upon your return home."

"Thank you," Ronnie said, walking sedately down the hallway to the spiral staircase. She didn't want to see Pieter—and she hadn't expected that he would want to see her right away. She had wanted to go straight to her own room and lie down and sleep and dream and preserve her memories. . . .

But this was better. Pieter was right. They had to face each other; they had to break the ice that must surely exist between them now.

She paused before the door to his sitting room and forced her hand to knock upon the varnished wood. She always knocked. There were times when Pieter wouldn't allow her near him; when he couldn't bear the sight of her.

"Come in."

Pushing open the door, Ronnie quietly entered her husband's darkened sitting room and stood still, waiting for him to turn and speak to her as he stood at his own vigil at the huge bay window. Obviously he had been awaiting her return; he had watched her walk up the gravel path.

He was silent for several minutes, his hands clasped behind his back, his tall form pathetically emaciated. But at least he wasn't in the chair today, Ronnie thought, her heart constricting with the pity she was careful never to·show. He was standing straight, his parchment skin tight across a countenance that had never been handsome but still carried a nobility, despite the ravages of illness.

A shudder rippled violently through her as she watched his back and remembered their last encounter. He had been wild on that day, adamant, telling her he no longer needed to seek a divorce because he had discovered, in his attempts to obtain one, that their marriage was illegal. The "notary" who had performed the ceremony hadn't been a notary at all. . . .

Pieter had been so hard, so cruel. But she knew his motives.

In his way he did love her, and he feared he was reaching the end. After five years, he had decided to cause her no more pain.

But she knew he needed her more than ever now, and she could be just as adamant as he. "Forget it, Pieter," she had told him stubbornly. "Even if you're telling me the truth, it makes no difference. I've been your wife for five years."

He had bluntly assured her he was telling the truth. And he had insisted upon the cruise. A taste of freedom might be the answer.

Ronnie understood him. To placate him, she agreed. Yet she had never bargained on meeting Drake.

"Well?" Pieter queried her abruptly without turning. "You went?"

"Yes."

"And?" His form twisted a degree as he waited for her answer.

"It was a pleasant little vacation," she replied simply.

"Good," he replied brutally. "Perhaps you'll see some sense."

"No, Pieter," she replied, her voice barely above a whisper. "I will not leave you. Nor will I allow you to cast me out."

Her words rushed sweetly to his ears, but he closed his eyes in pain. "You'll do as I say, Ronnie," he replied harshly. She didn't reply, and he almost smiled as he imagined the stubborn tilt of her jaw. Maybe she was happy. . . . *Happy*. The thought was ludicrous. Not after the years he had inadvertently put her through. . . .

"That's all, Ronnie," he clipped rudely.

His bony shoulders seemed to hunch forward for a moment with weakness, and Ronnie had to prevent herself from rushing to him. Now, more than ever, he would want none of her compassion. She stood quietly, suddenly feeling very ill herself but, although dismissed, determined to keep a fearful eye on him for the next few minutes. When the pause between them became unendurable, she ventured a question.

"Will we be working today?" She braced herself, in case he became angry. She had to stay by him, but she had already pushed him today with her determination to do so. . . . And her guilt was weighing heavy on her mind. She knew the facade he wore. Beneath it, he was a good man.

She curled her fingers into her fists, not noticing that the nails dug deeply into her flesh. In her own mind she was still his wife. She had entered the marriage, whether valid or not, with open eyes. And still she had grasped for her little piece of the moon. . . . God forgive her, but she had had to have it. . . .

"No, we won't be working today. I do not feel that I could do the marble justice." He finally turned from the window and stared at her with somber eyes. She realized he was trying to smile. "Nor could I do justice to you today, my dear."

Ronnie felt the ever-threatening tears welling in her eyes. If only he had been cruel, flown into one of his tantrums! A small sob escaped her and she left the doorway to come to his side, but he stopped her with a hand in the air, his eyes closing.

"No, Ronnie, please," he murmured. "I—I want to be alone. Tomorrow we will go back to work."

Ronnie halted stiffly in mid-stride, swallowed, and nodded. "Can I do anything for you?" she asked softly.

"No, I'm fine. Go to your room and rest. Tomorrow we will be receiving a house guest. You will have your hostess duties to attend to when we are not in the studio." For now, anyway, he was informing her that they would go on as usual.

Ronnie nodded again. "Who is coming?"

"The gallery owner who will be handling the marble pieces." Pieter gave her a crooked grin reminiscent of better times; times when he had been a young and sound man. "He's quite a tyrant, I hear, determined to light a fire under the great Pieter von Hurst. A fine connoisseur of the arts, and a ruthless business tycoon to boot. You'll have to be your most charming—and determined to spare me his lectures."

Ronnie smiled. "We'll keep him at bay."

Pieter suddenly sagged into the massive wing chair by the

window. Once more, Ronnie would have rushed to him, but he stopped her again with a hard stare and an uplifted hand. "Go now, Ronnie," he said gruffly.

Squaring her shoulders, she turned and walked softly to the door.

"Ronnie?"

"Yes?" She turned back to him quickly, surprised by the tenderness in his voice.

Absurdly Pieter von Hurst was momentarily tongue-tied. He looked over the exquisite beauty of the wife who could never be his, and he knew, as he always knew, despite his often atrocious behavior, that she had a beauty that went far beyond her regal physical attributes. Hers was of the mind, the heart, and the soul. He owed her so much! Rebellious and spirited herself, she quelled her own righteous anger when he bitterly raged into her, using her as a scapegoat when he sank into despair and lost control.

She had stuck by him through everything, maintaining the public image that was all he had left of a once-great pride, even when they had found out that the ceremony binding them together had been a sham, presided over by an unlicensed notary. In one of his moods created by fear, Pieter had practically ordered her from him. But Ronnie had understood, and remained solidly at his side. They had lived together as Mr. and Mrs. Pieter von Hurst for five years, she had told him. She was his wife. In the very near future they would reconcile the illegalities. . . .

"Ronnie," Pieter repeated, the thin, cracked line of his lips forming a bittersweet smile. "I know this is hard to believe, but I do love you."

"And I love you, Pieter," she answered softly.

"I know that, and I appreciate it. I . . . er . . . hope your cruise was nice." He had, compelled by ego, insisted she take the cruise before they "reconciled the legalities." "We won't speak about it again."

Ronnie nodded and moved swiftly for the door, unable to meet his ravaged eyes. She knew what his words had cost him, and the

41

fact that he had spoken them was more than she could bear on top of everything else.

"Oh, Ronnie."

She paused with her hand on the door, not looking back.

"I . . . uh . . . missed you. Is it good to be home?" For Pieter, it was quite a speech.

"Wonderful." She strove for enthusiasm in her tone, but the word still came out as a whisper. Forcing herself to composure until she could sedately open and close the door, Ronnie then tore down the hall to her own room and locked herself in, a cascade of tears finally falling in torrents of silent misery as she was at last able to throw herself into the peaceful, private depths of her huge fur-covered four-poster bed.

A bed she had never shared with her "husband."

Ronnie had met Pieter von Hurst in Paris. She was just twenty-two, in love with spring, in love with Paris, and in love with Jamie Howell, one of Pieter's specially selected students. Few were so honored, few were lucky enough to study with the man, the artist, who was already considered a master though still in his early forties.

Von Hurst was rich and famous; he moved in the elite circles of society, from the Continent to the States. But Ronnie knew he had a fondness for her from the moment he met her. He had told her she was charming, eager, and brilliantly attuned to life, and had hosted the young couple to many a dance and dinner, reveling in their youth and enthusiasm.

And he was there when her talented fiancé fell prey to one of the oldest hazards of youth and the artistic community—heroin. Jamie was dead before Ronnie ever discovered the demon that had hounded him.

Ronnie was aware also that Pieter found her desirable, but he did not take advantage of her fresh innocence and beauty. He had made it very clear that he simply wanted to care for her. And she had let him. She was an American orphan, alone in Paris, grieved and bewildered, but already forming that shell of poised reserve that would hide her emotions from the world. She had been working as an interpreter for English-speaking tourists, but Pieter's artistic eye discovered a way to care for her and benefit them both. She would become his model, he reasoned, and the world also would benefit because her unearthly beauty would be forever captured in marble.

Although rumor ran rampant, she never did become his mistress. It was apparent that his love for her grew, as hers did for him. But she always knew her love for him was different. He was her friend, her mentor, a paternal figure. The difference in their ages was vast. But he wanted to marry her anyway. He had argued that he could make her love change.

And then three weeks before the wedding that was to be one of the grandest in Europe, Pieter found out about the disease that would rob him of his manhood—and eventually his life. Disbelieving and astounded, he railed against fate and cursed all who came near, never admitting the cause of his horrendous rages.

Except to Ronnie. He had told her, feebly offering her the release he couldn't bear, but she wouldn't go. And then it was he who turned to her for strength, she who salvaged the artist, Pieter von Hurst, she who gave him back to the world—at the cost of her own happiness and life.

But she did love him. When her own world had fallen to pieces, he had been there to pick her up. He had given her himself. She could give no less.

After a very quiet wedding—recently proved *too* quiet!—they quit Paris society and retired to the small island Pieter owned off the coast of South Carolina. Ronnie knew he could not bear for the public that idolized him to see him dissipate into a shrunken old man, long before his time.

She accepted interviews. She gave the papers the story of a perfect, complete marriage, of a one-to-one commitment that sent them scurrying into privacy to devote themselves to one

43

another and to his art. And because of her, he did keep creating; he did find a reason to go on living.

At first there had been a natural fondness between them. The little that they had been able to share Pieter accepted—her touch, her lips, the glory of her beauty. But after the first six months of their self-imposed exile, his mind began to warp, the ravages of bitterness clouding all reason. To have Ronnie as his wife but *not* to have her, sent him reeling into a world of cruelty and anger. He lashed out at her constantly for no reason. Twice he had thrown things at her, drawing blood from her golden satinlike skin.

And still Ronnie tolerated him. She knew he would be contrite, knew she could never leave him. He needed her. And he did love her as he so often told her. She was a heaven-sent angel. He couldn't have made it without her then, but now he had acquired her strength and wisdom from their years together.

In his more lucid moments he had confessed that he also knew he had robbed her of her life, or at least of her youth. He told her that after his death, she would be well taken care of; she would be exorbitantly wealthy. But he was aware that money meant little to her, and that she was fiercely independent. Upon her insistence, the bulk of his estate had been left to world charities that benefitted children.

The recent passage of her twenty-ninth birthday had been more of a milestone for him than for her. He had finally been able to reach from his web of self-absorption to realize what he had done—sacrificed her for himself. She had uncomplainingly given him life, while he took hers. He had stifled all the joyous youth that had been rightfully hers.

And he had become determined to set her free, although it was proving a difficult task. She fought him, but he persisted in her taking the cruise, that she at least taste the pleasantries of life away from him and the depressing manor. She was impatient at his insistence, adamant against him, but he forced her to go. He repeated the same argument he had used for wanting the divorce. Her time for youth and love had been all too brief. He could live as a cripple for years to come. And if she refused to leave him, then she needed to have a season of happiness to recall when he inevitably took his turns for the worse. And though she knew that the bitterness ripped him apart at times, he fervently hoped that she would have a wonderful time.

Ronnie cried herself to sleep.

She woke to a crisp tapping on her door. "Just a minute!" she called out, aware that she was a sight. Springing into the bathroom, she washed her tear-stained face, resolving that she would have no more excursions into self-pity. Pieter must never know how wretched she was, nor how his insistence on the cruise had only made it all worse. No one knew the seriousness of his condition—except herself and his doctor. And she could weave illusion for him when others believed that he had a weak constitution, common among brilliant artists.

She had long ago schooled herself against tears. Only the cruise had brought them to the surface. They would have to be shelved again, with the new love that she had found.

Combing her hair back into its neat knot, she walked into her bedroom and called, "Come in."

Henri opened the door and stepped inside, a silver tray in his stiff arms. "Good evening, madam. Mr. von Hurst suggested I bring you a tray. He didn't think you'd feel up to dinner, nor did he desire to dine downstairs. I hope you find this satisfactory."

"Yes, fine, Henri," Ronnie said. "Thank you."

Henri nodded, his head as stiff as his arms. "Where would you like the tray, Mrs. von Hurst?"

For a whimsical moment Ronnie was tempted to tell him she'd like to see it dumped upon his proper head. In the five years of their living beneath the same roof he had yet to address her as anything except madam or Mrs. von Hurst. In this house, she mused, it was easy to forget she had been given a first name, much less a nickname. Pieter spent days enclosed when he didn't see her; when he did see her, often as not he didn't address her at all. The earlier encounter had been unique.

45

Ronnie did not tell Henri to dump the tray on his head. Instead she bit back the giddy smile that tinged her lips and replied properly, "Set it on the low table, please, Henri. I'll get to it in a minute."

"As you say, madam." Henri set the tray down as directed, clicked his heels with a little bow, and left her.

Ronnie could smell a delicious aroma drifting from the tray, and she was sure that Gretel, their surprisingly wraithlike cook, had intuitively prepared something to especially tempt her palate. Lifting the cover of the tray, she found a light and fluffy spinach soufflé. One of her favorite meals, as Gretel was well aware.

But Ronnie could do no more than pick at her food. Her head was spinning and, consequently, her stomach was churning. She should never have sought out Drake. She should have lied to Pieter.

The emotions and desires she had suppressed for years were now plaguing her with a vengeful agony. Touching her lips, she wondered if she imagined it, or if she could still really taste the sweet salt of Drake's kiss, if his scent still lingered on her own skin. . . .

She had known from the beginning that the cruise could only be a disaster. She had tried to tell Pieter, but he had become so agitated that she feared he would cause himself to have another attack, and so she had agreed, stricken that he should heap this new, inadvertent torment upon her. She had left, intending to come home cheerfully with a tan, assuring him she was complacent with her own world.

Then she had seen Drake. And in frank honesty she had simply wanted him. It had never occurred to her that the experience could so badly shatter her day-to-day existence.

Impatiently she set her fork down and gave up on the soufflé. She just couldn't eat. The memory of a previous shared meal was too close.

So as not to hurt Gretel's feelings, Ronnie guiltily flushed the remainder of the meal down the toilet. Then she unpinned her

46

hair and climbed into the shower, making the water as hot as she could endure it, before scrubbing herself from head to toe and lathering her hair twice, soaking it in the expensive rinse Pieter ordered for her each month from Paris.

She desperately wanted to rid herself of the haunting masculine after-shave that seemed to cling to her body. The scent was driving her crazy; its intoxicating appeal wrenching her apart, creating longings that could not be fulfilled again.

The shower helped, and then she had things to do. After slipping into a set of Chinese lounging pajamas, Ronnie sat at her desk and planned a retinue of meals for the days to come, mulling over the proper wines for each with great care. She and Pieter entertained for only two reasons: Pieter's art, and his determination to create a living legend. Every guest was special; indeed, they entertained a number of dignitaries throughout the year.

If an arrogant tycoon had been invited to stay, Pieter wanted him impressed, no matter what his own feelings were. He was allowed to be moody or rude—he was the artist. Ronnie was supposed to create the atmosphere of genteel southern hospitality, to smooth all ruffled feathers. Pieter liked to be envied for his lovely wife. She was part of the elegance with which he surrounded himself.

Chewing on the nub of her pencil, Ronnie decided to have the Blue Room opened for this dubious guest's stay. The room was exceedingly masculine, its decoration basically stained wood paneling. The bed was a firm king-size, and the fireplace a very macho brick. Macho brick for a macho tycoon. That sounded good. And settled.

She picked up some of the correspondence that had accumulated but she couldn't concentrate on the letters. She dropped them again and picked up a book by one of her favorite authors and climbed beneath the cool silk sheets.

But she couldn't concentrate on the words. They kept blurring before her eyes, and the heroine was having a perfect love affair. If there was anything she didn't want to read about at that moment, it was a perfect love affair.

Ronnie snapped off her bedside lamp and curled into position to sleep. But try as she would, sleep would not come. Instead an image of dark eyes kept coming to her, and the memory of tender hands that demanded as they seduced.

Just last night it had all been real. And the reality was so strong now that she felt she could reach out and touch Drake. . . .

But she couldn't. All she could do was toss and writhe and close her eyes to dream—and burn with the sweet, simple memory of being held and cherished through the night.

It was very late when exhaustion finally overtook her and allowed her a few brief hours of respite.

Morning was much better. She had things with which to keep herself occupied. Pieter did not appear for breakfast, and she assumed correctly that he was saving his strength. As she had also expected, he sent her a crisp note by way of Henri, telling her that, after all, they would spend none of the day working. Dave would be motoring their guest to the island at five o'clock precisely—she should please see to it that she was dressed and prepared to greet him.

"Do you wish to reply, Mrs. von Hurst?" Henri asked politely.

"Yes," Ronnie said sharply, dismayed by her own tired irritability. "Ask Mr. von Hurst to please make sure I know this man's name before I greet him!"

If he was surprised by his mistress's uncharacteristic outburst, Henri gave no sign. As usual, he clicked his heels, bowed, and left her.

Ronnie finished her coffee and wandered out to the garden, pacifying herself with the selection of flowers. She loved the garden and had nurtured it with tender care, giving her flowers the affection she needed to release. And although she did the planning for any entertainment or renovation, the house actually ran smoothly without her. The black-and-tan coonhounds that roamed the estate were well looked after by the kennel keeper, and the four American saddle horses were tended by a conscientious groom. Only the flowers really depended on her, and so they received her devotion.

Now she savored their sweet aromas, wrinkling her nose into their blossoms as the softness of the petals caressed her cheeks. She clipped and pruned a colorful assortment, planning a myriad display for the huge formal dining table, which would be used that night. Then, with a streak of impishness, she planned an arrangement for their guest's room. If the man was hard as tacks, she mused, a little flower softness might be in order.

Returning to the house, Ronnie set to her arrangements, dryly appreciating the fact that they were to have company. She so desperately wanted to keep her mind busy! To worry about Pieter brought about useless pain; to think about her excursion into the arms of Drake brought agony. To tangle with them both brought a torturous guilt. In the eyes of the world she was married, and she had willingly sought out another man.

But her heart cried out that it was impossible to be untrue to a husband who had never been one with her. She vaguely wondered what her life might have been like had Jamie not senselessly lost his life to drugs. But that was all so long ago. It was in her extreme youth; it was the past. She could barely remember Jamie's face. When she tried to recall it, another appeared—that of Drake O'Hara. And she was back to self-incrimination. . . .

"Mrs. von Hurst?"

"Yes?" Ronnie glanced up as Henri stepped quietly into the salon where she continued to absently trim leaves from her flowers.

"You requested the name of your guest. He is Mister Drake O'Hara of Chicago, Illinois, owner and proprietor of the American International Galleries. Mr. von Hurst would like you to be aware that—Mrs. von Hurst! Are you quite all right, madam?"

Ronnie wasn't all right. The room was spinning around her, going completely black, and spinning around her again. Her heart had ceased to beat. She felt as if she had been drained of blood.

"Mrs. von Hurst!"

49

For once Henri dropped his cold dignity to rush to her side, appalled by the parchment-white color that had overtaken his usually healthy mistress. He caught her just as her slender body wavered and angled toward the floor.

Ronnie snapped back into physical control at Henri's touch, numb, but aware that she needed to be coherent. Blotting the panic out of her mind and wondering what cruel trick of fate could make such a thing happen, she forced herself to breathe and to find a voice to reply to Henri as she straightened from his saving hold.

"The sun, Henri, I think I stayed out to long. . . . Could you please . . . would you get me a glass of water?"

"Certainly, Mrs. von Hurst," Henri exclaimed, loathe to release her until she was seated. "Certainly . . . immediately. . . ." Watching her with concern, he hurried to carry out his errand.

Ronnie closed her eyes and kept breathing deeply, willing her heart to beat normally and her blood to pulse regularly through her veins. It wasn't possible. It simply wasn't possible. There had to be another Drake O'Hara.

And yet she knew there wasn't.

She had been destined to meet the man she had chosen wildly as a companion in a clandestine affair long before she had ever seen his intensely probing, magnetic, dark-brown eyes. . . .

He's coming here! she thought desperately, struck by another wave of panic. *Oh, God, oh no, oh no. . . .*

Henri walked quickly back into the room with a glass of cool water. Ronnie accepted it with a grateful smile and drained it in a moment. Smiling up at the butler, she thanked him.

"Perhaps I should call the doctor," Henri said doubtfully.

"No! Heavens, no!" Ronnie exclaimed hastily. "I'm fine. Really fine, I promise you. It was just the heat. And Henri—I would prefer it if we not mention this little spell of mine to Mr. von Hurst. I fear it might needlessly upset him."

"As you wish, madam."

Henri was quick to agree with her. He knew that there were

days when Pieter von Hurst totally ignored his wife, but he also knew that the temperamental artist would worry incessantly if he thought anything was wrong.

"Now"—Ronnie leaned back in her chair with a bright smile affixed to her face—"you were telling me about . . . er . . . this man. Drake O'Hara. Was there anything else Mr. von Hurst wanted me to know?"

She listened, registering facts without really hearing. O'Hara, a man who dabbled in sculpture himself, owned the most prestigious galleries in the Midwest. His shows were legendary; he could make or break an artist with a single critique.

It was shocking, really, that she hadn't known the name. But, she had been in Paris and then on a remote island for many years.

"Thank you, Henri," Ronnie told him placidly, hoping she could trust her legs to carry her. "I think I'll go up to my room and rest for a bit."

"Shall I have Gretel send you a luncheon tray?" Obviously Henri was still concerned.

Ronnie smiled wanly. "Yes, thank you, that would be nice. . . ."

She made it up the spiral staircase to her room, where she sat numbly at the foot of the bed.

In a matter of a few short hours she was going to have to stand in the doorway and greet a man as a total stranger who she already knew more thoroughly than any human being. . . .

They would be staying under the same roof for God only knew how long.

It was impossible! What was she going to do? How could she endure seeing him day after day?

And, dear God, what was going to happen when Drake saw her? His opinion of married women who carried on affairs had been blatant. He had loved her so fiercely, and now he scorned her with equal fervor. Would he deem it proper to tell Pieter?

A laugh of hysteria was rising in her throat. Pieter, in his present mood, might be pleased to discover she had taken a lover

51

. . . but certainly not amused to find that he had invited his wife's impetuous lover into his own home.

All she could do was pray that Drake showed no sign of recognition until she could talk to him alone and convince him that upsetting Pieter could be dangerous to his condition. Supposedly the great gallery owner was visiting Pieter because he admired and respected the great artist. Surely he would do nothing to harm such an illustrious idol.

Ronnie's slender fingers wound into tense fists, her nails tearing into her own flesh. She pounded against the mattress with venom and despair, striking the thick padding until she wore herself out.

It was impossible! she kept railing in whispered curses to whatever deity lurked above. Incredible, impossible.

But it was happening.

And somehow she was going to have to not only live through it but carry the entire thing off without the hint of a hitch. She couldn't afford the luxury of more tears or hysteria.

She had to prepare herself to walk down the staircase with all the effortless poise of the irreproachably elegant Mrs. Pieter von Hurst.

CHAPTER THREE

Ronnie had probably never taken more care to dress in her life. But her clothes that night would be like a knight's shield of heavy armor. They would protect her from searing dark eyes that could thrust daggers into her soul.

Her hair, clean and fragrantly scented, was piled on her head in burnished waves of gleaming sable. Delicate diamond earrings dangled from her earlobes, catching and reflecting the deep midnight blue of her silk cocktail sheath. Loathe to play the coward, she had chosen the backless dress on purpose, knowing it displayed the shapely contours Pieter found so fascinating for his sculpture.

At five o'clock she was standing beside her husband in the elegant entry hall, her hand resting lightly on Pieter's velvet-clad arm, evidencing none of the turmoil that raged through her.

Pieter looked well that night. Despite his gauntness, he was a tall man and, with the shoulders of his tailored suit well padded, he enhanced the illusion of a delicate form of health—one that befitted a dedicated artist.

Ronnie's hand tightened in an involuntary shudder as Henri opened the doors. It was the first time in their married life that she had leaned upon Pieter. But her face remained impassive. Even as Drake O'Hara moved into the hallway, towering in the shadow of the encroaching dusk, she stood immobile, a polite smile of greeting frozen on her placid face.

"Drake!" Pieter moved forward to shake the enthusiastically outstretched hand of the younger, more robust man, and Ronnie blinked once as she realized the two men had met at some previous time.

"Pieter," Drake returned, a smile warming the sinister male darkness of his angular features. "You're looking good, damn good."

It was then that his eyes flickered with glittering anticipation to Ronnie, and then froze, locked, and turned to pits of the deepest dark hell.

Ronnie wasn't breathing. She waited, too numb to pray.

But though his telltale eyes burned her heart to quaking cinders, Drake's face registered no change, unless it was a wry lift to one corner of his mustach-covered lip.

She, after all, had been prepared. He hadn't.

"Forgive me, Pieter, for staring," Drake said, his cool smile deepening for Pieter's benefit. "Your wife"—he inclined his head to Ronnie—"has an uncanny beauty."

"Ah, yes." Pieter was pleased by Drake's statement, noticing nothing amiss. "Come here, my dear, and meet a longtime friend and comrade, Drake O'Hara. Drake, my wife, Veronica."

It took every ounce of willpower Ronnie had to raise her hand and have it engulfed by Drake's powerful, punishing one. "Mr. O'Hara," she managed coolly, "welcome to our home."

"Thank you," he replied, refusing to lift his burning gaze from hers. "Please, call me Drake. I believe the circumstances warrant a first-name basis."

Smiling wanly, Ronnie delicately withdrew her hand, tugging slightly. He released her with a casual finesse.

"Pieter." Ronnie turned to her husband. "Shall we adjourn to the salon for drinks?" Damn, she needed a drink. She was grateful that Drake had seen fit to hold his silence, and mercifully control his recognition, but still, if she was to endure the condemnation in his hell-fire eyes, she needed a drink. Probably several.

"Yes, by all means." Pieter was actually sounding jovial. He clapped his hand upon Drake's back, his bony fingers ludicrous against the imposing breadth. "Come, my friend, it's been years. We have a lot of catching up to do."

Ronnie sailed ahead of the two men, listening vaguely to their chatter about Chicago, the state of the arts, and the Von Hursts' home on the island. In the comfortably tasteful salon she hurried to the small but well-stocked rosewood bar and slipped behind it, feeling absurdly that she had found another shield. Any distance between herself and Drake was beneficial. She knew his eyes followed her relentlessly; she could sense them as if they were tangible fires, and she refused to look into them.

"Drake, what can I get you?" she inquired, busily setting up glasses. She dropped ice into only two of them, knowing that when her husband drank, it was neat Scotch. He still abhorred the American custom of cold liquor.

"A bourbon, please, with a splash of soda," Drake replied politely. He leaned his vibrant form against the bar, forcing her to an awareness of the leashed energy that composed him. His fingers closed over hers again as she pushed his glass toward him, tightening momentarily and drawing from her a shiver of apprehension. From the corner of her eye she could see that he had felt the shiver, and that it had given him grave satisfaction. His lips were twisted into a dry, hard grin.

Ronnie mentally squared her shoulders. She couldn't allow him to believe he could intimidate her. Moving serenely from the bar without glancing his way, she brought the crystal rock glass of straight Scotch to Pieter and, carrying her own highball of Seagram's and Seven, chose an encompassing provincial chair apart from the others. The men seated themselves after her and immediately fell back into comfortable, reacquainting conversation. Sipping on the drink she had made much stronger than usual, Ronnie let their words float around her head, learning that her husband and Drake had met years before: once in Pieter's Dutch homeland, and once in Chicago. The first American showing of Pieter's work had been at Drake's galleries, hence Drake's determination now to push Pieter to greater productivity.

"You've been hiding out on this island too long," Drake told Pieter. He seemed perfectly at ease, one long leg crossed over the other at an angle, his hand resting on one knee. Ronnie was sure she had been temporarily forgotten, but then he turned to her. "Of course, that's perfectly understandable. Had I your lovely wife, I might be tempted to spirit her away to an island myself."

It was a perfectly innocent compliment. Only Ronnie understood the undertones. *Keep her safely away from all others.*

Pieter was pleased as always when reference was made to his wife's beauty. He chuckled quietly, and, at another time, Ronnie would have been equally pleased to see the happiness that was easing the terrible strain of his pinched features. "Ronnie and I find great pleasure in our island. We seldom leave it."

"Ah," Drake inferred with a teasing tone, "but you must sometimes!"

Ronnie unfurled from her chair and rose gracefully to her feet. "I believe I shall fix myself another drink," she said smoothly, ignoring Drake's comment. "How about you, gentlemen?"

Pieter declined, but Drake grinned at her cruelly. "Please."

As hostess she had no choice but to walk to him and retrieve his empty glass. And at that moment she hated him intensely. It was obvious that her wishful assessment had been correct; Drake admired Pieter and would say or do nothing to hurt him.

But he didn't intend to let her forget a thing. It was evident that he was barely concealing his disdain, evident that he believed whatever torture he inflicted upon her was more than warranted.

Taking Drake's glass as swiftly as was conceivably polite, Ronnie met his gaze for an instant of open hostility, determined not to wilt before his fire. She spun away from him and retreated once more to the bar, grateful for the mechanical tasks that kept her moving with the natural autonomy of a brilliantly programmed robot.

She was also grateful for the years that had bred self-restraint. If she had had to depend on instinct, she would have run screaming into the night, hands clenched tightly to her head to drown out the clamoring emotions that pierced through the numbness that had claimed her.

Her heart bled for Pieter. And she hated Drake. Hated him for judging without knowing . . . hated him with even more vehemence, because she knew that by all outward appearances he had come to the only possible conclusions. . . .

Yet she hated him mostly because of her own sense of bewilderment and shame. When he looked at her, when his hands grazed over hers, when she inhaled the too-familiar drugging scent that exuded from his coiled frame, she wanted him again. Sensitivities that had lain dormant all those years had been reawakened by this man who now despised her, but God help her, despite his scorn, despite her honest but different love for Pieter, she couldn't stop her tormented mind from bringing her back to those cherished hours of curling against his magnificent naked form. . . .

Ronnie didn't attempt to meet Drake's eyes as she returned his fresh drink and once more took her chair. The conversation turned to the quality of various marble, and she found herself speaking occasionally, her tone deadened, but all her inflections in the right place.

This time her drink was almost straight Seagram's. She welcomed the choking heat that burned down her throat, blazing much-needed bravado through her system.

After dinner, she was going to lock herself in her room and get rip-roaring drunk. The next day's hangover would be a small price to pay for that night's solace.

Henri made one of his proper entrances to announce that dinner was served. Pieter and Drake both sprang to their feet to escort her graciously into the formal dining room. Despite the warmth of the liquor, Drake's touch on her arm was as hot as a branding iron; his sardonic grin as he towered above her as cutting as an unsheathed foil.

It was impossible for her to do anything more than pick at the excellent meal of stuffed grouse that she had planned for the evening. The crystals of the multifaceted chandelier swam together above her head, fogging the brilliant colors of the flowers she had cut with such complacency earlier in the day.

"Certainly," she suddenly heard Drake saying dryly. "A gem above all others."

Ronnie's eyes rose from absent concentration on her plate to glance quickly from man to man. They had been discussing her openly, and she hadn't heard a word that was said.

"An amazing talent," Drake continued, raising his wineglass a hair as he steadily returned her inadvertent glance. "Uniquely stunning; the most charming chatelaine. I'm sure all of her . . . ah . . . talents, are equally pleasing."

There was no way to prevent the rush of crimson that stained her face in a wild flush of fury. How could he be so insinuative with Pieter at the same table?

Because Pieter was blissfully unaware. The comment meant nothing to him. Only Ronnie knew the degrading implication. . . .

"Ronnie excels at nothing so well as being my model," Pieter was saying cheerfully, oblivious to the color of his wife's face as he studiously cut his food. "But you'll see what I mean tomorrow."

"What?" The squeaked question was out before Ronnie realized she had voiced it.

Pieter finally looked up, frowning. "I told you, Ronnie, Drake is also a sculptor. I intend to draw him into our work." His brooding gaze left her to travel to Drake with a hint of pride. "This young man could probably have far surpassed me in genius if his interests weren't so diversified. His hands war with his mind—art and business. But he has come to push *me*. I intend to push in return and involve him in our project."

Ronnie placed her fork down and reached for her water glass, dismayed by the trembling that assailed her fingers. She couldn't possibly model with Drake in the room. Pieter was carving the curves of her back into pink marble. Sitting for her husband was clinical. Sitting, clothed only in drapery, while the two chiseled

58

and discussed human anatomy, using her like the marble beneath their hands, would be enough to drive her over the brink.

She would be like a fish out of water, exposed, totally vulnerable to whatever verbal attack Drake chose to make.

And he knew it. He raised his glass higher to her as a single brow quirked high in cynical amusement. "I shall be looking forward to tomorrow."

Ronnie drained the entire glass of water, only to find that the effort still did nothing to dampen her desert-dry throat.

There could be no tomorrow. She was determined and adamant. But now was not the time to argue with Pieter. They did not argue, or even "discuss," in front of others, but this was one time she would make an unrelenting stand against the man she strove to please in all other ways.

Drake must have sensed her plan to protest. "Please don't be distressed, Veronica," he told her glibly. "I assure you that I am a legitimate artist."

Pieter waved his hand in the air with dramatic dismissal. "Don't worry about Ronnie, Drake. She's a very professional lady."

"And one who needs a bit of air," Ronnie declared, unable to sit still any longer and be discussed as if she weren't present. Rising quickly, she murmured, "If you'll excuse me for a moment . . ."

Pieter might be shocked that she was walking out on company, but that too would have to be brought up later. She was getting out of the room.

Both men rose quickly. "Certainly, my dear," Pieter murmured in response, concern in his tone. But there was also anger. Ronnie didn't really care. Maybe it was time she stopped catering to him.

"I'll rejoin you shortly," she promised, surprised by the cool determination of her own voice, "back in the salon for brandy. . . ."

She was sailing regally out the door before either man could give further contemplation to her abrupt departure.

But she wasn't out of earshot quickly enough to miss Pieter's damning words as the two reseated themselves.

"I doubt if Veronica will be modeling much longer for me, which means my project must be completed soon. Her loyalty to me has been excessive, but I'd like to see her pursuing a few new interests. . . ."

She was going to scream. Either that or bury herself beneath the fertile soil that harbored her cherished plants. . . .

But she did neither. She did flee to the garden, discarding her stately walk as soon as she had left the house behind. Her heels twisted in the dirt as she ran, wrenching her ankles, but she didn't care. She needed time desperately. Time to retrieve a measure of dignity.

She was panting when she reached the little tile paths that ran among her flowers and the fountains that played in the garden. Finding the wrought iron love seat wedged near the rear wall, she sank onto it, automatically straightening the tendrils of sleek auburn hair that had fallen loose in her reckless run.

Now, more than ever, she had to talk to Drake alone. Without giving away any of the truth, she had to somehow subtly convince this man who had torn into her life like a cyclone that he could endanger her husband's precarious health.

She never heard his footsteps. He came upon her as silently as a wraith, a shocking feat for a man of his size and robust vitality. Her first knowledge that he had come upon her was the result of his raw words.

"So—the 'Mrs.' that doesn't matter is Von Hurst. Tacky, madam. That name has mattered with incredible importance for almost twenty years."

"What are you doing out here?" Ronnie bit back sharply. She didn't need to feign civility out there.

"Pieter is concerned," Drake drawled mockingly, setting a polished shoe upon the love seat, his hands in his pockets, leaning toward her. "The poor man doesn't seem to know what's gotten into his precious wife. Actually, it seems there's a lot the poor man doesn't know about his wife."

Ronnie curled her nails into the iron pattern of the seat, wishing fervently that she could flail them across his hard, accusing, bronze face and draw the blood he seemed to want from her.

The metal grating beneath her fingers braced her with the illusion of strength. She lifted her chin high and forced her eyes to brazen into his. She clenched her teeth together, then parted them to speak with a collected firmness.

"And do you intend to inform Pieter that you have been previously acquainted with his wife?"

Dark eyes swept her contemptuously from head to toe. "I shouldn't answer that. I should let you worry." He planted his foot back on the ground, dusted the love seat, flung back his jacket tails, and sat beside her. Unwittingly Ronnie found herself shrinking as far to the side as the seat would allow.

"My, my, what are we afraid of?" Drake mocked grimly, catching her wrist with a coiled menace. "My touch? Ahhh, but there was a time when you begged for it, Mrs. von Hurst."

"Please!" Ronnie murmured, twisting her wrist within his crushing grip as her teeth sank into her lip.

"A note of distress? I'm truly touched!" His teeth flashed in a wicked grin as he brought his face menacingly close to hers. Again she thought that his eyes were like a black fire, capable of burning flesh with all the true heat of hell.

"Drake, please," she protested, wincing. He was so close that his mustache tickled the peach softness of her skin, tantalizing her, terrifying her. "Pieter is right inside—"

With a curt laugh he withdrew and dropped her hand as if it were poison. "You needn't fear advances from me, Mrs. von Hurst," he grated, his tone dripping the venom of his eyes. Apparently his mind was running along the same lines as hers. "My dear, sweet poison beauty. I happen to think the world of Pieter von Hurst. I wouldn't think of touching his wife. It was a vast pity I ever did."

Ronnie had to find a way to fight her tears and ignore his cutting cynicism.

"So you don't intend to say anything to Pieter?" she inquired flatly, unconsciously rubbing her wrist as she stared into the foliage before her.

"No, I don't. I see no reason to hurt the man. He has obviously been gravely ill."

Ronnie breathed a silent sigh of relief. "Thank you," she said stiffly.

"Don't thank me!" His hiss was soft, but to her ears it came as a roar. "I'm not doing anything for you. It's my sound opinion that you should be horsewhipped. My God, woman! Your heart must be chiseled out of marble! Running around on a man who has given you his adoration on a platter, a man who has been ill. A man like Pieter von Hurst!" His voice rang with his own self-disgust for having had the affair, and Ronnie inwardly cringed.

"I don't have to listen to your judgments," she said hollowly.

"Wrong, Mrs. von Hurst," Drake said, a gravel-like tone lacing his voice.

Ronnie tensed, aware of the extent of his anger, acutely sensing the depth of the coiled strength that breathed beside her, held in check by sheer willpower. She didn't dare breathe, or make a move herself, when he again picked up her hand, idly trailing his tanned fingers over the faint blue veins.

"I'm afraid, Ronnie, that you'll have to listen to every word I have to say—until I leave, that is, which could be awhile yet—because there is one thing that could make me tell Pieter about his precious wife."

"Oh?" Ronnie heard her own voice, coming with faint curiosity, as if it were very far away. "And what is that?"

"Well," Drake said, matter-of-factly, "the slightest implication that your excessive loyalty has turned to a few new interests."

Ronnie involuntarily attempted to snatch her hand away, but Drake held it securely. She tried to turn her head completely from his, but he caught her chin with his other hand and held it firmly, lowering his own autocratic features over hers again. "Let's not play this too cool, shall we, Mrs. von Hurst?" he lashed out icily. "I don't know what your personal game is, but I do hope you know what you're doing. Potential consequences, you know. Say, should you produce a child, I can guarantee you I'll be back—to claim it."

Ronnie gasped, shocked by his vehemence and firm determination, and the very idea. "There is no child," she rasped, adding with narrowed eyes. "And you couldn't."

"Try me."

"It's irrelevant," she grated, swallowing. "Pieter—"

"I'm afraid Pieter would have to discover at that point that his wife is a crystal angel with the devil's own heart."

"Don't worry, at that point—" Ronnie began desperately. She broke off her own words. To go further would be to betray the confidence Pieter had entrusted her with. "Could you please let go of my chin?" she demanded haughtily.

He shook his head relentlessly. "I want to stare into those beautiful blue eyes when I listen to your treachery."

Ronnie grated her teeth with fury, further irked because she feared she would soon start trembling. It was too easy to remember when those same dark eyes had stared into hers with tenderness, too easy to remember when his touch was gentle, tender, demanding nothing but that she love him with equal ardency. . . .

"Drake, please"—she searched his eyes for a shred of compassion and found none—"I swear to you. There is no child."

"And how do you know?" he queried sceptically, reminding her that forty-eight hours hadn't passed since they'd parted.

"Believe me, I know," she said with all the confidence she could muster. "I—" She faltered only a second. "I do know what I'm doing. This is the nineteen eighties."

He released her chin and hand and stood, annoying her as he towered above her. "Well, I don't know," he informed her curtly. "And I promise you, I'll be waiting to see. I'd hate to hazard a guess about you and Pieter, but the time you spent with me was wildly potent. You were a wanton. . . ."

Ronnie sprang to her feet, wilder than Drake had ever seen

her, any semblance of her regal cool shot entirely to the winds of mindless wrath. She didn't give a damn at that moment if her house guest reappeared inside with her hand print clearly etched on the side of his face.

But she never raised her hand. His arms locked around her body as soon as as she sprang up. "No, no, no, Mrs. von Hurst. No outraged violence. I won't tolerate it from a woman who literally asked me to take her."

Seething with frustration, Ronnie went limp. To pinnacle her wretchedness the shelter of his arms, even in anger, was dangerously enticing. She so desperately wanted to bury her head in the mass of hair that she knew lurked beneath the crisp tie and pressed dress shirt; so desperately wanted to blurt out everything that had happened, the way that everything was. . . .

She stiffened her slender spine and met his eyes. Exhausted, dejected, she spoke to him tiredly. "I think we'd better get in. Pieter might start worrying."

He let her go and, squaring her shoulders, she started back down the tile path.

"Ronnie."

She stopped and turned back without expression as he called her name.

"You will sit tomorrow."

She shrugged dispiritedly. Arguing with Pieter could have caused him a lapse anyway, and he was looking so happy.

"Yes, I'll sit," she said coldly, resuming her trip back to the house.

Drake watched her go in a torn agony himself. He didn't know what to think, but he couldn't help what he felt.

Logically she was poison. A cold-hearted temptress. A woman who would betray an ailing husband to partake in an illicit affair with all-out ardency, and, unwittingly, granted, use against that husband a man who was his most fervent fan.

Used. Drake knew he had been used more shockingly than ever, and it was that thought that fully boiled his blood to where the cap could barely be kept on his steaming temper.

But it was impossible to look at her and not be touched, not be swept back into a land of passion and tenderness.

She was still incredibly beautiful. And majestic. That proud lift of her shoulders and bracing of her spine when challenged . . .

She would never be cornered.

And then there were those eyes. Those beautiful blue eyes that had been haunting him since he first saw her. Eyes that could freeze with blue ice. Cold, assured, confident eyes, which every once in a rare while relented and lost their guard.

And then they could be beseechingly, trustingly warm—the eyes of a sensitive, sensuous woman. Eyes that lured him into a silken trap, made him fantasize . . . made him believe against all reason that she was all things good—love, devotion, and loyalty. . . .

But that was ridiculous—she was none of those things. And if his haunted body still yearned for her with an alien singleness and treachery, it didn't matter.

He could never touch her again.

She was Von Hurst's wife.

CHAPTER FOUR

As Ronnie hurried along the path she heard her name called again. Stopping, she saw that Drake was catching up with her, his long strides bringing him quickly along.

"Don't you think we should make an appearance together?" he suggested mildly, his expression now fathomless. "I was sent to escort you back in."

Ronnie watched him contemplatively for several seconds, then her dark lashes swept over her cheeks. "I suppose," she said indifferently.

He offered her his arm, and she accepted it lightly as they returned to the house. Pieter was already in the salon, where Henri was preparing stout snifters of a fine cognac.

"Ah—there you are!" Pieter greeted them jovially. His gaze alighted upon his wife with mild curiosity. "Are you quite all right, my dear?"

"Yes, fine." Ronnie smiled weakly, accepting her cognac with a nod of thanks to Henri. "I've a bit of a headache, though." She kept her gaze upon Pieter rather than Drake. "If you two will forgive me, I think I'll excuse myself shortly and retire for the night."

Pieter frowned and nodded his acquiescence. "My wife, I'm afraid, Drake, will need her rest. I don't go about much myself these days, so she'll be your escort around the island." His frown deepened and his brooding eyes turned to probe Ronnie. "I hope you didn't acquire sunstroke aboard that ship. Too much time in the sun is not healthy."

66

Ronnie tensed, sipping on her cognac. She didn't dare look in Drake's direction. "I'm fine, Pieter, just a little tired. I—er—I really wasn't in the sun that much." She winced at the folly of her last statement. If she had ever left an opening for Drake to pounce upon, that was it. But he said nothing. She couldn't see him from the angle of her chair, but she could sense his presence as he casually leaned against the bar.

Pieter turned to him in explanation. "Ronnie just sailed off on one of those Harbor cruises you see advertised." He lifted a gaunt hand in the air. "As I've said, I seldom leave the house myself. Veronica, however, is still young. I insist that she occasionally get out and enjoy herself."

"How nice," Drake replied, his tone betraying nothing. Ronnie could feel his dark eyes turn to·her. "And did you enjoy yourself, Mrs. von Hurst? I hear that those cruises can be very pleasant—offering every amenity."

"Thank you, yes," Ronnie replied coolly, rising, still refusing to glance his way. "I did enjoy the cruise. Pieter"—she moved swiftly to her husband to drop a quick kiss on top of his thinning blond head, certain he would not brush her aside with company in the room—"I'm going up, if you don't mind. Mr. O'Hara"— she finally lifted her eyes to Drake's with a daring shade of defiance—"I do hope you'll forgive me. However, I'm sure that you and my husband have a multitude of things to discuss." With the regality of a queen, Ronnie then sailed from the room with her head high.

"I wonder," she heard Pieter murmuring absently as she closed the salon doors behind her, "if I'm fair to Ronnie in many ways. . . ."

Ronnie grimaced as she started up the spiral stairway. Pieter couldn't know it, but his statement had probably given his guest quite a laugh.

The headache she had invented was pounding away in her skull as she reached the sanctuary of her room. Rubbing her temple assiduously, she kicked off her shoes and haphazardly began shedding her clothes, heedless for once of where things fell. She lay in her bed, clad only in her lace bra and panties, fighting the waves of nausea that assailed her and simultaneously discarding her idea to drink herself into oblivion.

The highballs, wine, and cognac she had already drunk hadn't done a thing to improve the situation, they had only added physical torture to mental! If she just lay still, very, very still . . .

Somewhere along the line she must have dozed off. She awoke with a start—and the immediate tingling, uncanny perception that she was not alone in the room. A scream rose in her throat, but before she could give vent to the sound a hand clamped tightly over her mouth. She knew instantly the scent and touch of the hand, as she did the deep voice that hissed, "Hush, it's me."

Shivering with both outrage and fear, Ronnie pushed at his hand and struggled into a sitting position, meeting his sinister dark gaze in the light of the moon with her own eyes snapping sapphire glints. "What are you doing in here!" she hissed furiously in return, wishing she had thought to draw down the covers before she had plopped on the bed. Her instinct was to grab something to clutch to herself, but there was nothing available.

"I haven't come to assault your dubious virtue," he commented dryly, his hips perched beside hers on the bed. "I want to know what's wrong with Pieter."

Ronnie's lashes fell, but she was quick with a comeback. "I think you could have found a better time to discuss Pieter!"

"Oddly enough, my dear Mrs. von Hurst, this seems to be the only time I can guarantee having an audience with you alone."

Ronnie blinked rapidly, highly aware of her state of undress, whether he was or not. Apparently he already knew beyond a doubt that she and Pieter did not share a room.

"Pieter has not been well," she said quickly.

"Obviously," Drake drawled. His arms on either side of her, not touching her, held her as if between bars. His dark face, ruggedly swarthy in the moonlight, moved within inches of her

68

own. "What's wrong with him?" It was a demand, not a question.

Ronnie clenched her teeth, meeting his stare silently as she played for time to think of an appropriate answer. His gaze momentarily left her face to sweep over her form and the cream of her silky skin displayed enticingly by the expensively cut underwear. Chills as vibrant as tiny electrical shocks seemed to prick at Ronnie's flesh, but his gaze returned to hers, cold and disinterested. "Well?"

"Drake," she began haughtily, "I'd appreciate it if you left my room. My husband—"

"Your husband isn't coming anywhere near here, and you and I both know it," Drake cut in coldly. "How long has Pieter been ill?"

"If you're concerned for Pieter, you'll get out," Ronnie retorted.

"I'll be happy to leave," Drake promised sardonically, "as soon as you answer my questions."

Ronnie blinked again, then released an exasperated sigh. She couldn't tell him anything, but she had to get him away from her. Her outrage was fast losing its intensity; the temptation to reach out and touch his harshly squared jaw was seeping through her to obliterate reason.

"I cannot discuss my husband's condition," she said flatly, fixing her vision upon his jacket sleeve. "Yes, as you have so brilliantly observed, Pieter has been ill. If you wish further answers, you'll have to ask him."

"Why?"

"Why?" Ronnie ejaculated, her voice rising with desperate annoyance at his persistence. "Because I have given Pieter my oath not to discuss him with anyone!"

"It would seem you have given him other oaths that you have seen fit to break," Drake grated harshly, pulling from her, his hand trailing a path insinuatingly across her midriff as he did so.

"Please, Drake," Ronnie begged, lowering her voice again with acute misery. "This is Pieter's house."

"I see—the place makes a difference."

"You wouldn't understand."

"I understand too well."

"Drake—"

"Don't fret, Mrs. von Hurst. I wouldn't touch you with a ten-foot pole." He stood abruptly, making her feel far worse and even more vulnerable as he towered above her, his broad shoulders rigid. "Is Pieter under a doctor's care?"

"Yes," Ronnie whispered, snatching her pillow from behind her back to clench over her torso. "The best."

Drake spun on his heels and quietly padded across the room to the door. He paused for only a second, his hand on the knob. In the darkness she could still see the burning glitter of his dark eyes. "Don't be a hypocrite, Ronnie. The pillow bit was definitely unnecessary. There isn't an inch of you I don't know better than the back of my own hand." His gaze raked over her one last time, fathomlessly. "See you tomorrow."

Then he was gone, and she was left to lie awake for the rest of the night, alternately feeling as if she were as hot as lava and then as frigidly frozen as a bleak stretch of Antarctic ice.

By morning Ronnie's nerves were sadly on edge. She was grateful when she dressed and cautiously walked downstairs to find herself alone in the dining room. There was no evidence that Drake and Pieter had eaten and left, but then she didn't expect to find any. Henri would have removed an empty coffee cup before the china had time to grow cold.

Intuitively certain that she would have a respite of peace, Ronnie decided she was famished. Making up for the meals she had barely touched, she piled her plate high with the cheese blintzes that were Gretel's specialty, lavishing them with thick mounds of strawberry jam and sour cream. She also prowled through the remaining chafing dishes, adding to her plate crisp slices of bacon, smoked Virginia ham, and a spoonful of the grits that Pieter considered "animal mash" but consistently ordered for the morning buffet. It was one of the small courtesies his continental mind tolerated for his born-and-bred southern wife;

one of the little niceties that tugged at Ronnie's heart. No matter how bitter, withdrawn, and cruel Pieter had been at times, she knew he never intentionally used her as a scapegoat. Remembering the little things, the trivial things like grits, was Pieter's way of apologizing, of telling her that he did appreciate all that she did, the untiring devotion she gave to him.

Because, despite the fact that Pieter seldom allowed her near him, and often exploded against her when she was, she had allowed him to keep the two things a desperately ill man needed most fervently: his dignity and pride.

Reflecting on Pieter now, Ronnie wondered if she would have actually married him had he not become so sick. With Pieter, she had always responded to respect, ardor, and compassion *with* respect, ardor, and compassion. Her brief, shining love for Jamie had been very different. They had both been young Americans finding the wings of adulthood and romance in the spirited streets of Paris. They were both explorers, adventurers. They fought with a verbal vengeance, and patched up their quarrels with tears and passion.

She could honestly say that she had loved Jamie. And Pieter had a part of her heart that he would hold forever. Yet neither began to compare with the intensity of emotion she felt for Drake. His touch stirred senses she hadn't known existed; the mere sight or sound of him sent her mind reeling. But it was more than a physical draw. During that one day that now played havoc upon her world in memory, she had come to love him for the man he was, for the honesty of his word and his actions, for the tenderness only a man of his character could freely display. . . .

Damn it! she thought with annoyance. It wasn't safe to think about anything anymore! All roads led to Drake O'Hara.

"Goodness, woman! How the hell do you stay so thin eating like that?"

Ronnie's eyes flew to the doorway, where Drake stood, dressed in a casual short-sleeved shirt and black pants, one hand stuck in a pocket, the other bracing his frame as he lightly leaned

71

against oak paneling. His lips were curled in a half-smile that tilted his mustache to a rakish angle, making the harsh contours of his face devilishly charming.

She wondered if the look was a form of peace treaty. He acted as if they had never exchanged words—or anything else for that matter.

Determined not to be the one to cast oil upon still waters, Ronnie answered him with the polite truth. "I don't usually get quite this carried away."

Drake smiled in return and walked to the buffet to pour himself a cup of coffee. Lifting the silver pot, he arched a brow to her. "Can I refill your cup?"

"Please." Ronnie pushed her coffee cup forward and watched as the dark liquid rose in a cloud of steam. She added cream and sugar to her coffee as Drake sat in the chair beside hers.

"This is a beautiful place," Drake commented.

"Thank you."

"Where are you really from?"

Ronnie shot him a wary glance, but the question was straightforward. At her look his lips curled even further, lightening his eyes. "I mean, you are from the South."

Slightly amused by her own rush to be defensive, Ronnie suppressed a full-scale grin and nodded. "Durham, North Carolina."

"Did Pieter choose Charleston for you?"

"No," Ronnie told him, glad for the comfortable normalcy of their conversation. "He owned this place long before I met him. I believe he bought it on his first trip to the States."

"Well," Drake mused, idly stirring his spoon in his coffee, "you fit it well. But then you also—" He stopped, and Ronnie bit her lip. His first nontaunting compliment had been unintentionally marred. She was sure he had been about to say that she had also looked well upon the cruise ship.

Not wanting to let the easy repartee that had come between them dissipate, Ronnie ignored the abrupt end of his statement.

She lifted her cup and sipped her coffee musingly. "I've never been to Chicago. What is it like?"

"New York"—Drake grinned—"except that it's Chicago."

Ronnie laughed, and Drake went on to describe the city, extolling the virtues of the midwestern metropolis, but also giving a blunt appraisal of the problems and drawbacks. "It's a good city for artists," he ended. "The community supports the theater and the visual arts."

Ronnie chewed thoughtfully on a last piece of cheese blintz. "Charleston is much smaller, but I would say it's a supportive community." She found herself talking about the charm of southern living, unaware that she became more and more animated as she spoke, and beautifully charming. Drake again found himself fascinated by her voice and her every movement. She was such a complex creature. So cold with that tragic reserve, part warm with a wealth of spirit and vitality. He began to forget his reason for seeking her out.

"Ah, I've found you both!" Pieter broke in from the doorway. "Ready?"

"Yes, I am!" Drake declared, rising and moving to Ronnie to pull back her chair. "Ronnie?"

She glanced to her husband with a hint of confusion.

"The sitting," Pieter explained with a hint of exasperation. "I'd like to work now. The afternoons drain me, I'm afraid."

"Oh," Ronnie murmured uneasily. She rose and followed Pieter with no further comment, her spine straight, her shoulders squared. She knew now why Drake had called his unspoken truce and she wasn't sure whether to be grateful or suspicious. He had known the idea of posing before him and Pieter had disturbed her, and he had tried to ease the situation. But had it been an act of kindness, or was it self-beneficial?

It really didn't matter. An hour later Ronnie had already endured the misery she had expected, and had withdrawn from it, setting her mind as far away as possible. She was posed upon a settee, holding her position exactly as she had been long and laboriously trained to do. A single movement could send Pieter into a tirade.

Stiff muscles meant nothing to him in his pursuit of art. When she modeled, Ronnie knew, she lost her identity completely. She was nothing more than a tool to Pieter. He would set her up with fingers of ice and bark commands until she was perfect in his mind's eye.

Today had been worse than usual.

She was actually clad with a fair amount of respectability. She held her drapery high over her breasts, and Pieter had tucked it securely over her legs. Only her back was visible, but it was a visibility that would inherently make one nervous. To turn one's back on anyone for any length of time was to feel uncomfortably vulnerable. Especially when that back was the topic of conversation. Pieter was instructing Drake in planes and angles and curves. Clinically. She might have been an inanimate object . . . and certainly not his wife.

All her reserves of inner strength were called upon as Pieter asked Drake to learn by sense of touch. And she had to wonder sickly as she stared straight ahead, not breathing, blinking, or daring to move an eye covertly what Drake was thinking and feeling as his hands moved over her back, their touch fire to Pieter's ice. . . . She was amazed that her body followed the strict dictates of her mind, and that she neither flinched nor constricted into a mass of helpless quivers.

But finally, after vaguely listening to two hours worth of discussion on her own contours and the virtues of Venetian pink marble, Pieter let out a drawn sigh. "I believe I've pushed a bit too far. We'll quit for the day."

A haze of grateful tears welled in Ronnie's eyes to be instantly flicked away. She fought the urge to gather her drapery and shoot from the room like a bat out of hell and rose gracefully instead, calmly heading for the door. She even risked a cool glance in Drake's direction, but his eyes were on the tools he was carefully cleaning. Thank God for small favors. . . .

* * *

By the end of the week, however, Ronnie had learned to be grateful for Drake's presence in the studio. She had sneezed once, and Pieter's chisel had gone flying across the room. Drake's shocked stare had brought Pieter to the instant contrition he normally wouldn't have found for hours.

The entire house seemed to breathe new life with Drake in it. Although Ronnie was careful never to see him alone, she began to look forward to mealtimes, when she knew she would see him. Since the moments they had shared at the breakfast table on the day after his arrival, he had made every effort to be constantly cordial, if distant. And now that the initial shock of his arrival had subsided, Ronnie had regained the composure to act the collected hostess of her training and old-time southern background. She learned a new discipline, one that allowed her to be remotely yet perfectly polite while still enjoying the sight and sound of Drake's lean body and the mellow twang of his deep voice when he spoke.

The nights were still hell. She couldn't forget the fact that he slept just down the hall, and her body would burn as she tossed and turned, engulfed with longing, yet awash with shame. Sometimes when she finally slept, she would awaken again with a start, and she knew that she expected—and hoped—Drake had entered the room. And it was so stupid, because she also knew he would never enter again, and that if he did, it would be senseless. He wanted no further part of her; he had made that clear. And even if he did want her, she couldn't want him. . . .

It was a pity that the existence she had learned to tolerate with complacency had been so completely shattered.

Pieter cut the session extremely short on Friday morning. Startled, Ronnie took an uneasy look at her husband.

His skin had turned a terrible gray pallor; his hands, when he did not hold them behind his back, trembled with palsy. The health he had been clinging to since Drake's arrival was surely draining from him, and Ronnie knew he was hanging on to his last reserves of strength until he could be alone. He would not want Drake to see him feeble and in the chair.

Knowing her husband, Ronnie began to excuse herself, tallying an account of the things she had to do.

"Forget it, Ronnie." Pieter waved aside her plans. "We've offered Drake so little! I'd like you to take him for a ride around the island today. He's an expert horseman—I'm sure you'll find him up to our most rugged paths."

Ronnie had no doubt that Drake would be an expert horseman; she bitterly decided he would be an expert at anything he chose to do. But she couldn't think of a more trying afternoon than being alone in his company.

"Pieter, perhaps I should be here," she began tentatively.

"For what?" he demanded, his voice sharp. He couldn't tolerate a statement that he might need her.

"It's up to you, Ronnie," Drake interjected smoothly, intuitively stopping a battle before it could begin. His dark devillike eyes looked into hers with the briefest glint of understanding. "I would very much enjoy a good look at the island, but if you do have plans—"

"Nonsense," Pieter declared. "Ronnie has no plans that cannot wait."

"Ronnie?" Drake persisted.

"I'll be happy to accompany you for a ride around the island," Ronnie said uneasily, covertly watching Pieter. She would have promised anyone a ride in a spaceship to ease the tension and the sunken grayness of Pieter's skin, which was increasing by the second. "I'll, uh, need about fifteen minutes. I'll meet you by the stables."

"Fine," Drake agreed, his face troubled, his eyes on Pieter.

But Pieter was watching neither of them. He was attentively studying the work Drake had done for the day. Realizing he was being watched by them both, he looked up with a short laugh. "That's amazing . . ." he murmured, his hands moving reverently over the marble.

"Oh? What's that?" Drake queried, striding to join Pieter and glance down at his own creation with a puzzled frown.

"Those dimples," Pieter muttered. His eyes were still downcast over the marble, so neither Ronnie nor Drake saw the pensive speculation that lurked within them. "Those dimples beneath the spine . . . you've captured them in a stunning essence, and I hadn't even realized the draping was that low."

Ronnie stood dead still, hoping Pieter hadn't heard the horrible rasping of her indrawn breath, and hoping that Drake would answer suavely. . . .

He did. There wasn't a fraction of a second's hesitation before he smoothly chuckled in return. "The draping *wasn't* that low. I was taking a little artistic license, I'm afraid." His expression became suitably sheepish. "I suppose I haven't reached the point where artistic license is in order, but the chisel just seemed to go that way."

"No, no," Pieter protested, "you have done excellent work. The intuition was marvelous. I think you are wasting your time in the business side of the field."

"Thank you," Drake said quietly.

Ronnie sprang into action. "I'll go change," she murmured swiftly, gliding to the door. Turning for a moment of uncertainty, she kept her eyes blank and unwavering. "Pieter, shall I get you anything first?"

"No," Pieter returned abruptly. "Send Henri to me. Then please do not disturb me. I wish to be alone for the day."

Ronnie slid out the door, nodding. He was being rude, as was usually the case when he had his bad bouts, but he wasn't angry. Nor did he seem upset. Apparently he had accepted Drake's knowledge of her anatomy as imagination. As she closed the door she could still hear him speaking with Drake and, if anything, his tone was warmer and more cordial than before.

Pieter's thinking, however, involved more than mere suspicion. He had been watching Drake and Ronnie all week, and today had been the final assurance. He had known Ronnie was in love with Drake shortly after Drake's arrival. She wasn't in any way obvious, but Pieter could remember the way she had looked before Jamie died. That marvelous sparkle of sapphire in her eyes was a giveaway probably only he could fathom. Today he had learned for sure that Drake loved his wife. No, not his wife. He had to stop thinking of her with that title. Somehow he had to force himself to make the break before he could expect her to.

The two had been lovers at some time, Pieter knew. Fate, or coincidence, Drake must have been aboard the cruise. It hurt, he admitted. It hurt badly. And yet he was touched and flattered. Ronnie did care for him deeply. Even with the love that people spent their lives dreaming about within reach, she was refusing to leave him. And he knew the two of them were never intimate in his house.

It was also strangely palatable to lose her to a man like Drake. A lesser man would never have done. His ego wouldn't have tolerated it; there were times when his pride now went raw.

The knuckles in Pieter's bony hands cracked, and he realized how tightly he was clenching his fists. It was time he let her loose. She had never been his, just a loan from compassionate powers. She had given him the strength he now needed. But she was a tigress. Pairing her with a black panther was going to be tricky business, and he would still have to watch himself, because it did hurt.

Once in her room, Ronnie chose to wear her fawn-colored riding habit rather than jeans and a shirt, which she would have preferred. The habit was formal; jeans were not. Formality and distance were essential when she spent time with Drake.

With her hair in a neat knot and her riding cap in place, she zipped up her high black boots, sought out Henri to send for Pieter, and hurried out to the stables to have the horses saddled. Ronnie's mare, Scheherazade, was a gently spirited bay. Sure that Drake was the equestrian of Pieter's compliment, she chose Black Satan, a seventeen-hand magnificent stallion who lived up to his name, to be saddled for him. The two, she decided, matched one another. They were both the devil's own.

78

There was also a streak of mischief in her choice. Drake would be very busy handling the independent stallion, so busy, he couldn't possibly plague her with questions.

Drake appeared just as the groom was leading the horses to the mounting block. He watched Black Satan prance and snort and toss his well-defined head, then turned to Ronnie with an arched brow and a glint of amusement in his dark eyes.

"Is this an attempt at entertainment"—he chuckled—"or have you determined I have overstayed my welcome on your island? Am I supposed to be cast from the cliffs to the sea?"

Ronnie pursed her lips enigmatically. "I wouldn't think of offering you anything but our finest mount." Spinning in a smart circle, she sprang onto Scheherazade with practiced ease.

Drake shrugged and repeated her action with equal finesse, not losing a shred of confidence as the sleek black horse attempted to sidestep the man mastering him. Drake held the reins with a firm hand as he spoke gently to the animal, in a low tone that soothed but conveyed absolute command. Granting him grudging admiration as chills overcame her from the sound of his voice, tenderly guiding as she had once heard it, Ronnie led her bay out of the stable yard. Drake followed her with Black Satan under perfect control.

"The island covers about two miles," Ronnie said informatively. "We can ride up through the cliffs, or take the beach route. Either is a nice ride—"

"Ronnie."

Twisting her head quizzically at his halting, low tone, she arched a brow in question.

"I want to apologize." His eyes were as darkly fathomless as ever.

"For what?" she demanded shortly.

"For several of the things I said. I can't pretend I'm happy about this situation, or that I could ever condone your behavior, but I know there's more here than meets the eye. I have no right to judge you."

Ronnie kept her eyes glued to the trail in silence. What could

79

she say? But he wanted a response. She heard an impatient oath from him, and then Black Satan trotted up alongside her. The house was far behind them now, hidden from their view by the dense foliage of the rising cliff. Drake passed her, reaching near Scheherazade's muzzle to catch her reins and stop the horse.

"Ronnie!" Drake persisted. "If you would talk to me, I might be able to do something."

"There is nothing that anyone can do," Ronnie said flatly, sighing as the horses strained at their bits. She raised her eyes imperiously. "I thank you for being so quick to assure Pieter. . . ." Then anger suddenly overtook her cool resolve. "What in the hell possessed you to sculpt—to sculpt—"

"More than met the eye?" Drake provided laconically. "I didn't do it on purpose, I promise you. I just knew, and my hands—"

"You sound like Pieter," Ronnie said with unintentional bitterness. "The hands of the artist just move."

Drake shrugged. "Something like that." His voice went hard and grim. "But I told you once I would never intentionally cause Pieter any pain. Whether you want to admit it to me or not, the man is dying. That is why I find it so terribly difficult to understand you."

"I don't remember asking you to understand me," Ronnie replied smoothly.

"No," Drake responded critically, adding in curt reminder, "but you are asking other things of me."

"Could you let go of my horse's reins, please?" Ronnie asked, preferring to ignore his statement. "I think we should take the beach path."

He had barely released his grip before she hugged her knees tightly to Scheherazade's ribs. The animal, attuned to her mistress's lightest touch, broke immediately into a smooth canter.

The black stallion was not far behind.

"Ronnie!"

Ignoring Drake's demanding shout, Ronnie continued on. She had no intention of enduring a question-and-answer period.

There was little else she could say to Drake; no way to redeem herself in his eyes.

The wind drove against her face, giving her a wonderful sensation of wild, abandoned freedom. Scheherazade moved beneath her with powerful magic. It was possible to believe she could race forever, away from the turmoil of her life, away from the man who now relentlessly pursued her.

"Ronnie!" he shouted again imperiously.

She glanced behind her quickly to see him scowling darkly. He was still shouting, but she couldn't make out the words. She didn't want to hear them anyway. The pounding of Scheherazade's sure hooves was tempestuous music to her ears. Breaking out of the trail through the foliage and onto the beach, she gave her horse full rein. Scheherazade, as exuberant for freedom as she, tore gladly into a thundering gallop.

Drake was still shouting. The mare was a powerful animal, but no match for the stallion. Ronnie was forced from her world of wind and speed to glance at Drake as Black Satan pounded abreast of the mare.

"Damn it, Ronnie—"

She turned back around. Racing along the beach, she thought with irritation, and he was still determined to give her the third degree!

Impossible. He was still talking, but she couldn't make out the words. Scheherazade could hold her own. Ronnie was not going to give in to Drake; she would run until both she and the bay had tired, and Drake could go hang.

Racing was one of her great pleasures. Either on Scheherazade, or in the Boston Whaler, she loved the feel of wind and sea in her face. Riding on the beach was almost like combining the two. She could feel and hear the wonderful, vibrant gallop of the horse; she could feel and hear the infinite rolling of the surf; salt spray sailed into her face, and sand flew behind her. . . .

And Drake was still shouting for her to stop. He was telling her something, but she had closed off. Purposely.

The great black stallion pulled alongside of her again. *"Ron-nie!"*

Still she ignored him. It was a contest of wills. It was one that she could win—they were on her turf.

He was furious, and she knew it. She loved it. She had enough of Pieter maneuvering her to his will, she'd be damned if she would find Drake anything more than mere annoyance.

She glanced to her right to give him a grim smile, but perplexity furrowed her brow instead. Something in his tone began to crack through the wall of of sound with which she had cocooned herself. "The gir—"

She lost the rest of his word, but she then noticed more than anger in his dark scowl. His bronze skin was stretched taut over his features, his brows seemed to meet in a single tight arch, and his lips were thin and white beneath the black curl of his mustache. He was concerned, frightened. . . .

Black Satan began to head her off into deeper water, forcing her to slow down just as a movement beneath her seat made her sickly aware of the word Drake had been saying. The girth was slipping on her saddle. In another few minutes she would be thrown under Scheherazade.

Drake reached for her reins just as she began to pull them in herself. The cinch belt gave entirely, and the polished leather saddle swerved awkwardly off the horse, dumping Ronnie unceremoniously into three feet of saltwater.

Sputtering, she thrashed around to regain her balance, and then stood, shivering despite the late summer heat. She was mortified—her appearance totally undignified—but embarrassment was far preferable to the broken bones that could have resulted had Drake not forced her to slow down in the deeper water. . . .

He leaped off his own horse, mindless of the water that filled his Frye boots and saturated his jeans, and strode toward her, grasping her in his arms as he reached her.

"I'm all right," she protested feebly as he lifted her off her feet and carried her to the white sand. "I'm all right," she repeated, gasping. But she didn't fight him. Her arms curled around his neck, she closed her eyes, unable to deny the pleasure of the stolen moment of being held by him, of feeling the pounding of his heart, of resting her head against the breadth of his chest and having his heat radiate new warmth through her.

All too soon she was lying on the beach. She lay still as his eyes raked over her, with tender caring. . . .

Briefly. Very briefly. A second later he was standing, legs apart and firmly planted in the sand, tight-knuckled hands clenched on his waist.

"Good Lord, woman! What the hell is the matter with you! Why didn't you listen to me? Of all the unmitigated fool things to do . . ." He railed on in the same tone, and Ronnie felt the chills—and any sense of grateful tenderness—drain from her swiftly as her own temper rose to match the dark, burning fury in his eyes. She took enough harassment from Pieter! And she took that for a reason! She'd be damned if she'd tolerate another man venting anger in her direction—deserved or not.

Springing to her feet and spraying Drake with water and sand with the the fury of her pounce, she marched straight to him, her own legs spread in a defiant stance, her arms flying with wild vehemence.

"Don't you dare—don't you dare!—speak to me like that! I won't have it. I will not have it! All right, so I should have listened, but how the hell did I know you had something to say that wasn't an insult or a none-of-your-business question? I have had it up to my neck, Mr. Drake O'Hara. You're right—you don't know a damn thing and you have no right on earth to judge me." Ronnie wasn't winding down at all. All the frustration and wrath she had so carefully bottled up rose to the surface and, before she knew it, she was pummeling Drake's chest with tightly clenched fists.

At first Drake was stunned. Then, absurdly, he broke into laughter, and continued to chuckle as he dodged her flailing fists and secured them easily with his own hands.

Then, as she ranted and raved and protested, newly infuriated by his amusement, he picked her up once more, carried her several feet in to the water, and dumped her back in, watching with that dry, sardonic smile as she sputtered again to the surface, gasping and incoherent as she slung a widespread string of oaths in to his face.

"Hey! Cool down," Drake protested, backing away from her with mock terror in his eyes. "I thought one dunking might do it, but another may be necessary."

"You dunk me one more time, Drake O'Hara," Ronnie dared, her eyes flashing with the brilliance of cut sapphires, "and I swear to God, you'll live to regret this day if it takes my entire lifetime!"

Her threat elicited nothing but more laughter, and she attempted to stomp a foot in the water before realizing how ridiculous she must look. Her cap was long gone with the waves, her hair was half up and half down with straggling pins, and her elegant fawn-colored riding habit encased her in drenched dishevelment.

Snapping her mouth shut for an instant, she drew herself to her full height and primly stiffened her shoulders. "Pray, Mr. O'Hara, be so kind as to tell me what you find so amusing about all this?"

He crossed his arms over his chest and slowly let eyes that still glittered with laughter roam with ill-concealed mirth from her hair-plastered face to the spot where her breeches met the water. "Besides the obvious?" he inquired innocently.

Gritting her teeth, Ronnie retorted, "Yes—besides the obvious!"

"Okay, my dear, dear Mrs. von Hurst," he replied, his mockery light as he surveyed her. "It's rather an inside joke, but I'll try to explain." He shifted his weight to launch into his explanation, and as Ronnie glared at him she was forced to hide a grudging admiration behind the wall of her anger. Even soaked he was magnificent, his form outlined by his wet clothing, his hair and mustache so black, they glinted blue.

"You see, I've always thought of you as a cat. So sleek, so

smooth, so independent . . . incredibly lithe, remarkably agile. From the moment I first saw you, I thought you possessed that sophisticated feline mystique. By whimsy I think I've just discovered that to be a little true." He paused for a moment, and Ronnie realized that he had been slowly advancing on her. His words had astounded her. They seemed to be compliments.

But that devilish twinkle was in his eyes. She began to back off further in to the water as he continued his approach.

"A cat, Ronnie," he continued. "An aloof creature, seeking to be stroked occasionally, only at her own leisure. Sometimes even purring with pleasure. Sometimes baring claws that scratch deeply, but always, always, so terribly independent."

He had woven a spell with his words as he came closer and closer. And even as she watched him with suspicion, he stopped directly in front of her and grinned, his teeth startlingly white against the damp mustache.

"Now I'm absolutely convinced you are a cat. Only a drowned cat could look so pathetic when inadvertently drenched."

Ronnie curled her lips over tightly clenched teeth, and her eyes blazed, shimmering like the sea beneath the sun. "Thank you, Drake," she enunciated with dry formality. "A cat, huh? I would watch it, then," she advised. "I've heard that cats are known to be exceptionally fierce when 'inadvertently drenched.' "

"Are they?"

"Oh, yes," she said pleasantly, basically back in control and wise enough to move with caution. "Especially when plagued by extremely dense, prying blackbirds." She certainly wasn't going to be able to use brute force against him, she decided dryly, but perhaps a little cat cunning. . . .

"Prying blackbirds," he told her with an edge to his voice, "only pry when they don't understand. It's an effort not to be dense."

She wasn't really listening, she was hiding a smile of satisfaction—he expected no retaliation. Shrugging dismissively, she stooped in the water as if to find a pebble in her boot, then leaned her weight abruptly against him as she shifted a foot behind his.

The effect was marvelous. Totally unprepared, Drake fell backward with a splash. Her self-satisfied smile of victory, however, left her face and was replaced with a yelp. He had recovered enough to catch her hand before he went down, and a split second later she was splashing down on top of him.

"Blackbirds can also be fierce when harassed by cats," Drake said, grinning as he maintained a grip upon her as they both surfaced. "Poor things. Especially when they fall prey to the deviousness of a cat. A second time." The grin suddenly left his lips. "Most especially cats who promise love in the dark, and forever in the daylight, while knowing all along that their promise of forever is nothing but a lark."

He still held her wrist; she couldn't escape him. The color fled from her face, and she lowered her lashes, but she didn't flinch.

"A part of me meant that, Drake," she admitted with a strange type of dignified pride. "I—I just never imagined—"

"That I'd appear at your house?" he demanded sarcastically, his grip upon her wrist tensing painfully.

"No." She straightened her shoulders and met his eyes. "I never imagined that you could possibly be serious."

Drake stared at her silently for several seconds, then cast her hand away from his with a strangled curse. God, he told himself with contempt, he was falling for her again, for her words that meant nothing.

"Oh?" he charged, knowing his anger rose even as he attempted to stay as cool as she was. "You're not going to ask my forgiveness—tell me you just went a little crazy? You had been contemplating leaving your cruel husband?"

"No." Ronnie didn't move. He had jokingly told her—before the conversation had turned grave—that she looked like a drowned cat. But she didn't. Pale, more regal than ever with her pride wrapped around her with her admissions, she still looked like marble, perfect, intricately sculpted marble. He was still in love with her, he still wanted her so desperately. Contempt was his only defense. He wanted to believe that she loved him, no matter how wrong.

"I have never once contemplated leaving Pieter," she said tonelessly.

There was misery to her voice, but truth; something so honest that he wanted to pull her comfortingly into his arms. But pain fed the fuel of his anger, the inner reminder that she had used him.

"Ahhh . . ." he murmured cruelly. "A greedy cat."

Ronnie felt as if she had been struck. Her entire body seemed to shudder uncontrollably. But she couldn't let Drake move in too closely—she had already offered what she could, an offering he disdained. "Have it your way, Drake," she said, shrugging.

He turned his back on her in the water, staring across the cliffs of the island. They must look like two idiots, he decided remotely, standing in waist-high surf, talking circles around each other. He had apologized for his treatment of her when they started out, and now he was back to it. It was sheer frustration that drove him, and he knew it. He hated home wreckers; he liked, respected, and admired Von Hurst.

If the man was a macho idiot who beat his wife, Drake could like himself better. But Von Hurst wasn't an idiot, nor was he insanely cruel. He loved his wife. The relationship wasn't right, but whatever the depths of emotion, Ronnie also cared for Von Hurst. Whether that caring was tempered by a vicarious hold on wealth and position, Drake just couldn't tell. . . .

Yet it was hard to question her beautiful, steadfast eyes; hard to convince himself she didn't love him, too. . . . For a moment he clenched his fists painfully at his side. With effort he released them. He turned back to find her motionless, watching him, still pale, still determinedly dignified.

"Sorry," he said simply, mentally giving him himself a shake. He would get to the bottom of everything, and he would live by his apology. She visibly relaxed at his abrupt change, and more than ever, he wanted just to touch her. "Oh, no!" he cried, quelling a grin.

87

"What?" she demanded quickly, concerned.

"My drowned cat is drying off!"

With the supple strength of a born athlete, he was swiftly upon her, lifting her in his arms a last time to dunk her thoroughly. She clasped her fingers over his head and dragged him down, too. They both emerged sputtering and laughing, their arms wound around one another as their eyes met. Such a contradiction! Ronnie thought, anger sparking in her. "Now, what do you find so vastly amusing?" she demanded haughtily, warily thinking of his lightning change of mood.

He sobered in an instant and his voice was strange when he answered. "You almost had me convinced that you were marble," he told her quietly. "I had begun to believe that I had imagined there had been a woman who walked, talked, and breathed with beautiful life and warmth. . . ."

He withdrew his arms tiredly and strode out of the water, whistling for the horses as he reached the shore. Ronnie stared after him, chewing her bottom lip. His shirt and jeans were plastered to his body, and it was impossible not to feel a tug at her heart and senses as she observed the striking tone and pride of his physique. But it would also be impossible ever to explain all that she felt. Still, all anger seeped from her, and she determined to grasp whatever straw of friendship that she could from him.

Ronnie began to chuckle, emerging from the water as Drake captured the bay, restored its saddle, and then went after the stubborn stallion.

Drake scowled at her as he made a second attempt to catch Black Satan's trailing reins. "You want to let me in on *your* amusement?" he inquired wryly.

Inclining her head toward the horse, Ronnie smiled. "Just the obvious."

Drake didn't look at her, but his own smile slipped slowly back to curve his lips. He moved one hand to gently pat the stallion's neck while the other snaked out to secure the reins. "Need a boost up?" he asked Ronnie.

She thought about saying yes just for an excuse to feel his touch, but she shook her head. "No, thanks. I can manage."

They began the ride back to the house in a silence that was strangely comfortable. Nearing the stable yard, Ronnie stopped him.

"Drake."

"Yes?" He turned to her expectantly.

"I—it's my turn to apologize. I could have been really hurt. Thank you."

He gave her a cocky, devilish grin that mocked his own emotion. "'Twas nothing, my marble beauty. A pleasure."

Their eyes met for an instant and then they both looked away.

Neither had anything more to say. They had reached the stable, and the strange, compelling interlude was over.

CHAPTER FIVE

Pieter did not appear for dinner that night, only his note of apology upon a filigreed silver tray. And, of course, the note was addressed to Drake, not Ronnie.

She watched as Drake's dark eyes scanned Pieter's flourished script quickly as they waited in the salon, and she did not avert her gaze when his eyes rose from the paper to her.

"It seems," he said laconically, absently folding the sheet of monogrammed note paper, "that your husband wishes a few days of rest. It's his suggestion that we spend the day in Charleston tomorrow."

Ronnie's fingers curled over the arm of her chair. She was sure Pieter was not issuing a suggestion but a command.

"Surely you've seen Charleston," she murmured.

He shrugged, tapping the note against a casually crossed knee. "Not much of it, really. I came here to see Pieter. I was a few days ahead of schedule, so . . ."

His sentence trailed away, but Ronnie knew the ending. Flushing unhappily, she lowered her eyes to the upholstery of her chair, where she watched a long glazed nail trace the pattern of the brocade material.

"I think we should go into Charleston," Drake said with a firm determination that made Ronnie's heart leap unexpectedly. His tone held an underlying menace. She was sure she was in for the third degree again, which Drake wouldn't administer in the house with the possibility of others listening in.

Stiffening, she answered indifferently. "If you wish." She resented him heartily. He must realize that if she protested, Pieter might become suspicious. Why the hell couldn't he do the gentlemanly thing and disappear into the blue—or at least think of sound reasons to reject his host's "suggestions" when he threw the two of them together?

"Yes"—he looked her squarely in the eye—"I do wish."

Henri appeared to announce dinner, and Drake rose mockingly, offering her his arm. Ronnie clenched her teeth as they entered the dining room together and sat down to their lone meal. Drake's conversation became impersonal and polite—the front he extended for Henri and Gretel as they entered and exited the room.

Ronnie knew his smooth mask would not slip, but she ate and spoke in stilted misery anyway. Each time she glanced his way she caught his dark eyes upon her, pensive and calculating. And she shivered with new apprehension of the morning to come.

Dave Quimby took them into Charleston Harbor on the boat at ten o'clock. Pieter kept a Ferrari parked in a private lot, and Ronnie suggested they pick up the car and head first for the old slave market.

Drake firmly shook his head. "I think we should start with a walk along the Battery. I want to talk to you."

Ronnie sighed with sheer exasperation, her gaze upon the shimmering harbor and the multitude of boats rocking lightly in their berths.

"Drake, you can talk to me until you're blue in the face! There is nothing that I can tell you."

"There's plenty that you can tell me," he insisted grimly, taking her elbow and starting briskly down the walk by the sea. "And I definitely intend to get some answers."

Powerless against his hold, Ronnie had no choice but to accompany him.

"For a man who proclaimed he'd never touch me with a ten-foot pole," Ronnie complained with bitter sarcasm, "you're doing quite a job on my arm." Though long-limbed herself, she was panting to keep up with his brisk pace.

"Merely expression," he replied laconically. "I think we both know to what type of touching I was referring." He halted abruptly. "This looks as good a place as any." Bowing sardonically, he dusted sand from the seawall. "Sit, if you will, please, Mrs. von Hurst." At her hesitance he raised a mocking brow. "Or might we crease our designer jeans?"

Ronnie glared at him coldly, then pointedly drew her eyes to the label of his black jeans before returning her eyes to his and caustically replying, "I don't know, might we?"

The darkness of his eyes suffused with a flame of mirth as his mustache twitched in a way she was beginning to know very well. "My dear Mrs. von Hurst," he replied gallantly, "I do give you credit for a marvelously ticking little mind." He crouched to the wall, deftly flinging his legs over the edge while dragging her down beside him. He didn't release her hand as she joined him with little choice, her attitude less than gracious, her teeth grinding.

He smiled at her annoyance. "This is a lovely view," he commented, his mustache tilting with a full grin. "The sea, the sky, the mist, Fort Sumter rising in the distance. Nice place for a talk."

Ronnie kept her gaze on Fort Sumter, rising in the mist as he had pointed out. "Lovely," she agreed dryly. "Talk any time you like."

"How long has Pieter been ill?"

Ronnie shrugged, determined to give him nothing. "Awhile."

Drake muttered something inaudible beneath his breath and his grip on her hand jerked painfully. "Damn it, Ronnie! I already know the man is desperately ill. I'm not asking you for the sake of conversation—I think I can help."

The explosive sincerity of his voice was undeniable. Ronnie glanced at him, reading the intensity of his dark stare, then shook her head with appreciative but sad resignation. "Drake,

I told you before. There's nothing that you can do, nothing that *anyone* can do."

"Ronnie," Drake said forcefully, "you're being fatalistic. I can help. I know a man from the center at Johns Hopkins who specializes in just this type of thing, the wasting diseases—sclerosis."

"But Pieter has seen dozens of doctors!"

"So he should see a dozen more."

Ronnie mulled his words slowly through her mind. Drake was right; she and Pieter had given up, accepted the inevitable. They should have never allowed themselves to do so. Such a fight should be fought to the bitter end. "How do we get Pieter to see this man, and will he see Pieter?"

"The doctor will see Pieter," Drake said assuredly, softening his features to a grin again. "He's an art lover. Pieter—well, leave him to me."

"No!" Ronnie cried. "He'll know I've been discussing him and he'll be absolutely livid."

Drake shook his head emphatically, and Ronnie suddenly realized he was no longer gripping her hand but holding it soothingly, his fingers working tenderly over the pale lines of her veins. "I promise you, Pieter will know nothing. . . ." His voice trailed away as they both thought of the other implication of such a statement.

Drake cleared his throat and continued in a businesslike tone. "I'll talk to Pieter and convince him of what is really the truth— I can see his condition. But what I do need from you is everything that you can tell me. I want to know when he became ill, how the illness affects him, and what has been said so far by his doctors."

"That's a large order," Ronnie murmured. "Where do I begin?" She wanted to help Drake, knowing he was serious and reaching tentatively for the ray of hope he was giving her. And she would answer him as truthfully as possible, but there were certain things she simply couldn't reveal, certain things about which Pieter would rather die than have become known. . . .

"Start anywhere," Drake prompted her, "and I'll insert questions when I want you to go further."

Taking a deep breath, Ronnie began to talk, telling him that the disease had begun at a slow rate of acceleration soon after their marriage. It was a small white lie, one which she hoped would make no difference. Drake's few comments and questions were intelligent and well spaced, and before she knew it, she became immersed in her monologue, telling Drake the things that worried her most, confiding in him as she had never thought possible.

They never had to discuss a sex life at all. Drake knew Pieter and Ronnie kept separate quarters, and although Ronnie knew Drake still condemned her for her affair with him aboard the ship, he was tactful enough at the moment to make no remarks. Ronnie stopped speaking suddenly and looked up into his eyes, which gazed intently at her. She wondered if she caught a spark of empathy, but it was gone so quickly, she assured herself that tenderness from him could only exist in her imagination. And yet, she felt good, as if talking had lifted a heavy load from her shoulders. She could easily hate Drake for his often disdainful treatment of her, but she also trusted him explicitly.

He was a hard man, a thorough man—a man she had stupidly fallen in love with—a man of fury and intensity, but one who would direct his energies tirelessly and relentlessly in pursuit of a goal. She felt a drained relief to know his goal at that moment was the life and health of Pieter von Hurst.

"It hasn't been easy for you, has it?" he asked, his tone surprisingly hard for his question.

"No, it hasn't," Ronnie replied bluntly, her voice every bit as matter-of-fact. Then the relief of having shared her burden washed through her and she impetuously grabbed his arm and stared into his dark eyes beseechingly. "Oh, Drake, do you really think there's any kind of a chance? . . ."

"Yes, Ronnie, I do. I believe there is always hope."

Hope. Ronnie dropped his arm and stared out to sea. For some things, perhaps, there was hope. Not for others.

Drake suddenly hopped to his feet with athletic agility and reached to give her a hand. "I've never seen Fort Sumter," he told her, still with a rather harsh, gravelly tone. "Can we go over? How do we get there?"

Ronnie stood beside him and answered his new line of questioning levelly, sounding something like an indifferent tour guide in relation to his manner. No matter what he said, no matter what had once gone on between them—no, not even the fact that they had become conspirators on Pieter's behalf—could change his opinion of her. For a wild moment of misery she was tempted to throw herself into his arms and explain everything, to unburden herself completely, to cry out that she wasn't a run-a-round wanton but a victim herself of desperate need . . . and love. But she could say none of those things. She simply couldn't do it to Pieter and, anyway, it wouldn't change things, she would still be Mrs. Pieter von Hurst.

Even with the slim ray of hope Drake offered, Ronnie would always be bound to Pieter by ties of her own morality. And so as her mind dwelt upon dreams unuttered she kept up a line of chatter about Charleston, talking as she led him to the Ferrari, which would be their transportation around town. She pointed out various old houses along the Battery as they drove to the ferry that would take them out to Fort Sumter, maintaining her cool, instructorlike stream of exposition.

As Drake listened to her, he struggled with an inward battle. He didn't mean to sound harsh each time he spoke; his cold brusqueness was a line of defense. It was impossible to look into the incredible blue depths of her eyes and not be touched—and painfully inflamed. He decided with a cruel twist of his lips that he was a masochist.

Every time he came near her, he was stricken with the wild desire to sweep her into his arms and take her with primitive passion—no matter where they happened to be. Remembrance of the satin softness of her skin, the perfect, harmonious fit her slender, lusciously curved form made with his body . . . being one with her . . . drove him to the brink of madness, and to a number of cold showers. And all the while he berated himself for his stupidity. She was Von Hurst's wife; a sophisticated woman who indulged in affairs for her own entertainment while married to the great, ailing artist. . . .

God, he groaned inwardly. Why the hell didn't she fit the part of the hard, calculating seductress? It would be so easy to forget her then . . . but no one could look into her unmasked, depthless, beguiling eyes and call her hard, or believe that she was—what she was.

A woman with needs, a part of his mind told him. One who endured a lonely, demanding life. One who sincerely cared for Pieter. But he had been deceived by her once, used by her once, because he had trusted the character and soul in those eyes, which had held him a willing prisoner of her grace and beauty.

He couldn't lower his guard to her for a second. She was Von Hurst's. But deep within himself he struggled with another thought. If—an incredible if—he could ever make her his, she would probably do the same—run around. She had learned the lesson, and surely cheating could only become easier and easier. He didn't even have any idea of how many escapades she had carried on like the one they had shared.

He shook himself mentally. She wasn't his. He had no right to be angry with her; her affairs or lack of them were Pieter's concern. Her *husband's* concern. He lashed out at her because of his own frustration and a haunting desire that overwhelmed him that could never be fulfilled again. . . .

Recognizing what ripped him apart—and admitting the root of his anger—suddenly calmed him. She was here with him today because he had forced her hand, both to quiz her on Pieter, and also to take a form of punishment out on her—to force her to be near him. Perhaps he wanted to force her to suffer as he did, because he loved her still every bit as much as he hated her for shattering the illusion of trust and happiness he had created with her upon his pedestal. . . .

"Drake."

He started as she said his name, obviously for a second time. "This is it," she said quietly as he stared at her blankly in return. "The ferry."

"Oh." Drake uncoiled his length and hastened dexterously from the car, suddenly determined to be courteous. But she was out of the driver's seat before he could reach her door. Not daunted, he slipped an arm through hers. The glance she gave him, peering at an angle through fringed lashes, was skeptical, to say the least.

"I'm opting for a pleasant day," he told her smoothly. "A tourist out with a native to see the sights. No past, no concerns. Deal?"

Ronnie slightly arched a doubting brow and pursed her lips in a small smirk, but nodded. "No past, no concerns."

And an hour later, as they crawled around the cannons and ruined brick of the island fort, she lost her cynicism and began to believe him. He was out to be charming.

They linked arms as they ambled about, occasionally listening to the guides, occasionally referring to the informative pamphlets, and reading aloud to one another. They discussed the war and the battle that had rocked Fort Sumter over a century ago, and from there the conversation progressed easily to present times. Without innuendo, Drake quizzed Ronnie on life in Paris, and she in turn discovered that he was well traveled and had a host of amusing anecdotes relating to difficulties for Americans in various European cities.

By the time the ferry took them back to the harbor, they were both comfortable with their strange truce. Drake assuredly plucked the keys from Ronnie's hand as they returned to the Ferrari, murmuring with a quiet firmness, "I'll drive."

"Oh?" she teased, obediently slipping into the passenger seat as he opened her door, "and where are we going?"

"I do know the town a little bit," he retorted. "And I know precisely where to go for dinner, dressed as we are."

Ronnie glanced ruefully at the jeans they both wore. She

hadn't thought that they would be dining out, but they had passed lunchtime without thought, and she realized she was ravenous. She was also happy to continue the day. It had had a shaky start, but the afternoon had been so pleasant; a sweet interlude of a dream coming unexpectedly to life. In time they would return to the island, her coach would turn back into a pumpkin, her prince would turn back into Drake, and she would turn back into Mrs. Pieter von Hurst.

But the bewitching time was midnight, wasn't it? she thought, closing her eyes dreamily. Drake was taking her to dinner. It was a pity they weren't dressed. She would love to dance every second away and, like Cinderella, not lose a precious second, but leave on the stroke of twelve. . . .

"Where are we going?" she asked, her lips slightly curled from the whimsy of her imaginings. "There aren't any really nice dinner spots I know of where we can go like this."

Drake sent her a dancing ebony glance. "It takes a tourist!" he groaned with mock disgust. "We are going to a little private club near the city center. A casual place with impeccable stuffed mushrooms and the tenderest steak tidbits you'll ever sink your teeth into. And"—his sizzling coal gaze came her way again as if he had read her mind—"they employ a top forties band that is great. They lean a little toward hard rock, but they are good, and lots of fun. Any objections?"

Ronnie shook her head and lowered her lashes to hide the extreme pleasure his words had given her. "No—no objections. It does sound like fun."

The club really wasn't little at all, Ronnie realized as they entered the comfortable redwood establishment. Like so many night spots, the decor was dark, basically black and crimson, and the lighting dim. It was split into several sections, with the band and dance floor a half level below the dinner tables. Ronnie approved of the design immediately. It was possible to talk with one's partner while intimately dining without being drowned out by the music, and then equally possible to fully enjoy the dancing and music without intruding on a voracious diner!

They were led up a short flight of thickly carpeted stairs to a secluded booth in a corner. The smiling hostess seated them across from one another, and Ronnie was grateful as she sank into the plush booth. It would be too easy to forget she was just a Cinderella if she had to sit next to him and feel the heat from his body vibrate along the side of hers. And she was sure Drake never really forgot who she was, no matter how pleasantly he behaved toward her.

A silence fell between them after they placed their drink orders, and Ronnie pretended a great interest in her menu while sneaking covert glances at Drake. He was marvelous—though somewhat chilling—just to look at. Tonight he almost matched the decor of the club; his snug jeans were black, his casually tailored shirt black-and-red-patterned. The top two buttons of his shirt were open, revealing a V of crisp black hair upon his chest. Matching it all were his eyes, seeming of the deepest, darkest, ebony fire. With his wavy dark-brown hair and devilishly curved mustache, high, gaunt cheeks and foreboding but fascinating profile, he had already drawn the recurring gazes of the club's female patrons.

Yet it was more than looks that brought eyes to him like magnets. A sense of indifferent confidence was part of Drake. He emanated a totally male assurance, and something even more intriguing: that beguiling, mesmerizing look of the devil—a dangerous look, as compelling as fire. . . .

A hand, long and broad and sporting neatly clipped nails, suddenly swept away Ronnie's red-tassled menu. "You're reading upside down," Drake told her dryly, adding as she flushed and parted her lips for an explanation, "And you don't need to read anyway. Trust me, I won't lead you astray."

Glad of any excuse to bypass his observation of her upside-down reading habits, Ronnie inanely murmured, "I trust you." Then, alarmed at the multiple meanings her tone could give to the simple words, she chatted on at an impetuous rate. "Stuffed mushrooms, right? And the most tender steak tidbits in the world. Served, I assume, with some type of deliciously seasoned

99

dipping sauce. And the mushrooms—stuffed with fresh crab-meat, delicately tipped with bread crumbs, and basted in seasoned butter to tempt, tease, and fully arouse the palate—" She broke off in confusion, wondering where she had found such words of description for food.

Drake was laughing. "They should hire you to write the menus. You just made a casual dinner sound like an erotic experience."

His laughter broke off abruptly, and it was he who stared down at his menu. They could both easily remember an erotic experience. Thankfully their drinks arrived at the table before an uncomfortable silence could lengthen. Drake glanced at Ronnie only once as he gave their orders. He already knew she preferred her meat rare, sour cream for her baked potato.

Ronnie staunchly pulled her flustered demeanor together as Drake placed the order for their meal. A long sip of the brandy alexander she now had before her helped her regain a measure of aloofness, necessary with their words taking on unintentional insinuation. She didn't want to mar the day with a tense exchange of hostilities should one of them step too far.

The sweet, mellow taste of her drink hid but didn't diminish the combined potency of the brandy and crème de cacao, which were mixed with only a hint of cream. A second sip steadied her while giving her the illusion of relaxation as a languorousness misted the world around her, taking away all the sharp edges. She almost giggled but stopped herself. She was floating on two sips of a drink, and she could only credit the sensation to her completely empty stomach.

She didn't want to giggle right now, though; she wanted to wear her cool image, her Mrs. Pieter von Hurst image. A giggle just wouldn't fit. Nor would the rumble in her stomach if it became loud enough to be heard. . . .

Placing an elbow on the table and resting her chin on her knuckles, Ronnie smiled distantly, unaware that the sparkling, wistful mist in her eyes was soft and bewitching. "Tell me," she said conversationally, "something about Drake O'Hara." She

100

idly picked up the swizzle stick that had been in her drink and pushed absently at the floating nutmeg. Ruefully, her eyes then on the drink, she added, "You know a little too much about me, and I know nothing about you. Except that your home is Chicago."

He quirked a brow as she met his eyes again. "Not fair. I don't really know anything about you. Not about the real Ronnie who hides behind the marble mask. I know nothing about your past, about your own dreams."

Ronnie bit down lightly on her lower lip in an imperceptible movement of an eyetooth. It was a damn good thing he knew nothing about her dreams. They were as far fetched as a piece of the moon.

"You first," she told him. "Were you born in Chicago?"

"Right in the heart," he replied wryly, lounging back in the booth, one finger running idly up and down the icy moisture on the side of his rock glass. "I grew up in a suburb, Des Plaines, and then picked up my B.A. at Northwestern." He grimaced ruefully. "My major was actually business, but I was offered an art scholarship to the University of Florence. I picked up a master's degree there and became passionately involved in what I had previously decided—wisely, as my parents had instructed—to be only a hobby: sculpture. It was impossible not to become aggressively and passionately involved, not with the works of Michelangelo and other great Italian masters within reaching distance. I used to spend hours in the Medici Chapels, just staring at his work on the tombs."

"I don't understand," Ronnie interjected. "You must be very good. Pieter says so, and he never flatters anyone, and you received a scholarship. Why do you only dabble in sculpture now?"

Drake shrugged. "Actually, I don't just dabble. I work under another name. Mero."

Ronnie had lifted her glass to sip at her drink and found herself taking a huge swallow—one that left her choking as the heat of the brandy catapulted to her stomach. "Mero!" she

101

gasped. He *was* well known in the world of sculpture, and highly respected. Pieter had many of his pieces, fine miniatures intricately wrought in flawless marble. "I had no idea . . ."

"Few people do," Drake said. "I prefer to remain anonymous. As a gallery owner and critic, it becomes awkward to be known. I would appreciate your keeping my alter ego a confidence."

"Certainly," Ronnie murmured, surprised and inordinately pleased that he should trust her enough to offer such a confidence. If only he could trust her a little as far as other things went. . . . Foolish. What good would it do? She couldn't change her own circumstances. She blocked her mind to pain and asked, "But then, why the galleries?"

He laughed. "I'm a little too self-centered to be a completely dedicated artist. My love of art is widespread. I'm fascinated by the work of others, by the ancient masters, by the promising greats of the future. When I can discover a talent, and force that talent to expand and improve, I receive my greatest personal rewards. And when I can work with or encourage a Pieter von Hurst, I find my own personal achievement."

"I don't find that self-centered at all," Ronnie murmured appreciatively, too enamored of his tale to make an attempt to sound indifferent. "I think it's wonderful."

Drake grinned. "Thanks. Your turn."

"My turn?" she echoed in dismay. "Not yet! You haven't really told me anything, uh . . ."

"Personal?"

"Well, yes, I suppose that is what I mean," she admitted. The drink, the cozy atmosphere, the muted sound of the band, all were making her unwittingly at ease with him, and bold enough to honestly pry. Her questions, she realized with a tug of pain, were part of a driving curiosity she couldn't contain, even as she accepted the fact weakly that the answers could cause agony. He said once, in another world, that he loved her. She didn't want to hear that he loved elsewhere, or that he had loved before, but with perverse voraciousness she had to know everything that she

102

could about him; about his life, about the things that made up the man that he was.

"Personal . . . hmm," he mused reflectively. "My parents are both living. They're a nice middle-class couple with a certain quiet charm who still reside in Des Plaines. I have two brothers and a sister, all younger, and the family meets each year for Christmas and the Fourth of July. You see, Katie lives in Arizona, Michael in Atlanta, and Padraic in northern Michigan. I have a lovely—if sometimes monstrous—collection of nieces and nephews."

Ronnie laughed at his monologue, envying him the obvious warmth of his family. Apparently Drake had everything: success of his own creation, wealth, power, and, most important, an abundance of love. The desolation of her own life threatened to sweep over her, so she quickly joked, "And are these lovely but monstrous little nieces and nephews all dark as Satan like their hell-bent uncle?"

Drake shrugged wide shoulders, flashing her a white grin at the comment. "Half and half. Perfect split. Padraic and I are dark like my father, Katie and Michael are blue-eyed blonds. Their offspring are all the various shades in between."

"Prolific family," Ronnie said dryly, sounding light in spite of the catch in her throat. "What happened to the oldest O'Hara? No little creations to date?"

"You would have known if there were," he told her bluntly, reminding her of the intimacy of their first meeting. Yes, he would have told her if he had any children. At that encounter, he had said that he wanted to marry her. . . .

"You could have been married at one time," she said defensively, playing with her swizzle stick again to avoid his eyes. "I mean, you are well over twenty-one, and a healthy, virile male . . ." Ronnie's voice trailed away and she was thoroughly annoyed to feel a hot flush rising to her cheeks again. She deserved this loss of cool reserve. She was asking leading questions that could only return in circular fashion to their own brief relationship, and consequently to the tension that lurked beneath

103

their best efforts to be continually pleasant. For her to make a comment about his being a healthy, virile male was abject stupidity. She knew what he was, but he also knew that she knew only too well what he was. . . .

"No," he replied bluntly, "I have no children. I was married once, though, when I was very young."

Ronnie waited for him to continue, but he didn't, and she was compelled to ask in a soft whisper, "What happened?"

"She died," he said shortly, then catching the quickly hidden flicker of pain in Ronnie's eyes, he added, "My wife was an Italian girl. I met her while studying in Florence. There was a cholera outbreak."

"I'm sorry," Ronnie murmured truthfully, her eyes misting ridiculously.

"It was a long time ago," Drake said gruffly, watching her eyes as they shimmered with that soulful tragedy he had sensed before. Intuitively he knew she had suffered a similar loss, a pain that was not related to Pieter. He reached a forceful but strangely compassionate hand across the table to take hers. "Your turn, Ronnie. What happened to you before Pieter?"

She looked for a barb in his tone, or cynicism in his eyes, but there was neither. She shrugged and smiled softly. "The same. I lost a fiancé." Her lower lip trembled slightly.

"What happened?" He returned her own question.

She bit her trembling lower lip to cease its action. "Drugs," she said faintly. "I never even knew until it was too late and all the signs were there."

Drake's handclasp on hers shook roughly, and with surprise she found an unusual and oddly harsh sympathy in his eyes. "Surely you don't blame yourself!" he said sternly.

"No," she replied, startled at the realization that she did in a way. "Not really."

"Not at all," he commanded. "No one can change a situation like that."

Ronnie broke his gaze with a tentative smile of thanks, moving her eyes with sudden interest to the stage. Their conversation had grown a little too personal, and she didn't want her soul completely bared to this man who still condemned her on one hand while offering encouragement on the other.

"The band is marvelous," she offered enthusiastically. "And, if I'm not mistaken, we no longer have to starve. I believe our waitress is coming our way."

Her intent to change the subject was obvious, but as their dinner arrived, steaming with succulent aromas, her switch to a lighter, more casual conversation seemed easily accomplished. But after munching into and savoring a large mushroom cap, Drake returned to his interrogation of her with a single-worded question.

"Parents?"

"Pardon?" Ronnie stopped uneasily, her fork halfway to her mouth.

"Your parents. Are they living?"

She bit into her mushroom and shook her head. "They were killed in an auto crash in my senior year of high school."

Drake offered no more sympathy; it wasn't needed, he knew. Still, he felt his heart constricting for her and was consumed with an overwhelming desire to take her into his arms and shield her, protect her, and offer her all the love she had lost. He understood now the strength of her marble beauty, the brick wall of dignity that hid the giving, sensuous woman he had known so briefly.

But she wasn't his to protect or love. She was Pieter's. And she had never denied the love she felt for the husband she saw fit to leave from time to time.

"Siblings?" he asked, continuing to eat.

"None."

"What took you to Paris?"

"After college, I had nothing to go home to," she said matter-of-factly. "I majored in the French language, so it seemed logical to go to Paris. I met Jamie at The Louvre one day."

"And Pieter?"

"Through Jamie. He was a student." Ronnie set her fork down for a moment, losing her appetite for the delicious food. Like she

105

had done, Drake was going to keep quizzing until he had all his answers. These were things she could answer honestly, so she might as well give him a quick story.

"Jamie and Pieter were close friends," she told Drake tonelessly, her hands folded in her lap, her eyes downcast. "When Jamie died, I was stunned, very young, and very lost. Pieter helped me through all the bad times. I'm—ah—I'm very grateful to him; I will never forget how wonderful he was."

"Von Hurst is an amazing man," Drake said simply.

Ronnie was still staring at her plate of half-eaten food, and so she didn't see the speculative look Drake covertly cast her way.

And he was speculating. For the first time since he had seen Ronnie beside his host, he had stopped envying Pieter von Hurst. Ronnie, he realized, did love the man. But not the way a man wanted to be loved. Her love for Von Hurst was gratitude, mingled with fondness and respect. It was not the all-encompassing passion and commitment that should exist, not the sharing, not two souls soaring . . . not the love, he, Drake, could have shared with her.

A savagery gripped Drake, an emotion he controlled by cruelly ripping at a piece of meat with his knife and fork. Ronnie had married Von Hurst, no matter what her emotions, for better or worse. But her vow hadn't held her when "worse" had come into being. All his speculations were absurd, they were to no end. . . . If she were suddenly as free as a lark, he wondered if he could ever learn to trust her.

He chewed his last piece of meat and pushed his plate aside, once more leaning back in the booth with crossed arms. "Enjoying the band?"

Ronnie glanced up to discover from his guarded ebony eyes that he had entirely withdrawn from her. "Yes, thank you," she replied coolly, "very much."

"Not too raucous for you?"

"No." She laughed. Drake had been right. The band, a five-member group consisting of a solid drummer, a keyboard player, two guitarists exchanging the vocal leads, and a talented saxophonist, tended to hard rock. They were careful to slip pleasant, mellow pieces into their repertoire, but they excelled at letting loose, playing popular pieces by The Stones, old Doors numbers, and other music that seemed tonight to stir wildly in her blood. Concentrating on the band, she forgot the air of aloofness that had settled over Drake and laughed. "I'm crazy about the band. They're making me feel very young."

Drake, caught by the vibrant yearning in her tone, laughed in return. "You can't be all that old!"

She tilted her head and quirked a shrugging brow. "I'll be thirty, and I know, that's not all that old. But they're making me feel really young—eighteen and, and . . ."

"Innocent again?" Drake supplied.

"Yes, I suppose that's what I mean."

Drake grinned with the satanish twinkle to his eyes. "Want to feel even younger? Let's try out the dance floor."

"Oh, I don't know," Ronnie demurred, watching the swirling dancers. "I'm not really sure what they're doing out there."

"Believe me"—Drake chuckled—"neither are they. These days, everyone does more or less what they feel like. Come on. Follow me, and I'll think of something."

He was on his feet, towering over her and reaching to escort her from her seat before she could protest further. His hand was on the small of her back as he led her down the short flight of steps and through the lower level to the shiny, light-colored wooden dance floor.

Just his touch was jolting. His hand upon her back sent traitorous tingles of anticipation and delighted memory racing along her spine. It was so natural to be touched by Drake, to drift into the warm masculinity of his arms, to curl her fingers at his nape.

The tune was a fast one, easily recognizable, and as he spun her about in deft circles, Drake laughingly informed her that the song had become popular after the movie *Saturday Night Fever*, and that it was a piece by the Bee Gees.

Panting as she dipped and swung and swirled, Ronnie haugh-

107

tily replied, "I knew it was the Bee Gees! Even on the island we have a television—several actually—and a stereo system!"

"Did you see the movie?" Drake queried when another swoop of his arm brought them facing each other again.

"No!" she admitted, chuckling. She couldn't begin to imagine Pieter sitting through an American movie. "Did you?"

"Of course. Several times, actually." His grin broadened deeply. "I told you I had a score of nephews and nieces."

Ronnie laughed again, breathlessly. It was fun out here with Drake. It was almost as if—as if they were back on the boat; as if they had returned to that magical day when it had been her right to touch Drake, to feel Drake's touch upon her. . . .

The music rose to a pitch and clamored to a halt. "Slowin' down now," one vocalist called cheerfully. "One for all the lovers out there. . . ."

Before the young man had finished speaking, Ronnie felt herself crushed closely into Drake's arms, her entire form pressed to the warmth of his hard, strong body. Instinctively she arched to his hold upon her hips, nestling her head in the inviting curve of his shoulder. They danced silently, their movements synchronized, fluid with the tender beat of the music. Drake's hands moved caressingly along Ronnie's back, and with intuitive volition, her hands, once more resting around his neck, began an exploratory return. The silky sheerness of his shirt enhanced the play of hot muscles beneath her fingers, and she thrilled as she trailed them over his shoulders, then thread them through the thick hair at the back of his neck. She was dimly aware that she was being foolish, following a path that could lead nowhere. But she couldn't help herself. Her own arousal from the dance had to be apparent to Drake; her nipples, brushing against the heat and breadth of his chest, attuned to the crisp mat of curls that tickled them erotically despite the material of their clothing, were hardening to impertinent pebbles that seemed to reach out for further delectable contact. And she was quivering . . . burning with the heat his body lent to hers. . . .

She was too close to him not to feel the desire rising inside him.

But he said nothing; he made no movement to draw away. If anything, he pulled her irrevocably closer. His warm breath fanned against her hair, stirring new sensations of longing. Was it wistful thinking, or did his lips form a kiss at her temple? She had no way of knowing. Her eyes were closed, her face pressed against his shoulder, feeling heat, feeling the beautiful, lulling pounding of his heart—feeling, absorbing, becoming one with every breath he took. It was torture, it was agony, it was wonderful. She was secure and content, ablaze with an unquenchable fire. It didn't matter. She wanted the dance to go on and on. As long as the music played with the incessant beat of the drums, she was in an exotically haunting heaven.

She must have had mind control, a powerful telepathic bond with the band leader. The next three numbers, which finished the set, were slow, romantic tunes. They came to her ears infinitely sweetly. Never once did Drake break his hold. She was immersed in him, cocooned in his drugging body heat, intoxicated with the woodsy scent he wore that combined so well with his essence of virility.

Unknown to her, Drake's mind was running along the same lines. As long as the music played on, he could forget the world, and luxuriate in sheer sensation. Each time he inhaled, the air was sweet with the light perfume of her hair; each time he moved she molded to fit his body, her incredibly soft but firm curves taunting him with captivation. God, he wanted her. No other woman had affected him so totally, stirring his blood intensely at mere sight, reducing him to yearning with a simple touch or a look from shimmering eyes as depthless as the oceans. . . .

If he had to think, it would be wrong. But as long as the music played, he didn't have to think. He could hold her, feel the sensuous femininity of her straining breasts against his chest, the undulating fluidity of her hips against his. . . .

No, he didn't have to think. He couldn't possibly think. This little bit of ecstasy was his.

But the music did stop. He didn't meet her eyes, and she kept

109

her head lowered as he swiveled her around and silently led her back to their booth, his hands still searing as they rested near the base of her spine. Without asking her consent, he ordered them each another drink.

He needed a drink. She must, too. Their contact was broken, and it was as if the sun had set on a cold day, leaving both empty and numb.

Drake glanced at his wristwatch with a frown. "We'd better drink up and head back. It's almost midnight." He opened his mouth and then shut it. He had been about to say "Your husband might be worried." But he couldn't phrase it that way. It would be a sacrilege at the moment. He started over. "I don't want Pieter to worry."

Ronnie smiled wryly in return, sighing silently with resignation. Midnight. Did everyone know that that was the bewitching hour? At the stroke of twelve, would all be lost?

Irrevocably. There was no glass slipper.

"Yes," she said smoothly, unconsciously straightening in the booth. Her chin tilted a little. "We'd better get going."

Drake payed the check and escorted her from the club. He took the wheel of the Ferrari without comment, so like Drake, always in charge.

They spoke little as they drove to the dock. Ronnie was exhausted. It was all she could do simply to stay awake. She didn't dare sleep; she was afraid she would convince herself that her dreams could be a reality and awaken to a devastating nightmare —reality.

Dave was sound asleep in the cabin of the Boston Whaler, but he cheerfully awoke as they came aboard, anxiously inquiring if they had had a nice day.

Even Dave liked Drake, Ronnie thought wearily.

Drake answered for them both, apologizing for being so late, assuring Dave they had had a wonderful day.

"No apologies necessary, Mr. O'Hara," Dave proclaimed with a proud grin. "Don't matter to me what part of the sea I'm on, so long as I can feel the water beneath me. As long as Miss

Veronica is happy and looked after, you stay anywhere as late as you like."

Drake voiced polite thanks and sat topside along with Ronnie. "Are you cold?" he inquired, his distant courtesy reinstated.

Ronnie shook her head. The night wind as they left the harbor was cold and brisk, but she welcomed its slapping chill and the salt spray it carried. The night and the sea were as dark and brooding as her heart . . . as fathomlessly, intensely, dangerously dark as Drake's ebony eyes.

At the clock's twelfth stroke they reached the island.

Thanking Dave, Ronnie was quick to hop from the Boston Whaler unescorted. As Drake watched her, her graceful, lithe cat movements, he felt a curious anger grow within him again.

She was once more cloaked in her cape of invincibility, her shield of marble ice. Following her up the path to the house, he felt his rage take on monstrous proportions. He wanted to shake her, to tell her to put on no airs around him. Damn it! He knew her. He knew her more thoroughly than any man alive, more thoroughly, he was sure, than the man who could rightfully claim her.

Something snapped in him as they reached the house and she set a slender, delicate hand upon the door. His arm shot out and he spun her around, nailing her to the wood with his body, pressing against her so that she was forced to adjust her form softly to his. Her eyes stared into his, naked for a second, startled and alarmed.

"Drake!" She whispered his name with beseechment, but neither knew if she pleaded for him to release her, or to carry out the action he couldn't control.

His lips were swift and harsh as they claimed hers, bruising and hungry. Her mouth had been parted and moist, and he found its plunder easy. She had no chance to resist, and his tongue drove deeply in demanding circular play that made response mandatory. She whimpered deep within her throat, and the sound brought out all that was primitive in Drake. His hands trailed her face and wove over her body, wedging space to cradle

111

her breasts possessively. His thumbs grazed over the nipples that had taunted him all night, and a savage satisfaction filled him as they rose instantly to his caresses. It was crazy; it was insane. He wanted to drag her into the garden, divest her of her garments, and gaze upon her exquisite marble beauty. She was his only, glowing with grace and majesty in the moonlight.

Drake ripped himself away from her as abruptly as he had wrenched her into the ruthlessly quick embrace. Ronnie stared at him, appalled, her knees buckling. Only the door kept her standing; only years of dignity kept her from quailing beneath the shocking ferocity of his dark scowl.

"Home, Mrs. von Hurst," he growled bitterly, bowing low with a terse mockery. "Once again, I thank you for a lovely time."

Ronnie pushed open the door and fled up the stairs, unaware that even her hasty exit was a regal, graceful sail and equally unaware that all of Drake's anger and mockery was directed at himself.

CHAPTER SIX

The simple task of rising and leaving her room the next morning was an arduous chore for Ronnie. Pieter, she knew, would not appear, and she would be left to face Drake alone. But she couldn't hide out all day, it would be cowardly. And God forbid, on top of everything else, Drake should call her a coward. . . .

Still, she stalled as long as possible, washing her hair leisurely, taking care to blow dry it. She showered for so long that she feared even their ample hot water supply would run cold, then convinced herself she needed a manicure and pedicure.

She was so perfectly primped, she told herself dryly, that she was like a young girl about to meet her lover. The thought brought a rush of miserable, ironic color to her cheek, and she quickly brushed it aside. Biting her lip, she knew she had to face the day, and Drake. Sweeping her hair into a severe knot, she finally opened the door and left her bedroom behind, hoping Drake had breakfasted early.

He had, but he was obviously waiting for her, drinking a second cup of coffee while he looked over the morning paper. As he spotted her entering the room he set the paper down and rose dramatically to greet her.

"Ahhh . . . my dear Mrs. von Hurst. Good morning."

The cynicism of his tone did little to improve her state of mind.

"Mr. O'Hara." She acknowledged him with a nod, hoping he didn't notice how tense she was as she glided past him to the sideboard. Her hands were steady as she poured herself a cup of coffee, and she decided toast was the most she was going to be able to stomach with his mocking gaze upon her.

He half lifted a brow as he reseated himself after solicitously pulling out and pushing in Ronnie's chair. "What happened to your appetite?"

"Not a thing," she said, stirring a spoonful of sugar into her coffee. "There are just days when I'm hungrier than others. Could I have a section of the paper, please?"

"Certainly."

Ronnie was careful to keep the print right side up as she accepted the front section. The news of the world, however, could not engross her, not when Drake was openly watching her with unfathomable eyes. Was he still angry this morning? He was sardonic, but not cruel; mocking, but not scornful.

It was best always to be on the defensive with Drake. Fairy tales were brief in duration.

"Did you have plans for the day?" Drake suddenly inquired.

She was taken off guard but answered quickly. "Yes. I'm behind in quite a bit of correspondence, and—"

"And I'm afraid you'll have to forget it." Drake grimaced ruefully and reached into his shirt pocket. Ronnie felt a queasy sensation as she saw him extract one of Pieter's monogrammed notes.

"What now?" she murmured skeptically. "We've already seen Charleston."

Drake pushed the note across the table to her. "Is this how you and your husband always communicate? You should hire a full-time postal clerk."

She stared at him while fingering the note, finding a dry, almost bitter humor in his eyes. "We don't need a postal clerk!" she snapped, unnerved by the note that promised another day in his company. He was dressed casually today, in dark pants and a white tailored shirt with rolled-up sleeves that not only accentuated his strikingly dark attractiveness and bronze tan, but emphasized the ample strength of his arms. God, it wasn't fair that anyone should tantalize so by mere appearance. She was

114

tempted to reach out and run a finger down the exposed length of bronze flesh. During those magical days on the cruise she would have impulsively done so. But they were no longer on the cruise. Her fingers curled resolutely around her coffee cup.

"I suggest you read the note," Drake advised, ignoring her waspish tone.

Her eyes darted warily from his to the paper. They flew back to his with the panic she was too surprised and dismayed to hide.

Pieter's request for the day was ludicrous. He couldn't be serious. In her glance to Drake, she unwittingly pleaded and demanded agreement that it was so. But his eyes gave her nothing in return; they were enigmatically dark.

"I won't do it," she said with flat finality, pushing the note aside. In his very precise wordage Pieter "asked" that they spend the day working. He was worried about the marble pieces, so near completion, actually reaching that stage. Drake knew what he was doing, while Pieter's hands "troubled him."

To Ronnie's surprise, Drake shrugged with a casual lift of his brows. "Then that's that, isn't it?"

"Yes," she replied, more forcefully than necessary.

He took a sip of his coffee and leisurely lit a cigarette, watching her all the while, giving her the prickly feeling that she was being baited. "You sound as if you mean it," he finally commented.

"Well, of course I mean it," Ronnie retorted, annoyed. "I usually do mean what I say."

She saw the cynical arch of his brow too late. He had been baiting her, and she had fallen for the bait.

"Funny," he remarked idly, inhaling deeply on the cigarette, "I seem to remember you saying several things it appears you didn't mean."

What had happened to the warmth they had shared yesterday? she wondered fleetingly, carefully freezing her face into a mask of indifference so as not to allow him the satisfaction of seeing how deeply his barb had struck.

"Rest assured, O'Hara," she said coolly, "I do mean what I say this time." She did mean it. Posing for Drake and Pieter was mortifying. Posing for Drake alone would be unthinkable. She couldn't even think of a word to describe it. Suicide might be most appropriate.

He turned his attention back to his newspaper. "Whatever you say, Veronica."

He didn't believe her, she thought with annoyance. Well, this time he was going to learn a lesson about her willpower.

And he would have, she assured herself later with marked bitterness, if only it wasn't for Pieter. Without finishing either coffee or toast, she had left the dining room, only to find herself summoned to her husband's room.

If Pieter were really adept at something other than sculpture, that something was using and manipulating her. Looking pale and gray in the monstrous four-poster bed that seemed to consume him, he told her how much the pieces meant to him, how they might never be finished . . . unless she cooperated. He became so upset that, as usual, she backed down, concern overriding all other emotions. She was shortly assuring him that she would do anything in her power to help. And consequently, she was posing for Drake, her mind seething, her teeth sunk deeply into her lower lip.

Strangely, though, once she had admitted defeat with glacial quiet and and a dare in the lift of her shoulders and tilt of her head, Drake chose not to taunt her. He had known all along that she would be posing, and though her challenging reserve did not daunt him, he said little.

"Your husband is a difficult man to say no to," he had said simply when she sought him out.

And now, careful not to watch him as she arranged the drapery around herself, he said nothing. The room was deathly silent, and she instinctively knew that his dark gaze bored into her; she could feel the heat of his eyes. But he didn't come near her to make any adjustments as Pieter would have done; he simply waited.

Finally she could hear the grating of the chisel. Each rasp upon the marble was a cut across her nerves. In time, she was sure, she would toss back her head and emit a hysterical scream of pain. . . .

Drake was barely aware of what he was doing. His hands moved carefully upon the fine marble, but his eyes kept hazing over. Light beads of perspiration formed on his brow and threaded beneath his mustache, despite the comfortable temperature of the air-conditioned room. He paused several times to swipe at his forehead with the back of his arm and to nervously erase the moisture that clung to the fringe of black upon his upper lip. He was as miserable about the situation as she, but what did one say to a skeleton of a man whose eyes burned with fever as he pleaded?

He had lost to Pieter. He had known Ronnie would, and he hadn't meant to mock her this morning; he had meant to apologize. But his apologies meant nothing, and guilt and frustration drove him on, as well as the raging desire that burned him whenever she was near. . . . He really wasn't sorry that he had taken her into his arms. The sensation was too fundamentally right to be wrong . . . or to be denied.

He looked down at his fingers. They trembled, and he had to steady them before touching the delicate marble again. One mistake at this stage . . .

How long had they been working? He didn't know. A thin mist of perspiration was now breaking out across the backs of his hands. It was amazing, but the marble was taking shape beautifully . . . and the shape he carved was beautiful—slender, but so shapely. Sleek shoulder blades, the spine that curved exquisitely to tempting hips . . . and at the base of those hips would be the slightly indented dimples he had previously formed from sweet memory . . . agonized memory . . . memory that was driving him to a torture his mind could control, but his body couldn't handle. Flames were lapping at his insides, searing him, crippling him. . . .

She breathed, evenly and deeply. She could never be a "tool" to him. Each breath that caused the tiny motion of the expansion of the fine, shadowed lines of her ribs reminded him that she was

117

not marble. She was warmth, fire, sweetness, unconquerable passion. . . .

Ronnie was reaching that point where she would scream insanely, like a demented shrew. The chisel grated, the chisel stopped. The silence between them was such that she could hear his every movement. The entire room seemed to have a life, that of his radiating presence, that of his heartbeats. . . .

The stillness was broken with a shattering impact when the chisel went flying across the room. Ronnie heard the strange whizzing sound, and jerked around quickly to see the tool crash into the far wall. Drake was staring at it with a disgusted look on his face, his hands planted on his hips. He glanced at her suddenly, aware that she was staring him. He didn't speak for a moment and offered no apology. "I think," he said finally, "that we have fulfilled our obligation. These pieces need only a few final touches—and Pieter should make those touches himself."

Ronnie nodded, only too happy to call it quits graciously. Drake had broken just seconds before she would have.

In her haste to scramble to her feet and escape the room, she stepped upon the long swath of silk drapery. The material jerked from her hands and fell to the floor, leaving her facing Drake totally naked.

She was too startled, too horrified, to make an instant grab for the material. It was not just her cheeks that suffused crimson; the color flooded her body from the roots of her hair to her pedicured toes. Still she didn't move; her eyes were held by a compelling prison of darkness.

It seemed like an eternity, but actually it was only seconds later that Drake came smoothly to her with a steady tread. He stopped directly in front of her, a semismile curving his lips. Crouching to his feet, he retrieved the drapery, rose, and carefully wrapped it around her shoulders. "Don't look as if the sky just fell," he said calmly, lightly tapping her chin with his knuckles. "I certainly didn't see anything I haven't seen before."

In mute misery Ronnie wrapped the material more tightly

118

around her, her clear sapphire gaze thanking him for the gentle kindness with which he had handled a moment he could have used to full advantage against her.

He did not linger near her but turned quickly to straighten the tools he had been using and to stoop and also retrieve the thrown chisel. "What's the story with that boat?" he demanded conversationally, as if nothing had ever happened and they were idly talking over afternoon tea.

The color was still receding from her body; her mind wasn't working quite as quickly as his. "What?" she murmured, disoriented.

"The boat," he said. "That Boston Whaler. Is it Dave's private property, or can I take it out?"

"Ah, no," she said quickly, rebounding from the incident. "I mean, no, the boat is for anyone's use. You're welcome to take her out. Just let Dave know you're going."

Drake wasn't looking at her, he was carefully covering the marble. "Want to join me?"

"What?" she murmured again, this time surprised.

"Damn, Ronnie," he said with a trace of amusement, "your eardrums must have turned to marble. I said, do you want to join me?"

"My eardrums are just fine," she assured him dryly. "It's simply that I find your invitation a shade peculiar."

"Why?"

"Why?" she repeated, amazed.

Drake laughed and looked around the room. "Is there an echo in here? I believe why was my question."

Ronnie sighed with exasperation and began to inch toward the door. "No, I don't want to join you. I want to avoid you as much as possible, and you know it, and you know exactly why. I don't think we make the most congenial of companions."

She had reached the door, and it appeared that he was advancing on her, but he wasn't. He reached for the knob. "Do you mind," he inquired politely. "I'd like to get by."

His acceptance of her refusal should have pleased her, but she felt curiously deflated. "Excuse me," she said, quickly stepping aside. Again she became disoriented.

Again she stepped on the drapery. And again it fell to her feet. She closed her eyes in rueful dismay, wondering bleakly why she should have chosen this day in her life to suddenly lose coordination. She felt Drake move to her feet and once more chastely redrape her.

Her eyes opened slowly. His were inches away, bright with laughter.

"If I didn't know better, Mrs. von Hurst," he said with dryly feigned chastisement, "I'd say you were trying to seduce me."

And she was doing a hell of a good job of it, he told himself. Far more beautiful than any statue ever created, the sight of her nakedness could tempt a cloistered monk. He knew her skin was like velvet. Even when frozen with dismay she stood proud, her breasts blossoming high and firm, her slender waist a handle of nature that knotted his fingers with memory. She was shadows, contours, curves, mystery, and enchantment. She was driving him nuts.

But she was as tormented as he was; he knew the trauma in her eyes so well. In spite of himself, he teased, he laughed, although the sound was a half guttural groan from deep in his chest.

She, however, did not find his teasing so amusing. He could see trauma simmering to anger. "Go on, Mr. O'Hara," she hissed, "you can get by now."

He felt his teeth grinding into his jaw. Damn her and her imperious reserve. Here he was, making light of a situation to save her feelings, and she was unsheathing her claws. "You first, Mrs. von Hurst," he drawled mockingly. "I'll make sure you get down the hall clothed."

"Please," she bit back, "it isn't necessary."

Drake didn't budge. Belatedly Ronnie saw by the hardening of his firmly squared jaw and the chilling intensity that swept into his eyes that she had made a mistake to snap at him. She was even dimly aware that her anger had been uncalled for. But

120

despite the fact that the fault was her own, she had been humili-
ated, and humiliation could best be appeased by anger. Understanding the situation was going to do little to help her now.

"I insist, Mrs. von Hurst," he grated harshly, taking her elbow
forcefully and propelling her out the door. "A lady should pre-
ceed a gentleman."

"I didn't know we had any present," she remarked beneath
her breath.

He heard her. "Ladies, you mean?" He purposely misunder-
stood with a cutting, cynical tone. "Oh, come, Veronica. I would
never refer to you as anything less than a perfect lady."

"Gentlemen," she retorted. "And I don't think I shall ever
refer to you as one!" He was walking quickly, and she was
breathless. It was difficult to keep up with his long-legged stride
and keep herself wrapped to avoid any further disastrous mis-
haps.

He stopped at the door to her room and pushed it in before
giving her a light shove inside. "I'll see you at the boat in thirty
minutes," he said casually.

"You will not!" she promised, swinging the door shut only to
have him prevent its closing with a quickly outstretched arm.

"Yes, I will," he said confidently. "We all know that Mrs. von
Hurst does everything Mr. von Hurst orders."

Ronnie sucked her breath in sharply. He was observant; he
was almost correct. But he was no better at denying Pieter than
she was.

"What's the matter with you?" she retorted. "You have a will
and a stubborn tongue—I can certainly vouch for that. You can
say no. You should have today; you should have yesterday—"

"I didn't want to," he said simply.

"And anyway," she continued, her wrath rising, "Pieter did
not tell me I had to go out on the boat with you. He asked me
to work. I worked. I'm done. Finished. You go out on the boat
if you want."

Drake wasn't sure himself what had gotten into him; she was
right, they should stay far away from one another. But the anger

121

he hated but could never quite control had him in its grip. He wanted to break her. He wanted to take her forcefully into his arms and make love to her with wild passion until she admitted she wanted him as badly as he wanted her.

He couldn't do that. He was stopped by his own morals as well as her denial. It was crazy—but then, he was a little crazy. Being in the house had slowly been driving him mad. He couldn't have her, but he wanted to be with her. Stupid and contradictory as it was, Drake was certain that she did love him in her way, and that that love would last forever.

As he looked at her, his face mirrored none of his feelings. It was hard, indomitable, ruthless. A devillike face—rawly handsome, sharply dangerous. Even more dangerous when he smiled slowly.

"You mean Pieter didn't ask you yet? It must have been an oversight. I'll go speak with him."

Ronnie really wasn't sure if he would go to Pieter, but she wasn't up to another meeting with him. It would be absurd. She would wind up promising anything. . . .

Soon, she promised herself, soon she would put her foot down. She won with him when she had the strength. More accurately, she won with him when she knew she was doing the right thing for his health.

Time was ticking by as she stared at Drake frigidly, indecisively. Why was he doing this to her? Didn't he realize how she loved just to be near him, to hear him talk, to watch him breathe? Maybe he did; maybe that was his way of tormenting her.

Yet she could have sworn that he had enjoyed yesterday as much as she had. He had held her as they danced with such genuine tenderness . . . but he had kissed her with repudiating violence. The best of their times together were destined to end that way.

Still, her choices were few. "I'll be at the boat in thirty minutes," she told him.

He made no effort to stop her as she slammed the door.

* * *

122

She had intended never to forgive him, and she hadn't really, she assured herself, as the Boston Whaler cut through the foamy indigo waves of the Atlantic. It was the sea that had broken the animosity between them; the swiftly changing depths of the mysterious ocean and the cleansing, healing salt wind.

It was impossible to be angry with anyone while speeding through the fascination of these elements. Especially when that someone was the devil's own spawn—a dark pirate at home in the wild winds, his angled, arrogant profile a dark bastion to challenge Neptune himself.

They had spoken briefly and curtly when they started out, but within fifteen minutes both were laughing gaily, recklessly. They spent an hour skimming over the open ocean in haphazard patterns, switching turns at the helm in unspoken agreement.

It was a glorious afternoon, hot for late summer in Charleston, but tempered by the relentless cool breeze that was part of the water sport. Drake had been farseeing enough to plan a basket lunch, but Ronnie was the one to suggest a sheltered alcove where the boat could be anchored while they ate their meal.

"No rocks!" Ronnie assured Drake as he watched her in silent doubt while she maneuvered the Whaler within twenty feet of the shore. "If she beaches, the tide will be with us. We can push her back out."

A moment later, with the anchor secure, Ronnie doffed the jeans she had worn over her bathing suit, rolled up the sleeves of her shirt, and hopped over the bow. The water, which came to her midriff, was delightfully cool after the heat of the sun. Shielding her eyes with a hand, she looked back to Drake. "Want to hand me the basket?"

He did, then hopped down beside her, holding a sheet procured from the cabin high above his head. Together they walked through the water to the beach.

"We're about a mile from where we brought the horses the other day," Ronnie remarked a little nervously. Drake hadn't said anything as he spread the sheet on the sand, and she was wondering if she should have suggested the alcove.

He nodded, looking down the beach. "That's about what I figured." He pulled his damp sport shirt over his head and tossed it to a corner of the sheet before taking the basket from her knotted fingers, setting it down, and sitting beside it. Rummaging through the interior, he found a cold-pack, unzipped it, and produced two bottles of Heineken. "Beer?" he queried her. "I hope it isn't too plebeian for your taste, but it seemed right for a boat excursion."

"It's fine," Ronnie said briefly, ignoring the mild taunt as she accepted the icy bottle. She seated herself on the other side of the blanket and once more bemoaned her impulsive suggestion. They had had no difficulty communicating aboard the Boston Whaler, but now conversation was stilted. They were also too close, too surrounded by primitive elements, and too near a state of undress. Drake now wore only a pair of cut-offs, and she wore only her rather skimpy bathing suit and the wet shirt.

She didn't move her head, but her eyes moved sideways. She wished she could ask him to put his shirt back on. He looked so much like that day she had first seen him by the ship's pool, casual but imposing, his bronze skin stretched tautly over a torso that was compellingly broad and sleekly muscled.

Ronnie looked quickly back to the sea. His savage kiss of last night seared her lips afresh with memory. His repudiation chilled her despite the heat of the sun.

"Why on earth did you insist I come with you?" she demanded suddenly.

He shrugged, and his eyes met hers. "I don't really know. But don't tell me you're not enjoying yourself. Your eyes light up like diamonds on that boat."

"You're capable of being charming on a boat," Ronnie admitted bitterly, digging her toes in to the sand. "It seems shorelines don't agree with us." She could feel herself winding up for an argument, and the prudent thing to do would be to find a sandwich and fill her mouth, but she couldn't control her harsh words. "Really, Drake. It amazes me that you find my behavior so atrocious. It never occurred to me that your type of man cared whom he sought for a rendezvous. I am not, after all, your wife."

"It's lucky for you, Ronnie, that you're not," Drake snapped scathingly.

"Really?" It was impossible to ignore such a blatant challenge no matter what the repercussions. "I suppose I would have been crucified by now?"

"Possibly."

"You'd condemn without a hearing?"

"I believe that marriage means fidelity."

So do I! she wanted to reply, but it would be ludicrous and laughable. "I suppose you had the perfect marriage yourself," she said derisively, immediately sorry that she had intentionally set out to wound him.

He stared at her calmly, but Ronnie intuitively knew that if his fingers hadn't been so tightly clenched around his knees, they would have been around her throat. "No, I didn't have the perfect marriage. I was only twenty-two at the time; rash and temperamental. We both took pleasure in outside flirtations when we fought, which was often. It was too late when we realized what we were doing to one another, how serious the games we played were. I swore when Lisa died that I'd never inflict such a relationship on anyone again—nor have it inflicted on me."

Ronnie could think of nothing to say to the direct reply she hadn't expected, but she didn't need to reply, she had gotten Drake going. His fingers left his knees to lash out for her arm, and she was dragged to the sheet so that he could heatedly stare over her, his weight half pinning her down.

"That's why I find your behavior so atrocious, Ronnie," he bit into her. "I spent fifteen years swearing I'd never marry again because it always involved games. Then I met you, and I believed you were guileless, completely sincere. You talked about love and forever. God, what a fool you made of me! Then I find out that you're not only married, but married to one of the greatest artists of our time. A man desperately ill. What were your prom-

125

ises for, Ronnie? Were you putting me on hold until Pieter kicked the bucket? That really wouldn't have been necessary, you know. I'm not worth quite what Von Hurst is, but my finances are fine."

Ronnie had remained stunned and still as he began his unleashed tirade, but the last was simply too much to tolerate. Where she had been chilled, she began to boil. She was shaking like a dry leaf in a winter wind. She exploded with a single word that well described what she thought of him, then went into a frenzied struggle against him. A worthless frenzied struggle.

His weight held her still and his arms fended her flailing limbs easily. He didn't even have to put forth much effort. He didn't speak, but smiled at her grimly until exhaustion brought her still again, panting, her eyes only challenging him with a blue ice that was as sharp as a glacier.

For several seconds she lay still, breathing, staring at his dark eyes. Then she twisted her lips into a smile as grim as his and sweetly hissed another sound expletive. "You're right, Drake," she finally told him, "absolutely right. I'd much rather be a widow wallowing in money than anyone's wife."

Drake released her roughly and stood, staring out at the sea, his hands planted on his trim hips. Ronnie watched his profile for a minute, cut sharply against the blue of the day, darkly rugged and uncompromising. Then she closed her eyes wearily. Nothing could change the facts.

Drake remained standing, watching but not seeing the sea and sky as he fought an inward battle for self-control. He didn't really know what he was after, except that he felt there had to be some sort of explanation. He wanted her trust. He wanted her to make him understand how she could have sworn such ardent love to him while knowing all along she would return to another man. He would so gladly understand, because in spite of everything, all logic, all absence of future, he loved her. He wanted to shake the truth out of her, but she didn't break, she didn't even bend. She tossed his accusations right back in his face. All he could do, he thought bitterly, was his best for her husband. His

126

damnedest to restore that husband's health. Possibly restore her to his arms.

He couldn't really believe she was after the Von Hurst fortune. But then, why not? She had deceived him once into believing in forever. She could still be deceiving him—and Von Hurst. He was a fool to drown himself in the crystal-clear blue of her eyes.

Ronnie felt Drake's weight as he lowered himself back to the sheet. She flinched slightly and heard a mirthless laugh. "Relax," he told her dryly, "I'm not going to attack you with a ham sandwich."

She opened her eyes to find him collecting the beer bottles that had spilled into the sand while he chewed on a sandwich. "Your choices are ham and cheese and egg salad," he said brusquely. "Which will it be?"

"I'm not particularly hungry," she murmured, rising on an elbow.

He tossed a wrapped sandwich to her. "Eat anyway," he told her curtly. "I don't want you getting seasick on the way back."

"I don't get seasick," Ronnie protested as he handed her another beer.

"No," he said almost musingly. "I guess you wouldn't."

Was it a form of apology? Ronnie wondered. Perhaps the best he could do under the circumstances. Not an apology, she decided; at best, an armed truce. She began to chew her sandwich automatically. Let him lead the conversation; perhaps he could keep them off forbidden topics.

Halfway through a second sandwich he finally spoke, as if suddenly remembering that he wasn't alone. "I called my friend at Johns Hopkins after breakfast this morning. I'm going to talk to Pieter soon."

"What did your friend say?" Ronnie asked anxiously.

Drake shrugged, his brow furrowing into a frown. "There isn't a cure for his type of dystrophy, but it can be treated and controlled. There could even be a remission."

He hadn't been watching her as he spoke. He had given his

127

attention to the lettering on the beer bottle. Silence followed his last words, and he turned to her with tense curiosity.

Her eyes were brimming with tears that she fought to blink away. For the split fraction of a second before she could hide her emotions, Drake saw into her heart, and his anger melted away, replaced by that instinct that touched him to the core of his being—the instinct to care for and protect her. Logic and situation meant nothing; he was overwhelmed by the primordial, male urge to give his strength to the woman his senses claimed to be his own.

She drew away from him, her lashes fluttering furiously, her eyes wary and defiant. "Drake—" she protested, but she was in his arms, and once more, two forgotten bottles of Heineken were emptying into the sand.

"It's going to be all right, Ronnie," Drake murmured. "Pieter is going to be all right," he said with soothing conviction.

"Thank you," she whispered.

He had taken her to offer comfort. He knew it; she knew it. But suddenly the embrace changed. Neither would ever be able to say who instigated the change; it just happened. One second he was holding her shoulders, the next he was touching her hair. She had been limp in his arms; his touch revitalized her as instantly as a driven current of electricity. It was as basic as nature, as compelling as the ties that bound them together in a relationship that defied the outside world and even their own conscious thought. Seeds of love had been planted in both of them that flourished and grew despite themselves, despite everything.

As they touched they forged a private world. It consisted of the sea and sand and breeze around them, spiraling into a relentless whirl. The pounding of the surf became that of their hearts.

Drake's initial kiss, falling on moist lips that parted sweetly for his, brought them both back to the sheet. He could hear nothing but the provocative call of the surf, feel nothing but the touch of velvet that was her skin. He was a man possessed, and possessing what was his. Slender fingers tangled through his hair, draw-

128

ing him ever closer as his tongue probed her mouth for all its secrets, all its warmth. The hunger that raged within him could not be easily appeased, and his lips left hers to travel to her cheeks, her throat.

Ronnie shivered and moaned as the moist heat of his demanding kisses moved slowly down to her cleavage. The slightly abrasive rasp of his mustache teased her flesh unendurably; like him, she was aware of nothing except the force that drove them together. Her fingers left his hair to splay across his back, seeking with wonder the breadth of muscles that quivered beneath them. Her body curved to his, arched, a perfect, natural fit, hips melded to hips.

The roar of the surf pounded louder and louder, intoxicatingly filling their bloodstreams. Drake found the tie that held her bikini in place, and his fingers deftly released it. His tongue reached out to touch a roseate nipple with reverence, then his mouth moved in sensuous and heated command to claim it entirely. Fireworks shot off along the length of Ronnie's spine. She moaned as she shivered with the intrinsic delight, so absorbed with his essence and raw masculinity that his being even eclipsed the sun. Her lips fell to his bronze shoulder. Her teeth grazed it with abject longing as her fingers played along his spine, moving with assurance to his hips, and slipping beneath the waist of his cut-offs.

"I love you." She whispered the words without conscious thought. They were right, they simply came to her lips and muffled into his flesh. It didn't even register into her mind that she had spoken. . . .

But her tender plea was as strong a deterrent to Drake as a bucket of ice water thrown heedlessly into his face. His desire didn't lessen—not with the length of her supple, silky legs tangled with his and the warm, aroused peaks of her breasts pressed to him—but he was jolted back to reality. He had heard the words before.

A groan, guttural, harsh, and tormented, ripped through him with a violent shudder as he jerked himself away, leaping with one movement, like a panther, to his feet. His eyes tore into her as she lay in the sand, startled, then awareness filled her beautiful eyes, confusion turning to pain.

He had never seen her more lovely, her form a delicately curving, still-welcoming silhouette on the sheet. Stooping, he plucked her bikini top from its landing spot in the sand and tossed it back to her.

"Get dressed," he instructed, and though he meant his tone to be soft, it was curt and hard.

She rose majestically, her sable hair a cascade behind her, making no awkward, embarrased attempts to shield herself, but quietly redonning her garment with dignity.

Drake turned and strode for the water. He submerged himself in the salty depths, wondering acidly if steam rose above him. Surfacing, he strode vigorously along the shoreline, chastising himself with each movement for his lack of control. Guilt riddled him as he thought of Pieter. He was a guest in the man's house and was coveting his wife.

He had settled nothing with himself when he returned to shore and, consequently, barked curtly at Ronnie, who waited, regally calm, their things gathered together.

"Let's go," he rasped, dismayed at the violence still contained in his tone. He hopped aboard the Boston Whaler first, then jerked her arm with an oath when she attempted to ignore his overture of assistance.

Her eyes flashed as his arm brought her leaping over the side.

"Stop it, Drake," she charged him. "You're a hypocrite. Don't take it out on me when you're responsible for your own actions. I've never held a shotgun to your head and told you to touch me."

She was right. Coolly, calmly, regally right. It didn't make him feel one bit better, nor soothe his savage mood.

"It would be better if you had," he retorted coldly, at least in a semblance of control. "And speaking of hypocrites"—he arched a high, scornful brow—"I thought, Mrs. von Hurst, that *you* loved *your husband.*"

Ronnie blanched as if she had been struck. "I do," she said weakly.

"You bandy that word around a lot, madam."

"I don't bandy it about," she said tonelessly, turning from him. "I do love Pieter, and"—her voice became a whisper—"I do love you."

They were frigidly silent as they returned to the dock, keeping a safe distance of several feet between them that might have been miles, both riding the wind with a secret misery.

Drake seemed to have forgotten her completely as he moored the boat. He was so distant that she was shocked when his hand came to her arm to spin her around and into his arms before she could leave the deck.

"You're a witch, Mrs. von Hurst—a seductress, a temptress, a lying Circe." His fingers drove into her hair at the base of her neck, and he ravished her mouth quickly but with astonishing, intense demand. "But God help me, madam, I love you, too."

He hoisted her into his arms and set her on the dock, then released her to jump up himself.

He brushed past her, and his long strides swiftly put a breach between them.

Ronnie trudged more slowly to the house. His meaning had been perfectly clear. He loved her, but he despised her, too.

They both dined in their rooms that night.

CHAPTER SEVEN

Drake spent the following morning closeted with Pieter. Ronnie learned from Henri when she awoke that the two men had already been together for hours and that Pieter had left instructions that under no circumstances was he to be disturbed. He had requested, however, that she not leave the house.

"Thank you, Henri," Ronnie told the butler, turning her back to pour a cup of coffee from the buffet. She didn't want him seeing the ill-concealed unease the situation was causing her. Had Pieter summoned Drake, or had Drake insisted on an audience with his host? Whichever, she didn't like the idea of the two alone together for hours. No matter how she attempted to assuage her worry with self-assurances that Drake, knowing the truth of Pieter's condition, would say nothing to aggravate him, she simply couldn't control her nervousness. Drake had very strong beliefs as to right or wrong, and in his eyes she was wrong. They were both wrong. If Pieter was to press Drake, he might find it impossible to lie.

Morning became noon, and still neither man emerged from Pieter's suite. Ronnie gave up all efforts of pretending constructive industry in the house, and trailed upstairs to her room, halfheartedly agreeing to a tray when Gretel insisted she have some form of lunch.

Pieter and Drake were dining in Pieter's room.

After picking at her lunch, Ronnie settled herself in the fur comfort of her bed and forced herself to read a recently ordered novel. It was by an author she loved, and Ronnie usually found his books absorbing and engrossing. That day she went through the first chapter before realizing that the words had not congealed in her mind at all and that she had no idea of what she had read. Guiltily she set the book aside. It was too fine a novel to be fluffed through.

At least, she thought idly, she had killed more time. The digital clock on her dresser informed her it was past two. Surely the men would break soon, and she would know what was going on before she started climbing the manor walls or sitting on the bed like a child and screaming hysterically with frustration.

Restlessly prowling her room, she recalled for the zillionth time Drake's contrasting behavior each time they were together. He could be charming, occasionally kind. He could also be mocking and ruthless—all within seconds. He called her witch while claiming to love her.

But it was a love she couldn't—wouldn't—dare trust. She could stir his passions—savage, fundamental passions—but it was as if he despised her and scorned her even as he reached for her. . . .

Her hair received the brunt of her own ravaged pride and emotions. Thinking of Drake, she brushed the lustrous sable mass with a ferocity that was certainly beneficial to her scalp, if somewhat haphazardly. As her arm tired she chided herself— she had to settle down.

The secret meeting going on was a good one. Drake was going to convince Pieter to see the specialist he knew. Pieter would have hope. She should be ecstatic. But they had to be talking about more than a specialist. It had been hours . . . and hours. . . .

She stood perfectly still as she heard a knock at her door, wondering at first if wishful thinking had conjured the sound. But a tap came again, followed by Henri's tentative "Mrs. von Hurst?"

"Yes?" Ronnie flew to the door and flung it open expectantly, her hair falling about her face in thick, fluffy waves.

Henri stared at her blankly for several seconds and Ronnie,

having no idea in the turmoil of her mind that he was seeing her as he never had before, her face flushed, her hair wild, her manner reckless and impatiently vibrant, repeated herself anxiously. "Yes, Henri. What is it?"

Henri snapped his jaw back together, returned to the present, but still thought of his mistress with a new dawn of comprehension. She was young, beautiful, and spirited. Funny how the years of steadfast poise had always blinded him. Her rigid composure had made him think her far older, far more prepared to take on the desolation of the island and its inhabitants.

"Mr. von Hurst, madam," Henri said quickly, shuttering his thoughts with the rapid blinking of his eyes. "He requests you in his suite at your earliest convenience."

Ronnie laughed aloud, further startling Henri. Earliest convenience! Nice words for a command. Well, for once she and Pieter were attuned. Her earliest convenience was now! Even facing Drake after yesterday's stunning show of strange possession was preferable to enduring one more second of this awful, nerve-racking curiosity.

She didn't pause for an instant to check her appearance or bind her hair. With a brief nod of thanks, she swept past Henri, mindless that her gait was less than truly dignified as she sped down the corridor to Pieter's door and rapped on it briskly. She could hear the murmur of words from within, but a hush echoed to her after her first rap.

"*Entrel!*" Pieter called, his use of the French word sounding almost studiously nonchalant.

Ronnie forced herself into a semblance of calm as she twisted the brass knob and pushed on the wood. The scene she came upon looked as if it had been purposely set. Pieter and Drake both sat in fan-backed chairs by the beveled window, comfortably leaning into the chairs, their legs crossed negligently.

They might have been discussing the weather, except that Ronnie knew better. There was tension in the fingers that rested on Drake's knee, an evasiveness in Pieter's light eyes. Yet oddly, Pieter seemed to be the happier of the two—almost complacent.

Drake was rigid . . . radiating that dangerous energy even as he sat. Ronnie covertly lowered her lashes to form crescents on her cheeks and watched Drake from beneath them. She caught a glimpse of his dark eyes and felt her breath depart her body. Unwitting chills assailed her.

He was furious. And, she realized as his arrogantly accusing stare came to rest upon her with explosive menace, it was not Pieter with whom he was furious. His wrath was directed at her.

Why? she wondered desperately. He had been angry yesterday, but surely not to this extent! Nor was there a hint of the yearning desire he had displayed yesterday despite his roughness . . . or the underlying core of a heated passion that burned with or because of the anger. . . . No. His wrath was brutally cold. It seemed to touch her like the tangible chill of an arctic wind. What could she possibly have done?

"Ronnie! My dear, you do remember Mr. Simmons, my attorney from Charleston?"

With one of his natural but dramatic hand gestures, Pieter motioned across the room, and Ronnie suddenly became aware that there was a third party in the immediate vicinity. She turned to the new guest, quickly hiding her surprise.

"Mr. Simmons, yes," she murmured graciously, extending her arm with a feigned pleasure. "How nice to see you."

Mr. Simmons was a dignified white-haired old charmer of legendary southern gentility. He accepted her hand with a slight squeeze and a small bow. "Dear Mrs.—von Hurst!" he replied in a low, modulated tone, "I assure you the pleasure is entirely mine." Ronnie noticed that he stuttered over her name.

Drake chose that moment to cough discreetly. Ronnie couldn't see him as she faced Mr. Simmons, but she could feel his scorn searing through her. She would have loved to politely excuse herself to Mr. Simmons and turn around and just as politely dump a bucket of ice water over Drake's head, or slap his mocking face, or, better still, drop him in a kettle of boiling oil. . . .

"Mr. Simmons has some papers for you to sign, Veronica,"

135

Pieter said, indicating his varnished rolltop desk. "Would you take care of it right away, please?"

"Yes, of course," Ronnie murmured automatically, pivoting to the large desk, her own bewilderment and curiosity quickly being replaced by a seething fury. Simmons must be there so that she and Pieter could legally fill out a marriage license. And Pieter, damn him, was nonchalantly carrying off this piece of very private business with Drake in the room. Had he let Drake in on their "family secret," or was his behavior so smooth that Drake would think it to be any document requiring both signatures?

Tears of humiliation were blurring her eyes, and she picked up the document to enable herself to read it, but her eyes refused to focus. A heavy band seemed to be constricting around her stomach, a band of inescapable steel that stopped her heart and closed in around her lungs. After signing this document, she would become Pieter's wife in truth. She had always claimed to herself and Pieter that the illegality of their original marriage had meant nothing.

But it had.

It had made it possible for her to spend that magical time with Drake—possible to grasp at interludes of happiness, and to dream and love.

There would be nothing faulty about the marriage this time. It would be legally registered in the State of South Carolina.

Pieter and Drake both rose simultaneously and came to her with swift strides—an amazing accomplishment for Pieter. Startled from her reflections, Ronnie dropped the document on the desk, her eyes widening with confused alarm as the two men seemed to swoop down on her like vultures. She emitted a little gasp as they neared her, and almost imperceptibly they slowed, and Pieter smiled. A quick glanced passed between him and Drake, and Drake changed course, walking across the room to Mr. Simmons—nowhere near her.

Had she imagined that he was coming for her? Ronnie wondered fleetingly. His change of direction had been so smooth. . . .

"Don't bother reading the thing, Veronica," Pieter instructed, securing a pen from the desk and slipping it in to her fingers. "I have more business to take care of, so I'll need you simply to hurry. And don't forget to use your, ah, proper name."

Proper name—maiden name. Uneasily Ronnie leaned over and signed Veronica Jane Flynn. Pieter immediately slid the paper from her and retrieved his pen, sighing. "That's that," he said with satisfaction.

Did the room reek of tension, or was she falling prey to the desolate life on the island and becoming paranoid? Pieter smiled at her benignly, Mr. Simmons casually glanced out the window, and Drake stood near him, quietly questioning him about growth along the Battery. Picture perfect. She *must* be growing paranoid. Drake had not been coming for her, he had just happened to rise along with Pieter.

With the document in his hand, Pieter suddenly seemed to wilt before her. The normal pallor of his face took on a gray tinge, and for a moment Ronnie feared he would crumple to the floor. Ronnie forgot all the peculiar behavior surrounding her; she even forgot that Pieter usually shrugged off her touch sharply. She gripped his arm with naked concern, supporting him.

"Thank you, my dear," he murmured. "I think I do need a little help over to my chair."

He had spoken softly, but Drake was at his side in a minute, nodding to Ronnie over his head with unspoken instructions in his eyes. Together they led Pieter back to his chair by the window.

"Thank you," Pieter murmured again.

Once more Drake's eyes met Ronnie's. The mutual agreement they had shared so swiftly in regard to Pieter was gone. The hostility was back. Burning, scorching hostility. The look was deadly, but she couldn't seem to tear her eyes away from the flame. Thankfully Mr. Simmons broke them apart.

"I think that's all that I need," the older man said cheerfully, taking the paper from Pieter and placing it in his neat nondescript briefcase. "Mr. von Hurst"—he shook Pieter's hand—"I'll return in three days. Mrs. von Hurst, if you'll escort me out . . ."

"Certainly," Ronnie replied, "Pieter? . . ."

"You'll come right back here, please," he commanded.

"Excuse me," Drake interrupted. "Perhaps I should see Mr. Simmons out. I'm sure that whatever you have to say to your wife must be personal, and I can leave you two alone now—"

"No!" Pieter protested firmly. "I want you here, Drake."

Ronnie was surprised by Pieter's vehemence, and stunned by his words. She felt an uncomfortable coldness implacably settling in her limbs. Pieter hadn't wanted her to read the paper. What in hell had she just signed?

"Pieter." Drake set his jaw with the protest. "I don't think—"

Pieter lifted a hand weakly, and Ronnie had a slow dawning, and astounding suspicion, of what was going on. He was feigning part of his illness now, using it deviously to manipulate Drake. He knew the other man—the stubborn, indomitable, Black Irishman—had a will to fight anything, except his weakness.

"Drake, please," Pieter insisted, and if she didn't know him better, Ronnie could have sworn he hid a satisfied smile. "Mr. Simmons is waiting, Veronica."

"Yes," Ronnie said, challenging him with a hard stare. "Yes, I'll be right back. Mr. Simmons . . ."

She exited the room politely with the lawyer and waited until they were halfway down the staircase before turning to him bluntly. "Mr. Simmons, what did I just sign?"

Brilliant color flooded the older man's face, and he began to stutter. It was obvious he hadn't expected the question. He lowered his head and hurried down the remainder of the stairs, stalling for time.

"Mr. Simmons," Ronnie persisted, keeping pace with him as he stretched his strides to reach the door. "You are an attorney, sir. I believe I have just put my signature upon something important without proper legal counsel."

"Mrs. von Hurst—Veronica." Simmons still seemed to be fumbling with her name, but then he was aware of the circumstances. "Please speak to your husband. To—uh—Pieter."

Ronnie sighed with exasperation. "Can you answer me one question, *please?* Is Mr. O'Hara aware of anything?"

"Oh, no, no!" Simmons was able to assure her. "I just arrived —I drew the papers up long ago. Mr. von Hurst summoned you for your signature as soon as I entered the room."

Ronnie was sure from Simmons's conspiratory and sympathetic look that he was placating her for all the wrong reasons. He imagined that she found her invalid marriage a horrifying embarrassment; after all, she had been living with Von Hurst for five years, a situation not actually shocking in the society of the eighties, but still not entirely palatable to the Bible Belt of the Old South. She hid a dry smile. She was far too concerned about Pieter to give a damn about propriety, but Simmons couldn't possibly comprehend her feelings. He could imagine what he wanted.

But if Drake knew nothing about the paper, why had he jumped to prevent her from reading it? She hadn't imagined his action—it wasn't paranoia.

Simmons, awed by the straightforward, cool confidence of the elegant young woman, suddenly found himself spilling far more than he intended. "I assure you that the document is in your best interests and protects you completely. I admit, Mr. von Hurst did plan to trick you, and that he did ask Mr. O'Hara's assistance. . . ." Simmons's voice trailed away inaudibly. Von Hurst was the main client of his office—the main income. He wasn't to be offended, and if that had meant joining in a small deception . . . Oh, well, *he* hadn't stopped her from reading the paper. . . .

"Mr. Simmons," she charged him bluntly. "That was not an application for a wedding license, was it?"

"No," he murmured unhappily, praying she would ask him nothing more.

139

She didn't. "Thank you for that much honesty. Good afternoon."

Very unhappily Simmons left the house and started down the path for the Boston Whaler, his ticket off the island.

Ronnie watched him for several seconds and then turned with forceful steps to the staircase. It was time for a confrontation, and she was ready to battle Pieter. There would be no more humoring.

She charged into Pieter's room without knocking, startling both men who awaited her. Casting a quick, hostile glance at Drake, she turned the flow of her force to Pieter. Her voice was a low, controlled growl. "I insist on knowing what is going on here!"

Pieter smiled. "I'm divorcing you, Ronnie."

His reply momentarily stunned her. How could he be divorcing her when he knew they weren't really married?

Then she understood completely. Somehow, *Pieter knew.* He knew that she was in love with Drake, and was determined to play matchmaker. This announcement in front of Drake was a show. The tides were changing again. Pieter was trying to take care of her, at his own sacrifice. She loved him for it, but she couldn't let him do it. Tears misted in her eyes as she approached him, facing him squarely. "No, Pieter, I simply won't let you do it."

He turned from her, and in his life he had never been more callous. He had to be. "I'm afraid you have no choice, my dear. You have just signed a document absolving me of any responsibility for you. I will be leaving shortly for Maryland and this Johns Hopkins doctor Drake has arranged for me to see. I want you off the island before I return."

Ronnie knew Pieter; she knew what he was doing and her heart went out to him. Nobility fit him well.

Drake gasped, and Ronnie cast him a quick glance. He didn't know what was going on. His countenance was brilliantly hard, his eyes laser-sharp diamonds. He was seeing the great Pieter von Hurst cruelly strip his wife of everything. "Pieter," he began harshly. "Lord, man, this is extreme. What we had was a brief affair . . . the woman really loves you."

It was Ronnie's turn to gasp. Drake had told Pieter about their shipboard romance.

"Oh, God! Pieter!" Tears streamed down Ronnie's face for the man she had called husband, the man she had hurt so badly, who was now staging this whole thing for her benefit, not realizing how Drake despised her for the affair to begin with . . . and how she despised him now for the pain he had caused with his admission. She rushed to the huge fan-backed chair in which Pieter had wearily sat. "I'm so sorry, Pieter," she cried, clasping his terribly gaunt hand once again with no thought of being rejected. She caught his sad blue gaze, strong now with his determination, and her tears continued in a waterfall torrent. She couldn't stop them. "Pieter," she choked, "you still can't do this, I won't let you. . . . Oh, Pieter . . . you can't. I know that you need me. . . ."

He looked at her with love and tenderness. "No, Ronnie. No more."

Drake couldn't see his host's eyes, only the humble tears in Ronnie's. And he was furious. Von Hurst had tricked him into admitting the affair, smoothly bribing him. He would go to Johns Hopkins only if Drake would accede to the fact that he was in love with Pieter's wife. And with the admission necessary to offer the great artist life, Drake had felt his rage rise at Ronnie, who had deceived him from the beginning. Ronnie, who had no life with Pieter . . . Ronnie, who had sworn her love for him. . . . Ronnie, who, now offered complete freedom—no, forced into complete freedom—was groveling at the feet of the man who had callously cast her out. Good God, he was being used by both of them! But what hurt him most was the fact that she didn't turn to him. He couldn't love her as Von Hurst's wife, but if Von Hurst was sworn to repudiate her . . . she should accept it. Supposedly she loved Drake, too.

Drake could literally feel his heart harden. He had been deceived all along. Ronnie cared for Pieter, desired him, but really gave her love to no one. There could be only one reason that she pleaded so fervently with Pieter: She liked being Mrs. von Hurst. She couldn't part with the prestige and promised wealth.

She was still crying, and oddly, Von Hurst was trying to soothe her. "I know what I'm doing," he told her.

"Oh, Pieter" was all that she could mumble. She stumbled to her feet, still murmuring, "No, I won't let you. . . ."

Then, with her beautiful sapphire eyes glinting like a multi-faceted crystal chandelier, Ronnie turned a weary, scorning gaze to Drake. The air between them was thick and charged with tension.

She was angry enough to stare Drake down, angry enough to meet his contempt—angry enough to really boil him in oil, if only she had a big enough pot.

But she also felt as if she were bleeding within, and the room was closing in on her. She couldn't bear any of it anymore. Ripping her eyes from the electricity of Drake's, she strangled a sob and raced out of the room, down the staircase, and out of the house.

Both men were silent for several minutes after she left the room. Drake began to pace, running his fingers through the raven wings of his hair. Damn Ronnie! How could she have put him in a position like this? Morally, he was bound to argue that the man keep his wife—a wife Drake's heart felt to be his.

"Damn it, Von Hurst!" he finally exploded. "I don't think you understand Ronnie—"

"I understand her perfectly, O'Hara," Pieter responded. "And I understand you, my friend." Pieter sighed wearily. He was not all that good at being generous. It was becoming harder with the two of them fighting him. "Always follow the command of your heart, Drake. There is a season in life for everything. In this season of my life I am following my heart."

"Von Hurst," Drake began heatedly, "if you're following your damn heart, keep me out of it! You used me today—"

"Yes." Pieter waved a hand that was truly growing weak. Watching the younger man was tiring. He was a panther on a leash, exuding vitality, restraining himself. Von Hurst knew Drake would love to bash his fist in his face. He also knew he wouldn't do it.

"Would you go find . . . Veronica, please," Pieter requested. "I do not want her alone." His wife. His dearly beloved wife. He would never use the term again. "You will find her by the sea. She has probably taken one of the horses."

Drake stormed out of the room gladly. He wasn't sure it was such a good idea for him to find Ronnie at that moment, but it wasn't a particularly good idea for him to stay with Pieter. In his present mood he wanted to throttle them both. He felt like a volleyball they had been passing back and forth, and for the life of him, he couldn't begin to figure out what the hell was going on. He had spent the morning convincing Pieter that he should see another doctor. Pieter then had charged him very politely with having an affair with his wife, never once losing his temper. To the contrary, he had seemed pleased. . . . He had assured Drake then that he would see the doctor. Then he had become excessively weak and begged Drake to help him force Ronnie's hand, and then the attorney had appeared. Then Pieter, who hadn't even been angry, was telling his wife he was divorcing her . . . then . . .

The entire situation was mad, and he couldn't even get out of it. He was too involved—and too much in love, as well as frustrated, confused, and terribly furious—and suddenly, very, very determined to find Ronnie. They were going to have it out once and for all.

His fists clenched into iron vises at his sides, Drake stalked down the stairway in pursuit.

143

CHAPTER EIGHT

Pieter did know Ronnie much better than she would have ever guessed.

Her first instinct was to run to the stables and to the bay mare. Startling the elderly groom, she slipped a bridle over Scheherazade's head herself and shunned the idea of a saddle, grasping the mare's mane to swing herself astride in a reckless but practiced leap.

Her second instinct was to race to the sea. She followed the trail through the lower foliage until she broke out on to the beach. There she gave Scheherazade free rein, and allowed the pounding of the surf and the horse's thundering hooves to drown out the throbbing in her head.

Finally Ronnie realized she was overtaxing the mare, and she reined in. Scheherazade slowed obediently and came to a halt.

Ronnie slid from the horse's back and walked numbly to the water's edge, heedless of the waves that saturated her loafers, washing over them like slender, receding tentacles. She sat and lay backward, throwing an arm over her eyes to shield them from the sun.

Not since Jamie's death, so many years before, had she been at such a loss. And not in the five years of their pseudomarriage had she ever felt closer to Pieter. Yet never in her life had she encountered the love she felt for Drake—an emotion that overwhelmed all else, including her own will.

It was such a fiasco. She knew damn well that Pieter would never force her off the island, and she also knew, no matter how noble his gestures, that he would need her to endure the trauma of once again searching for hope.

She felt the approach of Black Satan reverberating in the sand even before she heard the sound of his galloping hooves, and she winced. She was in no mental condition to do battle with Drake.

Twisting her head and covertly opening an eye beneath the shade of her arm, she watched with an almost detached admiration as the horse and rider came nearer. Black Satan, huge, powerful, and magnificent stallion, like a war horse of another era, thundered down the beach. His rider was equally powerful, equally magnificent. As if it had been staged, Drake was in black today: black jeans and a black silk shirt, with sleeves that rippled in the wind. Drake too had shunned the use of a saddle, and he seemed to sail down the beach, one with the stallion. A black knight.

So much for Cinderella tales, she told herself grimly. She would have laughed if she didn't fear the laughter would turn to hysteria. This was certainly no fair prince coming to wipe out the misery of the past with a single kiss of loving tenderness. It was Drake, his dark, brooding scowl a countenance as foreboding as his appearance. She could already see the dangerous gleam of anger glinting like black diamonds in his eyes.

He wasn't coming to give her a tender, loving kiss.

The stallion came to a rough halt about thirty feet from her. Drake was off the horse's back in an instant, his long strides carrying him swiftly to her. He gripped both her hands with thin-lipped determination and jerked her curtly to her feet, releasing her as she stood. Ronnie automatically rubbed sore wrists as she stared at him, inwardly strengthening herself as she noted the harsh irregularity of his breathing as he glared at her.

They stood like that for several seconds, just staring at one another, both unaware of the sea that foamed over their feet or the horses that wandered aimlessly in the background.

Drake finally spoke as he saw her chin begin to tilt. Even now, with her sable hair whipped by the wind and her jeans and tailored shirt spattered with water and wet sand, she was regal.

"I want to know," he grated harshly, his words enunciated crisply between the clench of his jaw, "what the hell is going on here."

Ronnie shrugged with cool eloquence. "Why are you asking me? You seem to be privy to more information than I. You also seem to be giving out more."

"I didn't tell Pieter a damn thing he didn't already know," Drake growled with low menace.

"But you did tell him something?"

"I had to."

Ronnie did laugh then, a short, bitter sound. "You once told me, Mr. O'Hara, that I did everything my husband instructed. How does it feel to find yourself in the same position?"

It was the wrong question. Ronnie gasped with alarm as Drake's hands came to her shoulders, gripping them with barely controlled intensity. His eyes were a dark, savage fire as they seared into hers, seeming to scorch her soul. "I'll tell you how I feel," he clipped. "Used. Used in some travesty between the two of you. You were terrified that your husband would discover your little indiscretion. Because of his health, so you tell me. Well, I don't wish to blatantly insult you, madam, but your husband seemed ridiculously happy to hear about your outside affairs. He seemed thrilled for a good excuse to get himself an easy divorce.

"Now, on the other hand"—his pressure on her shoulders increased as he pushed her back to sit in the sand and crouched before her, barely losing a beat in his dissertation—"I have you. You claim to love your husband, but you weave me into your little spell at the same time. I'm supposed to believe that you will do anything, sacrifice all, for the husband you so adore, while carrying on with me as if I were some sort of a stud service—and, oh, you forget to tell me the conditions!"

His words had finally gone past the boundary of endurance. She instinctively followed one of the oldest impulses of time and slapped him with every ounce of seething strength she could muster.

146

He appeared almost not to notice. He stopped for a single second, procured both her wrists with a not-too-gentle wrench, and continued speaking. "Now we have our bountiful little princess of charity faced with a divorce from a man she is benignly staying with because he is an invalid. A man she couldn't possibly have slept with for some time. A man who wants nothing more to do with her."

"Let me go!" Ronnie hissed.

"Uh-uhn, princess. You're going to hear this one out. Then you're going to do some talking."

Ronnie made one quick attempt to extract her wrists from his grip, and then realized the futility of the effort. She went motionless, closed her eyes, and ground her teeth together.

"There really is only one deduction that can be made here," Drake went on, his tone still harsh and bitingly academic. "Mrs. von Hurst may enjoy an occasional excursion into the carnal delights of life, but she is very fond of being Mrs. von Hurst. Luxury is easy to become accustomed to, even though our magnanimous lady claims she also loves me—our third party in this little drama. Being the humble lover, I even tried to convince Mr. von Hurst that a divorce was a bit drastic—that his beautiful wife found me merely a diversion and was still deeply in love with him. But I failed, madam. Your husband is cheerfully determined to be rid of you. He will get a divorce."

"You are an idiot!" Ronnie hissed explosively. "A complete fool."

"Obviously," Drake drawled, "I'm involved in this. But be thankful you did involve yourself with an idiot. No matter what Pieter does," he added with a bitter note, "I will take care of you."

Ronnie laughed again. It was all so ridiculous. "Don't be absurd, Drake!" With his scorning attitude she'd die before he ever took care of her. "I repeat," she charged, her sapphire gaze challenging his dark one as she made a rash, foolish attempt to free herself, which only served to tighten his constricting hold, "you are an idiot. That entire scene in Pieter's room today was

147

staged. I can guarantee you, my dear Mr. O'Hara, that I will never need you to take care of me. Pieter will not throw me off the island. Nor will he divorce me. He can't divorce me, because we're not really married."

Shock did for Ronnie what all her struggles could not. Drake's hands went cold and limp; his bronze face went paper-white beneath the tan. In contrast, his eyes became blacker than the night, his mustache and hair perfectly etched lines of ink against parchment. The reddening imprint of her hand became clear against the high, angular line of his cheekbone.

"What the hell are you talking about?" he rasped.

"Pieter and I are not really married," Ronnie repeated furiously. She was no longer in the least bit numb, but in the full heat of a long-withheld rage herself. She jumped to her feet, still careful to put a little distance between Drake and herself. "I told you, that entire scene was staged for your benefit. I suppose Pieter used the term *divorce* because he was afraid you would think less of me for living with him for all these years. It's a pity the poor man doesn't realize there is no way you could possibly think any less of me."

She had moved down the beach as she delivered her stunning retort, hoping to escape the touch that sent shivers down her spine even as it imprisoned her with demand.

But there was no escaping him today. He was on his feet with agile, lightning speed, and by her side to grasp an arm. "Don't walk away from me, Veronica—you're far from done."

"The hell I'm not!" she asserted. "You seem so great at judging everything. You take it from here!"

"Sit, Ronnie," he grated, "or shall I help you?"

She hesitated just a moment too long, which was foolish. She knew he never made idle threats. A slight movement of one of his powerful thighs swept her feet from beneath her and she was in his arms, being lowered back to a sandy seat. Just to be certain she didn't move again, Drake crooked an elbow over her waist and settled his head into his hand. His weight was held off her, but it was a very effective prison nonetheless. There was no way

148

she could move the bar of his arm or push past the broad chest that hovered in front of her. "I'm listening," he reminded grimly as she stared at him, silently seething.

"All right, your honor," she grated mockingly. "But you're not going to understand—"

"I'm dying to understand," he interrupted dryly. "Try me."

Ronnie sighed and clenched her eyes shut for an instant. It was ridiculous, but in the midst of all this, her fingers itched to reach out and touch the crisp, smattering strands of black curls that rose above the two open buttons of his silk shirt. She was tempted to draw a tender line along that of the mustache that could quirk with his laughter, tease her flesh with exotic torment. . . .

Her eyes flew open. They met the relentless dark glare of his.

"Pieter and I were married in Paris as I told you," Ronnie said. "We came here right after—Pieter didn't want to be seen anymore. It was very rough on him at first, as you can imagine. He was impossible for a long time, but—contrary to what you believe—I did love him. Maybe not in a way you would condone, but I did and do love him. About a month ago he went into a period of brooding, and I finally learned it was about me. He got this thing in his head that he had ruined my life and he wanted to give me a divorce so that I could have a life of my own. He contacted his attorney, and consequently discovered that our marriage wasn't valid, because the notary who had performed the ceremony wasn't a notary at all." She smiled dryly. "He wanted a secret ceremony to avoid the press, and it was so secret, it wasn't even real."

"Go on," Drake prodded briskly as she fell to silence.

"That's about all there is to tell," Ronnie said blandly, focusing on the waves behind Drake rather than on his eyes. "I told Pieter from the beginning that I wouldn't leave him. Whether we were or weren't married was irrelevant. I consented to be his wife in Paris because I knew that he loved me, and he needed me very desperately. I don't think that that has changed. Pieter has sim-

149

ply decided that I want you, and he is determined to give you to me."

Drake became the still one. He was silent for so long that Ronnie forced her gaze from the sea back to him. She became aware of a chill as she watched his face, and she wasn't sure if it came from the damp sand and her soaked feet or not. He had regained his color, and he was in complete control now of his actions. The face she stared upon was hard and implacable, darkly grim, giving away nothing.

"You knew you weren't married at the time of the cruise," he finally said. His tone was no more readable than his face. Did he intend to forgive her on a legality? She couldn't allow such a falsehood.

"I knew about the marriage being invalid," she said bitterly, forcing herself to meet his demand squarely without tears forming in her eyes. "But"—her voice grew hard with the effort to be cold—"don't go absolving me of adultery or 'game playing,' as you call it. Whether that marriage in Paris was legal or not, I entered into it with wide-open eyes. I made all the vows. So you see, to me, I was married. I was Mrs. Pieter von Hurst."

"Then why me?" he asked hoarsely.

Ronnie swallowed carefully, and despite herself, she could answer in no more than a strained whisper. "I—I never intended there to be a you. Pieter forced me to take the cruise—you are right; he can use his illness to get just about whatever he wants— because he assumed a taste of freedom would make me agree to allow him to die alone. He feels the end is near." She had to stop for a minute to breathe deeply in order to continue without sobs choking in her throat. "When I met you, I thought we would share a drink. I knew what I was coming home to, and knew that no matter what Pieter did, I couldn't just walk out on him. I never thought I would see you again. And I—and I—" God, it was so hard to explain! "I just wanted you so badly." Her voice wasn't even a whisper, it was a feeble gasp for air.

Drake lifted his head and straightened himself, releasing her from the prison of his body. She stared at the sea; he stared at the cliffs. His long, strong hands moved to his face, and his fingers tiredly massaged his temples.

"How many other 'cruises' have there been?" he asked obliquely.

The question should have made her angry, but it didn't. Her anger was spent; her heart was torn in pieces.

"No other cruises, Drake. That was it."

He still wasn't looking at her and he asked his next question almost absently. "Do you really love me, too, Ronnie?"

Her throat constricted completely. He had stripped her veneer, plundered the depths of her life. It would be foolish to lie now, foolish to hold on to any false pride. Things were out in the open now, but they hadn't changed. Nor did she feel Drake's basic beliefs could change. Of her own admission, she had carried on an affair while still being, in her own mind, a married woman. It was a vicious circle. She couldn't leave Pieter despite his noble gestures; Drake would never trust her, even if she could leave Pieter. So none of it mattered . . . except that it did. She did love Drake with all of her heart, and now she couldn't bear a lie between them. Soon enough the time would come when she would never see him again.

"Yes." All of the warmth and yearning of the love she bore him came out in the barely audible whisper of the word.

Drake rose to his feet, a little unsteadily. He continued looking out at the cliffs, his profile as ruggedly indiscernible as the terrain he surveyed. He didn't soften, he offered her no tenderness.

He turned back to her and grasped her hands almost as roughly as he had originally. She came to her feet, and only then did his eyes meet hers.

"I'm going to marry you, Ronnie," he told her in a voice that was devoid of any emotion.

"No," she murmured in confusion. "You still don't understand. You can't."

He shrugged, peculiarly remote. "Yes, I can," he said distantly, "and I intend to."

Ronnie shook her head, her brows knit in confusion, her teeth nervously chewing the tender flesh of her lower lip. She was sure he had lost his senses, but he portrayed nothing to her now, not anger, not mockery, not sympathy, not love. He spoke with the absent courtesy of a casual acquaintance.

"You're not listening, Drake," Ronnie said firmly. "When Pieter leaves for Maryland, I'll be with him. I can't leave him to face hope—and possible disappointment—by himself. I will be with him."

Drake ignored her and let loose a shrill whistle. Black Satan obediently left the outcrop of grass he had discovered and trotted to the man, as acquiescent as a well-trained and beloved dog.

Soul mates, Ronnie thought with a shade of resentment for both man and animal. The fiery horse and arrogant man did deserve one another.

Drake swung over the stallion's back with expert ease. "Where's Scheherazade?" he asked her curtly.

Ronnie searched the area quickly with a sweep of her eyes. Her resentment for Drake's charismatic influence over the usually aloof Black Satan increased as she realized she had been deserted by Scheherazade—an animal she had owned for five years.

"Probably back at the stable, munching sweet alfalfa," she answered in annoyance.

"Then you'd better hop up," Drake suggested, sliding back to give her room over the horse's withers.

Ronnie stared at him uneasily. He hadn't responded to her announcement that she would be leaving with Pieter; in actuality, he hadn't responded to much of what she had said at all.

He had given her his bland yet determined offer of marriage, and then nothing else. He had ignored her commitment to stay with Pieter. Probably because he preferred it that way, she thought with dry misery. He might now believe that she did love him, and he might even still love her in return, but he didn't really want marriage. It was probably a moralistic, noble gesture —the type Pieter was proving to be so proficient at.

She was back to her vicious circle, and suddenly just as happy as Drake to drop the subject, which had so recently overshadowed all else. She wasn't, however, very happy to mount the black stallion with Drake. She was drained and more vulnerable than she would ever have him see her.

He held the reins with one hand and offered her the other. "Mrs. von Hurst—" He caught himself. "But that isn't your name, is it? What is your surname?"

"Flynn," Ronnie murmured, touching his hand but not accepting it. "I, uh, can't jump up that way," she explained with lowered lashes. "Black Satan is a lot higher than the bay—"

"Take my hand," Drake interrupted impatiently.

She did so and was surprised to find herself lifted high enough to swing a leg over the animal's neck and shoulders, in front of Drake. Careful of Black Satan's comfort, she scooted back to unnerve her own well-being. She fit like a glove to Drake's body, and was able to feel the slightest twitch of his muscles, from his strong thighs to the shoulders that sheltered her back. She could feel the expansion of his broad chest against her flesh with each breath, the thud of his heart. She could almost feel the racing of his blood through his veins. . . .

"Ready?" he queried crisply.

She nodded, and he nudged the stallion toward home. Black Satan, knowing the direction indicated offered a meal, tossed his huge, well-sculpted head, snorted, and attempted to take the bit between his teeth.

Drake was ready for him, clearly the master, but he allowed the horse a fleet canter. Ronnie clamped on to a handful of the sleek black mane, her thighs, like Drake's behind them, holding Satan while they moved with him.

Drake's arms were around her as he held the reins, loose but secure. She and Drake were one, and one with the horse. The wind whistled by them, the sun splayed down upon them, and the scent of the sea filled their senses.

Her life was a fiasco, but as they rode, Ronnie shared a brief, intimate pleasure with Drake. She realized poignantly how very much alike they were. They were both attuned to the joy of the

153

wind, of the animal beneath them, of the wild and voluptuous summer beauty of the craggy island. And no matter what the tumult was between them on a mental or verbal level, they would always find harmony in their bodies, a rhythm that claimed them as they rode, a rhythm that would claim them eternally in one another's arms. . . .

Drake brought the stallion to a trot as they broke the trail foliage on the return and approached the stable. Ronnie became even more acutely aware of the perpetually strong and secure arms that held her, of the heartbeat she knew better than her own, of the delicious scent that was uniquely his, as crisp and clean as the sea, as enticing and enigmatic as the wind. A scent entirely masculine. . . .

The ride was over. The house loomed before her like a luxurious monstrosity. But she couldn't blame the house; the chains that bound her existed in her own heart and soul.

Suddenly she couldn't bear another second with Drake touching her, so close, yet miles out of her reach. The days they had shared before in tentative friendship and disastrous discord had been shattering. She needed time to mend the cracks that were threatening to tear down the facade of indomitable marble she must have to maintain her existence.

Black Satan stopped a few feet from the watering trough. Ronnie pushed Drake's arm aside and slid from the stallion, just catching herself from stumbling.

She didn't look back at Drake but turned her steps toward the house. Drake made no attempt to stop her. She could hear him vaguely as he talked to the groom. The bay had indeed returned and was safely in her stall. Mr. von Hurst, having heard the horse had returned riderless, was beside himself with worry.

Ronnie sighed with a breath that trembled. Drake could go and assure Pieter that she was fine. She had had it for the time being. Both of the willful men who tried to manipulate her life could go hang.

She was a mess, mentally and physically. Bareback riding had left her jeans covered with bay and black hairs and the damp

154

lather of the horses. Her feet were cold and aching from the wet shoes, and she was splattered with seawater and sand.

A long, hot, revitalizing bath was in order.

Despite her dishevelment she was able to sail coolly by Henri with a brief greeting of acknowledgment. "Mr. von Hurst is quite concerned, madam . . ." the butler called after her as she glided up the stairs.

Ronnie paused a second, her hand barely touching the banister. "Mr. O'Hara will see Mr. von Hurst," she answered calmly, wondering idly what Henri was going to think of her grimy footprints on his shiny wood floors. "I'll be in my room," she added firmly, never more than now the mistress of the house. She started walking again, then, aware that he watched her in puzzlement, she turned, no sign of turmoil in her face. "I'll also have dinner in my room, please, Henri. You may convey my regrets to Mr. O'Hara and my—Mr. von Hurst—if he should appear."

"Yes, madam, certainly. . . ."

She stripped off her clothing haphazardly in her room and immediately filled the large tiled tub in her bathroom with near-scorching bubbles. As she soaked she was gratified to feel tension ebb away, and warmth replace bitter cold. Her eyes were dry now, resigned and very tired. She had thought herself too upset ever to sleep again, but the opposite sensations were engulfing her. All she wanted to do was sleep.

She finally left the bath to dry herself with a large, snowy towel and slip into a floor-length burgundy silk caftan. Gretel appeared with her meal, a tender steak, which she surprisingly wolfed down. When she came to retrieve the tray, the slender housekeeper and cook glanced at her with concern.

"Mr. von Hurst and Mr. O'Hara both send their regards," Gretel said slowly, careful to pronounce the English she seldom used. "They instruct you to take care not to catch cold."

Ronnie gave Gretel a dry smile. "Mr. von Hurst went down to dinner tonight?"

"Yes, ma'am."

"Thank you, Gretel." Ronnie watched the middle-aged

155

woman leave her room and close the door before she chuckled. It was definitely a different night: the master had appeared and the mistress hadn't!

Her chuckle turned into a catch in her throat, and she curled onto the fur spread of her bed without removing the cover. Exhaustion took its toll, and as her mind continued to race with worry and pain her body gave up. She drifted into a sleep so deep that she wasn't plagued by a single dream.

The tapping on her door was light, so light that it was the persistence of the sound and not its echo that woke her.

She lifted her head, puzzled, groggy, and disoriented, then, alarmed as the noise continued, she hopped to her feet and flew to the door and threw it open.

Drake was standing in the dimly lit hall, as devastating as she had ever seen him. He had dressed for dinner in black velvet and white, an image of raw masculinity only semicivilized by nonchalant, but stunning, elegance.

Ronnie stared at him for a timeless second, unable to speak, enmeshed in the enigmatic, compelling demand of his dark eyes. Everything she had ever wanted stood towering in her doorway, motionless yet so very alive; arrogant and hard, yet strangely haunted and tender.

"I'm leaving in the morning," he told her, the assured timbre of his voice barely touched by a husky catch. "I came to say good-bye."

She had known the moment would come, but it caught her completely unaware. Her body congealed on her and she seemed detached from it, as if she had no control over limbs that felt like stone.

She finally forced a stiff nod, not trusting herself to speak.

"Oh, God, Ronnie!" he emitted in an explosive rasp. The door was pushed aside with a spontaneous shove, and Drake was in the room. She was enveloped into shaking arms that felt like bands of steel, and her cheek rested against the warm velvet texture of his jacket.

"Ronnie," he whispered, his hand stroking hair that was as silky as her caftan.

She looked up into his eyes. The vivid sapphire blue that met his gaze was clear but tremulous. Her lips were quivering, parted, sweetly moist.

He lowered his own to them, tenderly, lightly, reverently. He drew away, searching out her eyes, then the band of his arms tightened around her, and she was crushed to him, his kiss this time passionate, giving, taking, thirsting, bruising with intensity.

He would devour her.

Yet she met him with equal fervor, her fingers clinging to his broad shoulders, her nails digging into velvet. She noticed no pain as his lips consumed her, only the hunger and need that grew within both of them like wildfire. She accepted, she demanded in return, her tongue seeking his in a harmonious duel of longing that deepened with endless space. His fingers wound tightly through her hair, arching her neck, holding her for his driving demand in a grip from which she desired no escape. And when his mouth finally left hers, it moved tenderly down the exposed length of her throat, tasting, touching, flowering soft butterfly kisses.

He suddenly released her, only to lift her into his arms. Ronnie was delirious with him, drugged in the sensuality that was his tenderest touch as well as his passion. She was ready to forget everything. . . .

But she sensed a withdrawal from him as he laid her gently on the fur spread. Not the harsh withdrawal he had often displayed before, but a controlled, determined withdrawal that wrenched apart her heart and left it as torn and bleeding as his. Wild, passionate lovers, they were oddly, uniquely, moralists. It was Pieter's house.

He touched her forehead with his lips and moved away. For a moment longer he watched her, drinking in, absorbing, her beauty: the exquisite form molded by the silk caftan; the burnished sable hair softer, more lustrous, than the fur it was spread upon; the clear blue eyes, clearer than the sky, deeper than

157

indigo; her face, delicate, regal, more finely sculpted than any piece of marble, ingrained with indomitable character.

The woman who had taught him the meaning of love, of loyalty and devotion.

He turned and left the room, a panther disappearing into the night.

Ronnie watched him go with a sense of emptiness that was overpowering. Her fingers moved shakily to her bruised lips, to the flesh still feeling the ravishment of his mustache and slightly rough cheeks.

She didn't cry—the pain was beyond that. And she didn't sleep again that night.

CHAPTER NINE

"I thought I'd never live to say it, Veronica, but you do look like hell."

Ronnie glanced up sharply from her third cup of coffee, praying the caffeine would put life in her veins.

Pieter looked surprisingly well.

She attempted a smile for him. "I thought I'd never live to say it," she retorted, "but you are a conniving, devious, and very, very wonderful man." She sobered. "But it's no good, Pieter. I'm going with you to Maryland."

He had been standing too long, even for the good health he was displaying. He took a chair beside her and tenderly touched a lock of her hair with a sigh. "I expected that you would fight me. You and Drake."

Ronnie closed her eyes, stricken afresh with a tug of war in her mind that was half guilt and love for Pieter, and half pain and love for Drake.

"Forgive me, Pieter," she murmured quietly. "I never meant to hurt you—"

"Veronica," Pieter interrupted, lifting her chin. "You are a priceless gem, so very rare, so very fine. I have nothing to forgive."

"Oh, Pieter, it wasn't right—"

"No!" he protested with a righteous vehemence that reminded her fleetingly of the great artist and man he had been before the illness had played havoc with his emotions and mind. "What wasn't right was us, Ronnie. Me in particular. The years you gave me, a sick old man clinging to a goodness and youth too devoted to do anything other than accept self-centered abuse. But no more, Ronnie. I will never throw you out of this, your home, and I will love you as my dear friend for the rest of my life and thank the gods for the time that you gave me. I will be delighted to take you to Maryland with me, as my very good friend, but we never will make our marriage legal. You and Drake are very right for each other, Ronnie. You will make him a marvelous wife."

She had thought herself cried out, but the encouragement, coming from the man she had betrayed, brought a flow of wetness down her cheeks. "Pieter . . ."

"There, there," he soothed, able to touch her now with his newly directed love. As husband and wife they were stilted strangers; as friends they could care with unstinting empathy. "Don't cry, Ronnie. Your future will bring all the happiness you have been denied. You must marry Drake."

"And what of you?" Ronnie charged through her tears.

"I am going to return to Paris," he told her, "for whatever time I do have. I am going to face the world. I am going to live as the great Pieter von Hurst!"

Ronnie smiled with sad admiration. "You are the very great Pieter von Hurst," she said softly.

"But first"—there was actually a twinkle in his pale blue gaze—"I shall attend your wedding. The papers will love it! We will tell them that we are divorced, of course. I will allow no scandal attached to your name!"

"Oh, Pieter!" Ronnie laughed. "You are the priceless one! I don't care about scandal, I care about your health. I care about—"

"Drake O'Hara." Ronnie flushed unhappily, and Pieter continued. "Please, Ronnie, no more sadness. You gave me all I could ever ask for—the spring of your life. But it's winter now for me, Ronnie, summer is left for you. A season for you to love."

"Pieter!" Ronnie protested. "I will not accept winter. And though you want now so much to give, you can't give me Drake.

He's gone. There are other things between us that can't be settled."

"He'll be back," Pieter said with conviction. He cleared his throat, and his next words took a great effort. "I have never held you in my arms, Ronnie, not as a man, but if I had, I know I would defy heaven and earth to hold you again."

Ronnie winced inwardly, flicking away the final trace of tears with her lashes. The immediate future was before them, and nothing would alter the course she planned to take.

"I think," she said, rising in a businesslike fashion, "that we'll have to discuss Paris and my future at a later date." She poured a fourth cup of coffee for herself and the first for Pieter, adding the heavy cream he liked. "We have a doctor to see first."

"Yes," Pieter said lightly. "We have a doctor to see." He drummed thin fingers on the table. "Ronnie?"

"Yes?"

"Whether the prognosis is good or bad, I am returning to Paris. Alone."

She nodded, her fingers trembling slightly as she set the coffee cups down. He reached out bony fingers to clasp her hand. "The prognosis may very well be good."

She nodded again, gulped her coffee down, mindless that she scalded her tongue, and left the dining room on a mumbled pretext of packing.

Pieter watched her, praying for her sake more than his own that the prognosis would indeed be good.

Four weeks later they were again sharing coffee, again talking as they had so belatedly learned to do.

But the dining table was different, the place was different, even the lifetime and dimension seemed to be different.

They were celebrating Pieter's forty-third birthday, and the celebration was a real one. Just that afternoon Ronnie had held his hand in hers as they waited for the verdict from a team of doctors. Their hands had been clammy together, but their expressions stoic. Only the two of them knew how their hearts beat

161

with hope—a hope granted this time. The disease was still incurable, but new treatments could give Pieter an unknown lease on life. A life far easier. With new medication, his existence could be almost normal.

Now they sat in the coffee shop of their hotel, looking out of the veranda on the magnificent display of fall colors that were adorning Maryland in a natural beauty. It wasn't the peak of autumn yet, but the reds and golds of the trees had never seemed brighter, nor the grass greener.

And Ronnie was laughing. Pieter hadn't seen her laugh during the entire month. Her eyes, though, even as her lips curled, remained haunted. And he knew why, but he couldn't reassure her. He could only play God so far.

He reached a hand across the table and enveloped hers. "I would like it very much, Veronica," he told her, "if you would go upstairs and don your prettiest gown. An old and grateful man would like to take you to dinner."

"Old, never," Ronnie protested. Pieter now was ageless. He was still going to die, and he knew it, but as he pragmatically told Ronnie, they were all mortal, all subject to only so many years of life. He had been given many more and he intended to live each day to the fullest.

"Well, then, you must dress up for a very dear friend."

"I'll be glad to." She squeezed his hand back.

"Go on now," he persisted. "I shall call at your door in an hour."

Ronnie left him and returned to her room, which was actually a luxury suite. She wasn't really in a mood to dress elaborately for dinner—the last weeks had been filled with tension and strain during the day and fitful dreams of yearning and loss at night—but it was Pieter's birthday, and he was a new man, so like the kind and mature patron who had adopted her and Jamie all those years before.

She mechanically stripped off her tailored navy suit and adjusted the water for a shower. Beneath the steaming spray of heat and mist, she wondered what she would do. Pieter had given her the island, but she didn't intend to return to it after he left. The house off Charleston could bring nothing but somber memories. She would have stayed with Pieter if he had wished it, but he was adamant, and determined that they split soon. Dependency, he informed her, was no life for either of them. He was putting all his affairs in order, and although he would have to return to Maryland several times a year, Paris was going to be his home. He had finished the marble series with her as his model before they had left, and he had given the press release that stated he and Ronnie were divorcing. It was wonderfully worded. She would always be "his dearest and most beloved friend."

Ronnie wondered as she listlessly showered if Pieter still imagined Drake would come back. She had dreamed of it at first, but as the days passed and no word was heard from him, she had to accept the truth.

Drake had gone home where life was normal, where women were in abundance, where he could forget his strange encounters and affairs on the remote, forbidding, windswept island. He hadn't even called to inquire about Pieter's health. He had entered her life with passion and a searing temper, and he was gone like a winter's thaw.

Leaving the shower, Ronnie surveyed her reflection with a grimace. She was terribly pale, and purple shadows were tinging beneath her eyes. She had to perk herself up; she would do nothing to ruin the wonderful night for Pieter.

After a careful application of makeup, she was more than satisfied. A brush of light blush had colored her cheeks; three-toned shadow and then mascara had subtly improved her eyes. A gloss of lipstick, and she could fool anyone, she promised herself.

On a whim she pulled the pins from her hair and brushed it loose. Another improvement. She could look almost young, almost gay, almost carefree. Pieter would love it.

She chose a dress of metallic blue that highlighted her eyes and complemented the waves of rich dark hair that cascaded over her shoulders. It was a daring dress for the one-time totally dignified

Mrs. von Hurst. The skirt drifted about her shapely legs like sheer mist while sporting a long slit that bared a glimpse of nyloned thigh when she walked—but again, she decided that Pieter would love it. Always the artist, his once purely aesthetic eye was now laced with warmth. He still appreciated a beautiful woman—even one he no longer called wife.

She slipped into a pair of matching heeled sandles, grabbed her evening bag and stole, and gave herself a final critical glance in the mirror.

Clothing and makeup, she thought with a sigh. They could do wonders. She looked fine, and when she smiled, she looked happy, which she was. Very happy for Pieter. He was eagerly looking forward to his new life.

She wanted him to believe she was happy, but she wondered if she ever could be again. Pieter did not hold her heart, but while he had needed her, she had cared for him and busied herself so industriously that she had managed to push her sense of loss to the back of her mind.

Tonight it was upon her full force. Drake had never really been hers, but she had been his completely. No matter how she tried to convince herself that a real love would come one day, she knew she lied. She was in love with a one-of-a-kind Black Irish devil. He would never come again.

A knock sounded at the door, and Ronnie focused her blurring eyes once more on the mirror to adjust her drooping smile. She wouldn't have Pieter see her with anything but the brightest face.

"Coming," she called cheerfully, spinning away from the full-length mirror and walking briskly to the door. She threw it open, and her heart missed a beat and seemed to stop entirely.

It was not Pieter at her door, it was Drake. She stared at him blankly for a moment, wondering desperately if she had conjured his image with sheer yearning. But she hadn't. No mere image could be as resplendent as Drake in a three piece, vested navy suit and elegant powder-blue French-cuffed shirt. Only Drake could wear such attire with such assured, raw masculinity. He was towering, beautiful, magnificent.

"Miss Flynn." He greeted her with a grave nod. "Are you ready?"

She wanted to throw her arms around him, to ignore everything but his presence, question nothing.

She chose fury instead. "Drake O'Hara. How nice to see you, except you're a little late, aren't you?" The weeks of loneliness, worry, and pain had driven her to the frenzy she felt now. "You've only come in time for the grand finale. Pieter has seen his doctors—the ones you arranged for—and he has already sweated through the diagnosis. It was good, thank you. He has finished his work. I'm afraid you left Chicago merely for a dinner."

Drake was laughing, pushing his way into the room.

"Stop it!" Ronnie hissed, fruitlessly pitting herself against his chest to prevent his entry. "You could have called, you could have written—"

"Damn!" he replied with amusement, catching her wrists to fend off her feeble pummeling. "To think I ever compared you to cold marble! You're as hot as volcanic fire—not that I don't love it!"

Ronnie stopped her assault with ired awe. "How dare you walk in here joking after—after—"

"Leaving when it was the only possible thing to do?" he supplied. He briskly led her to the carved love seat that dominated the salon of her suite. "Sit down, Miss Flynn."

"I will not—"

"Yes, you will." He smiled. "We've been through this before." Ronnie sat.

Drake pushed back his jacket to plant his hands upon his hips as he paced before her. "For your information, Miss Flynn, I have been in Maryland since the day you arrived. I have been in constant contact with Pieter."

Ronnie felt her jaw fall in a most undignified manner. He laughed and tapped it closed, then his expression sobered.

"I left when I did, Ronnie, because I knew you had to see this through with Pieter. I felt like a complete fool that day on the beach. You were right, I hadn't understood a thing. But dear God, Ronnie, I was in love with you, and I couldn't do a thing about it. How could I take you from a man like Von Hurst? I was continually frustrated, and I lashed out at you. I judged you because I couldn't bear the situation, and I had to have someone to blame. Then, when it appeared Pieter would do anything to be rid of you, you still didn't want me!"

He stopped his pacing and knelt on one knee before her, tenderly taking her hands in his. "I told you I was going to marry you, Ronnie. I meant it. I have Pieter's happy blessing, and nothing is going to stop me, not even you. I'll drug you and drag you down the aisle if I have to."

Moisture burned in Ronnie's eyes and she carried Drake's hands to her lips. "Oh, Drake! We still can't marry one another! You'll never trust me, and our lives would be a disaster."

Drake emitted an impatient oath, but Ronnie noted incredulously that it was directed at himself. "Ronnie, you have to forgive me for being an insufferable bastard. Trust you! I would trust you with my life—it's yours anyway—my heart, and my soul."

"But—"

"Ronnie," he interrupted, caressing her face with tender fingers and shaking it slightly as if he could force sense into her. "I believed at first that you and Pieter had had a very normal marriage, and that you had turned from him when he became ill—still caring, but not enough to endure a little chastity for the sake of his love and pride. I felt horrible when I entered his house and discovered I had had an affair with his wife. I admired the man, I respected him, I cared for him—and I had taken the one thing from him that a man doesn't take from another. I was furious with you, and I loathed myself, because even when I thought you were his wife, I wanted you still. I went through torture every night in that house. I wanted to run down the hall and ravish you—willing or no—in your husband's own home."

166

He stopped speaking abruptly and rose to sit beside her. His black eyes were on her with all the love and trust she could ever pray for. "I have to kiss you, Ronnie. I've gone crazy staying away this last month."

She did not protest as his lips touched hers with hungry reverence and his arms encircled her with firm possession. After a sweet infinity that threatened to grow dangerously passionate, he pulled away, gruffly explaining, "We are meeting Pieter for dinner."

"Oh, Drake," she choked, finally realizing the impact of what was happening through her reeling senses. "I can't believe this."

"I doubt if I'll ever stop being amazed at the sight and touch of you," Drake responded huskily. "You haven't said anything. Am I abducting you and dragging you down the aisle, or are you coming willingly?"

"Not willingly, eagerly." It was ridiculous; she wanted to run in wild circles, shouting for joy, but tears were streaking her cheeks.

Drake smoothed the dampness from her cheeks with the slightly rough touch of his thumbs. "What is it, Ronnie?" he demanded.

"Nothing, Drake," she assured him quickly, fingers trembling as they came to rest tentatively on the texture of his jacket. She laughed, wiping her own face with the back of her other hand. "I seem to cry so easily these days! But right now I'm happy, so happy. I never believed you wanted to spend your life with me. I thought you felt a proposal was the right thing to do—since you believed I'd be out in the cold. I wanted you to believe in me, forgive me, so badly, and I never thought it could happen."

"I was a pompous ass," Drake said baldly. "It is you who need to forgive me."

She thought of him, then, patiently waiting this month, on the sidelines all the time if needed, while she had carried out the commitment of her heart to another man. He had never left her, even when she sent him away. He had loved where she had loved,

167

given her a depth of comprehensive understanding that went beyond all speech and explanation.

"Drake," she cried suddenly, flinging herself onto his lap, mindless of her dress and his impeccable suit, to cling to his chest and bury her face in his neck, where the heady scent of his crisp and wild after-shave assailed her senses like a potent drug and sent delicious shivers to her spine. "I love you."

"I love you, sweet marble seductress," he hoarsely returned, cradling her to him and running a possessive hand down her spine. The shattering ferocity of his love took hold of him as he held her, his own now, his incredible creature of warmth, gentleness, and beauty, of quiet, stubborn pride and steadfast loyalty. His arms tightened around her. "No more tears, Ronnie. I'm going to make you happy, or die trying. We're going to do everything together, go everywhere together. We'll go anywhere you want. Rome, London, back to Paris. The honeymoon will be your choice. Where would you like to go?"

She raised eyes to him that now shimmered with crystal laughter. "Everywhere—eventually," she told him. "But for a honeymoon I want to take a cruise out of Charleston Harbor."

His own eyes twinkled and his mustache took on a lopsided twitch. "I'm crazy about cruises out of Charleston. I can guarantee you, I'm one man who will never knock southern hospitality —or charming southern belles." He planted a kiss on the tip of her nose. "Right now, we do have to get down to the lobby. Pieter is waiting."

"Drake." Ronnie paused with her fingers unnecessarily straightening his tie. "There's something else I'd like to do very much."

"And what is that?" He raised a querying brow.

"I want to go to Chicago." She raised impish eyes to his. "I want to meet your family, and all the little monster nephews and nieces. I want to meet the parents who could create such a creature as you!"

"I'm not sure how to take that, Miss Flynn," he replied with mock severity. "You have to have respect for your future husband. I will be a man who insists upon you toeing the line!"

"As long as he toes it in return!" Ronnie said demurely.

"Oh, he will," Drake said airily, lacing his fingers through the hair at her nape. "But you, young lady, you keep in mind that he—your future husband—is a temperamental Irishman, prone to irate rages and use of a horsewhip on erring wives."

"I'll bear that in mind!" Ronnie promised gravely, ruining the effect entirely by bursting into a fit of giggles. She couldn't imagine Drake, who went into self-torture for control, horsewhipping anyone—not even a horse.

"Laugh at me, woman, would you?" he challenged sternly, adding a threatening "You will get yours."

Ronnie smiled mischievously and raised a doubting brow. "I guess we had better meet Pieter." His last statement, had she retorted, could have become very leading. They could have explored the potential meanings of his words for hours.

Pieter himself was magnificent in his own way that night. Slender and gaunt, he nevertheless made a handsome picture in his brocade jacket. Pride soared in Ronnie's heart for him, and she deserted an understanding Drake to slip her arm through Pieter's and plant a loving kiss upon his cheek.

His eyes were more alive that night than she had seen them in years. He smiled at her and squeezed her arm, but directed his comment to Drake. "You see, O'Hara, I told you she wasn't entirely unreasonable."

"I'm not quite convinced of that, Von Hurst," Drake replied, the curl of his lips obliterating his attempted frown. "But she has consented to marry me."

"Who needed my consent?" Ronnie charged with an indignant sniff, her chin tilting but her eyes sparkling. "It seems I'm the only one who hasn't known what's been going on. You two have obviously been conniving. I suppose I should consider myself lucky you brought me in on everything tonight!"

Drake met Pieter's eyes over her head. "Maybe we should feed her," he said innocently. "Is she always this cranky when hungry?"

"Hmmm . . ." Pieter replied absently. "Even when she isn't hungry. But dinner might cause an improvement. Let us go. I have a taxi waiting outside."

Dinner was Pieter's choice; it was his birthday, and a very real celebration of life. He had discovered a wonderful French restaurant near D.C. that he swore was "almost like dining on the Champs-Élysées."

He was right. The meal was authentically French, from the champagne to the delicate fruit dessert. The decor was intimate and pleasant, the room dimly lit, and a strolling violinist added just the right touch as he moved unobtrusively through the trellised vines that gave the lush wicker-and-velvet room a hint of the feel of a true terrace.

Drake and Pieter did most of the talking, and as she listened Ronnie marveled that her life could have held two such wonderful men, who both loved her deeply in their own special ways. Such a short time ago she could never have imagined such a scene, her relationship with Pieter turned to a binding friendship, her love for Drake turned to a commitment that would last forever. And Pieter and Drake, her two magnificent men, fast, sure friends.

It was a fairy-tale romance. She had her prince, but there were no evil warlocks. Only a magnanimous and benign king.

"Is that all right with you, Ronnie?"

"Pardon?" she realized guiltily that her mind had drifted from the conversation.

Drake smiled tolerantly. "You accuse us of not involving you," he complained teasingly, "but when we do, you don't pay any attention! Pieter and I were discussing the wedding taking place in three days. Pieter has made all the arrangements. It will be in the little chapel down the street from the hotel."

Ronnie's eyes flitted from Drake's to Pieter's. Pieter was grinning like a very smug Dutch cat. Ronnie felt tears coming to her eyes again, tears she couldn't dare show. Impulsively she jumped to her feet, threw her arms around Pieter's neck, and kissed both his cheeks.

A crimson blush filled his cheeks and he admonished her gruffly through the grin he couldn't force to fade. "Really, Veronica, such behavior is most undignified."

"Oh, I know!" she agreed with wide eyes. "Don't you just love it?"

"Yes," he mumbled into his demitasse cup, "yes, I do."

By the time Drake walked Ronnie back to her room that night, the future she had worried about had been settled. She and Drake would spend a few days in Chicago after the wedding, then fly back to Charleston to arrange for the transport of Pieter's marble sculptures. They were not going to be sold but dispersed to various museums. Von Hurst had taken his place with the masters.

As soon as Drake made the shipping arrangements Ronnie and he would leave for their honeymoon, and Pieter would shortly leave for his new life in Paris.

Henri and Gretel would be going with Pieter. Drake and Ronnie would take the horses and dogs. And Dave would care for the pleasure boats Drake kept on the Great Lakes.

Dreams could come true, Ronnie realized, her head spinning with the details the men conscientiously considered, with all ends tied up nicely.

Ronnie wasn't surprised when Drake followed her into the suite, but she was somewhat startled when he comfortably removed his jacket, vest, and tie and slung them casually over the arm of the love seat before seating himself to remove highly polished shoes.

He caught the consternation in her eyes and smiled with wicked amusement, answering her unvoiced question. "Yes, I am staying the night. This is not Pieter's house, and I can't stand one more minute of propriety. I'm not that much of a gentleman. And besides"—he moved toward her with slow deliberation, his feet soundless on the carpeted floor as he gapped the distance

171

between them—"there is one thing I learned from Pieter that far surpasses any wisdom he gave me pertaining to sculpture." He took her face gently between his hands and looked deeply into her eyes. "Life is a very precious gift, not to be wasted. Love is even more precious. I am a very lucky man. I have them both. I don't intend to lose another second of either."

"Oh, Drake." Ronnie trembled as she circled her arms around his neck.

He smothered her against him, his hands raking the silklike hair down to her spine and beyond, to the two shadowed dimples he knew he would find at its base. "Ronnie," he groaned, the sound a thundering from deep within his chest. "You're crazy if you think I could leave you tonight. I haven't slept nights, dreaming of you the way I left you, your hair splayed across the fur, your provocative, beguiling shape so visible beneath that misty garment. In my dreams your eyes invited me, they were sparkling with liquid, sensuous beseechment. . . ."

She pulled away from him and asked wistfully, "Like they are now? Can the reality live up to the fantasy?"

"Reality," Drake said, pulling her back to his chest, where the beating of his heart combined with hers, "outshines the most fervent imagination in your case, my love." His kisses fell to the eyes that held such enchantment, they covered her face, and grazed the long slender column of her throat. A very familiar heat filled him, one only she could create, one only she could satisfy.

Ronnie felt as if her body melted to his like mercury. She could feel his rising desire, and her own spiraled to meet it. Her hips formed to his tauntingly while she arched to work at the buttons of his shirt. Her face tilted to his; her eyes became those of a cat, gleaming, exotically narrowed, seducing subtly with the hint of wild abandon. "Tell me more about your fantasies," she urged him, pulling his shirt from his waistband and allowing her fingers to provocatively run along the newly exposed flesh.

His satanic smile came into play as he caught her hands deftly and reversed the aggression, finding the zipper of her dress,

172

releasing it, and allowing the fabric to fall to her feet like an ocean wave.

Indeed, he could well imagine she was Venus rising. Breasts of alabaster cream rose proudly over the lace of a teal-blue bra, her deep rose nipples peeking through the lace. He bent to remove the matching slip from her, allowing his hands to glide along her smooth midriff, over her hips, and down the velvet of her shapely legs as the slip too joined the dress on the floor. He heard her soft moan as his hands grasped her hips firmly, and his lips followed the course they had so recently taken. The sound of her pleasure sent his pulses racing to a fiery speed, and an urgent, fundamental, totally masculine, wildly primitive need to hold and conquer the exquisite feminine beauty that was his gripped him with shattering intensity. The dark depths of his passion showed in the taut lines of his face as he rose to meet his Venus, wordlessly sweeping her into his arms, leaving behind the discarded clothing as he swiftly walked her into the next room and lay her upon the bed. His eyes continued to hold hers as he impatiently doffed his clothes.

Ronnie watched him with unabashed longing, the warmth in her body growing as she anticipated the rough touch of the hair upon his chest against her breasts, which tingled and peaked in expectation. A quiver began to ripple through her. The extent of his desire was unmistakable, the sight of his long sinewed legs intoxicating.

His kisses ravaged her breasts as he hovered over her, even as he lifted her to him and sought the snaps to release the bra. Ronnie moaned and shuddered as he moved on to remove her last remaining garment, gossamer panties that slid sensuously down her legs. The heat in her was intensifying, but Drake found the core of her longing and stroked it languorously with knowing fingers that found in return complete reception. His eyes found hers again as he gave pleasure and sweet torment, and with a strangled cry she gripped her fingers in his hair to bring his face to hers. Her tongue traced the line of his mouth, then jutted into the demanding warmth. She felt as if she were going mad with

173

her own desire, whirling into endless space with a burst of sensation. Her mouth left his to bite lightly into a bronze shoulder, her body undulating to his, speaking a plea of its own as she beseeched him with barely comprehensible whispers to make her his.

"Fantasy, my love, or reality?" he whispered hoarsely.

"A little bit of both," she sighed. "Drake . . ."

He moved from her for a brief moment, one well used. His kisses covered her body moistly, feverishly, seeking all the places his hands had discovered and reawakening them even further into a flame run so rampant, it threatened to consume her. Each of Ronnie's pleasure-filled responses drove Drake to heightened desire, and he lowered himself over her, spreading thighs that wound to his own sinewed ones with the sweetest of welcomes.

"Forever, Ronnie," he groaned, shuddering fiercely with the wonderful release of taking her, becoming one with her in a volatile entry. "All this forever, my love."

Her answer was a moan, inaudible, but heard by him. "Forever." It was forever. Stroking, gliding, sailing into the stars. Drake's passion and desire were such that he was rough, but his aching love guided even that ardor, and he took her with him every step of the way. Their rhythm was mutually combustible, wild as the wind they both adored, as natural and primitive as the inevitable predestiny that had brought them together as man and woman.

The tempo increased, madly, sweetly, aided and abetted by the fact that neither could keep their hands still. Their lips would cling and part, their tongues touch, duel. The end, the beginning of heavenly oblivion, came upon them together as a crescendo of tenderly violent impact that left them both in trembling awe, satiated, saturated with wonder. They did not part but held tight together, waiting in languorous pleasure for their breath to return and the quivering of their limbs to subside.

The satisfaction of their union, tenfold sweet with the admission of a binding love, had exhausted Ronnie. Her eyes began to close in a rest that was overwhelming with the release of all the tensions she had suffered—pain, worry, denial. She had cast them all upon Drake's broad shoulders, and in the wild and chaotic beauty of their union she had found peace.

She blinked, realizing she had dozed off, to find Drake seated Indian-style on the bed, drawing idle patterns around her navel. A very slow smile crept into her lips as she watched him through lazy, half-closed eyes. A smug thrill of feminine satisfaction invaded her; there was something boyish about his pose as he sat vulnerably naked, yet there was nothing boyish about his sinewed physique, taut over his bone structure even as he leaned forward.

He knew intuitively that she had wakened, asking without glancing at her face, "Are you happy, Ronnie?"

She nodded and caught the hand caressing her skin to kiss it. "So happy, and scared. Can this really last?"

His strongly planed features grew grave. "Yes, it can. Not every minute can be ecstasy, or blind passion, but love can be—and ours will be—a shelter against outside storms. Love is trust, and peace and security in that trust. It's a wonderful thing, even in the worst of times."

Ronnie absorbed his words without speaking, her eyes downcast. When she opened them, she found Drake watching her with a brooding intensity.

"Why didn't you tell me that you'd never made love to Pieter?"

She caught her breath and watched him blankly for a second. "How did you know?"

"He told me."

Ronnie gasped with surprise. Her voice quavered. "When?"

"We had quite an interesting dinner that last night. Pieter told me a lot I already knew—about Jamie's death and your marriage in Paris. He also told me a lot you didn't. He told me that you knew from the very beginning that you were entering a platonic marriage." Drake paused for a minute. "He also told me how bad it was for you all those years, how he used and abused you,

175

and how you withstood it all with unbreakable patience and endurance."

Ronnie's hand tightened convulsively on the one she held. Her lashes lowered and she held her voice steady. "It wasn't that bad, Drake. You see, I always knew the real Pieter von Hurst. I knew he would never really hurt me. I knew that no one else could understand what he went through as I did. I—" She stuttered momentarily. "I never told you that our marriage had always been platonic because one thing Pieter clung to was his pride."

Drake adjusted his weight over hers and gently took her chin in his hands. "Look at me, Ronnie," he commanded with tenderness. "I'm not angry or upset that you didn't tell me. I admire what you tried to do. All these wonderful quirks of that crazy proud personality of yours are what make me love you so very much."

Her heart was in her eyes as she met his, offering the depths of a soul that had remained innocent and pure through everything.

"Oh, Drake," she murmured with loving gratitude, placing kisses of tremulous emotion in the hollows of his collarbone. "And I love you so much for all that you are!" Her voice softened. "For all that you've done for Pieter."

Drake smiled at her. "I have to admit, it's been a lot easier to be Pieter's friend now that I know you two were never lovers. You can't imagine what it's like to sit at a dinner table with a man and try to carry on a normal conversation when you know you've made love to his wife."

Ronnie chuckled and sobered. "Drake—you know I'll always be concerned for him."

"Yes, Ronnie," he said gently. "I do know. And I'll always share that concern with you."

He shifted back to a sitting position abruptly, pulling her with him into his arms. "Enough of this deep conversation for the night!" he charged severely. "If one of us slips on a robe, I think we might find a bottle of champagne chilling outside the door to the suite."

"Champagne?" Ronnie arched a brow with amusement. "Mr. O'Hara, you do know how to treat a fiancée!"

"Of course." Drake grinned, lifting her slightly to give her underside a light swat. "And since I thought of the champagne—French, of course—I think you should run out and get it."

Giggling, Ronnie jumped from the bed. "This time, O'Hara. But don't get any ideas that I'll always jump when you swat!"

Drake laced his hands behind his head and made himself comfortable on the pillow while Ronnie grabbed a robe. "Hurry!" he ordered imperiously, ignoring her comment. "By the way—I hope you had a lot of sleep last night, because I don't want you to count on much tonight."

"Promises, promises!" Ronnie said mockingly, sighing.

Drake threw a pillow at her but missed. He grinned fully, his face a devil's mask.

"I always keep my promises."

CHAPTER TEN

They were married as planned three days later.

Pieter von Hurst did attend the wedding. The papers, of course, got hold of the story, but the three involved found outside perplexity over the situation nothing more than amusing.

Drake and Ronnie then flew to Chicago, where she met his parents. They were a charming couple, accepting her immediately with open arms. Drake's mother, an incredibly tiny woman to have produced such a son, was an attractive and spirited lady, literally pooh-poohing any fears Ronnie might have had about her being concerned with Ronnie's notoriety.

The senior O'Hara was a Gaelic charmer, and Ronnie could easily see where Drake had inherited his size, coloring, and dangerously charismatic eyes. His speech enchanted Ronnie; he still carried the lilt of a brogue after almost forty years in the States.

Drake watched with tolerant amusement as his parents and Ronnie instantly endeared themselves to one another. He had expected nothing less, and he thanked God fervently for both his mother and father when he saw the happiness in his bride's eyes that night. "Oh, Drake," she told him wonderously, "not only do I have you, but a family, too! It's been so long. . . ."

He chuckled and enveloped her in his arms tenderly. She was so terribly strong, yet so sweetly vulnerable. "You definitely have a family," he replied ruefully. "They've adopted you already. In fact, I think they prefer their new daughter to their son!"

They weren't able to see much of Chicago, as Drake had spent too much time away from work and had to put some time in at the main gallery. Ronnie didn't care. She assured Drake that the city wasn't going to go away, and spent her days between her in-laws' house and her own new home.

Drake's house was like the man—tasteful, fastidious, yet very warm and masculine. It was a split-level modern house done in brick and wood that complemented both the manicured lawn and rock garden and the untouched woodland that stretched behind it. A terrace of three-sided glass looked upon the rock garden, and Ronnie found herself continually drawn to the spot, trying to convince herself that the magical place was really her new home.

"Like it?" Drake asked, slipping his arms around her waist and resting his chin on her head.

"Love it," Ronnie replied, slipping her hands over the pair that held her.

She ran her eyes over the room. Drake's love for art was apparent everywhere: exquisite sculptures adorned the tables, paintings decked the walls with clever display. A strong macrame swing extended from a brass fitting in the corner of the room like an intricately woven birdcage. Earth tone throw pillows were nestled into the seat, and Ronnie blissfully imagined hours of curling into its circumference with a good book, swinging lightly, looking up now and then to view the garden through the spotless glass.

"Change anything you want," Drake directed with a smile. "Hell—find a new house if you want! I am fond of this place, though. We have five acres, and we're still only a thirty-minute drive from the heart of the city."

"I love the house," Ronnie assured him, "and I don't want to change a thing. Except maybe the—"

"The what?"

"The bedroom." Ronnie grimaced ruefully. "Not that I don't like it"—she thought of the room with its high platform bed, polished oak bookshelves and dressers, and rich chocolate drapes and bedspread—"it's just a little too male!" She smiled slowly at

179

his confusion. "I want anyone who walks into that room to know that you do share it with a wife!"

Drake laughed, but while he was gone that afternoon a package arrived for her. It was a huge luxurious white alpaca spread. Drake hadn't signed his name, just the word *fantasy*.

Ronnie laughed delightedly and quickly changed the spread. It made a wonderful change, coupled with the feminine articles she now had resting on her dresser, it made the room very intimate, very much that of a couple. White drapes, she decided, would be the finishing touch. But they could come later. . . .

When Drake returned home, his fantasy was fulfilled. She waited for him, swathed in the sheerest of black negligees, stretched languorously on the fur, her hair a startling contrast of thick sable waves. Her eyes were those he had always imagined, captivating, seductive, heavy with a passion uniquely for him. . . . She was his marble beauty, half kitten, half tigress.

Later, when their bodies had cooled and they clung together beneath the fur for warmth, Drake tugged lightly at a strand of silky hair tangled in his fingers. His eyes were deeply brooding as Ronnie stared into them.

"Do you miss Von Hurst?" he asked softly.

"No," she answered with honesty, meeting his gaze before issuing light kisses on each corner of his mustache. "I went days without ever seeing Pieter when I lived on the island, and . . ."

"And what?" Drake persisted, willing his mind off the lips that were stirring his senses again.

She flushed lightly and buried her head in the black curls on his chest. "When I'm in your arms," she muffled softly to him, "I don't miss anything. I don't even remember that there is an outside world. . . ."

He stroked her hair, the contours of her back, and marveled at the wonderful combination of modesty and passion that was his wife. He had asked the question because they were returning to the island tomorrow. She had told the truth, and yet he still worried slightly. She had been away from the man she had cared

180

for only a week, and she knew she would see him again. Her loyalty was deep, not easily broken. Would seeing him again tear her apart all over? There would be a finality to the break up of the barren island off Charleston's coast. . . .

He thought no more. Like her, he forgot there was an outside world when they came together in one another's arms.

The next days were grueling. Though Von Hurst appeared fit, and pleased to see them in an admirably friendly fashion, he could take little part in the work ahead. Hired labor took care of the transfer of animals and furniture, but as artists, neither Drake nor Pieter would trust the packing of the marble pieces to anyone else. Ronnie learned in those days that her new husband had a streak of perfectionism that was amazing. At least, she thought with dry tolerance as she repacked a box for the third time, he had the will and strength to ask no more than he gave.

He looked up suddenly from the pile of insulating material he separated with his strong, sure hands and laughed.

Ronnie sent him a querying frown.

"You'll never be able to accuse me of chauvinism." He chuckled to her dryly. "How many men would allow their wives' backs to be on display in museums all over the world?"

"The back is attached to a head," Ronnie retorted.

"And a derriere," Drake reminded her sternly.

She watched him for a moment, wondering if there were just the hint of a curl to his lips. "*Do* you mind?" she asked him.

He crawled through the various debris on the floor and held her, one hand molding over the anatomy under discussion. "No," he said, and there was a decided curl to his lips. "Not when I was in on the creation. But I do think the world has seen the end of the modeling career of Mrs. Drake O'Hara. If you get any professional urges, you'll have to come to me."

"You are a chauvinist," Ronnie informed him.

"Do *you* mind?"

181

She shook her head with mischief in her eyes. "Not at all. I can handle you."

Drake was undaunted. "That's right," he said gravely, fingering the band he had recently placed on her finger. "You can handle me whenever you like."

He teased her through all the work they did, and even when Pieter was present, the mood remained light. Meals were pleasant affairs with conversation running smoothly. But as the inevitable time to leave drew near, Drake knew that Ronnie was straining to remain cheerful.

The hour of their departure came. Ronnie was as beautiful and elite as ever, her apparel a smart beige suit with a vest that emphasized her slender curves beneath the tailored jacket. She wore shoes and a hat of complementing tan, and Drake thought with an admiring amusement that Ronnie was a clotheshorse. She had an instinctive ability to choose clothing, and each accessory was always perfect. Her hat dipped low over one eye, and he was reminded of the first time he saw her. She would always be innately regal, mysterious and intriguing. And always wear her pride like her clothing, a valiant shield that was impenetrable. Except to him. He concealed a tender smile, suddenly completely secure.

"Go say good-bye to Pieter," he told her.

"Alone?"

"Yes, I'll carry the bags and meet you at the boat."

Ronnie tapped at the door to Pieter's suite for the last time. She smiled and bit her lip as she heard his imperiously clipped, *"Entre!"*

She opened the door and found him by the window, looking out, his thin hands clasped behind his back. His light eyes turned to her, and a soft smile curved into delicate lips.

"Everything is ready!" she began cheerfully. Then the effort failed. Her lips quivered and her eyes started to fill. "We're leaving."

His arms extended to her as they never could have before. She rushed to him, and the tears fell as he held her.

"Don't cry for me, Ronnie. Please, don't cry." He wiped the tears from her cheeks. "You gave me my art; you gave me life when I desired to end it. You must give me one more thing."

"What is that?" she asked, trying to smile again as she wiped her own eyes.

"The promise that you will live long and happily, and take all that Drake can give you."

Ronnie nodded, fearful that if she tried to speak, the tears would fall again.

"I haven't lost a wife, you know," he told her, pale blue eyes searching hers. "A man cannot lose what was never rightfully his. I have, instead, gained a friend, and a very talented protégé to boot."

Ronnie nodded again, the shimmering beauty of her eyes giving him a love he would cherish to his dying day.

He kissed her forehead and shoved her lightly for the door. "Go now, Veronica. And don't cry. You will see me again."

She walked to the door with her head bowed, pausing before she whispered, "Take care of yourself, Pieter."

"You too, Ronnie."

She swung around like a water sprite and flew back to him with a strangled cry. He held her for second, and pushed her away. "Stop it, Ronnie," he said gruffly. "You're getting tears all over my shirt, and it's silk. Go now and tell that protégé of mine that he'd better take care of you and make you happy."

Ronnie fled the room. Perhaps she had given Pieter his life, but he had also given her hers. He had given her Drake.

She moved swiftly out of the house, and in the garden that had once been her sanctuary, she reconciled all that her life had been with all that her life would be. Plucking a single rose, she held it to her cheek, then slowly left the garden and walked the pathway to the dock.

Her footsteps quickened as she neared the boat. Drake was already there, patiently waiting, his tall dark form a towering bastion of strength. He reached out a bronze hand and took hers, enveloping it with warmth and a tender, secure pressure.

A promise to love and share into eternity was in the grip of that bronze hand, and as it led her onward Ronnie knew she would always follow without looking back, loving and trusting in return.

EPILOGUE

Statuesque. She was still a marble beauty, but like the exquisite marble work of the masters, she was alive, warm, vibrant, and bewitching.

She watched him, and he knew it; he returned her appreciative gaze.

They had had enough sun; it was time to fulfill the messages of their eyes.

He executed a perfect dive into the pool, and so did she.

His touch upon her satiny skin in the water was sheer agony to nerves heightened with anticipation. His breath, as he whispered in her ear, was a stimulant that sent her senses reeling. "I'm Drake O'Hara, madam, and don't you ever forget it. I'd like to buy you a drink, but not poolside—in *our* cabin."

"That's nice," she murmured in return, nibbling at his lower ear and feigning a mock defiance, "then I can buy you one—in *our* cabin."

"If you don't stop that," Drake warned, pressing against her so that she gasped with the evidence of his desire, "we won't make it out of the pool."

Laughing, they broke apart, but they were scarcely through the cabin door before Drake pulled the string of her bikini top, robbing her of the garment as she glided ahead of him. Uttering a startled chastisement, Ronnie swung around to him.

She was a golden-tanned, exquisite, perfectly molded, proud beauty, the breasts he had bared high and firm, her waist a wraithlike thing of satin that led to lusciously carved hips. Her

185

chin was tilted in mock query and indignation for only a second, and then she was in his arms, her soft breasts crushed to his hair-roughened chest, sensitively hardened nipples teasing and teased by the crisp depth of black curls.

"Ronnie," he whispered with a groan that rippled a shudder through his torso. He caught her head and looked deeply into the pools of sapphire that had long ago bewitched him, and then he kissed her, softly at first, then deeply with an exploding passion, seeking every sweet crevice of her mouth with a plundering tongue. She returned his play with a fire of her own, moaning as their bodies meshed together with heat, taunting him further with gentle nips upon his lower lip to be followed by the tantalizing and healing balm of the moistly tender tip of her tongue. It was she who pulled away to search out his eyes and demand with panted breath, "What do you want, Drake?"

He grinned but his eyes held warning. "I want you," he growled, scooping her into his arms with a steellike force that advised her there would be no more teasing. "Now, and forever."

"Sir," she returned meekly, "you have got me—now and forever."

She was aflame for him as he deposited her upon the bed, impatiently divesting her of the bikini bottom, and exploding with incoherent murmurs of desire as he planted kisses into the newly exposed hollows of her hips. She began to quiver uncontrollably, and he continued his assault almost savagely, claiming her flesh with moist, heated lips from the tender rise of her breasts to the invitation of her sleek thighs, alternately demanding fiercely and grazing with the utmost reverence.

Ronnie's fingers clutched feverishly into the thick black luster of Drake's hair, trying to bring him to her before the longing he had elicited drove her wild. "Drake!" she pleaded desperately, moaning delightedly with each intimate assault. "Oh, Drake. . . ."

His weight moved firmly over hers, pinioning her with the incredibly toned form that enveloped her into another, permeating world of sheer mindless delight. His heated flesh quivering like hers seemed to combine them in endless time and space. But though he pulsed against her and teased with taunting proximity, he again gripped her face firmly between his hands and gratingly countered, "What do you want, Ronnie?"

"You," she whispered, searching his eyes.

"Forever?" he queried, then touched her lips. "It isn't just a word."

"Forever," she vowed gravely. "Oh, God, Drake, no, it isn't just a word. Forever and ever and ever. . . ."

Her answer satisfied his mind, her movements satisfied his body. He had loved her from the beginning, but now that love was his, rightfully his, and the emotion guided their lovemaking. Their coupling was passionately wild, abandoned as the sea, as deep and obliterating as the sizzling dark depths of his eyes. But it was more than that. The intimate rhythm that drove them to the highest peaks of ecstasy was that of a combining of two perfectly attuned bodies; it was also the consummation of two minds that worked as one, two souls in harmony, two hearts that gave endlessly, unabashed to take in return. . . .

They crested upon that pinnacle of sheer ecstasy together, their release so volatile, it almost stole consciousness, leaving them to shudder delightfully in one another's arms as they left their solely private dimension to travel together back to solid earth. Drake was loathe to move from her, even as he relaxed with the sense of fulfillment. He was a part of her, physically for the time, and it was right, it felt wonderful. He would stay where he was, savoring his love.

She opened sapphire eyes and stared into his with a tender smile. She understood, she felt the same. Dusk began to fall as they lay contentedly together.

Later, comfortably situated, Ronnie's burnished sable head resting in the tender embrace of her husband's shoulder, they began to talk, to laugh, to plan their lives. Funny, though, they didn't really need to speak to communicate. Their silences were always companionable.

It was during one of those silences that Ronnie realized the vision of dark eyes would always impose upon any other. She would never forget the pale blue—she didn't want to. But those wonderful dark eyes that had haunted her from first sight would beguile her for eternity with love, with tenderness, with the understanding that would last even beyond youth and passion. . . .

Drake adjusted his length, as always, sensing her moods.

Dark-brown eyes stared into hers even as she envisioned them, gentle with the understanding she cherished.

"I love you," he said softly. It was all that was necessary.

"Forever," she returned with a smile.

His lips descended upon hers with gentle, overwhelming command, and there was no past. Only a glittering future of love . . . together, forever.

QUIET WALKS THE TIGER

For Mom
with many thanks

PROLOGUE

Grace, poise, and magic . . . she was all of these, the epitome of all the beauty that the physical body of woman could be. She had been born to dance, her body trained to utilize the natural talent to the utmost. As she swayed and dipped and swirled, the muted lights enhancing the unusual mixture of brunette, red, and gold that mingled in her flowing hair, she was a creature in her element. The music was in her slender form, a goddess sheathed in a shimmering bath of violet-tinged clouds. The love of the music, the instinct to follow it, glowed radiantly in her face. It touched her feet until it seemed she flew, no servant to the laws of gravity. She allured and enticed as she danced, emitting a message as old as pagan ritual, as natural as man himself.

To most who watched her, she was simply a part of the magic of the evening, a striking member of the prestigious Fife Dance Company. They would go home and remember the enchantment of the theater, the fascination of the dance, and then take off their gloves and cloaks and bask in pleasant memory until another night out in dress-up enlivened the monotony of day-to-day life. They would think of those on stage as something more than mortal, incredible beings of sheer physical perfection. They would shake their heads and momentarily wish that they too were so agile, so taut of muscle, so fleet of foot. They would envy without thinking of the endless years of commitment and work, and then they would forget.

One man in the audience would not forget. He knew the woman who had taken center stage, exhibiting the full and intoxicating physical expression that was dance.

He had come because of her. He didn't plan to try to talk to her; he just came to see her. He knew she was married, and

191

because of the man he was, he truly wished that marriage all the luck in the world. But he was in love with her. They had dated only once, but that one night had hopelessly entangled him. She had invaded his bloodstream and dreams ever since.

He was a bit like an out-of-date Lancelot, he told himself ruefully as he watched the performance. She belonged to another, but she held his heart. And so he was sworn to her, to love and forever cherish her from afar.

He wasn't at the theater alone, and he knew his companions would have a hell of a laugh if they knew what went on in his mind. He and the two with him were also creatures of physical perfection—a different kind, and at the moment, more famous than any of those on the stage would ever be.

They were football players and the backfield of the team that had just won one of the greatest American quests for glory—the Super Bowl.

And here he was—the macho, rugged leader of the pack—the quarterback, mooning over a slip of a girl who moved like quicksilver over a stage. . . .

The performance ended. The three tuxedoed men in the audience, friendly giants of virility, were asked for as many autographs as the dancers.

Backstage the girl changed. She hadn't a single thought of the audience on her mind; she was anxious to see her husband. She had marvelous news for him. Intimate, wonderful news. They were expecting their first child.

The football players were heading for a party. He might have sworn his heart to her . . . but hell, a man had to live. . . .

He wouldn't remember the name of the woman he was with that night or the color of her hair. But he was gallant. He always was. Charm was as much a part of his nature as power and the innate magnetism that drew respect from men and women alike. . . . He had a good time at the party.

He didn't see his dancer until five years later. And on that occasion he remained in the background again, although his heart was breaking for her.

She was a solemn figure that day, ramrod straight and proud. Slim and hauntingly beautiful in black.

The last earthly remains of her husband were interned into the earth. Ashes to ashes, dust to dust. She was surrounded by people who loved her, but she would be led away by none. She stayed as the first shovels of earth fell on the coffin. She stood straight and unyielding until she was alone.

Then her knees buckled and she fell to the carpet of green grass that encircled the mound of newly dug earth. Her hands flew to her face, and even from his distance he could hear the terrible sobs wracking her slender frame.

He knew he couldn't go to her; he knew he couldn't help her. He just stood there, railing against his helplessness, watching until the sun sank in a burst of crimson behind the hills.

It would be another two years before he would go to her.

CHAPTER ONE

The band in the dinner lounge was really very good. They were versatile and had done everything from Sinatra to Blondie and managed to complacently oblige almost any request for a song from the thirties to the eighties—spacing them to please the young hard rockers and the mature dinner clientele.

Sloan Tallett had been on the dance floor, twirling beneath the lights, for the majority of the evening. She was a beautiful woman, never more regal than when on a dance floor, and with her escort being the head of the dance department from the college where she taught, she had provided the patrons of the lounge with visual entertainment as well as acoustical. Eyes riveted and stayed upon the handsome couple, which was what Jim Baskins intended. They were the best advertising he could manage for the College of Fine Arts.

The number, a breath-stealing piece from the late sixties, came to a halt. Sloan laughed gaily to Jim as they wove their way to their table, hand in hand. She was flushed as she sat, her blue eyes as radiant as sapphires. Someone stopped by to issue a compliment, and she smiled with lazy thanks, the full-lipped, seductive smile of a temptress.

She had been born to dance—her friend and escort was thinking—but she had also been born to captivate. Only someone close could ever see the hard line of reserve and pain that lurked beneath the stars in her eyes and the radiance of her smile.

"Another scotch and soda?" Jim asked.

"No!" She chuckled, but her answer was firm. She glanced at her black-banded wristwatch with a frown. "It's too close to pumpkin time, I'm afraid. I'd love a plain soda, though, with a twist of lime."

194

"I'd probably better order the same," Jim said with a grimace, motioning to their waitress. "You're good for me, Sloan, do you know that?" he said after putting their order in. "You keep me on the straight and narrow."

Sloan smiled at her companion. Jim Baskins was twenty years her senior, and she was sure he had traveled the straight and narrow all his life. He was her immediate supervisor, and a more gentle, understanding man couldn't be found. A confirmed bachelor, Jim had dedicated his life to two demanding mistresses —dance and teaching. Approaching fifty, he had the look of a much younger man. An inch or so over Sloan's five feet seven inches, he was thin and wiry, the touches of silver in his thick blond hair adding an air of distinguished maturity. Most people who saw them together decided there was a romantic interest between the two—which wasn't true. They were co-workers and friends who enjoyed one another's company.

"I think it's the other way around," Sloan told him. "You keep me on the straight and narrow."

"Two damn straight and narrow, if you ask me," Jim replied. "You should be dating, Sloan. You're a young woman, and it's been two years . . ." His voice trailed away; he hadn't meant to remind her of the husband he had never met.

Clouds passed over the sapphire of her eyes, but Sloan kept smiling. "It's all right, Jim. It has been two years since Terry died. And I do date occasionally. When I'm interested. But society has picked up a little too much for me. Every time I date someone a second time, they seem to think I've said yes to hop into bed."

"It wouldn't kill you to have an affair," Jim advised, surveying her over his soda. "And you should consider a second marriage—"

"I don't want to marry again," Sloan interrupted softly. She had had a good marriage, and anything shallow to follow would be sacrilege She looked at Jim to see him, miserable, before her and realized she was extending her own unhappiness to him. And she wasn't really unhappy. She had her job, she had the children. "Why would I want to marry?" she queried cheerfully. "I have enough of my own problems! I don't need someone else's!"

195

Jim didn't look quite so miserable. "Bad attitude, Sloan. You share the good along with the bad."

Sloan laughed easily. "Jim—it's not something I have to decide immediately. I don't exactly have a score of suitors pounding down my door. You'd have to be a rich man to contemplate marriage to a struggling thirtyish widow with three children age six and under. Come to think of it, you'd have to be a lunatic as well."

"I'd marry you, Sloan," Jim said softly.

Sloan chuckled softly and stretched slender fingers across the table to envelop his hand. "You are a lunatic," she told him with warm affection. "And I do believe you mean it." Jim was aware that her life was rough—finances were low, and her job schedule, while trying to be a good mother to three young children, was grueling. "But I love you as a very dear friend, as you love me—and like I said, I don't want to get married. I'm a very independent lady—I run my own life."

Jim shook his head sadly. "You're a beautiful woman, Sloan. Someday some man is going to come along and crumble that shell of yours—and I hope I'm around to see the day."

"Only if he has a fortune!" Sloan teased. "Come on, boss," she added, rising. "Walk me to my car. I don't like to keep Cassie waiting. She expects me home no later than ten."

Sloan's sister kept her children on Friday nights so that Sloan could have an evening out. Usually, it was dinner and dancing with Jim or the occasional date that intrigued her. Friday nights were her only fling. She needed them to remind herself that she was still shy of thirty, still young. She enjoyed her evenings with Jim and the few "real" dates she accepted, but that was as far as she would venture from the wall she had carefully built around herself after Terry's death. Life was too serious a thing for her to take the time to really unscramble her feelings on love, sex, and affairs. It was—at this point—a fight for survival.

"Okay, gorgeous," Jim said amicably, signaling for the check. "We'll get you in for curfew. It's supposed to be twelve, though —not ten," he teased, dropping a few bills on the table and rising to assist her from her chair. "But I guess it's about the same. 'Beautiful, sexy, seductive dancer goes home and turns back into household drudge!' "

"Thanks," Sloan said dryly, grinning as she accepted his arm. "Just what every woman needs. A boss with a sense of humor."

Jim guided her from the still-thriving lounge to the parking lot. Since they could shower and change in the dance department, they went out straight from work, and both had their own cars. Courteous as always, Jim saw her into her Cutlass and closed and locked the door for her.

"Beautiful night," he mused, sticking his well-kept frame, nicely suited in a double-breasted jacket, through her window. "You should be enjoying it with some nice knight in white armor."

"I had my knight!" Sloan said with a wistful smile. "They don't come charging through a life twice—there is a shortage of white horses!"

"You're a cynic, Sloan," Jim said with a shake of his head. "Grown hard as nails."

"Oh, Jim!" Sloan protested, smiling. "I'm not a complete cynic! I know the games people play, and I merely prefer to play them by my own rules. I set them down squarely first. And if I'm hard—" she shrugged, but straightened in her seat, her chin tilting a shade, her eyes glittering like blue crystals in the night— "it's because I have to be."

"Lost cause!" Jim muttered, pecking her forehead with a brotherly kiss before pulling his torso from the car. "Have a nice weekend. Give the kids a kiss for me, and I'll see you on Monday."

"Thanks, Jim," Sloan replied, twisting her key in the ignition. "Have a nice weekend yourself!"

Waving, she pulled out of the parking lot and onto the highway, breathing deeply of the crisp air. It was a beautiful night— the type that made her happy she had left Boston after Terry's death and returned home to Gettysburg. Stars dotted the sky like a spray of glittering rhinestones against a sea of black velvet. She passed the gently rolling landscape of the national park and smiled to herself wryly. It was the type of night when lovers should stroll together across fields of green in the tingling, crisp coolness.

But, she wondered briefly, would she ever really love again? Sloan hadn't lied to Jim. She had dated. Nice men, good-looking men, men she had even found attractive, at first . . . she had kissed them, felt their arms around her.

But remained absolutely untouched inside. Jim was the only person she saw steadily, and that was because he was a friend. He never pressured her.

Sometimes she felt as if her heart had frozen solid. She was hard, she was cold, she was cynical. She had to be a dead set realist. There were times when she still hurt too much, but she had to shelve loneliness and pain. Terry was dead. Point-blank. Fact. She had managed a life for herself, a fairly good one. She liked people, she saw people, she looked forward to the future. To a time when she could leave the survival pay of the college and work for a professional dance troupe again. Hire some help . . .

"What am I worrying about?" she asked herself impatiently as she drove up to her own house. She glanced at the pretty white building with the green trim with pride. She had purchased it herself, a great deal that her brother-in-law had found for her. She had made a good down payment, and now she only had the mortgage and taxes . . . and damn! A payment was due.

Sighing, Sloan decided to deal with that problem later. She walked briskly to her door and started to use her key, then thought better of the idea. Cassie startled easily. Better to knock than to scare her sister half out of her wits.

"Hi, kid!" Cassie greeted her, opening the door. "How was your night?"

Sloan shrugged as she tossed her purse onto a chair and bent in the doorway to slip off the straps of her heeled sandals and nudge them beneath the same chair. "Nice. The usual. Jim is a dear." She smiled at her older sister with resignation. "I do enjoy the evening out. Jim may not be exciting—but he is adult companionship!"

"I've got a pot of tea on," Cassie said. "Want some?"

"Naturally." Sloan laughed, following her pretty, slender sister into the kitchen. The women, only two years apart, were best friends. They shared the same tall, graceful build, but there the similarities of their appearances ended. Cassie had huge, saucer brown eyes and hair so light as to be platinum. At thirty-one, she

198

was still looked at and asked for identification when she ordered a drink.

"Any problems?" Sloan asked as she accepted a mug of tea and curled her legs into a chair at the sunny yellow kitchen table.

"Not a one," Cassie replied, leaning her elbows on the table. "Jamie and Laura crawled into bed right after their super-hero program. And the baby, well, he's always an angel. He was sound asleep at seven."

Sloan warmed her face comfortably with the steam from her cup. "They know better than to mess with their aunt!" She chuckled. "Anything else new?"

Cassie hesitated, and Sloan watched her sister's beautiful brown eyes, puzzled. "What is it?"

"A man called for you, a Mr. Jordan."

"And?" Sloan prompted her sister casually, then held her breath as she waited for her answer. Mr. Jordan was with a professional dance company in Philadelphia.

"He said the job was yours," Cassie told her with troubled eyes. Then Sloan began to understand her hesitance.

"The salary?" she asked, holding her features in composure.

Cassie named a figure, and Sloan's heart sank. She couldn't accept the job. She sighed as she realized she would probably be with the college dance department for years to come—she couldn't afford to quit. Not that she didn't like her job; she did. It was just that she so dearly longed to dance professionally again!

"Well then," Sloan said briskly with a forced smile. "That's that, I guess."

Cassie looked as if she were about to cry. "If only you hadn't had so many children!" she exclaimed miserably. Then she hastily added, "Oh, Sloan! I didn't mean that. I love the kids. But it's so hard for you alone."

"Well," Sloan said wryly, curling her lips a shade so that Cassie would know her words had been understood. "When Terry and I planned the children, we didn't intend that one of us would be raising them alone."

Terry had been a dreamer, and she had dreamed right along with him. They seemed perfectly mated, a dancer and an artist. In their first years they had struggled. Then, while Terry had

199

been making his name as a painter, Sloan had gotten a terrific job with an ensemble in Boston. Luck followed the dreamers. When Sloan became pregnant with Jamie, Terry's oils caught on with the flurry of a storm. They lived happily. Terry was established; Sloan was able to combine her professional dancing with motherhood. They planned Laura and the baby, Terence, for his father.

But Terry didn't live to see his namesake. He was killed when his flight home from Knoxville in a friend's small Cessna failed to clear the Blue Ridge Mountains. It took searchers three weeks to find his body, and when they did, Sloan was in the hospital, in labor two months early due to shock.

Dreamers never think to buy life insurance, and artists have no benefits. Sloan was snapped out of her grief by desperation—she had to support herself and her family. The baby, so premature, ate up any savings as he clung to life in his incubator. Terry's last pieces drew large sums as their value increased, ironically, with his death, but even that money did little but help Sloan return home to Gettysburg where her only comfort, Cassie, awaited.

Sloan buried the young dreamer she had been along with Terry's mutilated remains. In the first year she had mourned her happy-go-lucky husband with a yearning sickness that left her awake long nights in her lonely bed. She had gone through all the normal courses of grief, including anger. How could he have died and left her like he did? Resignation and bitter sadness followed her anger, and now she lived day to day, finding happiness in simple things. But she *had* closed in. The vivacious and beautiful woman whom people met was a cloak that concealed her true personality. She had toughened, and reality and necessity were the codes she lived by. She was friendly, sometimes flirtatious, but when anyone looked beyond those bounds, he would find a door slammed immediately in his face.

"Lord, I almost forgot to tell you!" Cassie exclaimed suddenly, sensing her sister's depression and trying to cheerfully dispel her gloom. "Guess who is in Gettysburg?"

Sloan chuckled. "You've got me. Who?"

"Wesley Adams."

200

"Who?" Sloan frowned her puzzlement. The name was vaguely familiar, but she couldn't picture a face.

"Wesley Adams! The quiet quarterback, remember? He's a couple of years older than I am, but the whole town knew him. He graduated from Penn State after high school, then went on to play professional ball. About four years ago he retired because of a knee injury and disappeared from public view." Cassie gave Sloan a wistful smile as she curled a strand of blond hair around her fingers. "I was secretly in love with him for years! And he asked *you* out! I think it was the one time in my life I absolutely hated you!"

Sloan frowned again. "I went out with Wes Adams?"

Cassie groaned with exasperation and threw her hands in the air. "She doesn't even remember! Yes, you went out with Wes Adams. He had just finished at Penn State, and you were eighteen, about to leave for Boston and your first year as a Fine Arts major. It was the summer before you met Terry. I set up the date—by accident, I assure you!"

Sloan laughed along with her sister. Cassie could easily talk about her memories; she was married to one of the most marvelous men in the world. George Harrington loved his wife and extended that love to encompass his sister-in-law. It was George who insisted he care for his own two boys on Friday nights so that Cassie could allow Sloan her evening out.

"I remember him now," Sloan said, wrinkling her nose slightly. "He reminded me of Clark Kent. Beautiful body, face enough to kill. But quiet! And studious! Our date was a disaster."

"Hmmph!" Cassie sniffed. "He was simply bright as all hell. And you, young lady, your head was permanently twisted in the clouds. You didn't like anyone who wasn't a Fine Arts major!"

Sloan quirked her brows indifferently. "Maybe. I was eleven years younger then than I am now. We all change." She rubbed sore feet. "Brother! I feel like my soles are toe-to-heel blisters. I must have been spinning half the day!"

"You're losing your appreciation for your art," Cassie warned with teasing consolation. "I seem to remember a comment you made once as a kid that you 'could dance forever and forever, into eternity!' "

"There's a slim chance that I did make such a comment,"

Sloan admitted dryly. "But if so, I must have been a good twenty years younger than I am now—and twenty times as idealistic!"

The ringing of the doorbell interrupted their idle chatter. "Gee . . . George already," Sloan mused.

"No . . ." Cassie was blushing and flustered. "I forgot to tell you . . . well, actually, you changed the subject before I got a chance." She was talking hurriedly as the bell continued to chime. "It's Wes Adams. I told you I saw him today and he asked me about you and I told him and . . ." She raised her hands helplessly. "I asked him over."

Sloan's mouth dropped with dismay. "To my house?"

"Don't be angry!" Cassie begged in a whisper. "He and George are old friends too. I thought we could all chat awhile. In fact, I even broke down and asked my mother-in-law to break up her beauty sleep and go watch the boys so that George and I could both stay out. And you know how the old battle-axe needs that beauty rest!"

"Cassie!" Sloan wailed.

"Oh, Sloan! What do you want me to do? I know that that's Wes at the door." Cassie bit her lip as she watched her sister. "Damn it, Sloan! Give the man a chance. He's a better prospect than anyone else around here. This is a small town. And"—she grinned mischievously as she rounded the kitchen corner to answer the clanging of the bell—"he's absolutely loaded! He moved to Kentucky when he retired and bought a Thoroughbred farm. He breeds racehorses."

"Terrific!" Sloan mumbled as she trailed after her sister. "He was dull to begin with, and now he's a farmer in Kentucky."

"He's not a farmer, he—"

"I know, I know. He raises Thoroughbreds. It's all the same to me."

"Put your shoes back on!" Cassie hissed.

Sloan grimaced painfully and slipped back into her heels after diving beneath the chair to retrieve them. "Only for you, sister dearest!" she teased. "But give up on your matchmaking," she added in a low and serious tone. "I'm a twenty-nine-year-old widow with three children. I am too far-gone for romance!"

"Hush!" Cassie narrowed her brows, ran a hand over her

smooth blond hair, and threw open the front door. "Wes!" she exclaimed happily in greeting. "I'm so glad you could make it!"

Wesley Adams returned her greeting with a warm smile and a friendly kiss on the cheek. "Thanks for inviting me, Cassie." He turned sea-green eyes to Sloan. "Sloan. How are you?"

"Good, thank you, Wesley." She accepted the hand he offered her and shook it briefly. "Come in. Sit down. *Cassie*"—she smiled pointedly to her sister—"will be happy to get you a drink."

Cassie shot Sloan a quick, murderous glare behind their visitor's back. "What can I get you, Wes?" she inquired extra sweetly, attempting to atone for Sloan's ill-concealed lack of hospitality. Her grin became impish. "You and *Sloan* can have a seat, and I'll play cocktail waitress."

"Terrific, thank you," Wesley said smoothly. "I'd love a bourbon, if it's in the house supply."

"Certainly," Cassie murmured. "Sloan—a scotch?"

"A double—please." Sloan returned her sister's grin through clenched teeth as she politely took a seat beside Wesley Adams. He was still, she noted apathetically, a strikingly handsome man, probably more so with age. His shock of wavy hair, so dark as to be almost jet black, created an air of intrigue as it dipped rakishly in a natural wave over a brow. Faint lines etched his probing, intuitive eyes, lines which increased when he smiled with full lips. His face was bronzed and rugged; despite his navy suit and crisply pressed powder-blue shirt, he carried the definite air of an outdoorsman, an air which fit in well with his broad, powerful-looking shoulders and imposing height.

"I was very sorry to hear about your husband, Sloan," he said softly, sincere compassion in the sea-green eyes that met hers easily.

"Thank you." His unpatronizing sympathy touched a chord in her heart she had thought long since dead.

"I'm sorry again. Maybe I shouldn't have said anything."

"No, no, it's all right." She grudgingly gave him a faint smile. "Terry has been dead for two years. I assure you, I don't become hysterical at the mention of his name."

"You've changed," he remarked oddly.

203

"Have I?" Her smile became ironic. "I didn't realize you had known me well enough to judge such a thing."

The friendly smile he had been wearing remained glued to his face, but Sloan saw his facial muscles tighten as the warm spark in his eyes went cold. She winced imperceptibly at her own behavior. There was no need for her to be so uncivil.

Wesley Adams shrugged as he withdrew a pack of cigarettes from his vest pocket. He lit a cigarette, returned the pack to his pocket, and exhaled a long plume of smoke. His eyes were still on her, speculative and cold. Absurdly, she shuddered. Low-keyed and polite as he was, she had the strange feeling he could be dangerous if crossed.

"I didn't know you very well," he said casually, "but I do know that you never used to be out-and-out rude."

Sloan straightened as if she had been slapped. Of all the nerve! What a comment to make in her house! She drew breath for a caustic reply but snapped her mouth shut as Cassie gracefully sailed in from the kitchen with a tray of drinks.

"Wes," Cassie said as she placed the tray on the mahogany coffee table. "That's your bourbon on the left. Sloan, scotch in the middle."

Sloan fell silent as Wes and Cassie began to converse with a pleasant camaraderie. Moments later, George put in his appearance, and after kissing his wife and sister-in-law, he accepted the Wild Turkey and soda his wife had precipitously prepared and assured her the boys were safe in bed and his mother happily ensconced before the television set enjoying an oldie about a monster that was threatening to eat New York. He, too, readily joined in the light banter, and the talk turned to football. Sloan allowed her mind to wander.

She admitted to herself that she had been rude and wondered why. Wes Adams meant nothing to her, yet he disturbed her. She had the strange feeling that he saw more with those unusual oceanic eyes than most people. He watched her as if she were an open book and he could read her every weakness.

Ridiculous. There were no weaknesses. Not anymore. She had learned to rely on Sloan Tallett and on no one else. She didn't know, not in her conscious mind, that the very goodness of her marriage now blocked an open heart. Terry had loved her; Terry

204

had been wonderful. Terry had left her in the terrible mess she was in now. If someone had realized what lay in the uncharted recesses of her heart, they might have pointed out to her that she was blaming love for pain; blaming Terry for his own death as desertion. And if she could see, her eyes would widen and she would wince with horror at the reasoning that had left her as cold and as hard as steel. But she didn't see, and so she stiffened and went on.

And Wes Adams, the all but forgotten intruder who sat in her living room as if he belonged, was ruining the well-structured format of her life with his simple presence and cool words. It didn't matter, she told herself. He would be gone soon. And so would the inane feeling he gave her that she was losing control in some unclear way. She was always in control of any situation.

"And of course Sloan always joins in too," George was saying, his kindly gray eyes on her. He winked. "She's the high point of the summer!"

They were all looking at her now, and she flushed guiltily. "I'm sorry, George. I'm afraid I wandered. What do I join in to make this high point of the summer?"

"The school's annual summer dance!" Cassie hopped in impatiently. "Wes said he'd love to see you in a performance, and we told him he came at just the right time!"

"Oh," Sloan murmured, annoyed to feel herself blushing again as she met Wes's unfathomable, soul-piercing stare. What was the matter with her, she wondered impatiently. For the sake of the dance department she should be pushing the performance—glad of anyone who purchased a ticket and helped fill the immense auditorium. And by her own volition or not, Wes was a guest in her own home. A little cordiality wouldn't hurt. She slowly smiled and found it wasn't difficult at all when Wes curved his lips in return. "Our summer dance is quite a show," she told him, her enthusiasm growing. "We have some wonderful students."

He laughed easily. "I'll be looking at the teacher."

Absurd, but she felt herself blushing again, only this time the feeling wasn't uncomfortable. "What are you doing back in Gettysburg, Wes?" she asked, anxious to change the topic of conversation to anything other than herself.

205

"Business," he replied with a grimace. "And, of course, a little pleasure. This will always be home in a way. Mainly, I'm here on a buying trip—there's a man on the outskirts of the city who I do a lot of buying from. He has a knack with up-and-coming Thoroughbreds." Once again, Sloan was treated to a slow, subtly alluring smile. "At the moment," he continued, "I can honestly say I've never had a more pleasurable business trip."

Sloan managed not to blush again. With the hint of an enticing smile on her own lips, she inclined her head ever so slightly. Touché. He had learned to be a charmer when he chose.

From that point the night passed with surprising swiftness. Wesley, whom she had once found so boringly dull, proved to be an interesting speaker. His voice was a low tenor which still penetrated the room when he spoke, his words so appealingly phrased that Sloan was later shocked to realize she had listened to information on horses and football without once wandering from the conversation. It was after midnight when George finally looked at his watch and groaned that they had to leave.

"I'm sure New York has either been long consumed or saved by now," he said dryly, "and that my mother probably has her eyes propped open with toothpicks. How long will you be here, Wes?"

"A couple of weeks," Wesley replied, rising to shake his old friend's hand. "I'm sure we'll be able to get together again." He kissed Cassie lightly and took Sloan's hand. "Thank you, Sloan, for a pleasant evening."

"Thank you for coming," she parroted politely.

"Perhaps, if we have dinner one night, you'll join us."

Sloan wasn't sure if the invitation was sincere or not. She was being scrutinized by those uncanny eyes again, and the firm hand holding hers was mocking in its gentle but undeniable pressure. She smiled vaguely. "Yes, perhaps. But I have a problem with the children."

"I'm her only nighttime sitter," Cassie explained. "George's mother is too nervous to handle all five."

"That's no problem!" Wesley laughed, and for a moment his eyes seemed very warm and tender. "My housekeeper is with me, since I'm staying at my folks' home. They've been in Arizona for years now, so I assumed I'd need a bit of help with fixing up.

206

Florence adores children. She'll be thrilled to watch them for us."

"I . . ." Sloan faltered helplessly. She didn't want to tell him that she didn't leave her children with just anyone—it would sound frightfully insulting.

But Wesley astutely sensed her dilemma. "I'll bring Florence by at your convenience so that you can meet her and she can meet the children. Then, if all goes well, we'll make a definite date for Saturday night, a week from tomorrow. Does that suit everyone?"

A little awed, Sloan nodded. It didn't just suit her, it sounded lovely. One of the reasons that she so seldom went out was the lack of available, trustworthy baby-sitters and a determination not to take advantage of her sister. She would also have trouble affording a regular sitter. "Loaded" Wesley was solving all her problems.

Wesley released her hand. George and Cassie kissed her goodnight, and she was alone in her silent house with her sleeping children.

She was reflective that night as she showered and donned a light flannel gown, studying her face in the bathroom mirror. She winced at what she saw.

Although faint, tiny lines were forming around her eyes. Unlike Cassie, she certainly couldn't pass for eighteen. At least, she thought, giggling at her mirrored image, if she were to go prematurely gray, no one would notice. Her hair was already composed of too many colors.

Anyway, the hell with vanity. She was the mother of three. Still . . . her hand slid over her flat stomach. She was lucky. She had borne three children, yet come out of it without a scratch. Her figure was tighter than that of a teenager, her skin as smooth. Dancing, she told herself wryly. Her passion had kept her in shape.

But what difference did it make. There was no longer a man in her bedroom to tell her she was beautiful, to tell her what he loved about her. . . . No one to try to please. . . .

Sloan snapped out the light and peeked in on six-year-old Jamie, four-year-old Laura, and two-year-old "baby" Terry. They all slept soundly, their even breathing peaceful. Unable to resist, she tenderly kissed each little forehead. They were beautiful children, plump and healthy. Again, she reminded herself that she was lucky, and that she should be grateful and fulfilled.

I am fulfilled! she told herself sternly. There is nothing more I need than their love.

But she didn't sleep well that night. She was plagued by dreams of worry and emptiness.

Sloan pressed her hand over the mouthpiece of the telephone. "Jamie!" she wailed. "Quit torturing your sister! Give her back her doll! And hush up for five minutes!"

Jamie pursed his little lips, shot his mother a baleful glance, and returned his sister's doll. With a sigh, Sloan returned to her conversation.

"I'm sorry about the payment, Mrs. White, it must have been an oversight. I'll put it in the mail immediately. Please don't turn off the electricity!"

The woman on the other end spat off a few epitaphs about people who didn't pay bills on time and finally agreed to give her four days to have the payment in. Sloan hung up the receiver and rested her head tiredly on the phone.

"Mommy?" A tiny hand tugged on her sleeve, and she opened her eyes. Jamie—her devil, her love. "Mommy, I love you."

She picked him up and hugged him. "I love you, too, sweetheart. Now run along and see what your brother is doing."

She set him down and rubbed a hand across her forehead. No wonder she was getting wrinkles. She was always frowning.

"Mommy!" It was Jamie again. "Terry is putting the laundry in the toilet!"

"Eeeeeek!" Sloan screamed, racing into the bathroom. Lord, what next? She unstuffed the toilet and washed the baby, who gurgled happily with pleasure and lisped a few words. Then she returned to the kitchen to morosely sip her coffee, slumped into a chair.

"The morning," she told herself aloud, "is not going well at all."

Her mind, for no explicable reason, turned to Wesley Adams. He was a handsome man, polite and gracious. She unconsciously moved a hand over her face. He was attracted to her; she knew it intuitively. And he *was rich*. Wheels began to turn in her mind.

She sprang to her feet and raced back into the bathroom to anxiously study her reflection again. She smoothed the worried frown from her brow and smiled brightly. That was better. Much better. Maybe Jim's ideas for her future weren't quite so bad. . . .

She continued to stare at herself unseeingly for several seconds, oblivious to the playful ramblings of the children.

"I don't love him, I don't really like him, I hardly even know him!" she told the face that was forming before her, the face that had a bewitching but frighteningly predatory cast.

The children . . . I have to think of the children . . . and I'm so dreadfully tired of dealing with it all!

The face wasn't really predatory, she assured herself. Conniving, maybe, devious, yes perhaps . . . and hard. But not *predatory*! She swallowed, wincing, ashamed of her thoughts.

Sloan closed her eyes and turned away from the mirror, burying all sense of shame with purpose and determination as she did so. Like a marionette she jerked back to the phone and dialed her sister's number.

She chatted idly for a few minutes, then casually brought up the subject on her mind.

"What do you really know about Wesley Adams?" she asked.

Cassie rushed on with enthusiasm. Wes was wonderful. He had led his team to victory in the Super Bowl. He donated to charities all over the country. He had a beautiful spread in Kentucky where he raised his horses and held a summer camp for deprived children every year. . . .

"Does he really have that much money?" Sloan queried innocently, thankful that her sister couldn't see her face over the phone.

"Tons of it!" Cassie laughed. "His salary was unbelievable, and he seems to have the Midas touch with investments. Everything he touches turns to gold, silver, and green. They had a big write-up on him in *Fortune* magazine when he left pro ball a few years ago. . . ."

Cassie had more to say, but Sloan was no longer listening. A slow buzzing was seeping coldly through her. She couldn't allow herself to think; she couldn't afford to moralize.

"Sloan?"

"I'm here, Cass."

"So—you've decided you like him after all! I knew you would. He's such a super guy! And he's interested in you. Half the women in this country would sell their souls to be in your place!"

"Yes, Cass." Sloan held her breath for a minute. She wasn't much of a liar, and she had never lied to Cassie in her life. Suddenly she felt hot, dizzy, and nervous—what she was planning was preposterous. She might have joked, but the idea of actually doing it had never occurred to her. Until now. And it had hit her with a jolt. It would be wrong; she couldn't . . .

But the last two years of her life flashed through her mind in a split second—a tumult of events that was dark and sobering. Terry's disappearance, the baby's premature birth, her own long haul back to health, having to quit the Fife Dance Company, moving back to Gettysburg and teaching at a salary that was more than she had made with Fife but still barely allowed her to make ends meet. "Yes, Cassie," Sloan repeated. "I think I like Wes very much now. I'm looking forward to our dinner."

"Sloan! I'm so glad! It's obvious that he still has some kind of a thing for you. . . ."

Cassie went on talking, but Sloan heard little of what she had to say. Somehow, she made all the right responses.

". . . fate and a little time . . ."

"Pardon?" Sloan inquired. Her mind had wandered a little too far.

Cassie sighed. "I said, 'who knows? With fate and a little time . . .?'"

"Yeah," Sloan murmured. "I'd better get going, Cass. I have to go see what the little darlings are up to."

"Go!" Cassie chuckled. "I am so glad that you like him! Oh, well! Bye!"

"Bye. . . ." Sloan murmured faintly. She pulled the receiver slowly from her ear and sank into a chair, feeling light-headed. She did not replace the phone correctly, and a dull hum sounded to her ears.

Fate and time. She intended to give both more than a little push.

"God, I hope that I do like him!" she whispered fervently to herself. She rose, a puppet again, and very meticulously adjusted the phone, cutting off the hum. Her plan took substance, and she spoke it aloud.

"I'm going to marry him."

Her voice was light, toneless, but the grim edge of determination rang clearly through.

CHAPTER TWO

She hadn't actually done anything, but with her plan set in her mind, she felt the first pangs of guilt.

Rationalizing was in order. She put the baby and Laura down for their naps, supplied Jamie with pails and shovels for his sandbox, and moved into the back of the house, her studio.

The studio had been the one extravagant concession she had allowed herself to retain her art. The floor was an expensive wood to save wear on her feet and knees. A heavy metal exercise bar stretched the length of the left side, backed by a study mirror which covered the height and breadth of the wall. The right side of the room held huge bay windows which opened on the lawn, allowing her to work while watching the children at play. To the rear lay her stereo system, a good, complex one purchased when Terry had sold an elaborate set of landscapes.

When teaching, Sloan covered dance from classic form to aerobics. But to her the base for all dance was ballet, and when she engaged in her rigid workouts, it was to ballet exercises that she turned. Between stretches, pliés, and relevés, she came to terms with herself.

She planned to marry a stranger, a man she didn't love. It wasn't because she craved riches for herself, but because she would be able to provide a *decent* life for herself and her children.

And she swore she would never hurt Wesley Adams. She would never love again, she was sure, but Wesley would never know it. She would be everything he could possibly desire in a wife.

Her mind began to race with turmoil. How could she even think about doing a thing as despicable as marrying a man for his money? Marriage meant living with a man, sharing his life, sleeping in his bed. . . . A sick feeling stabbed her stomach. She changed the Bach on the stereo to a modern piece by a hard rock group and whirled about the room in a series of furious pirouettes and entrechats, hoping to exhaust her mind through strenuous dance. Sweat beaded on her brow, but it was as much from her thoughts as from her leaping jetés.

For a mother of three, she was painfully naive. Most of her friends had had one or two serious affairs before settling into marriage. Several were divorced and involved in new affairs, one after the other.

But for her, there had been only Terry. They had met when both were eighteen, married while still in school before either was twenty. It was all planned. A little over three years later they had their first child, Jamie. And in her years of marriage she had learned what intimacy between a man and woman truly meant. It meant giving oneself completely, trusting, opening up to vulnerability, accepting and loving—a part of a total commitment.

How could anyone even contemplate such a thing with a stranger?

She fell to the floor in a perfect split and stretched her nose to her knee. Don't be absurd! she snapped silently to herself. Sex was just a normal body function. Plenty of women she knew could easily sleep with any attractive male body. She closed her eyes, pushing such thoughts to the back of her mind. She would deal with her problems as she came to them. A little chuckle escaped her lips as she switched legs and her dark head bounced down to the other knee. *She* was planning a marriage. Maybe she wouldn't get to first base with Wesley Adams. According to Cassie, he could have his pick of females. Why should he *marry* her? Even if he was attracted to her. She was a twenty-nine-year-old widow with three children. He could probably have any number of bright, sweet young things—women who demanded no commitment and had no responsibilities to tie them down.

And then . . . Another thought nagged her. What if Wesley didn't get along with the children? She would never marry anyone, madly in love or not, unless he cared for the children and they for him.

Life, she decided with a wry grin, was a bitch.

But it could be so much better if she could only marry a kind, plia le man like Wesley Adams. She wouldn't always be worried about having to make a buck. She would be a good and true wife, but she would also be free to go her own way, to play with her children, to dance as she longed.

At that moment she closed her mind to right and wrong. Her heart hardened, not callously, but desperately. The dream of a good life was too sweet to allow for sentiment. She would use every one of her feminine wiles in the pursuit of Wesley Adams. And there was no time to lose. He only planned to be in Gettysburg for two weeks.

"Mommy!"

Jamie's voice, screaming over the stereo, jolted her from her reflections. Her head jerked up guiltily, and she looked to her son in the studio door and then gasped with dismay.

Jamie was standing with the man who had so completely filled her thoughts, Wesley Adams. The man she had planned to captivate and sweep off his feet. And here she was, no makeup, sweat-streaked hair glued to her forehead, clad in a black leotard that had long since faded.

"Wesley!" she croaked, scrambling to her feet and unconsciously smoothing back a stray tendril of hair. Then she turned to her son with reproach. "Jamie, I told you never to answer the door! You must always get me."

"It wasn't the boy's fault," Wesley Adams explained with a crooked grin. His eyes were friendly, laughing, almost matching the knit, forest-green shirt that outlined his broad chest and well-muscled biceps. It wasn't difficult to return his grin.

"I rang," Wesley continued, "but no one came to the door. I heard the stereo, so I walked around back and found your son." He tousled Jamie's light brown curls and hoisted the boy into his arms. "I convinced him I was a legitimate friend."

"Oh . . ." Sloan stammered weakly. This second meeting wasn't working out at all as she had planned. "I'm sorry I'm such a mess. . . . I need a shower. . . . I—I wasn't expecting you this morning!"

He laughed easily, and she marveled at what a comfortable man he was. "I think you look stunning." His eyes roamed unabashedly over the trim but enticing figure so vividly displayed by the tight leotard. Yet his gaze held nothing licentious;

it was one of teasing but respectful admiration. Foolishly, Sloan found herself blushing.

"Well, er, can I get you something?" she asked, laughing a bit nervously as she walked to the stereo to carefully lift the needle. "A cool drink? I have iced tea, lemonade, and oh, I think a few beers—"

"Run and take your shower, first," Wesley suggested, smiling at Jamie. "Then I'd love to have a glass of tea with you."

"Thanks," she smiled wryly. "But I can't. The baby should be waking up any minute."

"I'm the proud uncle of four nieces and six nephews," he told her. "If your little one wakes, I'm sure I'll be able to handle him."

"No!" Sloan protested. "I can't have you watching my children—"

"Sure you can."

Sloan smiled uneasily. That lopsided grin of his could be most endearing and, and unnerving! He really was an attractive and ... what? ... man. Vital. The word sprang to her mind, followed by one even more disturbing—sexy. He may have retired from pro ball, but his sturdy structure and lithe movements proved him to be every inch an athelete.

"All right," Sloan murmured, confused by her jittery reaction to him. *I'm* the one out to entice him! she reminded herself. "Thanks. I'll just hop in and out. I'll hurry."

"Take your time. I'll be fine."

She smiled faintly as she sidled by him, warned Jamie to be good, and hurried into the shower. Once there, she did take more time than she had intended. She scrubbed her skin pink and worked her hair into a rich lather with scented shampoo. It wouldn't dry, she realized as she fluffed it with a towel, but clean wet was better than sweaty wet! She splashed herself with a light daytime cologne that smelled of fresh fields and applied a touch of low-keyed makeup. Satisfied with the results, she slipped into a pair of hip-hugging jeans and a cool halter top. Although the nights were cool, the Pennsylvania summers could be murder in the day.

She emerged from the bathroom feeling much more confident. The role of femme fatale was played more easily in the right

215

costume. Affecting a brilliant smile, she moved into the living room with a calculated walk.

The children were all awake, all ensconced on Wesley's lap as he sat on the floor with them, embellishing a worn book of fairy tales. A painful little tug pulled at her heart as she watched the scene.

Wesley hadn't lied; he was a natural with children. Even two-year-old Terry sat with wide eyes glued on the storyteller's face.

Sloan forget all about her bewitching smile and swinging walk as she paused in the hallway, an erratic pulse beating through her veins. *He liked the children. He hadn't even let a day go by without coming to see her. The more she saw of him, the more she liked.*

The tale of Cinderella, told in his deep, compelling voice, came to an end with the prince and princess living happily ever after. Laura jumped to her feet, demanding another story.

"Not now, my pet," Sloan said softly, coming to scoop her daughter into her arms with a laugh. Laura's eyes were huge and blue like her own, and they snapped with outrage, causing Sloan and Wesley both to chuckle.

"Mommy!" Laura began her protest. "Go back to the bathroom."

"Hey, young lady!" Sloan chastised her. "Don't you talk to me like that."

"Remember our promise!" Wesley intercepted quickly, sneaking a wink which encompassed the three children.

"Pizza!" Jamie happily expounded to his mother. He never could keep a secret.

"If it's all right with your mother," Wesley said sternly. "And if you behave for the rest of the afternoon." He glanced at Sloan apologetically. "I hope you'll forgive a bit of bribery."

Sloan bit back a chuckle and sank gracefully to the floor beside them. "The best of us stoop to it now and then. Kids," she said, praying they chose to obey without argument, "go on into the playroom for a while now." She glanced at Wesley with raised "you asked for it" brows. "Mr. Adams will read you another story later."

Surprisingly, the children grudgingly wandered toward the

playroom, baleful glances at their mother their only sign of pique. Sloan waited until they had cleared the room to look to Wesley, breathing deeply as she reminded herself she must move with all speed.

"Thank you," she murmured, unnerved to find it difficult to meet his frank, unwavering green gaze. "That was kind of you."

"I told you, I like kids."

Sloan didn't try to look at him again. Running a slender hand along the shag of the rug, she continued, "I want to apologize for last night. You were right. I was being rude and I'm . . . I'm sorry."

He laughed, the slow easy laugh she was coming to like so much. "You're totally forgiven. I did rather barge in after a long day. But I'll extract a payment if I may. I supply the dinner, but I get to stay for it. How's that?"

"All payments should be so amiable!" She crossed one foot over the other and rose. The light, masculinely pleasant scent of his after-shave was drifting to her nostrils; she was becoming too fascinated by the display of his long rugged fingers as they lay casually upon a muscled thigh. "Come on, I'll get our tea."

Wesley proved to be a perfect guest. He didn't seem to mind in the least that the afternoon was spent checking on two-year-old Terry, nor was he adverse to wiping tomato sauce from little faces after the pizza arrived. When bedtime rolled around, he insisted on giving the boys their bath, after which he expertly taped a plastic overnight diaper on newly potty-trained Terry. True to his word, he read the children another story and tucked them into bed. They barely remembered to kiss their mother, and Sloan wondered with amusement whether to be offended or pleased.

She perked coffee while she waited for Wesley to finish with the children, arranging a tray anxiously to bring to the living room table for a more relaxed setting. Where did she go from here? Things were going too well. Wesley, by appearing at her door without warning, had thrown her completely off course. What was it he was after? She couldn't play too hard to get, or he might disappear for good. Yet she couldn't be an easy conquest. Marriage was her game, nothing else, or all was wasted.

Wesley sauntered into the kitchen as she placed a ring of

crackers around small squares of cheddar and Muenster cheese. "They're quite a handful," he remarked with a long stretch. "You must be a veritable powerhouse of energy." He nonchalantly reached for a cracker and slice of cheese. "How do you do it all?"

Sloan cocked her head with a short, convincing laugh. It wouldn't do to let him know that she wasn't managing well with "doing it all." "They are actually pretty good kids," she said. "They go to a great day-care center when I work, and Cassie lets me out on Friday nights. It's not such a bad life and I . . ." Her voice broke off suddenly.

"What?" The sincere compassion in his eyes urged her to go on.

"I wouldn't trade a one of them for anything in the world," she said softly.

"I don't blame you." Wesley picked up the tray and preceded her to the living room. "Good coffee," he commented as he sat comfortably on the sofa. The crooked grin softened his rather severely chiseled features, blending the angles of his high cheekbones and square, rugged jaw. "Good coffee is a sign of a good woman, you know."

It was easy to laugh with him, and she needn't have worried about the evening. He made no move to touch her as they talked, and she again found him interesting as they discussed a number of subjects. He wasn't Terry, he didn't fill the air with imaginative views and vociferous dreams, but as the time passed by them, she slowly forgot to make comparisons.

"So tell me more about you," he said suddenly, disarming her with the question thrown casually into general conversation.

"There's nothing to tell," she said, fiddling with her empty coffee cup as he lit a cigarette. Remembering what she was up to, she batted murky lashes with a sweet smile. "You've spent the day here; you've seen it all."

"Why did you give up dancing?"

She feigned a cough. She certainly couldn't tell him her strained finances were the cause. "I haven't given it up. I teach now. As for going back and joining a company full time . . . I'd have to head for a larger city, and with the children small, I like the size of Gettysburg."

"You danced when your husband was alive." It wasn't a question, but a statement of fact. Sloan replied slowly, puzzled at his sure knowledge.

"Yes, when Terry was alive he could be with the children nights. He painted at home, and his work was doing very well—" She broke off swiftly, frightened that she had come so close to giving herself away. Falling into another radiant smile, she hastily turned back his question. "How did you know that I was dancing when Terry was alive?"

Tiny dimples appeared in Wesley's bronzed cheeks. "I saw you in Boston. About seven years ago."

"Oh!" His revelation was startling. "What were you doing in Boston."

"Celebrating with friends. My team won the Super Bowl that year, and we were about crazy after the hectic season and grueling training." The dimples flashed again as he grimaced. "I think I fell in love that night. You were absolutely magnificent. Half the audience must have known from my shouting that you were a girl from my own town."

"Really?" Sloan laughed, but she eyed him nervously. He was teasing her, of course, flattering her. "Why didn't you come backstage?"

"Because I knew you were married."

"Oh." A silence hung heavily on the air between them. Sloan reached awkwardly for the tray to return it to the kitchen, but Wesley's hand came over hers. She started nervously and met his probing green gaze. His touch had felt like an electrical charge.

"Tell me about your husband," he said softly. "It's obvious that you loved him very much. I'd like to hear about him."

"Terry?" Sloan's eyes clouded to a misty blue. "Terry was a dreamer, a happy-go-lucky dreamer. He was a wonderful man; he loved the world. He was very talented and"—she couldn't lie about Terry—"yes, I loved him very much."

"Do you have any of his work?"

"Only one piece," she said lamely. How could she explain that she'd had to sell the others? She couldn't. She'd have to spin another notch in her web of lies.

"Terry lost most of his paintings in the accident."

"I'd like to see the painting that you have."

219

"I'm afraid it's of me," Sloan said apologetically, rising. "It's in my bedroom." She turned to lead the way quickly, annoyed to find that she was blushing again.

The painting, she believed, was Terry's finest piece. He had caught her in a graceful pirouette, her hair spinning red and gold around her, her dress of sheer gauze fluttering in touchable folds. The painting seemed to live, the radiance of the dance immortalized for eternity in the vibrant blue exuberance of her eyes. No amount of poverty could ever bring her to sell the painting. It had been a special gift from Terry, a tangible link to the essence of what they both had been.

Wesley stood staring at the painting for a long time. "He was a very fine artist," he finally said, "A brilliant one." He turned to her suddenly. "I assume it's not for sale."

"No," Sloan said. Then she moistened very dry lips. It was time to take a shot in the dark. "No," she repeated with what she hoped was a sensuous smile. "I'm afraid the painting goes with me. You can't have one without the other."

"Oh?" His brows raised slightly, and there was a definite, mischievous glint in his eyes. "Well, I have already determined to have the one."

Time hung suspended, and static rippled the air as Sloan stared at him, not breathing, mesmerized. Who is seducing whom here? she wondered briefly.

Wesley broke the invisible bonds that stretched between them. "I've got to get out of here." He chuckled, glancing at his watch. "I've way overstayed my welcome." He glanced back to Sloan, his eyes light yet strangely guarded. "What do you do on Sundays?"

"Uh . . . laundry, usually," Sloan stammered, annoyed that she should give him such a humdrum reply, but not as quick as he to break the spell of the unnerving moment.

Wes grinned with lazy ease. "Could I twist your arm into doing something else?"

Sloan laughed sheepishly. "You could twist my arm easily, but I'm afraid I still can't go out. Cassie and George spend the day with his parents and—"

"And the children would need a sitter," Wes finished for her.

"But they might as well meet Florence and get to know her early."

Not quite sure what he meant by such a comment, Sloan offered another weak protest. "Wesley, how can we just spring three children upon this lady? I'm sure she's busy with your house—"

"Florence would rather be busy with kids any day. And I promise you, she's a wonderfully unique person. She doesn't just tolerate little ones—she loves them."

Sloan lifted helpless hands. "What did you have in mind?"

"That, Mrs. Tallett, is a loaded question!" Wes warned teasingly. "If I answered you honestly, you'd throw me out." He was serious, bluntly, appraisingly so, but his winning grin took the sting out of the words. Even so, Sloan blushed. "Since I don't dare answer you honestly," he continued without apology, "what would you say to a picnic in the park?"

"A picnic sounds nice," Sloan mouthed automatically.

"Good," Wes said quickly, before she could think. "I'll be by tomorrow about ten with Florence. Is the time okay?"

"Fine. . . ." Sloan murmured, dazed. She was supposed to be the aggressor here, but so far she wasn't working very hard.

Wesley smiled and kissed her cheek lightly, as he had her sister's the previous evening. "Good night, Sloan." His long strides brought him quickly to the front door. "Thank you for a wonderful day."

"Thank you," Sloan called, but he was gone. Still dazed, she returned to the living room and picked up the coffee tray.

Everything was working out perfectly—to her benefit. Even in her moments of highest confidence, she had never imagined that Wes would make it so easy for her to set her little marriage trap. Instead of feeling wildly victorious, she was nervous as hell. As pleasant as Wes continued to be, there was a quality about him that was quietly powerful.

He had been a professional football player, she reminded herself. Such a sport bred a man who was innately domineering, physically fit . . . threatening with that primitive, almost untamed masculinity.

"What a ridiculous thought!" she chastised herself aloud. She was turning Wes into a charging tiger that might pounce in a moment of brute force. He was nothing like that. And she wasn't a member of an opposing defense to be tackled or plowed out of the way.

Still, there was something about him. She had sensed it that first night. Something that hadn't been there in his youth. A confidence and control that allowed him to be pleasant because he would have the strength to handle any situation that did get out of control with quick, ruthless ease.

She shivered suddenly, and the shivering brought her out of her mental wanderings. She realized she was still rinsing a well-rinsed cup. "I'm inventing things!" she whispered to herself. "Wes is the nice guy he appears to be. And he likes me. . . ."

But how did he "like" her? He was thirty-four, but he had never married. She was sure—simply from that virile masculinity that he exuded—that he had had a multitude of affairs. He was a sensual man—she was already keenly aware of his effortless magnetism. He was probably thinking of nothing more than an affair now.

"It can't be just an affair!" Sloan spoke aloud to herself again, her tone desperate. He had to marry her!

He wanted her. Even if her instincts had been faulty, he had come right out and said as much. Yet how badly did he want her? Enough to marry her?

A flash of heat washed over her from head to toe as she thought about the strange moment when they had stood together in her bedroom doorway. Admittedly, she had felt stirrings she hadn't experienced in over two years. Her senses had reeled more from his mere nearness than they had from any kiss by a would-be suitor.

Sloan dropped the saucer she had been holding into the dishwasher and crouched to the floor, circling her knees with her arms. She was attracted to Wesley, and the feeling was terrifying. She had to keep the upper hand; she had to be able to deny and demur all the time.

"And I will!" She fought the dizzy confusion that had assailed her like a forceful wind and stood, shaking herself. Lord! she told herself impatiently. I'm a twenty-nine-year-old widow! Not some naive half-wit! Not the type of sweet innocent to be led stupidly like a slaughtered lamb into a bed of seduction!

Semiconvinced, she straightened her shoulders unconsciously. She wasn't exactly an overly humble fool, either. She was aware of her assets—a dancer almost had to be. She knew how to play the games of flirtation and seduction herself. Granted, she had never set out to be the vamp before, but it was a role she could—and would—assume.

This was a game she was determined to win.

Sighing, she wiped the kitchen counter and slowly folded the dish towel. There was no way she was going to be happy and at ease until . . . until the game was over. Her mind was waging too many wars. It was wrong . . . she knew it was wrong to purposely set out to marry someone for money, no matter how she swore to herself to be a good wife. She should bow out of the game before it ever began. She couldn't begin to imagine what had possessed her in the first place to come up with such an idea.

But she had come up with it. And now it had become a dream . . . a dream of security that was so good she couldn't forget it, couldn't pretend that it had never existed.

Sloan bit into her bottom lip so hard as she walked into her bedroom to slip into her nightgown that she drew blood. There was no going back now. Wesley might not know that he was now engaged in the biggest game of his life, but he was. Another Super Bowl.

And this time, he was going to lose.

Sloan slipped between her sheets and turned off her bedside lamp. Even with her mind irrevocably made up, it was a long time before she slept. She tossed and turned and woke several times. She had been dreaming, but she couldn't quite put her finger on just what it was in her dreams that kept awakening her.

Finally, as the pale light of dawn crept slowly through the windows telling her that her fitful night was almost at an end, she realized what was bothering her.

She was no longer seeing Terry's thin, carefree face in her dreams. She was seeing Wesley's. The penetrating, oceanic green eyes. The pitch black hair with the wings of silver. The hard, angular, strong planes of his face. The rugged jawline. The full, sensual lips curving over perfect white teeth.

223

For the first time in two years she was actually dreaming of another face. Wesley's smiling face.

But a smiling face that was very disturbing. Because in her dreams the smile was cold. It didn't reach to eyes that were as sharply condemning as a jagged dagger of ice.

CHAPTER THREE

Perversely, with the coming of light, Sloan found herself finally able to sleep. Waking fully to recognize her dreams had put them to rest. Wesley had been nothing other than charming to her, and, if he continued with his persistence, the next two weeks would prove to be enjoyable and exciting.

It seemed that her alarm went off as soon as she was deeply encircled in a comfortable sleep. Grudgingly Sloan rose—her usual scurry of morning activity was about to begin.

The children had to be bathed and dressed and fed, and then today she had herself to worry about. Most Sundays she didn't bother with makeup but simply scrubbed her face, tied back her hair, and threw on a pair of jeans. The laundry didn't care much what she looked like.

Today was different.

Today she very carefully applied just the right amount of makeup to enhance her own coloring while still appearing natural. She heated her curling wand to tighten the light waves of hair which escaped her ribbon to fall about her face in delicate tendrils. She hesitated long over her casual clothing before choosing a pair of flattering shorts and a cotton, kelly-green blouse with puff sleeves and sash closings which tied in front between the breasts.

As she had hoped and planned, the effect was perfect.

She looked young and carefree, as charming and natural as a wood nymph. No one would ever take her for a mature matron about to complete her third decade of living.

That dash of excitement she had been feeling gleamed brilliantly in the sapphire of her eyes. She laughed exultantly. "Careful, girl!" she warned herself. "Looking like a teenager doesn't mean you should be acting like one!"

She had stooped to tie her sneakers when the doorbell rang. Jamie—remembering his lesson of the previous day—called to her, "Door, Mom!"

"Thank you, Jamie," she told him, tweaking his cheek as she passed him. "That's going to be Wesley and his friend who is going to watch you. Please be good, Jamie!"

"Ahh . . . Mom!" Jamie declared indignantly. "I'm always good."

"Oh yeah?" Sloan raised a doubting brow to him but smiled. Jamie was good—old for his six years, a stout defender for his younger sister and brother. He had been young when he lost his father, and his world had turned around, but he was a sensitive child, like the father he lost, and he intuitively knew when things were going especially rough for his mother.

"I'm going to be a living doll!" he promised with wide eyes.

Still smiling, Sloan opened the door. Wesley stood there in faded, tattered jeans and an old football jersey, his rich, dark hair gleaming like a raven's wing in the glare of the sun. A broad grin stretched across his face as he greeted her with sparkling eyes of appreciation.

"Good morning. Am I too early?"

"No . . . good morning." Why am I always stammering around him? Sloan wondered. She had seemed caught in the spell of his eyes again, frozen into forgetting who she was, where she was. . . .

"May we come in?"

"We?"

"Yes, I'm sorry. Florence—" Wes turned from the doorway, and Sloan saw a tiny, middle-aged woman who had previously been hidden by Wesley's broad, sinewed frame. "Sloan, this is Florence Hendry. Florence, Sloan Tallett. And those little faces peeping around her knees are Jamie, Laura, and Terry."

Sloan smiled hesitantly, suddenly as shy as the children who withdrew their curious heads quickly. But the tiny woman had eyes as warm as the sun, and the smile she gave in return was full and heartening. "Sloan," she said softly, taking the slender, outstretched hand firmly, "what a pleasure. Wesley has spoken

226

of nothing but you since we arrived." Her crinkled face dimpled. "I will admit, though, that I'm most anxious to meet the children."

Sloan stepped aside, realizing that her company was still standing in the doorway. "Mrs. Hendry, the pleasure is mine. Please, come in. Jamie, Laura, Terry—say hello to Mrs. Hendry. She'll be staying with you today—" Sloan bit lightly on her lower lip and glanced quickly from Wes—standing benignly amused in the background—to Florence. "Are you sure this isn't too much trouble for you? Opening a house must have you busy—"

"I have no schedules!" Florence laughed. "And please, call me Florence. I'm pleased to death to spend a day with your children. I miss all the little ones at home."

Sloan couldn't prevent her startled glance from flying to Wesley's face. He read her unasked question and threw up hands in mock protest. "Not mine!" he laughed. "I told you I was riddled with nieces and nephews—four of whom live with me. I went into the Thoroughbred business with my brother."

"Oh," Sloan murmured, feeling a flush rise to her cheeks. "Well, uh, Florence, let me show you a bit of the house. The refrigerator is stacked with sandwich meat—"

"Which we won't need," Florence supplied cheerfully. "We're going to have our picnic here. Wes had them make us two baskets at the deli," she explained. "So you just tell me any special instructions."

"I really don't have any special instructions," Sloan murmured, leading Florence on a quick tour of the downstairs. "If you need anything, Jamie will help you. Their rooms are full of toys and books. . . ." Sloan grinned sheepishly as they returned to the living room. "I'm not sure what else I should tell you."

"We'll get along famously," Florence said with assurance.

Sloan was sure that they would. The little woman who had breezed into her life along with Wesley was like a fairy godmother. Mature, confident, cheerful. The type person who made you immediately feel as if everything was all right.

"Well . . ." Sloan murmured again, surprised and a little disoriented to see that the children had already lost their shyness. Jamie was having a very mature conversation with Wes, and Laura and Terry were looking at Florence with eager anticipation. "I'll just get my sunglasses . . ."

No one seemed to notice as she ran back into the kitchen and searched the ledge above the sink which was a catchall. She dug her glasses out of a pile of coupons and savings stamps, pausing for a breath of air.

She felt as if she were walking on clouds. It was actually Wes who had brought the magic into her life. He lifted a hand, went poof, and all her problems were solved. He thought of everything. Their day stretched brightly before them—free and clear.

Of course, her problems would all come back in the morning. But she was—all scheming aside—exhilarated by the idea of the picnic she was about to go on. She was anxious . . . eager . . .

"Sloan! What are you doing, having those sunglasses made?" Wesley's demand, called from the living room, rang with a teasing tolerance.

"Coming!" she called in return.

Sloan paused for a second as she entered the living room unnoticed. Florence, despite her rather severe, hawk-shaped nose and the ramrod posture of her tiny frame, was perched easily on the floor while she drew the children out, telling them about Kentucky and all the horses, ponies, and dogs and cats that lived on the farm. Wesley was beside her, allowing a giggling Jamie to climb upon his powerful shoulders.

"Mommy!" Jamie cried, seeing her at last. "Wesley is giving me a ride."

"So I see."

Wesley grinned up at her a little sheepishly. "All set?"

"All set."

"Okay, Jamie," Wes said, setting his small charge down. "We'll be back in a bit. Take care of Florence."

"I will," Jamie vowed gravely.

Sloan kissed each of her kids and followed Wes to the door. She glanced back to Florence and started to open her mouth.

"I'm fine!" Florence insisted before she could say anything. "You two get going and have a nice day."

"We are going," Wesley answered for her, clamping a hand

over Sloan's mouth, which brought a burst of laughter from the children. "Bye—and you all have a nice day too!"

Sloan was giggling as Wesley led her out to his car, a plush, comfortable Lincoln, with his hand still clamped over her face. He released her only to usher her inside. "You," he accused as the car leveled onto the highway, "are a very protective parent."

"I'm sorry—" Sloan began.

"Don't be sorry," Wes interrupted, his right hand momentarily squeezing hers before returning to the wheel. "I think it's a wonderful trait. If I ever have kids—which I hope to one day—I think I would be every bit as protective."

Sloan smiled a little uneasily. She wondered what he would think if he knew she was already planning on his having kids—three, ready-made. But she didn't spend much time brooding. Even the weather seemed to benignly assist her in her secret quest. The sun shone golden in the sky, and a gentle breeze stirred to keep the heat from becoming oppressive. The grass at the park had never seemed greener, the day more lustrously blue, the air more exhilarating.

"Shade or sun?" Wes asked after the Lincoln was parked. He handed Sloan a small cooler from the trunk as he grabbed the heftier food basket himself along with a wide blanket.

"Shade, I think," Sloan chose. "I'm out so little that I have to be careful not to burn."

Wes smiled noncommittally and led the way to a draping sycamore that provided a broad and gentle shelter. "Okay?"

"Perfect."

Sloan was overwhelmed by that strange shyness again as Wes competently spread out the blanket and adjusted the basket and cooler. Absurd sensation! she told herself with an inward shake. Some vamp I'm shaping up to be!

Determined not to behave like a gauche, tongue-tied girl, she sat leisurely on the blanket and started the conversation rolling herself. "You were right about your housekeeper. She's wonderful. Where did you find her?"

"I didn't." Wes grinned, half reclining beside her and opening the cooler to pull out a pair of semifrosted glasses and a bottle of Chablis. "Grab the glasses, will you? As to Florence"—he poured wine for them each—"she raised me. Her husband was

229

killed in World War II, and she determined never to marry again, but she was crazy about kids, so she went to work for my mother. When my folks decided to move to Arizona, they sent Florence after me. They were worried—a little belatedly, since I was thirty at the time—but they thought a bachelor football player might not take care of himself properly."

"Too much of a wild life, eh?" Sloan chuckled, sipping her wine and feeling relaxation steal over her.

"Not too wild," Wes replied. "Thirty in sports is middle-aged. As a dancer you must know that there's only so much you can do to a body and expect it to keep functioning properly."

"You must have quit shortly after," Sloan observed. She hesitated slightly, hoping she wasn't traveling into troubled waters. "Cassie mentioned you had a knee injury. Was it serious?"

Wes shrugged. "Ligaments," he replied casually. "I could have just sat out a season, but I'd had enough. I played for ten years. I wanted to get into something else while I was still young enough to give it everything that I had. Dave—my brother—had started with the horses on a small scale a few years before and so"—he lifted his shoulders and dropped them, turning lazy eyes to her as he took a sip of wine—"there's the whole story."

Sloan chuckled. "By what I hear from Cassie—she's one of your staunchest fans, you know—there's a lot more to the story than that."

He shrugged again and plunged into the picnic basket. "Nope. That's about it. A lot of monotony in between a few broken bones and sprained ankles."

"But you never married." The words were out before Sloan realized what she was saying. Prying a little was one thing—pushing too fast could get her into hot water.

"No, I never married." His glance was cool and fathomless. "What would you like to start with? We have all kinds of salads, fried chicken, fried shrimp and—I am good at this if I do say so myself—I have a honey dip for the chicken and a choice of tartar or cocktail sauce for the shrimp."

"I think I'll start with everything," Sloan murmured, a little uneasy since she had so openly pried and thinking it might be to her benefit to keep her mouth busy for a while with food. "I just realized I'm ravenous, and . . . you are very good at this!"

"Thank you." Wes dunked a shrimp into the plastic container of cocktail sauce and popped it into her mouth. He laughed at her surprised expression, and the unease she had been feeling slipped away.

They both talked as they ate, and they began to learn a great deal about one another. While she managed to draw information diplomatically from Wesley about his summer camp and the battering years of pro football, he managed to get her talking about Terry. It was strange that she could talk about her deceased husband with Wes, a man she was supposedly seducing, when she found it difficult to talk about Terry to anyone. But he seemed interested, genuinely sympathetic. He seemed to offer her strength . . . silly. It was simply the way he was built, and the character that the years had ingrained in his face. Next to such a man it was easy to feel that he could take away the cares of the world and set them upon his own broad shoulders.

It was later in the day, after a bottle of wine and a half of the feast he had provided had been consumed, that Sloan contentedly made an admission to herself.

She was happy. Honest-to-God happy. Wesley had made no passes at her, but she felt herself drawn to him, at ease with him, comfortably so. He sat beside her, his compelling green eyes laughed into hers, his strong hand brushed over hers often, naturally. And she could feel him, his heat, his suppressed strength, his handsome frame so close to hers that it almost made her dizzy.

No, it was the wine making her dizzy. No, it was Wesley. . . .

She blushed suddenly as they lay in lazy companionship, comfortably relaxed beneath the sycamore. She realized where her thoughts had been taking her.

She had been wondering what it would be like to be held in his arms . . . to feel his lips commanding hers . . . to lie beside him, flesh against flesh, and feel the mastery of his superb muscles. . . . It was more than a blush, and she was glad his astute green eyes were idly upon the sky instead of her. Crimson splashed its way through her body, heating her from head to toe. What's the matter with me? she demanded of herself. I'm not that sort of person!

231

But something else inside of her was crying out. *What* sort of a person. It had been so long . . . and she was a mature woman, a normal woman. It was only natural that she should feel the need for strong, masculine arms around her, revel in the faint and intoxicating aroma of after-shave and . . . and . . . simple *maleness.*

"Shall we?"

"What?" Startled, Sloan glanced at Wes. He was no longer watching the sky; he was watching her.

"Sleeping on me, huh?" he teased, knowing full well her mind had wandered. "Nice. Real nice. I take the girl out and put her right to sleep! I said, 'Shall we take a walk?' "

"Oh—uh—yes, sure." She smiled quickly. "A walk sounds nice."

Wesley rose, moving with the agility that only an athlete could possess, and extended a hand to Sloan. She unwound her own legs and gracefully accepted his assistance up, her mind beginning to race.

Where was he leading her . . .?

It was a public park, she told herself coldly. He wasn't leading her anywhere. But she began to feel a tinge of fear, and it had nothing to do with Wesley's far superior strength or what he might attempt to do.

She was afraid of herself. The touch of his hand on hers was warm, commanding . . . inviting. She wanted to accept that invitation; she wanted to feel more and more of him. . . .

Face it, she was attracted to him. Very attracted to him.

Which was a damned good thing! her mind hollered out even as she faced him with a smile on her lips and a guard carefully cast over her eyes. She was plotting to marry him, rationalizing the action by telling herself she was going to be a good wife. If she was going to be such a good wife, it was an awfully good thing she was going to be able to respond. . . .

"How about the trail?" Wes queried, pointing off into the trees. "I think it offers a little privacy."

"Wonderful. . . ." Sloan heard herself saying weakly.

His arm was around her shoulder as they started off on the pine path and ambled into its delightful coolness. For a while they walked in companionable silence, speaking only occasional-

232

ly in whispers as they pointed out the little gray squirrels that skittered in starts from tree to tree. Then they reached a small glen, hemmed in by the graceful fingers of pines, carpeted by beds of lush, green grass. Wesley sank down and pulled her beside him, face to face, half-prone on nature's chaise.

Sloan's nerves were as taut as piano wire. She was frightened; she was eager. Her pulses were racing in a crazy zigzag of yes and no while her heart pounded so loudly she was sure it must echo through the quiet of the surrounding forest. He was going to kiss her. She was no longer going to have to wonder about the feel of his corded arms because they were going to come around her. . . .

But they didn't, not right away. He smiled at her, an incredibly sensuous, lazy smile as he lay back in the earth's soft cushion of the glen and openly relished the simple pleasure of watching her, the sea of his eyes languorously moving from the delicate lines of her profile—hesitating at the enticing hint of firm breast displayed to such advantage by the knot of her blouse—to the angular plane of her hip and along the slender but dancer-shapely length of her long legs.

A bird chirped somewhere in the branches above them, but Sloan was barely aware of its cheerful cry. It was part of the hypnotism this man was exuding, part of the compelling aura that seemed to make an island of the glen, an isolated place of beauty where all that was real was the shelter of the friendly pines, the encouraging whisper of the breeze, the soft, earthy bed of green and brown, and—the dynamically handsome man who lay before her, emanating an undeniable virility.

He dropped the blade of grass he had been idly chewing and stretched a tanned finger to outline the softness of her lips. They trembled at his touch and parted, and the finger went on to rub gently the edge of her teeth as he watched, fascinated. A shudder ripped through Sloan, one of such abject longing that it left her shocked by its vehemence and quivering in its wake. But still he didn't reach for her, but spoke instead, and his voice was part of the breeze, a whisper as compelling and hypnotic as his piercing sea-jade eyes.

"You're exquisite," he said. "Incredibly beautiful," and his eyes were still locked with hers; his finger still touched her lips.

233

His head moved toward hers until it was just an inch away, and he murmured, "I want you to know that my intentions are entirely honorable."

"What?" Sloan mumbled, confused and deep within the spell of the moment. She knew she should be listening; she should be talking; she should be coyly denying his touch. But all her scheming seemed worlds away. There was something else at stake, but she couldn't remember what. A pulse was beating erratically through her system. Her veins felt as if they were composed of a silvery liquid which raced like mercury in response to the simple feel of his finger; her nerves were so vibrantly alive that she could feel every touch of the gentle breeze, every blade of grass that brushed her skin. Her whole body was crying out, silently pleading for the excruciating pleasure of the muscle-rippled bronzed arms which must surely take her into their demanding security soon.

And they finally did, like lightning. A powerful hand crushed her lithe softness to his lean hardness as he groaned. "I'm crazy about you," he murmured huskily. "I always have been, And you're more beautiful than ever . . ." He intended to say more, but the moist, inviting lips parted tantalizingly before him were too much. He kissed her, nibbling her lower lip, probing with tender but firm command until she moaned and fell entirely acquiescent to his seduction of her mouth. Then the kiss became wild and passionate, and everything was forgotten and unreal as she strained against him, a willing prisoner of the all-encompassing, delightfully sensual sensations he was arousing. His lips left hers to create a burning trail along the sensitive flesh of her neck and down to the partially exposed mounds of her breasts; the unhurried, assured exploration of his hands sought her intimately, discovering the lean muscles of a thigh, delighting in the slender slope of a hip, creating an inferno of yearning along the bare flesh of her midriff. His seeking moved upward so that he might cradle the lushness of her breasts, and she made no protest as he fumbled with the annoying knot that kept material between his pleasure-giving hands and the rosy nipples which were hardening, demanding to be touched. She was, in fact, too deliriously busy herself, exhilarating in the feel of the crisp, dark hair that fringed his collar, stroking the tensed muscles that rippled and heated beneath his shirt as her hands and fingers feathered and caressed them. His breathing, she noted with vague, sensuous pleasure, was as ragged as hers; their hearts seemed to pound together in a furious, deafening roar, and even the pines that cushioned them seemed to disappear. All that she was aware of was him—the weight of his hard, lean form pressing into her soft one, molding her to him, demanding and giving. The knot finally gave; his hot kisses came to her breasts as they fell like exotic fruits to his hands. His thumb, gentle but ever so slightly rough, taunted one ripe-hard nipple while his teeth reverently grazed the other, and a sob of sheer, exquisite physical pleasure escaped Sloan as she instinctively clutched his head to her with fevered fingers imbedded in his dark hair.

A twig suddenly snapped, as loud as a rifle shot in the silent glen. Sloan started, but it was Wesley who pulled away, his expression tenderly sheepish.

"Just a twig," he chuckled, after perusing their haven with a keen and astute eye. His smile was wide with understanding amusement as he watched Sloan redden and hastily retie her top with nervous, trembling fingers. "Just a twig," he repeated softly, drawing a gentle finger along her cheek.

Sloan met his tender gaze briefly, then her lashes fluttered and she stared at the ground, shielding her confusion from his view. He thought he understood, but he didn't. It was not the idea that they may have been discovered in their intimate embrace that wracked her mind with horror and left her heart sputtering erratically, her nerves tense with torment.

It was the embrace itself; the wild abandon in which she had so eagerly fallen into his arms, willing—no! desperately desiring —to give him all.

In the middle of a public park.

What had happened to her?

Had she been so lonely that she had simply craved the first attractive male to come her way? No, she had dated a number of men, persistent ones at that! They had always left her feeling nothing, not even pleasant sensations. Wesley had awakened desires which had long lain dormant within her; his touch had brought to life a warm, feeling, responsive woman—a woman Sloan had thought long dead.

In fact, in all honesty, he had aroused her to greater passion than she had felt in all her twenty-nine years, and they hadn't even . . .

Sloan breathed shakily. She had to get a grip on herself! Some huntress she was! But there was no denying the fact that Wesley was a supremely powerful and sensual man or that an undeniable chemistry existed between them. And, in a way, that was good. She would be able to bring him something honest in their marriage. Her blush, which had begun to recede, came back full force.

She wanted him with every bit as much fervor as he wanted her. She could openly give him passion.

But as he laughingly helped her to her feet and brushed away the pine needles and grass that stuck to her hair and clothing, she guiltily realized that all she could offer would not really be enough.

Wesley was a good man, an exceptionally good man—kind, gentle, understanding, and unassuming. He had survived celebrity status and wealth and retained compassion and kept a solid, worldly-but-uninflated head upon his shoulders.

He deserved everything that a wife should give; friendship, partnership, passion and—love.

Yet even as remorse filled her heart, he was tilting her head with firm persuasion, forcing her tremulous blue eyes to meet his sea-jade stare.

"Please don't look like a maiden in shock," he entreated earnestly, the dimple flashing in his cheeks. He was still amused, but her silence was causing him considerable concern.

Sloan opened her mouth to speak, but the ache in her heart caused the words to freeze on her lips. He shook his head, his smile stretching across his taut, bronzed features. She wondered fleetingly why he had to look so darned attractive just then, so masculine and virile, yet boyish with his dark hair disarrayed, his eyes dazzling mischievously, his crooked smile engagingly intent. He was twisting her apart.

But again, he was—luckily for her!—misinterpreting her reactions.

"I love you, Sloan," he said huskily. "I told you before, my intentions are entirely honorable. Years ago, I fell in love with a wisp of a girl, an infatuation, if you will. But the dream of that girl has stayed with me all my life, paling all others. And she had her own dream, and it had to be followed.

"But now, I've found her again. We're both older and wiser. And now I know I can help her with whatever her future dreams might be. I have no intention of letting her get away again!" He kissed her again, very lightly, very tenderly, very gently. "You may think I'm crazy, Sloan, and maybe I am. I may be totally insane where you are concerned. But I do love you. I want to marry you. I know it's too early to expect an answer from such a crazy proposal, but after what just happened, I thought I should let you know how very much you do mean to me."

Sloan managed a sick, weak smile. She had won, just like that. She had taken the victory before the battle, accomplished everything she had set out to achieve—in less than three days.

Then why, she wondered miserably, was that victory so bitter-tasting, her triumph so hollow?

Had he really been in love with her for years? Was that why he had never married? Or was it talk, the bantering type of talk that lovers often used?

She really didn't know which would make her feel worse, but now, for certain, she couldn't let Wesley go.

But nor could she rid herself of a nagging feeling of . . . of . . .

Was it fear?

CHAPTER FOUR

Sloan slid a towel around her neck and closed the door to Fine Arts 202 behind her. She shook her head slightly. Melanie Anderson and Harold Persoff were in that studio practicing to Steely Dan, while the strains of Bach were also filtering through to her from Fine Arts 204 where Gail Henning—a student determined to be the next American prima ballerina—was also at work rehearsing.

Sloan's lips curved into a slight smile. She didn't mind teaching; in fact she loved it. Gail Henning was going to make a fine ballerina, and Sloan was playing a part in making the girl's dream a reality. It was a nice feeling.

Her smile slipped and she sighed. The problem with teaching was the college. The Fine Arts department was on a low budget —in the present economy state-funded schools couldn't afford much for the arts. Theater, dance, and music—and even visual arts—were just not practical courses of study in the world the kids would face when they left. Sloan agreed with the theory that her students—even the best—should have a sound education to fall back on. She, more than anyone, knew that they would have a struggle surviving in their chosen field. But although Jim Baskins was a great department head, he was under the chairman of Fine Arts, who was under the dean, who was under the vice-president of the school, and so forth. The politics in her job drove her crazy.

She mused over the budget wars recently fought in the last faculty meetings as she entered the ring of offices shared by theater and dance, thanking the student secretary for her messages and following the labyrinth of cubbyholes until she found her own—an eight-by-eight square with a small desk and two chairs. The rest of the proposals for dance finals awaited her approval, and she slipped into a sweat shirt, chilled now by the air conditioning in her damp leotard and tights, before seating herself to concentrate on the projects. A chosen few would be previewed on Saturday when she and Jim made their own contributions to the welfare of the Fine Arts department at the annual performance. And time, Sloan thought with a grimace, was slipping away. Wrinkling her nose with distaste at the loss of time she so often endured with the red tape of the paperwork, Sloan focused her attention on what actually constituted teaching.

Sloan picked up the first folder and pursed her lips in a tolerant grimace as she saw that Susie Harris wanted to tap her final to the Doobie Brothers' "A Fool Believes." The music wasn't conducive to tap, but Sloan believed in letting the kids—kids! they were eighteen to twenty, young adults—try their wings and learn from their own mistakes. Besides, she had seen some very good work come out of the highly improbable.

Sloan scribbled a few lines of advice on Susie's folder and set it aside. Dan Taylor wanted to do a modern ballet to Schubert.

. . .

Sloan set the folder down. Her effort to concentrate was fading. Chewing the nub of her pencil, she thought back to the previous night and Wesley. He hadn't mentioned marriage again; he hadn't touched her again. He had returned their relationship to a casual one, idly discussing the upcoming school performance. At her home he had played with the kids, picked up Florence, and left, saying nothing about seeing her again.

. . .

The tip of the eraser broke off in her mouth, and Sloan wrinkled her face in distaste before ruefully plucking the rubber from her tongue. She was going to have to stop being such a nervous wreck—and definitely improve her hunting technique. Wesley was supposed to think of nothing but her all day long, not vice versa. And she had been thinking of nothing but Wesley all day, to the extent that her students must be thinking Mrs. Tallett was mellowing. She was considered the roughest taskmaster in the department, knowing that only grueling work could take even the most talented to the top.

In all dance classes, you perspired.

In Mrs. Tallett's classes, you *sweat*!

Sloan was aware that her budding Nureyevs thought her a strict drill sergeant, but she was totally unaware that they were devoted to her and many considered her a miracle in a small college. Half the males in her classes were also in more than a little bit of puppy love with her. She was beautiful, tall, svelte, sophisticated, and although her voice could be a cutting whip, it was a soft-spoken voice. She was tireless and demanding, but she had the grace of movement they all strove for, and she participated in her own strenuous workouts.

If you got out of Mrs. Tallett's classes alive, you had a good chance of making it as a dancer.

Today, she had been mellow. She had been busy throwing her energies into furious movement, hoping she could exhaust her frame from remembering the burning touch that had made her forget everything else. . . .

A soft tap on her door became persistent and sharp before she heard it. "Come in," she called quickly.

It was Donna, the student-assistant secretary, and her pretty round face seemed somewhat in awe.

"What is it, Donna?" Sloan asked.

"He's here, Mrs. Tallett. To see you," Donna said disbelievingly.

Sloan frowned, sighed, and forced herself to be patient. "He *who* is here to see me, Donna?"

"Adams. The quarterback. Wesley Adams, the quarterback!" Donna said the name with awe, then rambled on, "Oh, Mrs. Tallett! He's gorgeous! What a hunk! And so nice. And he's here! Right here in Gettysburg. To see you. Oh, Mrs. Tallett, what do you suppose he wants?"

Sloan couldn't prevent the rueful grin that spread across her features. She lowered her eyes quickly, not to allow Donna to view the self-humor she was feeling. She might be the attractive and judicial Mrs. Tallett, but she was still a teacher, a mature if sophisticated woman.

Wesley was a national hero, living in the never-never land of eternal youth. It was hard to accept the fact that her students would think of her as a Cinderella chosen by the godlike prince

240

in a miraculous whim of luck, but that was how they would see it.

"Donna," Sloan said with tolerant patience, "Wesley Adams is from Gettysburg—and he no longer plays football. And yes, he is a very nice man. Show him back, will you please?"

"Sure thing!" Donna's huge, cornflower-blue eyes still held wonder, and she hesitated as she backed out of the room.

"What else, Donna?" Sloan asked with a raised brow.

"Could you . . . would you . . . I mean, I'd love . . ."

"Love what?" Sloan prompted, holding in her exasperation.

"An autograph," Donna breathed quickly.

"I'm sure he'll be happy to give you an autograph." Sloan smiled. "He can stop back by your desk on the way out and write whatever you wish. Okay?"

"O—kay!" Donna grinned and disappeared.

Only as the door closed did Sloan realize she was once again a mess. Her leotard, tights, and leg warmers were at least new and unfaded, but her hair was drawn back in a severe bun, and the sweat shirt she wore was an old and tattered gray one. Her makeup had been through Monday's schedule—Ballet III, Jazz II, Modern I, Advanced Tap, and Aerobics. So had her body.

And it would take Donna about fifteen seconds to walk back to the central office, another fifteen or twenty to return. . . .

Sloan made a dive beneath her desk for her handbag and hastily gave herself a light mist of Je Reviens and glossed her lips quickly with a peach-bronze shade that matched her nails. Tendrils of hair were escaping the knot at her nape, but it was too late to worry. She had been thinking of Wes all day, but never expecting to see him.

The raps came on her door again, and she shoved her purse back beneath the desk. "Come in."

A giggling and blushing Donna pushed open the door and led Wesley in. Sloan could immediately see why the girl had been so taken. Wes had dressed for business today, and he was stunningly, ruggedly good-looking in a way which could let no one wonder which was the stronger, virile sex. In a navy three-piece suit, stark white shirt, and burgundy silk tie, he looked every inch the cool, shrewd businessman while still exuding an aura of

241

an earthy power. Very civil—his omniscient-seeming green eyes were light, his grin warm—while still conveying that raw, almost primitive masculinity that women, no matter how liberated, sought in a male.

He smoothed back the breeze-ruffled silver-tinged hair that was the only thing out of context with his sleekly tailored appearance as he entered her office, overpowering everything in the small space. "Hi. I hope I'm not disturbing you. Do dance teachers get off at five like the rest of the work force?"

Sloan rose and smiled. "Not always, but you're not disturbing me." He was disturbing her, but not as he thought.

Donna still stood in the doorway, agape at their casual greetings. "Thank you, Donna," Sloan dismissed her gently. She cast a quick, apologetic glance Wes's way. "Mr. Adams will stop by your desk on the way out."

Wesley quirked a puzzled brow but agreed with her, smiling to the girl. "Sure, I'll stop by on my way out."

"Thank you," Donna murmured, flushed and pleasantly pink as she closed the door. .

"Why *am* I stopping by on my way out?" he asked playfully as he took the one chair before Sloan's desk and they both seated themselves.

"An autograph. I hope you don't mind."

Dark brows knit loosely above Wes's ever-changing green eyes. "I don't mind at all, but I wasn't planning on leaving. Not without you."

"Oh?" Sloan felt her heart begin to pound harder.

"I was hoping you'd come to dinner with me."

The pounding became thunderous. She certainly couldn't pat herself on the back for playing the femme fatale too well, but he was coming to her anyway. Had he really cared something for her all those years? It was impossible to tell whether he spoke with meaning or if his words were the pleasant, teasing games that all men—she thought—played. All men except Terry. She couldn't think about Terry right now, but unfortunately, neither could she accept Wesley's invitation. She had nothing tangible to go on yet, and she had commitments she couldn't disregard even if she did.

"Wesley," she murmured unhappily, "I'd love to go to dinner

242

with you, but I can't. Jim and I do a dance as well as the students, and I need a little practice time by myself. And I have to pick up the children and spend time with them and feed them—"

"I've already taken all that into consideration," Wesley interrupted her, giving her his dazzling, lopsided grin. He leaned his elbows upon her desk to draw closer, and the effect of his nearness was mesmerizing. "We'll pick up the kids together and run to your house so that you can shower and change. Then we'll take the kids over to the steak house, come back so that you can spend time with them and practice, and then we'll go out. Florence will be ready anytime we are. And you won't have to worry about your time with your children—they'll be in bed before we go. We won't stay out late—I know morning comes quickly on working days."

Sloan stared into his eyes feeling a bit of awe and wonder herself. She may not be in love with Wesley, she decided, but she couldn't recall liking or even respecting a man more! He was one of the most sensitive men she had ever met, understanding in every way, not just tolerating her children, but taking great care to keep their needs at the top of his priority list.

"You are marvelous!" she whispered, and she meant every word. Another smile spread slowly across her delicately boned face, erasing the tension and strain of the day. "Thank you, Wesley," she murmured tentatively, strangely humbled by his thoughtfulness.

"For what?" he demanded, his gentle, probing green stare telling her all that she needed to know even as he brushed her gratitude aside as unnecessary.

"For understanding," she said softly.

He chuckled, but his strong features were intense, and she was left to wonder about the depths of his sincerity. "I don't have much time to convince you that I'm madly in love with you and should forever after be the only man in your life. Come on, we'll take my car and worry about yours later."

Sloan smiled a little uneasily and straightened the folders on her desk. She would deal with them in a much better frame of mind in the morning. "The entire evening sounds beautifully planned," she said huskily. "Just give me two minutes to check out with Jim and five minutes to hop into the shower."

"Take fifteen," Wes laughed, rising. "I'll go take care of your dancing football fan."

There was more than one fan in the office by the time Sloan had slipped out the back of the maze to the showers and returned to go over a few notes with Jim. Some type of student radar had gone out, and an ensemble of dancers in tights and actors in various stages of costume from the drama classes had formed in a loose circle around Wes.

As she listened to him deal politely and quietly with the students, Sloan realized that the pleasant, low-timbred quality of his voice was truly becoming dear to her. Wes Adams did have everything; sinewed good looks, personality, charisma.

And a fortune.

She must have been blind all those years ago, but then they had been young. Neither had been what they were today.

Nervousness rippled through Sloan as she silently watched him. Cassie had probably been right—Wes could crook a little finger and have any woman he wanted. For some obscure reason he wanted her, and God help her, she wanted him too, even if the feeling wasn't love. But he had to love her, really love her, because it had to be marriage . . . she *needed* him. Desperately now, now that she had let the dream grow.

Her fingers clenched at her side. She was going to have to be so very careful . . . he had to keep wanting her. For a lifetime. And he had to keep believing in the illusion she hoped she was weaving.

An illusion of assurance, of sophisticated confidence. Of having every bit as much to offer in a relationship as he.

Green eyes suddenly met hers over a sea of faces. The lazy, incredibly sexy grin curled its way back into the strong line of his jaw. "Excuse me," he murmured to the students, and then he was at her side, leading her out as young men and women watched and echoed good-byes to them both.

For a moment Sloan was tempted to laugh. Wesley would probably never realize how he had just elevated her in the eyes of the student body.

"Nice kids," Wes said as he steered her to his Lincoln in the parking lot. "They filled me in quite a bit on you."

"Really?" Sloan raised a curious and surprised brow.

"Ummm." He grinned with amusement. "They say you're the sexiest tyrant ever to head a dance class. I assured them they were probably quite right."

"Oh," Sloan laughed, wincing as she felt a blush creep over her cheeks. "About being a tyrant—or, uh . . ." Damn! What was she saying?

"Sexy?" Wes supplied, chuckling as he shut her door. He walked around and slid into the driver's seat. "Both," he said, smiling at her. "I know you're sexy as hell, and I can bet you can be a tyrant."

"Worried?" she queried in as light and teasing a manner as she could.

"Not at all. I can fight fire with fire, my dear."

Sloan smiled, the right reaction since his answer had been teasing in kind. Yet a little trickle of unease worked its way up her neck. Had there been a hint of steel beneath his velvet tone, or was that only an illusion of her overactive imagination? She remembered the first night at her house . . . how bluntly he had called her rude. He hadn't really been angry; he had been in complete control. Yet she shuddered at the vision of a man who possessed his dynamic force and depths of passion losing his temper.

"Where are we going?" he asked.

"Pardon?"

"Your children," he replied, patient and amused by her wandering.

"Oh . . ." Sloan gave him directions to the day-care center.

Three hours later—having fulfilled all obligation to family and art—they were back on the highway driving to a hotel outside the city limits that offered rooftop dining and dancing. It was odd, Sloan thought, casting Wes a covert glance as he drove, that she had really only known him four days. She had known him years ago, of course, but that was a vague memory. On Friday night she had thought his appearance nothing more than a nuisance. The intensity of their relationship since was strangely comforting—while also disturbing. She was nervous—one couldn't be planning on marrying a man who had no idea he was being baited without being nervous—but she was now beginning to relax. For whatever heaven-sent reason, Wesley seemed to be sincere. His patience with her situation was astounding. He also seemed to be determined to pander to her every whim with tolerant amusement. Little by little, it became apparent that her inexpert vamping was working—she could almost hope she was winding him around her little finger.

It was over rainbow trout, tenderly seasoned and cooked and perfectly garnished, that Wesley began to quiz her about Terry again.

"When you talk about your husband there's a little light in your eyes," he told her, his eyes darting to hers from the fish. "It sounds like you had the perfect marriage. Didn't you ever argue?"

Sloan smiled, still curious that it was so easy to talk him. She sensed that the questions were relevant to their own relationship, although she wasn't sure why. She answered him honestly—there was seldom a reason to hedge because he never brought up finances.

"It was a near perfect marriage, I suppose, but we did argue." She laughed. "Terry spent lots of nights on the couch."

"On the couch?" Wes seemed surprised.

Sloan frowned slightly, perplexed at his reaction, but still smiling. "Sure. He always knew when I was really angry because I'd throw his pillow and a blanket at him. By the morning—or the morning after, at least—we were ready to converse like human beings. I thought it worked well."

"You would," Wes said, and although he kept the teasing tone in his voice, Sloan noted an edge of sternness. "You weren't the one sleeping on the couch."

"I meant we both had time to cool down," Sloan said. "You disagree with such a tactic?"

"I don't believe you can run away from the issue," Wes said, signaling their waiter for coffee. "But tell me, why do you think the marriage worked so well? Take it as research, if you like," he added with a grin. "I've only heard of or seen three really good marriages—yours, your sister's, and my brother's."

Sloan mulled the question over carefully. This talk about marriage was very tricky. Perhaps she should have told him she and Terry never argued. . . . "I don't really know. I think with Terry and me it was a question of both being artists. We loved each

246

other, and also respected each other's need to love what we did. We both knew we wanted a family. Cassie and I lost our parents when we were just out of our teens—and I learned then, and again when Terry died, just how important sisters can be. I wanted my children to have each other. So did Terry. He was an only child, and his parents died when he was young too. We had a lot in common. And I don't think I ever saw Terry really mad. He simply didn't have a temper—which was good, because mine was terrible when I was younger!" Sloan chuckled a little sheepishly. She hadn't meant to say quite so much, and Wes was watching her now intently, the green eyes seeming to pierce through to her soul. She didn't want him seeing her soul. . . .

"You seem to have pulled yourself together," he said simply. He lit a cigarette and sat back exhaling smoke, his eyes never leaving her. "Sometimes, when people lose a loved one, they blind themselves. They forget that the person was human and turn them into a god. You remember all the good, which is wonderful, but you seem to also realize he was a man."

Do I? Sloan wondered. She wasn't sure. There was still that terrible ache in her sometimes, but oddly, since she had started seeing Wesley, it was fading. It wasn't love, not as she had known it, but she respected him, admired him, and felt a wild excitement in his arms when he touched her . . . when she heard his voice . . . when she watched his powerful, lithe movements . . .

Wes abruptly changed the subject. "Would you like to dance? Or is that a poor question after you've taught all day?"

"No." Sloan smiled. "I'd love to dance. The effect is an entirely different one on a dance floor."

It was entirely different. She loved being in this man's arms, inhaling his pleasant scent, feeling the rough material of his jacket and the hard muscles beneath her fingers. Curiously, he was a wonderful dancer, light and agile on his feet, especially for a man of his size.

Tilting her chin to his face, Sloan smiled with a lazy happiness. "You do quite well on a dance floor, Mr. Adams."

"Thank you," he replied with a shade of amusement, his hand

tightening upon the small of her back and pulling her closer. "I like to think it's because of the ballet classes I've taken."

"Ballet? You?" Sloan queried with disbelief.

"Yep." They made a dip, and Sloan found her form fitting to his with uncanny perfection. "My coach made the whole team take dance classes to improve our coordination." He shrugged ruefully. "I'm six four and two hundred and twenty pounds—small compared to half the team. Seriously, imagine a guy we called Bull Bradford. Six foot eight, three hundred pounds. If a guy like that fell on one of his own teammates, he could put a player out for the entire season."

Sloan laughed and her eyes met his again. It was so good to be with him, laugh with him, have him take the burdens of her life off her shoulders. Good to be held by him, even if she held herself in careful restraint. The heat of him aroused so much in her, and she wondered fleetingly if it was wrong to want a man so badly whom she didn't love. It didn't matter, because she couldn't have him, not until . . . until he married her. She just couldn't take risks. She had always been confident in her sexuality before, but she had loved Terry, and he had loved her. What if . . . what if she just didn't have the experience or expertise to hold a man like Wesley? She shivered suddenly. She would be confident of Wesley's love when she had his ring around her finger . . . when her ragged existence had been eased.

And somehow, somehow, she thought guiltily, she would repay him. . . .

He took her to dinner again the next night, telling her in his light, easy fashion that he was staging a whirlwind courtship. He had not taken her into his arms again with the same passion he had hungrily displayed in the park; he was restraining himself. He kissed her good-night with gentle, sensual persuasion, leaving her senses reeling, her body aching for the demand she had known so briefly.

Apparently, she thought ruefully as she tossed in bed after that night, her body was unaware that a winner-take-all game was being played. Thank heaven Wesley was treading lightly. She feared an edge of pressure could bring capitulation from traitorous flesh.

Summer was a big time for tourists in Gettysburg, and on Wednesday morning Sloan noticed the traffic becoming heavy, the streets thronging with visitors. Fairly certain that Wesley would appear after her last class and ask her out for the evening, she decided to take things into her own hands. With that resolution for initiative, she planned a barbecue at her home. Wesley sounded pleasantly agreeable when she called him at the business number he had given her—they could avoid any crowds.

Jim popped his head into her half-open office doorway just as she was finishing her call. "A barbecue, eh? Am I invited?" he teased.

"Do you know," Sloan mused, wondering if it would now be a good idea to chance being alone with Wes once the little Talletts were tucked into bed, "you just gave me an idea. Yes, you are invited. Most definitely."

"Sloan," Jim demurred, sliding into her extra chair and una-bashedly casting her legs—covered by woolen leg warmers—over the corner of her desk, "I was teasing. The student grapevine tells me—since you haven't bothered to"—he interrupted himself with the woeful aggrievance—"that Mrs. Tallett is running hot and heavy with Wesley Adams. Granted, I told you I was living to see this day; but seriously, shouldn't you be alone?"

"No," Sloan said firmly. "And I'm not running 'hot and heavy' with anyone." Her lips quirked into a dry smile. "I'm assuming that was a student expression?"

Jim shrugged. "Sometimes the students have apt expressions. I know you were out with him Sunday, Monday, and Tuesday. I think that qualifies for hot and heavy. Especially with you."

"Damn," Sloan murmured, "that's some grapevine. How did you know about Sunday?"

"Jeannie Holiday—my Monday Beginning Jazz class," Jim told her with a smile. "She saw you at the park."

Sloan flushed a little and made a show of straightening her desk, wondering exactly how much Jeannie Holiday had seen. "And Fine Arts majors are notoriously creative," she said light-ly. "Are you going to come?"

Jim hunched his shoulders. "Wouldn't miss it," he said with a broad grin. "Sloan Tallett finally gets her rich man."

"What?" Sloan's eyes flew to his guiltily.

249

"The man's as rich as Onassis," Jim said. "Surely you knew that."

"I knew he was . . . comfortable," Sloan said, finding it hard to hide her conscience before Jim. She returned her attention to her desk until she could compose her features into a mask of cheerfulness. "I'm going to have Cassie and George over too . . . and my nephews, of course. Since you're coming, Jim"—she gave him a conniving smile—"do you think you could just assign my last class to their rehearsals? I'd like to hop out a little early and plan."

"Sure," Jim said agreeably. "Leave when you're ready. I'm so anxious to see this, I'll even bring the wine."

Sloan graced him with a tongue-in-cheek smile. "Bring beer—Wesley's bringing wine."

"Will do, kiddo." Jim stood and shook his head in disbelief. "I didn't think even a millionaire could get you away from those memories of yours this fast."

Sloan watched him leave her office with surprise. It was true, and Jim had seen it. She hadn't lost her memories in the last few days, but she had shelved them away in a poignant past where they belonged.

Her last-minute midweek barbecue turned out to be a wonderful success. She had overextended herself a little on the preparations, but then she decided, as the saying goes, it takes money to make money.

And she wanted Wes to think her capable of hostessing a nice, if informal, affair.

The July sun stayed out a long time, enabling the party to eat on the lawn. Sloan was thankful for her sister's appearance; with Cassie and George coming early with their two boys, she had left the supervision of all the children to them and managed to do a nice job of sprucing up the house and herself. By the time Wes had arrived, she had been cool and collected, her mad dash to collect children, clean house, and primp a thing of the past. She met him at the door with a brilliant smile, casually dressed in jeans and a body-hugging T-shirt that lent her an aura of feminine nonchalance.

When the food had been consumed and the grown-ups—including an eagle-eyed Jim—were leisurely relaxing in various stages of comfort on the back patio, George, an avid armchair quarterback all his life, talked Wesley into a football game.

"I need a handicap, though," George admitted cheerfully. "I get Jim, and I guess I have to take Cassie"—he paused with a grimace as Cassie frowned and whacked his shoulder—"and you get Sloan."

Wes chuckled and angled his head toward Sloan. "What do you say?"

Sloan shrugged with a slow smile. "Sure. If you can play ballerina, I guess I can be a halfback!"

"Go easy, halfback," Jim warned, and Sloan was startled into seeing her friend's appraising eyes on her. "Don't forget we have a performance on Saturday. I'm not dancing with a partner on crutches."

Sloan smiled at him, but her smile was uneasy. She felt he was warning her about more than a game.

"Touch game, only," Wes said, a semismile, warmly insinuative, on his lips as he cast a protective arm around Sloan's shoulders.

"And watch who you're touching where!" Cassie interjected, giving her husband an elbow in the ribs. She looked at the group with feigned grievance. "I think the man would love to get his hands on my sister!"

"Cassie!" George and Sloan gasped the protest together.

"I'm kidding, I'm kidding!" Cassie moaned. She laughed, half in earnest, half in jest. "I don't think he'd dare turn the wrong way at the moment, anyway! Wesley could fell him with one twitch of the finger."

"Hey!" George grumbled as they ambled away to form their team. "I'm not in that bad a shape—am I?"

Neither Wesley nor Sloan got to hear his wife's reply. They were laughing and forming their own huddle.

Wesley spelled out their plans for action to a giggling Sloan, who didn't understand a single play. "Woman," Wes groaned, "I'm glad you were never on the team. However"—his arms tightened excitingly around her and his whisper, warm and moist against her ear, inflamed her body from head to toe—"I never enjoyed a huddle like I'm enjoying this one."

The mini football game was fun. She and Wes had the advantage of his speed and prowess, and George had the advantage of a third person. Even with her frequent fumbles, though, she and Wes won the game. Or rather, Wes won the game. She was almost useless, but all of Wes's grumbling was good-natured. Eventually, as the summer sun faded entirely, they all wound up back where they had started—lazily sprawled around the patio, hot and pleasantly tired and thirstily finishing up the beer.

The talk was casual. Sloan, drowsy from an entire day of physical activity and rushing, didn't say much, but listened to the chatter with a feeling of well-being. She was vaguely pleased that Jim and Wes had hit it off so well. Even if she were to leave her teaching job at the college—which she intended to do if her scheming worked—he was a dear friend, one she would like to keep. Perhaps—and she allowed her mind to wander off to dreams—the two of them could form their own school one day without the miles of red tape. . . .

"Sloan?"

"Ummm!" She was nudged from dreamland by Wesley prodding the shoulder that rested against his knee.

"I'm sorry." He chuckled with affection. "I hate to disturb you with that sweet smile on your face, but I need to use the phone."

"Oh!" She jumped up quickly and excused them both from the group to lead Wes through the living room, where Cassie's boys were curled asleep on the couches, to her room and the extension. "I'll leave you to your privacy," she said, starting to close the door.

"No, stay," he said huskily, his intense green gaze demanding and sensual. "This will only take a minute, and I want to talk to you."

Sloan's heart began to flutter with anticipation and the combination of wild excitement and fear that always seemed to assail her when she was alone with him. She forced herself to smile and shrug casually before sitting idly at the foot of the bed to await his call.

It was half social call and half business, she realized quickly. It was his brother he talked to, and he started off in a warm humor. He rattled off a few names which she assumed belonged to horses, and discussed prices and breeding stock.

Then he was silent for quite a while, listening. Sloan literally saw all warmth leave his eyes—they became hardened crystals of smooth green glass. The muscles in his face tensed and tightened; a vein began to pound furiously in the whipcord strength of his neck. His jawline was hard and squared, the total quality of his handsome features suddenly transformed into something more chilling than she had ever seen before.

A face more fierce and ruthless than she had ever imagined. Wesley Adams furious.

Despite his metamorphosis, he remained silent, his hand tightening around the receiver until his knuckles went white.

But not as white as Sloan was feeling. It wasn't directed at her, but his anger was the type that froze a person's blood. Just watching the apparent control he wielded, allowing only muscles to tighten, started a shivering inside of her that would not cease.

He spoke low—a deathly growl. "Fire him. And make sure he's off the place before I get back."

Apparently the person on the other end of the wire knew there was no mercy when that restrained, bloodcurdling hiss was used. Wesley listened again, but Dave Adams had little else to say.

The tension in Wes ebbed somewhat as he said good-bye, his anger not directed at his brother, but at the party being fired. Sloan would hate to be that person, but if she was the employee in question, she would definitely be long gone before Wes got back.

The receiver clicked precisely back into its holder, and Sloan found herself wishing he had not asked her to stay in the room. She didn't think she wanted to hear anything he had to say at that moment, not with that look of ruthless authority still on his face.

Wes turned to her suddenly, as if just realizing she was still with him. "I'm sorry," he said quietly. "We had a problem with a trainer."

For some ridiculous reason—perhaps her own shivering apprehension—Sloan felt pity for the unknown man and came to his defense, stuttering, "Wh—what happened? Perhaps you should give the man a second chance—"

253

Wesley interrupted her, his lips drawn in a tight white smile. "I don't give second chances. I gave him a chance when I hired him. He came in drunk, decided to take one of our most promising three-year-olds out, and caused the mare to break her leg. She had to be destroyed."

"Oh," Sloan murmured weakly. Besides the anger, she could sense the pain in his voice.

But Wes could make incredible changes. His smile and eyes became lighter as he walked to her and placed his hands on her shoulders, then tilted her chin toward his. "There's nothing more to be done about it," he said gently. "I'm sorry, I seem to have put a damper on your evening."

"No—" Sloan protested, but she didn't get a chance to say more. She was drawn up, inexorably, into his arms. There was a force to him tonight, a leftover of the coiled tension he had constrained, a shuddering that rippled through sinewed muscles and lent heat and passion to his rough but tender command. His lips taking hers with no question or persuasion but with need and mastery. His tongue invaded the moist intimacy of her mouth, expecting submission with absolute authority and receiving it.

Sloan was at first startled, and then mesmerized. She couldn't have denied him . . . had she wanted to . . . been able to . . .

His hands were as sure as his lips. With one he held the small of her back, curving her to him in an arch that made her even more aware of his burning heat and his need for her, a need she felt that she melted to like soft wax. The excitement and spark of fire she experienced near him suddenly burst into flame like an inferno. His other hand was firmly caressing her face, sliding down the silken column of her neck, fondling her collarbone, her shoulder, seducing with each firm movement. It crept between them with no thought of obstruction from her to crush against her breast, seeking as it enticed, a work-roughened thumb grazing a nipple with expert enticement until it hardened to a full peak, straining against the fabric of her shirt to receive the intoxicating touch. A moan sounded in Sloan's throat, a whimper of desire. She was lost in his onslaught, swept away in a great wash of desire that began as a burning need in the root of femininity and spread a weakness rushing through her like a

254

tidal wave. She couldn't think, only need and crave . . . from somewhere a voice inside her reminded her that she couldn't give, but it made no sense . . . she wanted desperately to give . . . and give . . . and keep on giving until she could quench the terrible storm of desire. . . .

Her fingers, limp at first, found life. They curled over his broad shoulders, marveling at the play of muscle, and moved on to the coarse edges of dark hair at his nape, pulling her ever closer as her mind whirled in sensation. She wasn't sure that she still touched earth. . . .

She never did think of her conniving that night. It was a sudden splurge of fear, spurred as his fingers slipped beneath her shirt to sear her flesh with new pleasure that finally jolted her mind. *What if she wasn't all that he wanted? What if she froze and just couldn't . . .?* It had been so very long. . . .

All the terrors that flitted through her mind were unnecessary. Wesley had remembered where they were and under what circumstances, even if she hadn't. He drew away with a shake, then pulled her close to his chest again with tenderness. Her head rested against his thundering heart as he spoke.

"There's so much I want to say to you, Sloan. But I think your other guests are going to start speculating as to what we're up to. I can't wait long, though. Saturday night, when your performance and the hectic pace that goes with it is over, we're going to leave George and Cassie early and find some place to be entirely alone. No crowded dance floor or restaurant, and no car. I want you alone. Agreed?"

Sloan nodded vigorously against his chest, not trusting herself to speak. Please God, she prayed hastily, let it be a proposal. I don't think I can handle this much longer. And if I'm his wife, I know I'll be okay, I'll have to be okay, because I'll know he wants me forever. . . .

Everyone left shortly after they returned to the patio, Wesley brushing a quick kiss against her forehead as he helped George carry out his sleeping sons.

Sloan slept soundly. She had weighed all Wesley's words and actions and convinced herself that he was sincere. Saturday night was sure to bring the proposal she so desperately needed.

And she had completely forgotten the other insight she had momentarily seen of the man when his temper had flared.

A man who gave no second chances and slashed offenders with a swift but merciless blow.

CHAPTER FIVE

For some inexplicable reason the traffic in town went mad on Thursday morning. Running late to begin with, Sloan found driving the short distance to work a tedious chore. Gritting her teeth but resigned, she wove her way through vehicles that appeared ridiculously confused.

Reaching the parking lot of the college, Sloan quickly collected her things and raced into the Fine Arts building. She and Jim had a rehearsal scheduled before their first classes, and they needed every second of time. The performance was only two days away. Depositing her street clothing and papers in her office, she moved straight into Fine Arts 202, where Jim was already engaging in warm-up exercises.

"Good morning," she called quickly, making her way to the bar where she began her own series of stretches starting with limbering pliés.

"Good morning, Mrs. Tallett," Jim returned her call, his voice laced with a teasing amusement. "Or is it soon to be Mrs. Adams?"

Sloan stretched high in a relevé, watching the graceful movement of her hand from side to over her head. "Do I detect a caustic note in that query?" she asked lightly.

"Caustic? Who me? Never," Jim replied, leaping away from the bar to approach the tape player, where he set the music for their number—a medley of classical, jazz, blues, and rock created especially for them by the music department. "Ready?" he asked.

"Ready."

The music began. Sloan whirled into his arms, then spun beneath his guidance in a slow pirouette with a high kick.

"Be careful, Sloan."

Sloan missed a beat of the music and almost fell instead of swirling back into his arms. She kept her expression implacable and swirled across the floor, not answering until she returned to his side to be lifted high in the air. "I don't know what you're talking about."

"I think you do."

"I don't."

"You've got a tiger by the tail, Mrs. Tallett."

Sloan stopped the dance and walked purposefully to the tape player to halt the flow of the music, crossing her arms and facing Jim. "Okay, Mr. Baskins, let's have it. What are you talking about?"

"Oh, Sloan, don't go getting indignant," Jim said with a sigh. "I'm your friend. I'm just warning you to be careful."

"With Wesley?" It was really more of a statement than a question.

"Yes, with Wesley Adams. I watched you last night, Sloan, and I know you. I saw all those seductive smiles and that lazy sensuous charm. You're snaring your beast all right; I just hope you know what you're doing."

She could have cut Jim off by simply telling him it was none of his business, but Sloan didn't want to. He was a friend, but more than that, she had to see what he was reading from her behavior, because if she couldn't convince Jim, she feared she would never get by the astute, probing eye of Wes. . . .

"I thought you liked him," she said innocently.

"I do," Jim told her. "He's the type of man you respect immediately, and he's natural—honest. But don't fool yourself," Jim advised. "He's nothing like your Terry."

"You didn't know Terry," Sloan observed dryly.

"But I know of him—just like I know of Wes Adams," Jim said with a sigh. "I just want you to be aware that you're not dealing with the same type of man."

Sloan frowned. "I don't understand what you're getting at, Jim. Are you trying to say Wes isn't the nice person he appears to be?"

"I'm not saying that at all. From what I've read, he's even a bit of a philanthropist. But"—the warning was clear—"he's not the type man you cross, or play with loosely."

Sloan smiled slowly but surely. Jim wasn't doubting her emotion—he was just wondering how far she planned to carry it. Scampering back across the floor to him, she planted a quick kiss on his cheek. "You can stop worrying—*Dad,*" she teased. "I'm not playing loosely with him at all. And I haven't a thought in the world about crossing him."

Jim flushed. "Okay—lecture over. And please! Put the music back on! We have about fifteen minutes left."

But it was Jim who kept talking as they rehearsed. It seemed he was as well-read on Wesley Adams as Cassie. Wes, according to Jim, was a veritable tiger when it came to business. He was considered one of the most ethical men in the field of Thoroughbreds, but demanding in return. He dealt fairly, and expected the same in return. Woe to the man who attempted anything less.

Sloan paid little attention to his dissertation. She was wondering if she had judged Wes to be similar to Terry. Not really, she decided. Terry and she had been little more than children at first, growing together, but still squabbling like children together. Both men were courteous, but Terry *had* been completely carefree, without a serious bone in his body, without that piercing vitality that was part of Wes.

She was startled to realize that in her comparisons, Wesley was coming out by far the stronger man. Silly, she told herself. Terry had died at twenty-eight . . . he had never had a chance to really be a man . . . not in that assured, virile sense that Wes was.

It was strange, she noted vaguely late that night as she sat with Wes on her sofa sipping coffee, that Jim had asked her if she was comparing Wes to Terry. Because Wes brought up the same subject, suddenly, abruptly.

He set his mug on the coffee table and took both her hands in his. "You know, Sloan, that I'm not Terry."

At first confused and disoriented, Sloan made a quick comeback. "Of course you're not."

He shook his head with a tender smile. "I'm mean, I don't

259

think—in fact, I'm *sure* that I'm nothing like Terry. I want you to understand that."

Still confused, Sloan smiled, quivering inwardly at both the electricity that shot through her with the sear of his gaze and the implications of the deep sincerity of his words.

"I know you're not Terry, or not like him," she said softly. The right answer was important now she knew; every man—or woman, for that matter—wanted to be loved for what he or she was. "Terry was part of another lifetime. I loved him, but I'd never look to replace him." A slight beading of perspiration broke out across her forehead, and her hands went clammy. She needed to say more. . . . "I love you, Wes." There. It hadn't been hard, it had been incredibly easy.

And it was out . . . it was said. He intended to have her, he had told her, so she waited with anxious anticipation for his response. Surely he would take her into a passionate embrace . . . or make a new declaration in return.

Wes responded neither way, yet the intensity of his voice and the tender reverence with which he lightly lifted her chin to meet his eyes left her trembling, her mouth dry, her senses paralyzed.

"I can't tell you what hearing that means, Sloan. I think I've waited half my life to hear those words from you, and I would have waited another eternity.

Sloan tried to smile but found that she couldn't. His eyes burned into hers, deeply green, deeply charged with electric emotion. She was unable to look away, unable to release herself even as she wondered once again if he was seeing through her, reading all the thoughts and sins that existed within her soul. No, he couldn't be, because if he could read her soul, he would not be sitting there, he would be racing out the door.

He did stand, breaking the moment's spell. "I'd better run," he said, his hand settling gently on the top of her head and lightly massaging her hair against her temple. "Tomorrow is a workday for you, and I have an eight A.M. meeting a few miles out of town." He reached to grasp her hands and pull her to her feet. "Come on, walk me to the door."

Rising and slipping into the easy shelter of his arm, Sloan allowed her worry to cease. Her mind turned to the comfort and pleasure she found with his touch and easy camaraderie.

He paused with his hand on the doorknob and looked at her with a rueful grin. "I guess this is it until Saturday night," he murmured softly.

"Oh?" Sloan queried, somewhat surprised that he wouldn't be with her the next night—and startlingly disappointed. Had she come to depend on him so much that a night away seemed like endless time?

"I have another meeting tomorrow night," he explained. "One that might not end till midnight."

"You're welcome to stop by." Sloan murmured, hearing herself say the words without thought.

"No." He smiled broadly, his eyes very gentle, as if the thought on her part had meant very much. "Your dance is on Saturday—I'm sure it's quite a rush with the children and then the students. I don't want to be the one to keep you from a peak performance, and"—he brushed a kiss against her temple—"I also have selfish reasons for wanting you well rested. I want to keep you out till all hours on Saturday night!"

"Oh," Sloan repeated, aware that her pulse was racing madly and she was anticipating his mind-numbing good-night kiss.

But again, he did the unexpected. Instead of pulling her into the tight embrace of his arms, he brushed her forehead again with the briefest of feather-light caresses. And yet, the passion was there, barely hooded by sensuously lazy lids over the ocean-deep eyes as he pulled away. "Till Saturday night," he said huskily.

Sloan watched as his tall form disappeared down the path and into his car. She was dismayed to realize that she was hopelessly frustrated. Her anticipation had taunted her senses unbearably. It was with a raw, physical pain that she watched him leave, a fervent prayer on her lips; let it be soon . . . please, let it be soon. . . .

But could she force a wedding soon enough while still pretending to be the one to fall heedlessly under the spell of a relentless pursuer?

Sloan would have never admitted it to herself, but no matter what appearances were, no matter what Wes said or did, no matter how much confidence she felt in herself as a human being and a woman, she was running a little scared. At first Wes had been little more than an appropriate pawn, but the more she saw of him, the more she became aware that she had stepped a little out of her league without really realizing it.

She would have to be very careful never to take him for granted, make any type of assumption. Ironically, where she often felt old at twenty-nine, he, just five years older, was young —no, not young, but at a "prime" age for a male. Twenty-nine wasn't old, she reminded herself—it was being a "widow" that so often made her feel so—that and the responsibility of the children.

Nevertheless, Wes had everything to offer someone, while she had nothing.

She slept in a torment that night, altering between the conviction that he really did love her, and the fear that he would wake up and discover that she was nothing but a liability. And then again she would be plagued by guilt—because all she had to offer was love—and even that she wasn't sure she could ever give, even though she enjoyed him, respected him, admired him.

The morning went all wrong, and she was glad Wes wasn't making an appearance at her house. Trying to keep up "perfect" appearances all week, she had let many things slide. She had "cleaned" every night by stuffing things under the beds or into closets—and now, as she tried to dress the children, she discovered that she seemed to be missing the mate to every shoe she found.

And she didn't seem to have a clean sock in the house for Jamie.

But eventually everyone was ready. Sloan dropped the kids off at Cassie's—they would attend the performance with their aunt, uncle, and cousins—and hurried to the school, past the Fine Arts building today, and on to the main auditorium.

Where once again she met pandemonium. The dance was a major function for the school, and the students finally chosen to be a part of the performance were, naturally, nervous and jittery. They all needed a pat on the back as Sloan went over the program.

She had heard that time could stand still, but it dismayed her to discover today that it could flash by. She barely found the minutes to slip into her own costume, a mist of striking red and blue silks, before Jim was rushing past her to announce the students. The music department was out in full to lend support with accompaniment, and Jim waited with patience while the crowd quieted after the houselights dimmed.

She and Jim were the finale. As always for Sloan, she was immediately lost in the music. She loved to dance; she lived, came alive when she danced.

But today it was something more.

She knew that Wes watched.

Every movement was for him. Each kick was a little higher, each whirl and dip and spin a touch more sensual. For the first time in her life, her dance was a calculated one, planned to seduce one man into believing she was something special, that he couldn't live without her.

The lie came home to her as the music ended and the auditorium rang with applause. Sloan, her head bowed over her knee in a split, lost the magic that had been hers as she danced. She was just a widow with three children, scrambling for a dubious existence—not in the least special.

But Wes was for real. A football hero matured into a very special man, a man with dignity, pride, compassion, strength and humor and love. . . . And she couldn't let him fall out of love with her. He had to keep believing and loving. She would make it up to him.

"Sloan." Jim nudged her with a laugh. "You can get up now—I'd hate to see you stiffen in that position. Makes walking rough."

She gave her boss a dry grimace and accepted his hand to rise. Smiling along with him, she curtsied to the audience, and together they seemed to float off the floor. "So how did we do?" she inquired briskly, lest he inquire into her mind wandering.

"Why don't you ask Mr. Adams?" Jim suggested with an inclination of his head.

"Wes!" Sloan fought hard to keep her voice from shrieking as she saw him over Jim's shoulder. "I—I thought I wasn't going to see you until tonight!"

He was impeccable as he approached her in the busy backstage wing, his tan suit a striking complement to his dark hair and deep eyes. The bronze tone of his arresting profile was never more apparent, nor the muscle tone that lurked beneath its covering. Sloan was suddenly aware that her coiled hair was damp from exertion—as was her costume. But she didn't have much time to reflect on her own appearance; he was already at her side, already talking.

"You weren't going to see me," he murmured huskily, as if temporarily unaware that Jim—or anyone else for that matter—still hovered near. "But I couldn't leave without telling you that you were magnificent. Superb. Beautiful—"

"Thanks," Jim chimed in, drawing abrupt looks from them both. Sloan frowned with annoyance, but Wes laughed. "Sorry, Jim, you weren't beautiful, but it was a hell of a performance."

The two men shook hands, and Sloan was split between being glad of their friendship while also annoyed that Wes accepted the interruption so easily. He should be a little jealous of Jim, Sloan thought fleetingly. I was dancing with him. If Wes really loved me. . . .

He did love her. Really love her. And he trusted her. He knew she needed room for her own self-expression to be all she could be, and he had the confidence to allow it.

"I'm going," he told them both quickly, glancing at the students who awaited their instructors' words before dispersing. "Jim—be seeing you. Sloan—I'll be by at about eight. I'll get George and Cassie first." With a wave he was gone, his broad-shouldered frame drawing speculative and appreciating gazes as he retreated out of the stage wings.

"Watch it, Sloan," Jim muttered mischievously. "I can see your mind ticking. The beast is wrapped around your finger, but I think it's the tail you're wrapping, and if you're not careful, he's going to feel the pull."

"Jim—" Sloan began to protest with a frown.

"I'll bet you didn't know he was a Scorpio." Jim overrode her objection. "Scorpios are known for their sting."

Sloan smiled dryly. "Go dismiss the kids, will you, Mr. Astrology. I'm not pulling tails, and I'm not going to get stung. You tell me you like the man, but then you sound as if you think he is a beast!"

"No—you misunderstand. I do like the man—maybe because there's no hedging or backing down about him. But *I'm* not in

264

your position!" With that enigmatic advice, Jim quirked his brows and turned to the waiting students.

Sloan showered and dressed carefully, choosing a soft knit with a flaring skirt for the evening. She was nervous, knowing that this night was it—the make it or break it for herself. Qualms of conscience assailed her while she did try to convince herself that she had him wrapped around her finger.

After tucking the kids in, she returned to her own room to make a last-minute check on her appearance. The dress molded to her curvacious form like a glove; her hair, brushed from the chignon, fell about her face in soft waves, giving her the impression of innocence. Radiant happiness gave her face a beautiful glow, and she laughed uneasily.

"Maybe I am in love with him!" she told her reflection. Love was, after all, an elusive word composed of many emotions. It was also something which, nurtured correctly, could grow to endless bounds.

The doorbell rang, and she gave her dress a final straightening before running breathlessly to answer the clanging summons. Wesley filled the doorway with his imposing frame, causing her heart to skip for a second. In a black tux and sky-blue shirt he was impeccable, handsome beyond all earthly rights in a way that was still rugged and slightly savage in spite of his formal dress.

Sloan didn't realize she had been staring until his special teasing grin spread across his face and he murmured, "I think we should come in. Florence can hardly watch the children from outside!"

Sloan blushed, lowered her eyes, and moved away from the door. Wes ushered Florence inside, then followed suit himself.

"Any instructions, young lady?" Florence asked cheerfully.

"Ah . . . no," Sloan said quickly. "The kids are asleep, and you know where everything is. Make yourself at home, and Florence . . . thank you, very much."

"Nonsense!" Florence said briskly. "You two run along and have a good time. Your sister and brother-in-law are already in the car."

Sloan could not remember a more pleasant evening in her

265

entire life. A more congenial foursome could not have existed; wine and conversation could not have flowed more fluidly. Dancing with Wes, sitting beside him and receiving his casual, intimate touch, was the most natural thing in the world. For a time she was content thinking how lucky it was that Wesley seemed to belong with her group, then she realized, with a bit of awe, that it wasn't Wesley who had found his niche, it was she. She belonged with him. And she loved that belonging. No one had ever made her feel so very alive, so vibrantly aware. Not even Terry. No, not even Terry had held her with such competent arms, had thrilled and excited her with a simple glance or possessive touch on a shoulder.

Cassie suddenly stifled a yawn with embarrassment. "Excuse me!" she apologized.

"Company boring you, huh?" George teased.

"Oh, no!" Cassie protested. "This has been the nicest night! It's just that I'm not used to late hours."

"I think that's our cue," Wes told Sloan with mischievous eyes. "Time to take the Harringtons home."

George glanced at his wife, insinuatively wiggling his brows. "I'm amazed these lovebirds have taken this long, aren't you?"

"George!" Cassie remonstrated. "Hush! You're embarrassing them!"

"We're not embarrassed," Wes said with a leisurely smile. "And you're not keeping us. We've got all night."

Sloan felt as if her heart had crashed into her stomach. All night! Did he think she was spending the night with him? Her throat went dry and her hands clammy. Had she played the seductress too well? She couldn't have him pressuring her. If he pushed, she might capitulate! And then he might decide that there really wasn't anything so special about her after all.

. . .

But at the moment, she was cornered. The check was paid; they were rising to leave. And she had imbibed too freely of the wine. She shook her head. Her thoughts were fuzzy, and she needed a sharp, clear mind.

As they drove to drop off Cassie and George, she was quiet and withdrawn, mentally planning strategy with a desperate speed. She was still quiet when they were finally alone, until it occurred to her that she didn't even know where they were headed.

Moistening her lips and breathing deeply, she asked with a wobbly effort at nonchalance, "Where are we going?"

Wesley's jade gaze fell to her with a burning intensity. Although he grinned with his usual ease, his voice was hoarse and husky when he replied. "The nice romantic spot I promised. My house."

Sloan became dizzy with fear. Was he wrapped around her finger as tightly as she thought? She nervously smoothed already smooth hair. At any rate, she reasoned, the man wasn't a rapist. He wouldn't force her to do anything.

But she wasn't afraid of him using force, and she knew it. She was afraid of her own reactions. Heaven help me! she prayed fervently as he ushered her toward his darkened house. But would heaven help her after all that she had done? More likely, the powers that be would listen and laugh. . . .

Wesley switched on dim lights as they entered and calmly walked ahead of her. "Brandy?" he asked, as she stood in the doorway surveying the elegant room. Wesley's taste in decor was stunning—casual and warm, but elegant. The entrance hallway, carpeted in a creamy pile, led to a sunken living room, plush with thickly cushioned, wicker furniture. Palms and ferns unobstrusively added a beguiling hospitality, as did the glass window doors which led to a screened patio, complete with a sparkling, kidney-shaped pool and a whirling hot tub.

"Come in," Wesley invited with amusement, divesting himself of jacket, tie, and cummerbund and grimacing as he undid the top three buttons of his shirt. "The attack dogs have the evening off."

Sloan flushed as she moved uneasily down to the plush, sunken area. She sat, thinking she would have to remain seriously on guard in Wesley's territory. Her mind was so benumbed that she started when he handed her a snifter of brandy.

"It's me," he said kindly. "The same old Wesley you've been seeing all week." He sat beside her, sipped at his own glass, and took her chin gently with his free hand. "The same old Wesley who loves you very much," he added softly. "The same old Wesley who wants to marry you."

267

For some ungodly reason, she was close to tears. Without thinking, she blurted, "Why?"

"I could tell you a million things," he said, hypnotizing her with the gleaming jade of his eyes and the tender stroke of his fingers on the soft flesh of her face. "I can say because you're bright and beautiful and more graceful and lovely than any other living creature. And it will be true. But there's only one real reason—the only reason anyone should ever marry. Because I love you. I want to share my life with you. I want to be a part of yours."

The tears finally streamed down Sloan's cheeks. "Oh, Wesley . . ."

"Hey! I didn't mean to make you cry!" he exclaimed gently, setting their brandies aside and taking her comfortingly into his arms. He rocked her soothingly and stroked the lush tendrils of hair from her forehead. "Hey!" he repeated softly. "Don't cry. Just answer me. I won't rush you, but I'll go clear out of my mind if I keep thinking that maybe you will when you don't—"

"I will!" Sloan interrupted quickly. What the hell was she doing? she demanded of herself. She was crying like an idiot, feeling like a complete louse, just because he had said a few sentimental things. And why? He wanted her, he loved her. She wouldn't be twisting his arm.

The only reason . . . he had said. Love. That was why. She was betraying him in the most cruel way possible.

Hating herself, she lifted sapphire eyes to his. "I will marry you, Wesley. There's nothing I want more."

His arms tightened around her. "When?" he gasped hoarsely.

"As soon as possible," she replied. "Tomorrow, if we could. . . ."

He was startled, but pleasantly so. She knew he had expected her to set a date months in the future.

"Monday we'll get the license," he promised her. "And a week from today, we'll become man and wife." His lips fell upon hers with a passionate urgency, plundering the softness of her mouth. Sloan moaned faintly beneath his assault, in agony as she tried to keep a clear head. It was almost impossible. His crisp, clean scent was intoxicating her, his hands were arousing her to a feverish pitch as they roamed to secret places and sought her body through the field of silk.

Somehow, without her even knowing it, Wes had found the zipper to her dress and the silk fell from her with a whispered rustle. She heard his sharp intake of breath, then felt the pressure of his hands as he forced her down to the pillowy cushion of the couch. His hot kisses, hungry and out of control, blazed paths across her flesh. As if she were intoxicated, it slowly filtered into Sloan's mind that they were fast reaching a point of no return. Even as she stumbled mentally, Wesley's sure fingers found the front clasp of her lacy bra, and it joined the silk dress on the floor. His mouth found the firm flesh of her breasts, teased and raked her nipples until she cried out with an agony of despair and longing. She wanted him so desperately! To stop the excruciating pleasure would be to bring excruciating pain.

His hand ran along her leg, causing her to shake uncontrollably. Her slip wound around her waist; his hand found the elastic of her panties, and she gasped at the surge of desire awakened within her at the touch of his fingers so low on her abdomen, a touch which caused her to inadvertently strain toward him.

Then the ultimate warning in her head finally sounded. He was still clothed, but his knee was wedging firmly between hers, and his hand was subtly but surely exploring further. Bracing herself firmly, Sloan finally found her voice, begging him to stop.

At first she was totally ignored. Terror that she had played too closely with fire surged through her, and she gripped her fingers painfully into his hair. "Please, Wesley!" she sighed. "I beg you!" Tears formed again in her eyes and cascaded down her cheeks. "Please!" she whispered.

Wesley went rigid; his harsh breathing gave her the answer that he had at last heard her plea.

He didn't speak as he lifted his weight from her and tossed her discarded clothing into her lap. He didn't even look at her until she had reclasped her bra and slipped hurriedly back into her black silk dress.

Then he sat beside her, and she knew when he probed her face with an icy green stare that he was angry. But he didn't yell, he didn't make recriminations. He sat with folded arms and demanded, "Why?"

"I—I just can't!" she croaked shamefully.

"Go on," he prompted grimly.

Her abject misery was not, at the moment, a performance. Her hands were trembling so badly she could barely get a sip of sorely needed brandy to her lips. Yet still, her mind was ticking away with all speed. Her answer would have to be good. Looking tentatively at Wesley, she shivered and her eyes fluttered closed. *Think!* she told herself. She had everything at stake in the next few minutes.

"Please, tell me what's wrong," he persisted, and she chanced another glance into his probing jade orbs. He had gentled, his voice had become the kind one she was accustomed to hearing.

Taking a few deep breaths, she decided she could almost be honest. Looking straight into her brandy, she plunged ahead with a shy, very convincing explanation for her behavior which bordered on truth.

"I'm frightened, Wesley. I don't know what impression I give, but I've been alone for a long time." She knew she was blushing profusely. "The only man I've ever known was Terry, and—well, we were married. I know that sounds ridiculously old-fashioned, but . . ."

Wesley emitted a strangled sound, and Sloan glanced at him, cringing, fearing she had pushed his patience too far. But he was no longer angry, he was chuckling.

"What's so funny?" she queried with piqued exasperation.

"Nothing, darling, nothing," he assured her. He sat beside her again, ran his fingers through his dark hair, and took her hand to idly massage her fingers. "I don't think you're ridiculously old-fashioned. I'm kind of glad. I'd be insanely jealous if I had to learn about your other lovers. I'm even jealous of Terry, although God knows I can't begrudge the man a thing. He had heaven on earth and he had to lose it." His eyes met hers. "I laughed because you had me frightened too. I thought you might have a serious hang-up about *me*. If marriage is important to you before making a sexual commitment, I can honor that. That is"—he chuckled again, the throaty sound that was deep and endearing—"as long as you are sure that you do want me when we are married and as long as we do hurry with the wedding!"

270

Sloan stared at him with wide, blank eyes. "I do want you, Wes, I want you more than I've ever wanted another human being."

"I'm all yours, darling," he swore, with a light kiss on her forehead. "But I'd better get you home, because I want you to be all mine. All of you," he added, running a finger along the flesh of her bare arm. "Every delightful inch!" He kissed the tip of her nose. "Just one week . . ."

Sloan continued to shiver all the way home. Just one week. Then it would be pay-up time. And she had the strange feeling that, once she had legally sold herself to Wesley Adams, there would be no backing down.

Ever again.

CHAPTER SIX

Sloan called in late on Monday morning, and within an hour she and Wesley had filled in all the necessary papers and taken blood tests. Wes suggested they stop for a bite to eat before she went in to work as there were a few things he wanted to discuss.

"I've got to drive home for a few days," he told her as he folded his menu and handed it to the waitress. At her look of surprise he continued, "We'll be going on a honeymoon. I need to cover myself and get back to Kentucky and check with my brother on the farm. I also want to tell him about us firsthand and talk him and my sister-in-law into coming up for the wedding."

Sloan was startled. She had almost forgotten that Wes had another home and a family. "When are you leaving?" she asked unhappily. She was surprised at how it hurt to know they'd be parted. In a short time, Wes had come to pleasantly dominate her life, and she hadn't even realized it.

"Today," he replied with a cross between a smile and a leer. "I won't be back until Friday, which is probably best for both of us! I won't be trying to attack you every night, and you won't have to worry about fighting me off!"

"Oh, Wes!" Sloan murmured miserably.

"Hey! I'm teasing!" He chuckled, tenderly lifting her chin. "I have to take care of this now, though, because I don't want to worry about anything after the wedding. Where would you like to go?"

"Pardon?"

"Our honeymoon, darling," he said with a patient grin. "Is there anywhere particular you'd like to go?"

"Ah—no," Sloan stammered. She hadn't even thought about

a honeymoon. In fact, she hadn't really thought about anything beyond the wedding.

"Then I have a suggestion. I have a friend who recently bought a hotel just outside of Brussels. He swears it's one of the most beautiful cities in the world, and he's surrounded by hilly forests and sparkling little streams. We can spend a week there, and then a week in Paris. How does that sound?" Wesley sipped his coffee and watched her over the rim of his cup.

"It sounds lovely," Sloan replied with a slow smile. Belgium and France! She had never been out of the eastern United States! Wesley was opening doors for her which she had never even dreamed existed. "But, what about the children?"

"Florence will watch them, of course," Wes told her with a wave of his hand. "I'll have her move her things into your house tonight so that she can get used to your routine. Cassie and George will be around if anything she can't handle comes up, and hopefully, Dave and Susan will be here with their kids, and Jamie, Laura, and Terry can meet their new cousins and aunt and uncle. My sister lives in Arizona near my folks, so I doubt if she'll be able to make it or my mom and dad for that matter." He grimaced as he idly ran a finger over the top of her hand. "Dad has a heart condition, so he doesn't travel frequently. We'll fly out to meet them in a few months."

Sloan's head was reeling. There were so many things she hadn't taken into consideration! A small chill knotted in her stomach. "Wes," she said slowly. "What happens when we come back? Do we"—she licked dry lips—"Do we move to Kentucky?" Kentucky, away from everything she knew, away from Cassie and George. It almost sounded like an alien planet! And what about his family? What if they disliked her? What if they resented her barging into their lives with a household of children? What if they felt she were too old for Wes, too encumbered? His parents would want him to marry a younger girl, she was sure, one who would provide him with his own family.

Wesley's hand was warm over hers. As usual, he was reading the worries she couldn't voice aloud. "I promise you," he guaranteed her softly. "You'll love Kentucky. So will the kids. And my brother is a wonderful guy; Susan's terrific. We'll be in the same house for a while, but don't worry, it's huge. You don't have to see anyone else if you don't want to. I'll have George put my house here on the market while we're gone, but we'll keep yours and spend as much time in Gettysburg as we can. Okay?"

The secure pressure of his hand filled her with contentment. "Okay."

"And," he added with a conniving wink, "we have several good, professional dance companies in the nearby cities."

"Bribery will get you everywhere!" Sloan laughed happily. Wes *was* magic. He could work everything out.

Their sandwiches arrived, and Sloan found she had a good appetite for her ham and cheese. She was going to miss Wes terribly, but as he had said, his absence would be for the best. When he came back, there would be less than twenty-four hours left for anything to go wrong!

They discussed a few more details as they ate. The wedding would take place at Wesley's house with just their families and a few close friends in attendance. Sloan was to cater whatever she wanted, as long as she didn't put a strain on herself. After a quick reception, they would fly overseas right away.

"Oh! One more thing," Wesley added, his green eyes twinkling like gemstones as he reached into his vest pocket for a small jewel case. Flicking it open with one hand, he gently took her slim fingers with the other and slid the ring from the velvet box. "I'd like you to start wearing this," he said, extracting first the plain gold band which had adorned her finger since the day Terry had put it on. Then his ring went on, and Sloan stared at her finger with a mixture of nostalgia and joy. Terry's ring was gone. But Terry was gone, and somehow it didn't hurt so badly anymore. Oh, his memory would always sadden her; he had been her youth, her first great love, the father of her three children. But nothing could bring him back. She would always remember him with love, but . . . her eyes widened with shock. Water filled within them, but she was laughing too, with pure happiness. The loss of her love didn't hurt so much anymore because she had found new love without even knowing as it snuck up on her. She wanted to scream and shout with the joy of her realization, but Lord! Wes would never understand. Instead, she clutched his large hand in hers and covered it with tearstained, sloppy kisses. "Oh, Wes!" she murmured breathlessly, mindless if the other patrons of the coffee shop thought her crazy or not, "I do love you so!"

"And I love you, my dearest princess," he whispered in return, taking her hands tenderly to his mouth to kiss them reverently. Then the teasing glimmer leaped back into his eyes as he studied the ring objectively. "Perfect, if I do say so myself." It was a diamond, probably about two carats, Sloan judged, surrounded by a bed of sapphires. He traced the circle of blue stones with his fingers. "For your eyes, love. They match incredibly well." He released her hand reluctantly. "You'd better get into work so that you can quit, and I'd better head out of town. Or else, darling," he said huskily, one sensual dark brow raised in a rakish angle, "I shall carry you from this table and savagely ravish you in the back seat of the Lincoln."

Sloan half smiled with a rueful quirk of her lips and angled a furrowing brow herself. "I don't think I'd mind being ravished in the Lincoln," she murmured in teasing reply, fully aware that she now meant her words with no qualms. Love may not conquer all, but it did sweep away her doubts and insecurities. "But I've got a problem, Wes. I can't just quit my job. I'm a teacher. Jim can cover me for a couple of weeks, but I have to go back, at least until the quarter ends, which will be the end of summer. I have finals to give," she apologized lamely, hoping he would understand her commitment.

"Sloan," Wes reassured her quickly, sensing her distress, "the end of summer will be fine. I can set up an office in your house somewhere and catch up on paperwork. And phone calls. And I can fly in and out for emergencies. Just make sure they know you won't be back for the fall term."

Sloan smiled, astounded that he would so willingly arrange his life-style around hers. "Thank you, Wes," she said softly. "I promise I won't always be this difficult."

He laughed. "I promise I won't always let you be this difficult! Oh—one more thing," he added quickly. "How could I forget. It's about the most important thing!" He handed her a business card. "My attorney," he explained. "I've drawn up adoption papers for the children. I don't want to try to take Terry's place with them, but they can take back his name as adults if they choose. It will be to their benefit to be my legal heirs, insurance and all that. If you have any objection, I'll understand, but I knew we didn't have much time, so I set the wheels turning last night. Hopefully we can get a judgment by Friday." He grinned a little dryly. "Sometimes it helps to be well known."

Sloan suddenly felt as if she were shattering, breaking apart bit by bit. She had been so strong for so long, and now it was all being lifted from her shoulders. She was off-balance with the weight of burden gone, stunned by the depths of caring Wes showed her with his every thought. Tears glazed her eyes; she didn't deserve this wonder that she had schemed and deceived to bring about, but it was hers now, and she would cling tenaciously to it.

"Sloan," Wes began, his brow tight and features tense as he misread her silence. "If you prefer that I don't adopt the kids—"

"Oh, no!" Sloan protested hastily, shaking her head and squeezing her eyes tightly shut as she fought to weld the pieces of her self-control back together. "I think it's wonderful that you thought of such a thing," she said hastily. "I'll see the lawyer today for sure." She summoned up a sturdy smile. "And I'll get Florence on to the moving, and get George on to selling your house. And"—her voice fell deep and husky—"I'll have everything set for the wedding, and I'll be missing you like crazy until Friday night!"

Their eyes met across the table, Sloan's for once covered by no shields to hide deceit. They were star-glazed and incredulous. . . . She had never known simple feeling and happiness could be so damned good.

A moment later she was kissing him good-bye, clinging to his powerful frame with the real pain of parting. "It will only be a few days, sweetheart," Wes mumbled gently, his face buried in the silkiness of her hair. "Just a few days . . ."

Then he was gone, and Sloan was drifting on a high plateau of clouds. "Just a few days," she repeated to herself, and then she would have her newfound love forever, sanctioned by the laws of God and State. She didn't think it possible to be any happier.

Jim accepted her news with calm and pleasant resignation. "I admit," he said with a grin, "I didn't expect this all to come about so quickly, but"—he gave her a broad grin—"I wasn't really planning on having you for the fall quarter. You know," he mused, "I might not be here myself."

"Really?" Sloan queried, surprised. "Why not?"

"If I can swing the financing, I'm going to open a school and perhaps form a professional company."

"That's marvelous!" Sloan applauded him. "Maybe you'll let me 'guest' teach when I'm in Gettysburg!"

"There will always be a place open for you, Sloan," he assured her. "Anyway, at this time, it's only talk. . . . So when is the wedding? Saturday, you say? Do I get to be there?"

"Of course." Sloan grinned. "Family and adoptive family. You fit the latter category!"

The children—Jamie being the only one with a coherent memory of his real father—thought the idea of their mother marrying Wes and providing them with a new father was wonderful. They were thrilled that both Florence and Wes would be living with them, enthusiastic about moving to Kentucky where they could keep a pony.

The only person who accepted Sloan's news dubiously was—oddly enough—Cassie. Sloan wasn't sure exactly what went on in her sister's mind; Cassie didn't say much, but that was why Sloan was bothered. Cassie should have been as ecstatic as she—after all, Cassie had practically thrown them together.

Despite her unusual quiet and reserve, Cassie spent the days helping Sloan. She promised to handle all the catering arrangements for the wedding and also handle the details like cleaning, flowers, liquor, etc. George was happy to handle the sale of Wes's house; Wesley's attorney was a pleasant sort who seemed to take everything in stride, as if instant adoptions were a daily thing. He wished her the best of luck, smiling sheepishly as he told her he could well understand his client's rush.

With all that going on, Sloan didn't worry overmuch about her sister. She was determined to take all of her classes each day, since she would be putting such a burden on Jim when she was gone. Along with working, she was busy helping Florence move in and packing the few personal items Wes had in his house. They wouldn't be back in it once the wedding had taken place.

On Thursday morning Cassie called her at work. "I think you've forgotten something," she advised.

"What?" Sloan asked, frowning into the wire. She'd kept checklists on everything she was doing, and as far as she could tell, things were going fine.

"Shopping. If I'm not mistaken, your wardrobe isn't going to make a European trip."

"Oooooh." Sloan had been standing and she sat. Cassie was right; her wardrobe was practically nonexistent—she had been carefully pulling together her few decent outfits each time she saw Wes.

"I'll pick you up at work," Cassie said. "George can bring the kids to Florence for you, and you and I can have dinner and do a little spending."

Sloan thought for a moment. She had her paycheck in her purse, and now there wasn't any reason why she shouldn't spend it. By habit she hadn't cashed it, mentally balancing mortgage payments and bills. And now, suddenly, what was a huge sum to her was pennies to Wes. She chuckled softly. She could easily spend the entire sum, and Wes would still think her thrifty.

"Thanks, Cass," Sloan said. "Sounds like a good idea."

It wasn't until she set the receiver down that she realized Cassie had sounded funny. She wasn't really interested in shopping—she was interested in having dinner together and . . . talking?

Maybe she had been wrong, Sloan thought later as she and Cassie both decided on spinach salad at a local restaurant. Cassie was remaining as reserved as she had been about the whole thing. Several times as they chatted she was sure Cassie was going to say something about the problem bothering her, but she didn't. Still, it was odd. They talked about everything but the wedding.

Cassie livened up when Sloan went on her spending spree, giving harsh sibling advice on colors and styles. "This is fun," Cassie commented after helping Sloan put together several outfits that matched from the panties on out. "Buying anything you want . . ." Her voice trailed away. "Negligees!" she interrupted herself with a giggle. "I don't guess you get to wear them long, but that boutique across the street has some stunning pieces!"

Sloan followed her sister with her pile of boxes, frowning. She was ready to stop in the street and demand to know what was wrong, but Cassie was well ahead of her, and then they were surrounded by salespeople. By the time Cassie had made her try on a dozen garments, she was tired, and her sister's peculiar behavior had drifted to the back of her mind. She didn't think of it again until Cassie was dropping her at her car. "Sloan," Cassie began, stopping her as she walked the few feet in the school's parking lot.

Sloan turned back to her, balancing her stack of packages. "Yes."

"Oh . . . never mind." Cassie waved with a weak smile and drove away.

"What is with her?" Sloan mumbled to herself, shrugging as she fumbled to open the car door. When Cassie was ready to say something, Sloan figured, she would. Until then there wasn't much she could do.

At home she displayed everything for Florence's oohs and aahs and sternly told herself to go to bed. Once there, however, she was too nervous and excited to sleep. One more day and Wes would be back, then a single night before the wedding. . . .

She was still nervous when she awoke after her restless night. Knowing that he was coming made her want to see him desperately. Consequently, the day dragged. Classes which usually sped by for her seemed to be interminable. At three o'clock Jim caught her in her office and insisted she go home.

"I can't," Sloan wailed, "I have an intermediate ballet—"

"Which I can handle," he assured her.

"That's not fair to you, Jim," she objected softly.

"Ah, but the world isn't fair!" Jim chuckled. "Go home. You're driving me insane, and the students may never be the same again. They're limping around as if they've been working out for the Olympics! They aren't all floating on clouds of ecstasy, you know."

Sloan blushed. "I guess I did drive them pretty hard," Sloan murmured.

"That's okay." Jim chuckled. "It's good for them. But do us all a favor and go home! What time is Wes coming in?"

"I don't know," Sloan replied with a sigh. "But since you're being so magnanimous, I guess I will go home. Thanks, Jim."

"Thank you," he told her seriously. "I'm glad you're coming back to finish the quarter."

Sloan shrugged. "I like teaching," she murmured. "I like the students, and, well, I certainly owe you that much!"

"You owe yourself, Sloan, and you owe Wes," Jim advised softly. "Remember that. Now—" He stared at her sternly. "Get out!"

"Okay, okay!" Sloan laughed. "I'll get everything going smoothly!"

Her shower went smoothly; that was all that did. She burned dinner, knocked her iced tea all over the table, and put Terry's sleeper on inside out. After she stubbed her toe viciously while pacing the living room, Florence finally spoke up in the stern voice she used occasionally on the children.

"Settle down, young lady," she commanded. "You're wearing yourself to a frazzle. You'll be a pathetic-looking bride in the morning if you keep this up! Wesley *will* get here, but you can't make him get here any faster by chewing off your manicure."

Wincing while she held her toe, Sloan had to agree. "I think I'll fix myself a scotch and see what's on TV."

"That's a good idea. I'll even join you!"

Florence kept up a stream of chatter as they sat over scotches, tactfully keeping Sloan's mind busy. They slowly went over all of the arrangements together and arrived at the conclusion that nothing had been forgotten. Then, as the eleven o'clock news came on, Sloan caught her new housekeeper-friend yawning and winced. She had been so embroiled with her own thoughts that she had given no consideration to Florence!

"Okay, young lady," Sloan said gruffly, imitating Florence's own tone. "Up to bed with you! You've been a doll! An absolute doll. But I'm fine now, I really am, and I can wait by myself."

Florence was uncertain. "Are you sure?"

"Believe me." Sloan laughed. "I'm calm! Three stiff scotches and I'm not *just* calm—I'm almost out on my feet!"

"All right, then." Florence stifled another yawn and sheepishly admitted she was half-asleep already.

"See you in the morning," she said, kissing Sloan's cheek

affectionately. "Give Wes my love and a piece of my mind when he gets in! Although I don't think you'll get much chance to yell at him"—the housekeeper chuckled—"he'll probably just say hi and bye until tomorrow. It is getting dreadfully late, and it will be a full day."

Sloan grinned in return. "I'm not sure yet if I'm going to yell, hit him, or keep my mouth shut and kiss him in relief! Oh!" she asked, concerned for the graying lady who had cheerfully made her own life so much more pleasant with her courtesy, "Shall I turn off the TV? Will the noise disturb you?"

"Don't be silly," Florence protested, shaking her head. "In fact, you could blast it, and the neighbors would know before I did. I'm a heavy sleeper—you've heard my alarm clock. It's worse than a power drill because that's about all that will wake me up." She yawned again. "And all that scotch! My dear, I will probably pass out rather than fall asleep!"

Sloan chuckled. "Well, good. Then I won't worry if I do decide I'm going to yell at Wes."

"Yell away." Florence yawned, moving toward the stairs with a mischievous twinkle in her eyes. "Straighten him out on these late hours of his *before* the wedding!"

It was a good thing, Sloan thought wryly as she watched Florence walk up to bed, that she and Florence had imbibed in the scotches. Her emotions were running the gauntlet—from eager anticipation to anxious worry to frustration and therefore to growing anger. She really might be ready to yell her head off by the time he came in.

What was taking so long? Wes had called on Wednesday night, and everything had been fine. The "farm," as he called it, was running smoothly; his brother and sister-in-law were going to be able to make the wedding. The man had definitely said he'd be in on Friday night.

She was going to have a thing or two to tell him about phoning in the future if he was held up!

"Ummmph!" she said aloud to the clock with disgruntled anger. "He only has forty-five minutes of *Friday* night left!"

Sloan watched the clock for a few more minutes as she listened to the news drone on. With a sigh she despondently sauntered into her bedroom and changed into a slightly worn peignoir set.

281

Her new ones were packed, but if she was going to wind up sleeping in a chair as she fitfully waited, she might as well be dressed comfortably.

Tiptoeing, she checked on the kids and then Florence. Chuckling softly as she reclosed the older woman's door, Sloan had to agree that she slept like death; her soft snores were already deep and steady.

Downstairs, she curled into the sofa before the TV and, turning up the volume, convinced herself that she was going to pay attention to the old Boris Karloff movie coming onto the screen. It was something about a mummy, she realized, yawning with exhaustion herself. Then, somewhere along the line, she drifted into a doze. She awoke ecstatically to see car lights flashing across the walls through the drapes. The sound of tires on gravel assured her she hadn't been dreaming, and she leaped to her feet to throw open the front door with eager relief and an excitement that quickly turned to stunned surprise.

It wasn't Wesley walking up to the house, but Cassie.

Sloan whistled her sister's name in disbelief. "Cassie! What are you doing here? Do you have any idea of what time it is?"

Cassie shrugged, brushing past Sloan. "I came to have a cup of tea with my sister on the night before her wedding."

"Oh, I see," Sloan murmured sardonically, crossing her arms over her chest and following Cassie into the kitchen, still so surprised she forgot to close the door. "Clear as day." Cassie was calmly filling the kettle with water. "That's what you told George," Sloan stated.

"That's what I'm doing, isn't it?" Cassie questioned serenely.

"Precisely," Sloan acknowledged dryly. "Okay, Cass, what is this all about?"

"You have to call off the wedding," Cassie said bluntly, not watching Sloan as she set mugs on the table.

"What?" Sloan shrieked.

"Will you hush up!" Cassie hissed. "You're going to wake your whole house."

Sloan waved a hand in the air impatiently. "No one is going to wake up. The kids have been in bed for hours, and Florence is in another world. Now what in the world are you talking about?"

"You know what I'm talking about," Cassie said miserably. You can't marry Wes. You're my sister, Sloan, and I love you, but I can't stand by and watch you use a wonderful man like Wes because you'll only make both your lives miserable."

"What do you mean?" Sloan asked thickly.

"You're rushing things, Sloan," Cassie said, her brown eyes deep with unhappy turmoil as she met her sister's gaze squarely. "I've wanted to talk to you all week, but I keep telling myself I'm not your parent, guardian, or conscience. And I'd hoped from the moment I saw Wes and knew he was interested in you that something would form between you." She stopped speaking, bit her lip, and drew a long breath to begin again as Sloan stared at her blankly. "Sloan, I *know* you. I've known you all my life. Even when we were kids, you could charm the pants off of anyone you set your mind to. You were never cruel or malicious, but you could turn on that smile and connive just about anything. I saw you get your way with that sweetly subtle cajolery with Mom and Dad and Terry—and me! And it's not bad, Sloan, it's tactful and polite and no one usually knows he or she has even been taken! I'm sure that sometimes you don't even know you're doing it. But this time I'm sure you do, Sloan," she said gravely. "This time you've turned on the charm for all the wrong reasons! You're marrying Wes for his money."

"Cassie!" Sloan gasped, stunned by her sister's intuitive grasp of her initial motives. "Cassie, you're wrong!" she insisted, but she had never lied to her sister, and the fact that she was right about the original scheming made Sloan's protest weak.

Cassie shook her head, her eyes sad. "You said yes to a proposal in a week, Sloan, to a man you were barely polite to at first."

"Oh, Cassie," Sloan murmured, loving her sister and unable to bear her condemnation. "You *were* right. But not now." The screaming hiss of the teakettle momentarily halted her explanation—and also covered all other sounds in the house. Sloan grabbed the water and poured it over tea bags in the mugs and curled into a kitchen chair before continuing. "Cassie, everything was going to hell! I was overdue on the mortgage, the electricity—everything. So yes, I did set out to charm Wes. I had to get him to marry me; I needed his money."

"Oh, Sloan!" Cassie admonished miserably. "Without love?"

Sloan was fumbling for a way to explain how things had changed. "No, I didn't love him when I knew I had to make it be marriage. I—"

The sharp sound of the front door closing froze Sloan before she could go any further. "Wes!" she exclaimed to Cassie in a quiet hiss. Her sister had taken her so off guard that she had forgotten his expected arrival. "Cassie—I'll finish explaining later," she begged in a whisper, her eyes wide and pleading.

Cassie might attack her on moral grounds when they were alone, but as a sister she was true blue. Her voice rose cheerfully. "Sloan—I think he's finally made it here!"

Both sisters set their mugs down and almost knocked each other over in their guilty haste to reach the living room. "Wesley!" Sloan cried happily as she saw his tall form in the doorway. She raced across the room to embrace him, unaware in her own exuberance that he accepted her stiffly.

"You're late!" Cassie teased from her distance. "I'd better get on home so that you two can have your words out!"

Wes brushed Sloan's forehead with a kiss and smiled at Cassie. "No, Cass, don't leave on my account. I did run late, so I'm just stopping by to say that I'm here."

"Stopping by?" Sloan questioned him with a frown. She blushed slightly, not sure how to phrase her confusion with Cassie present. "Wes, your things are all here. Florence and I cleared out your house except for the things we'll need for the wedding. I—I thought you'd stay here tonight," she stammered.

Wes slipped an arm around her and tilted her chin. He smiled, but she noticed how hard the angles of his face could be, how tense the bronzed skin that stretched across them. He was tired, she realized, very tired. His eyes also had a peculiar light, one that glittered icily in the dim light of the doorway. "I wouldn't dream of staying here tonight," he teased, his voice husky. "We want to get that wedding ring on your finger, my love, and they say it's bad luck for the groom to see the bride before the wedding. I don't think we'll be needing any bad luck, do you?"

"No, of course not," Sloan agreed slowly, the chill his eyes had given her dissipated by the intense heat radiating from his body. Actually, she didn't give a damn about bad luck; he was here, and she wanted nothing more than to stay in his arms and quell the terrible aching she felt for him to hold her, to kiss her, to touch her. . . . "It's just that I've missed you so!" she whispered, loath to release him.

"Listen, I really am going—" Cassie began.

"No, no," Wes protested with firm haste. "I haven't had any sleep, and I think I'm going to need some to deal with my charming bride." He turned to Sloan, the smooth curve of his lip forming a smile that didn't reach his eyes. "Kiss me quick, love. I think I'd better get out of here"—his smile broadened, but there was a dry twist to his words—"before I lose my control with you completely, Sloan."

Sloan laughed, unaware that there could be a double meaning to his words. She kissed him, relishing the commanding feel of his lips upon hers, sensing something warm and combustible in his restrained passion. Tomorrow, she told herself, reluctantly allowing him to pull back from their embrace. Less than ten hours would see them man and wife. . . .

"You should have called," she chastised him huskily. "I was worried."

"Were you?" His grip on her shoulders was strong, almost painful; his kiss had been bruising. Neither bothered Sloan. He had missed her as much as she had missed him. "Yes, of course," he murmured. "The wedding isn't until tomorrow."

Sloan frowned. "I know, but you said you'd be in tonight—"

"I am going!" Cassie interrupted.

"No, I am!" Wes chuckled, pulling Sloan to him once more so that she felt the thunderous pounding of his heart. He pulled away just as abruptly. "Cassie—good-night. Sloan. . . ." He ran a finger along her cheek, a tender movement that became tense. "Tomorrow, love." He turned and exited before she could make another protest or chastisement.

Both sisters were silent for several seconds, Sloan mainly because she felt the sun had warmed her only to be covered by a cloud, Cassie because she was relieved that they had heard the door and hushed their conversation. She finally cleared her throat, wondering if Sloan, who was still staring at the door with brilliant, longing eyes, remembered that she was there.

Sloan spun around to face her. "Cassie!" She chuckled, running to hug her sister. "Don't you see? Everything is all right!

I did set out to use Wes, but I did fall in love with him! Hopelessly. Completely. If he didn't have a penny to his name, I would feel the same way about him. He's wonderful and—oh, just everything! I think I'm the luckiest woman in the world!"

Cassie breathed a sigh of happy relief. "I believe you," she said sheepishly. "No woman who isn't in love can carry stars in her eyes like you are now. I'm all for you, sis—I wish you both the best of everything. And I'm going home now, with a nice clear conscience. George already thinks I'm crazy for streaking out of the house in the middle of the night like this. Go get some sleep, kid! You'll be a bride in the morning."

The sisters hugged again, and Sloan watched until her sister was safely in the car. Then she locked the door and waltzed into her room.

She slept easily, ecstatic that Wes was back, and even if he wasn't with her that night, there would never have to be another night when he wasn't. She dreamed of her wonderful luck.

CHAPTER SEVEN

Sloan didn't see Wesley again until the ceremony, which was, according to their desires, simple but beautiful. Fragrant displays of summer flowers were the only decoration; the lilting strains of a single guitar the only music. Cassie acted as matron of honor, Wesley's brother Dave as best man. Sloan, in a cloud of excitement and euphoria, barely heard the words spoken, and although Wes's replies were strong and sure, she had to be nudged by Cassie to speak at the appropriate times.

Then the brief ceremony was over; they were officially man and wife. Wesley bent obediently to kiss her; and as his lips claimed hers, Sloan felt a tension and hint of punishment in the pressure of his arms.

It's the time we've been apart, she thought with loving tolerance. He released her, and their eyes met. For a second it seemed as if Wesley stared at her with cold, fathomless disdain. Then the look was gone, and she dismissed it from her mind as fancy. She was smiling up at *Wes*, handsome and as benevolent as an ancient god in the formfitting tux and exquisite laced shirt which seemed but to enhance every majestic line of his masculinity. Sloan reeled with the impact of his return smile, drunk from his aura and presence. She felt like Sleeping Beauty; awoken by a kiss only to find the real prince of her dreams. Was it a dream? she wondered blissfully. It was all too good to be true. Or did every bride feel the way that she did at the moment, even if it was the second time around?

The reception passed in as much of a blur as the wedding. Wes's brother and sister-in-law were an attractive, charming couple; Dave was a slimmer version of his brother and every bit as personable; Susan, a vivacious, down-to-earth woman Sloan immediately liked. The children pranced about gleefully, delighted to be participating in grown-up affairs, stealing sips of champagne from any available glass that fell their way. Before she knew it, Sloan, higher than ever on her cloud after several glasses of the delicious champagne, was being ushered into Wes's room to change for her honeymoon.

"Oh, Sloan!" Cassie marveled breathlessly as she followed her sister into the room and closed the door behind her. Tears of happiness formed in her deep brown eyes. "You're so beautiful today, so radiant! I'm so happy for you." Flying across the room, she embraced Sloan with a strangling hug.

"Thanks, Cassie," Sloan whispered. Then they were laughing and crying together, and Sloan's dress was spotted by their joyous tears.

Cassie finally extracted herself and smiled at Sloan from arm's distance. "I'm going to miss you. . . ."

"I won't be gone long, and I'll deluge you with postcards—"

"That's not what I mean," Cassie said, choking on a sniffle. "You'll be gone for good when you get back."

"Not for good!" Sloan protested, feeling nostalgic pangs of departure herself but determined to cheer Cassie. "We'll be living in Gettysburg part time!"

"Yeah," Cassie agreed, forcing a smile. "What am I doing?" she moaned. "I'm not supposed to be making you weepy on your wedding day!"

"Zip my zipper then," Sloan directed. "We've a long ride to the airport."

Sloan's travel outfit was a tailored, powder-blue dress with a matching jacket for the sound possibility of cooler weather when their plane landed in Belgium. The sisters chatted as Sloan retouched her makeup and unnecessarily straightened her clothing for a last time. "I'm ready, I guess," Sloan finally said.

"You sound reluctant," Cassie laughed. "Nervous?"

"Yep."

"Goodness—why?" Cassie demanded.

Sloan had to stop and think. "I don't know. Aren't all brides nervous?"

"To a point," Cassie agreed. "But not all brides get to marry

Wes! He's the nicest man . . . always so calm and gentle! I'd trust him with my life and—" Cassie broke off, blushing.

"And what?"

"I'll bet he's a hell of a lover!"

Sloan started to giggle. "I'll bet you're right!"

Just then Laura came racing into the room, tears flooding down her little cheeks. Sloan scooped her daughter into her arms. "Darling! What's the matter?"

It was difficult to understand Laura's garbled sobbings, but Sloan eventually deciphered the cause for her daughter's misery; Laura had just realized that her mother was actually leaving her for two weeks.

Crooning into Laura's silky-soft hair, Sloan assured her that she wouldn't be gone long and that Florence and Cassie would take good care of her. Laura continued to cry.

"What's the problem?"

Sloan looked up to find Wesley leaning in the doorframe. Raising her hands helplessly, she explained, "Laura doesn't want us to go."

Without another word to Sloan, Wes took the little girl from her arms. In a soothing voice, but one which he might also use on an adult, Wesley patiently told her that they were going on a honeymoon, and people usually did when they were married. He promised sincerely that they wouldn't be gone long and that they would send postcards and bring home special presents for everyone. Laura's sniffles slowly subsided, and before long she was asking Wesley to make sure he brought her a doll. She was all smiles by the time he set her down, eager to kiss them both good-bye.

Sloan and Wes had no further problems leaving. Jamie told them good-bye and to have a great time in a very adult manner; Terry was happily crunching crackers his aunt had given him and barely brushed his mother with a gritty kiss. To the happy strains of laughter and a shower of rice, Wes led his new bride to the car.

Sloan's nervousness increased as Wesley silently drove. Unaccountably, she was becoming terribly uneasy in his company. Remembering her sister's words, she tried to settle comfortably into her seat. Wes was a terrific man, always calm and understanding. And he would be, she was sure as a thrill of heat raced through her at the thought, a superb lover. If "previews" meant anything . . . Yet even as she deliciously contemplated the night, a vision of the icy hardness of his eyes as he stared at her after the ceremony rose unbidden to her mind. Stop! she warned herself. She could relax now, feel young.

Sitting up abruptly, she shook her head as if to clear it and turned to her new husband with a smile. Her wanderings were absurd and ridiculous! She knew Wes, she loved and understood him completely. He was the nicest, most wonderful man in the world, and any suspicions to the contrary were pure imagination on her part! They loved one another, and love was comfortable, secure . . . fun! She had invented his look of this morning in her mind; it had been a trick of light.

Resting her hand lightly on his thigh, she said, "Thanks for handling Laura so well. She was breaking my heart."

Wes shrugged, his eyes planted squarely on the road. "I'm crazy about the kids, you know that. And they're not your children anymore; they're *ours.*"

"I love you," Sloan said softly.

"Do you?"

Whatever reply Sloan had been expecting, that wasn't it. She studied him, puzzled. "You know I love you," she said, hurt. "Why else . . ."

Wesley's arm came around her neck, and he ruffled the hair at its nape. "We all like assurance," he said, and he glanced at her quickly. His eyes were full of their sea-jade warmth, and Sloan relaxed. Everything was all right.

"Why don't you settle down for a bit of a nap," Wes suggested, idly stroking her hair. "We've still got quite a drive to the airport, then a long flight, and it will be morning all over again when we land. Might be some time before we get to bed, and then—" He juggled his eyebrows insinuatively, and Sloan blushed like a girl and chuckled.

"Well, hell!" he grumbled with a wink. "One of us is going to need a lot of energy!"

"Okay, okay," Sloan retorted, stretching across the car and resting her head in his lap. "I'm napping!"

After the excitement of boarding the plane and moving out

over the Atlantic had also diminished, Sloan again cuddled into her reclining chair, her hand resting possessively in Wesley's, and slipped into another catnap. It was easy to sleep with the clouds out her window and the faint hum of the engines lulling in her ears. So easy, in fact, that Wesley was shaking her awake before she could believe the long flight had passed.

An hour later they were standing in the middle of Brussels' magnificent Grand Place while her citizens busily scurried about. Sloan stared in awe at the breathtaking visage of the city center. The buildings, though grayed and sooted with age, were spectacular. In the brilliance of the summer sun, they shone like a fairy tale, all white and glittering gold and carved with exquisite artistry.

"We'll just walk around a little and get the feel of the city," Wes said, taking her arm, "Feast on a delectable meal of French cuisine and head out for the hotel. Tomorrow we can start sightseeing."

"Tomorrow," Sloan laughed. "It is tomorrow."

"Not here." Wes grinned.

Wes pointed out certain of the gold-gilded buildings as they walked, reading from a tourist manual. The city was founded in the 500's, and many of the structures still standing dated back to the 1200's. They viewed with wonder and excitement the old Hotel de Ville, the Church of Saint Gudule, and the more modern Palace of Justice.

"I know it's here somewhere!" Wesley suddenly muttered, his eyes roaming studiously around the market square. "Off the Grand Place . . ."

"What?" Sloan asked curiously, following his line of vision. All she could see was the beautiful square, the bustling people, and a sky full of careless gray pigeons.

"The Kissing Fountain."

"The what?"

Wesley smiled roguishly and set his arm around her waist. "I swear to you, it's one of the 'must sees' in Brussels. Well, it's semifamous. Among honeymooners, anyway."

Sloan raised a brow. "Because the fountain kisses?"

"That's right."

"I don't believe you."

291

"Well, it's true," Wesley promised solemnly. "And do you know how?"

Sloan stared at him skeptically. "Somehow with water, I assume."

"You got it!" Wes grinned. "Come on, let's find it."

Laughing happily in the comfort of her husband's arm, Sloan ambled along the street with him. She was in for her first surprise when Wesley stopped a passerby and asked what she assumed were directions in what sounded like perfect French.

"It's on a side street off the Grand Place," Wes explained, without blinking an eye after he had been answered. "Follow, my love, and I shan't lead you astray."

"You never told me you spoke French," Sloan said reproachfully.

"You never asked."

Sloan smiled. "I guess we'll make surprising discoveries every day."

"Ummm . . ." Wes stared down at her, and for a fraction of a minute she thought she caught that strange coldness in his eyes again. Then it was gone, and he hugged her to him. "Discoveries are amazing, love. In fact, my darling, you never fail to amaze and surprise me. . . ."

After a few wrong turns, they came upon the "famous" Kissing Fountain, and like teenaged lovers they fell into one another's arms with uproarious laughter. Privately owned, the fountain was a tiny thing, composed of a chubby little girl and an equally chubby little boy, gilded beautifully in Brussels gold. As the water pressure rose from the ground, the pair turned to one another and "kissed," then swiveled again in their elegant garden with pretty pursed lips—to spout a misting flood of water upon any audience.

"This is a 'must see,' huh?" Sloan demanded, giggling as she wiped water from her cheeks. "I'll bet it's not listed in the majority of the tourist manuals!"

"Hey! What do you want?" Wes retorted good-naturedly. "Some world traveler you make! I told you, this *is* one of the things one does in Brussels!" His arm tightened around her waist, and he pulled her closely to him. "But now that we've done it . . ." His voice was low and husky. "Now we'll go for that French meal and head for our romantic room. . . ."

The restaurant Wes chose was right on the Grand Place, and they were quickly ushered to a discreet table which still allowed for a marvelous view of the quaint glittering buildings. The daytime light was muted to mellow the room and necessitate the use of a single, mood-setting candle at each table. Garlands of roses highlighted the intricately carved, heavy wood furnishings and contrasted with the velvety black booths. Sloan sank into the comfort of the booth gratefully and relished in the delight of Wes's hard body against hers. She acquiesced with a pretty grin when he suggested he order for them both and gave herself completely to the elegantly romantic mood surrounding them. It was so nice! So easy to rest against the sure shoulder beside her and put herself into the hands of the man she loved with no doubts or second thoughts.

"Well, darling"—Wesley turned to her and raised his glass when they had been served a delicious, dry white wine—"to that ring upon your finger." In the candlelight, he had a decidedly rakish expression, like that of a pirate, smiling with secret triumph as he gloated over his gold. It was odd that the wavering shadows of the candle could cause such an effect; Wes appeared almost scary but, Sloan thought as a warm shiver of anticipation bubbled in her veins, oh, so sexy!

"To us!" she corrected, raising her glass to tip to his. "That gold thing on your finger is a wedding band, too."

"Ummm . . ." But Wes's mind wasn't on his own finger or the gold band that adorned it. He was watching Sloan with his pirate expression, his eyes now as brilliant as the gilded buildings outside. With his left hand he held his wineglass, with his right hand he stroked her cheek in a feathery light caress. His thumb rubbed her lips with a tantalizing combination of roughness and care, persisting until she smiled and returned the sensual taunt by grazing her teeth over the thumb. "Ummmm . . ." Wesley repeated, "And I ordered escargot. You, my love, are all the appetizer, entree, and dessert I think I really require at the moment—"

"I thought you were starving," Sloan interrupted.

"Oh, I am," Wes retorted, brushing her lips with a kiss. But the arrival of their escargots—aromatic with subtle seasonings and dripping in a delicious butter sauce—curtailed any explanation of just what he was starving for.

The escargots were followed by an untouchable onion soup baked with a blend of cheeses and toasted cubes of French bread to perfection. Sloan moaned at the arrival of their main course, delicately seasoned fish, swearing she would never be able to finish the food. She did, however; it was all too delicious to consider leaving a mouthful.

Sloan demurred on dessert, but agreed to join Wes in ordering coffee and Grand Marnier. Twilight was falling as they sipped their cordials, and the muted blendings of gold and crimson added to the mystical romance of the evening. Sloan was marvelously comfortable and at ease. The liquor she had consumed made her feel as if she were truly floating on clouds, her body as light as a feather but superbly attuned to the touch and feel of the man beside her—the man who was now her husband and would soon be claiming all of his matrimonial rights. The thought made her shudder with delicious anticipation, and yet she was willing to savor every minute, to let things follow their dreamlike path slowly so that each step on the way to ultimate fulfillment could be cherished and heighten all that was to come.

. . .

She was almost in a trance by the time Wesley reached for her hand and escorted her from the restaurant. He was strangely silent as he guided their rental car out of the center of the city and into the surrounding hills, but Sloan barely noticed. Her head was resting on his shoulder; her hand rested lightly on his thigh, and ~he was secretely thrilling to its rugged, tense feel beneath her fingers. His breathing, she noted with misty satisfaction, was growing ragged, and a pulse was visibly pounding in the length of his corded neck. A smile of pure feminine pleasure fitted its way seductively into her lips. Wesley had power over her—he could prove that at any time with the slightest touch!—but she also had power over him, and she knew it. She loved him, desperately, but something as old as love and even more primitive held her in its grasp. Tonight she would play the seductress for real; the sensual vixen to the hilt. In the most ancient of feminine games, she would wield her power with subtle mastery until she had driven Wesley to the brink of insanity. Then, of course, they would surrender to love's sweet fire together. Still, she decided with the wiles of her sex, she would keep the upper hand. It would never do to let Wes know that he could be the eternal victor, while still the game was for them both . . . two winners.

She almost forgot her game when they arrived at their hotel. As Wes had promised, the place was secluded and enchanting. The old and new were blended together delightfully. Their room, furnished with French provincial pieces—the dominating one being a huge, four-poster bed—was also equipped with ultra-modern conveniences. There was nothing outdated about the beautiful marble bath or the plate glass windows which overlooked lush green hills and a blue stream. Flemish tapestries lined the walls, enhancing rather than contrasting with a thick shag rug of creamery-pure beige. Sloan clapped her hands with delight at her surroundings and spun on Wes with the enthusiasm of a child shining her eyes to brilliant sapphire.

"Wes!" she cried happily, lifting her hands inadequately as she sought for words of description. "It's beautiful—wonderful—marvelous!"

A smile tilted his lips, but he turned from her wordlessly to tip the boy who had brought their luggage in. The two exchanged a few words in French, then the boy left, grinning deftly as he pocketed Wes's francs. Then the door closed behind him, and Sloan was at long last alone with her new husband.

Wesley came behind her at the window. Darkness was enveloping the land, but a full moon was steadily rising to cast beautiful, luminescent shadows over the rippling water and nearby foliage. As they stared upon the view together, Wesley's hands spanned her small waist, and he began a series of erotic nibblings on her earlobe which surely found their way down her neck and collarbone. Then he was firmly turning her from the window, and his lips found hers with insistent demand.

Sloan moaned as her lips parted beneath his assault. His tongue plundered the recesses of her mouth mercilessly as his hands began a slow attack of their own. Instinctively Sloan responded, arching her body to his, running her fingers from the crispness of his hair to the strength of his back, luxuriating in the play of muscles beneath her fingertips even as his heat began to consume her. His fingers found the zipper of her dress, and as she heard the rasping sound of its release, she remembered, somewhat vaguely, her game. As his calloused hands found her bare flesh and began a possessive exploration, Sloan gently maneuvered from his arms. Having artfully escaped, she smiled at his look of frustrated confusion. Moving quickly before he could reclaim her, she impishly planted a kiss on his chin and sprang from his reach. "I'm going to take a quick shower, darling," she murmured. "I won't be long."

But she was. She allowed the hot water to run on and on, lathering herself richly with scented soap, her lips curled all the while as she gloated over the excitement of her taunting. Finally, she rinsed herself thoroughly and emerged, chuckling in her throat as she noticed the knob of the door twisting. She wasn't ready yet. Taking her time, she assiduously brushed her hair until it fell in silklike waves, then donned one of her new gowns, a deceptive piece of black gauze which covered her from neck to toe yet teased enticingly with slits that ran all the way to her hips. She continued chuckling as she stepped into a pair of black string bikini panties and completed her outfit with the matching black pegnoir. Then she reached for the doorknob, her heart beginning to flutter tremulously.

Wesley was not panting by the door as she had expected. He had discarded his own clothing for a velour robe and was leaning nonchalantly on the bed, one arm behind his head to form a comfortable crook for it, the other resting on his kneecap as he held an iced drink. He had turned on the television set and was watching a newscaster. "I ordered you a scotch," he said, idly motioning toward the dresser. He barely glanced her way.

"Thanks," Sloan said, bewildered. She walked slowly for her drink, swaying as she did so, but she received no response from Wesley. Frustrated, she sipped the scotch and sat at the foot of the bed. If he was giving no notice of her, she certainly wasn't going to jump into his arms! The voice of the newscaster droned into her ears. "That isn't French he's speaking," she said, growing increasingly nervous.

"Flemish," Wes supplied conversationally. "This is a bilingual country."

"Oh," Sloan murmured. Then acidly, "And I suppose you speak Flemish, too?"

"Not really," Wes said absently. "I understand a fair amount."

Sloan heard the clatter of ice as Wesley calmly drained his glass. Still, he didn't move. So! Sloan thought petulantly, he wants to play games, too! Well, she had already decided on winning this one. She drained her scotch in a gulp and winced as the burning liquid made its way down her throat. Then she stood, stretched and yawned, surprised at how dizzy she was. Gulping the scotch had been a mistake. Clutching the bedpost, she steadied herself and stole a glance at Wesley. The black hair on his chest curled provocatively over its expanse as it lay exposed from the V of his robe. The knotted muscles of his calves, thrown so carelessly over the coverlet, gave a breath-catching hint of the physique beneath the draped velour. . . .

Damn him! Sloan thought. She whirled from the bedpost and ripped the covers from her side of the bed. She was squirming with heat and anger. It had never occurred to her that two could play her game. . . .

Flouncing into the bed, she turned her back on him and stared at the bathroom door, fuming. His ensuing chuckle, deep, low, and from the throat, was the finishing touch. She determined furiously that whatever the cost to herself, Wesley would go to sleep on his wedding night with nothing more fulfilling than a hot shower!

His hand wrapped around her arm like a vise, and his next whisper was hot and tantalizing against her ear. "No games, my darling," he murmured, his lips moving along her neck and shoulder, searing her skin through the gauze. "You're my wife now. Legal possession."

"Possession!" Sloan shrilled, spinning around so quickly that her hair neatly slapped his face and momentarily curtailed his kisses. The evening was not going at all as planned! Wesley was calm and sedate, taking his own sweet time, and she was a bundle of nerves and frustration. He was supposed to realize she was elated, yet ever so slightly frightened despite her stance, needing him to cajole. Instead, he was calmly telling her that she was a *possession*.

297

"Ummm," Wes drawled lazily, his nibbling kisses moving over her breasts, warm and moist over the black material. "That's what you are now, you know, a possession."

"No!" Sloan squealed breathlessly. Her fury was mingling with her desire and the undeniable arousal he was so easily eliciting. Mind and body waged a silent war. She had to stop him before it was too late, before she lost herself in the steadily increasing vortex of pleasure he was confidently creating. Her fingers dug into his hair, and she pulled his face to hers with all the strength her anger could muster.

"Ouch!" he exclaimed, and then she saw his eyes and the amusement that sparkled within them.

"You've been teasing me!" Sloan accused, relaxing somewhat but maintaining her punishing grasp of his hair. "You . . . you . . . you . . ." She couldn't think of a fit name to call him.

"How about 'Lord and Master,' " Wes taunted, placidly circling her wrists with his hands and creating a pressure which forced her to gasp and release her hold. Then both of her wrists were firmly held by one of his hands and pinioned above her.

"'Lord and Master' my foot!" Sloan retorted, squirming and wriggling her wrists to free herself. The effort was ludicrous. "I'll get you for this, Wesley Adams," she said tartly, panting but unwilling to accept defeat.

"I do hope that's a promise," he drawled languorously. "Now," he continued, his tone lowering hoarsely, "just how do you plan to get me? Like this?" She felt the rough fingertips of his free hand delve beneath the black gown to travel with tantalizing leisure up the length of her thigh. "Or perhaps like this." With a force belying his subtle tone, he deftly drove a wedge between her legs with a firm thrust of a knee and lowered his weight over her body, imprisoning her completely.

"Wesley!" Sloan's calling of his name was a combination of amazement, irritation, amusement and—despite her firm resolve to remain unmoved by any of his advances until she was in control again—exquisite pleasure.

"Maybe you could 'get me' something like this," he went on, undaunted. He showered her throat and breasts again with the moist, nibbled kisses that were driving all rational thoughts from her mind as they ignited a fire within her that raged rapidly to every tingling nerve of her body. "Maybe more like this," he muttered darkly against her skin, and then before she knew his purpose, his teeth sank into the material of her gown as his hand momentarily halted its wanderings to rip the black gauze cleanly in two, leaving her slender form bared to his sensuous view. "What the hell are these things?" he demanded, slipping a finger beneath the elastic of the black panties. "Oh well, what the hell." A single twist of his fingers ripped the string, and he tossed them to the floor with a nonchalant flick of his hand.

"Wesley!" Sloan gasped again. The word was meant to sound indignant, reproachful, but his name came out instead as a groaning plea. "Stop it!" she murmured weakly, renewing the struggle for freedom of her hands.

"Stop what?" he teased. "This?" His fingers began a feather-light caress on her belly, drawing circles that became larger and more inquisitive as he shifted slightly and continued to the sensitive silk of her thighs. "Or this . . ." His voice grated on the last, and the hands and fingers that sought the secrets of her femininity were no longer fluttery and teasing but hungry and demanding as was the mouth that claimed her breasts, arousing them to rigid peaks.

Sloan shivered uncontrollably, writhing and squirming, but no longer to escape his hold. She wanted to get closer to him, closer and closer, become one with him and allow the fire that now pulsed through her like a living thing to burn to its height of shimmering flame and ultimately consume them.

"Wildcat," Wesley murmured to the roseate nipple his lips caressed. His face rose above Sloan's, and she was dimly aware that his eyes glittered like a jungle cat's and that his features were taut with his own desire. "My game, now, wife, and then no more games," he muttered darkly.

"No more games," Sloan echoed in a husky whisper, shuddering as if charged by electricity and arching to feel the crisp hairs of his chest against her breasts and the pulsating hardness of his masculinity that blatantly proved his own arousal. "Wesley . . . please!" Her words were almost a sob.

But he wasn't through with his exquisite torture yet. He released her wrists, but only to allow his lips further exploration of her flesh. Freed, Sloan's hands moved of their own volition, clinging to him, digging into him, seeking and desiring. And then, when she thought she would surely die of wonderful agony, Wesley's hands moved to her buttocks and lifted her to him.

"Surrender?" He was gloating, but his demand was uttered in such a raw rasp that it didn't matter. It didn't matter anyway. He had driven her to an absolute frenzy.

"Surrender," she croaked, parting her lips and hooking her arms desperately around the hard expanse of his shoulders. "No more games. . . ."

Skyrockets of dizzying ecstasy exploded throughout her as Wesley completed his conquest, taking her with a rough urgency that matched the wild passion flaming hungrily between them. Wesley's pulsating rhythm took them higher and higher to peak after peak, bringing them finally to a boundless precipice of sweet satiation that was so wonderful that Sloan could not move at its conclusion, could not disentangle her limbs from Wesley's nor willingly draw away from his overwhelming heat.

It was he who finally moved, but only to shed the robe that still encased his shoulders. He tugged at the remnants of Sloan's black gown. "Get rid of that," he commanded softly.

There was no more fight left in Sloan, just loving, dazed obedience. She knew she had lost the upper hand—if she had ever had it! But she didn't care. Her body still burned with the aftermath of pleasure; the memory of Wesley's demanding possession still throbbed divinely where his virility had split her asunder. Filled with loving contentment, she dutifully cast aside the remainders of the black gauze and curled to his naked side, reveling in the feel of his lean, sinewed body. A sigh of sheer peace and satisfaction escaped her as her eyelids fluttered closed.

"Sleepy?" Wesley queried with a throaty chuckle, stroking her damp hair from her forehead.

"Ummm . . ."

"What? On your honeymoon?" he mocked. "My passionate little wildcat giving out already? Un-unh!"

"Wes," Sloan protested drowsily. "I'm half-asleep . . ."

"I'll wake you up," he promised, and proceeded to prove he could do so. Slowly, more gently this time, with Sloan able to return every spark of arousal and explore him with equal intimacy. He demanded things of her, coaxing her with enticing whispers to tell him everything that pleased her most and exciting her to almost unendurable lengths by encouraging her own shy administrations with hoarse groans and gutteral exclamations of her perfection.

"I think I married a sex maniac," she told him euphorically as he swept her to his heights again.

"No, darling," he muttered, his face taut with desire, "*I* did, little wildcat."

"I never knew it could be this way. . . ." Anything else she had to say became incomprehensible as moans obliterated her speech.

Later, countless eons later, she drifted off to sleep in the ageless, dreamlike satisfaction of one filled to the brim with enchanted satiation, held in the security of her lover's arms. The night had been more than she had ever expected, even in her wildest imaginings. She had given herself to Wesley completely, and learned the superb sweetness of surrender. It was good, so wonderfully good, to be his and know that he was hers and that a man like Wesley slept beside her. She had been conquered, but the thought bothered her not at all. She didn't need a superior edge anymore; she loved and trusted him totally.

She awoke in the middle of the night, keenly attuned to his touch. She was coiled against him, her back fitted into the curve of his stomach, sheltered by his arms. For a minute she was confused, wondering why she had woken. Then she realized that he was insistently fondling her breasts; the pressure of his powerful chest and his hot, probing masculinity telling her the rest.

"Wes!" she murmured with awe and surprise, a remnant of guile prompting her protest. A laugh escaped her. "We have tomorrow, you know."

"Never put off till tomorrow," he quoted as his teeth grazed her earlobe. Had she been more awake, she might have noticed the slight hesitance before his teasing statement. As it was, she merely mocked a sigh of resignation and succumbed to his advances, shocked by the vehemence of her response and the wild abandon with which she eagerly returned his lovemaking when by all rights she should have been exhausted, spent, and still sound asleep.

Wesley chuckled softly when she shuddered in his arms again.

"Go back to sleep, darling," he whispered. "I promise I won't wake you again."

Sloan obligingly rested her head upon his chest. A thought nagged at her, but she was so tired, she couldn't quite put a finger on it. Then it hit her, but by then she was caught in the twilight between sleep and consciousness and she dismissed it immediately.

In all his words of coaxing and passionate encouragement, in all his whispers of hungry pleasure, never once had Wesley said he loved her.

What a ridiculous thing to be thinking about, Sloan thought dimly in her subconscious. She knew Wesley loved her; he had told her so many times, even when she had been setting her "trap" and was totally unaware of her own, intense feelings for him.

And so she slept again, soundly and perfectly happy in her newly discovered joy and fulfillment, blissfully unaware of what the morning would bring.

CHAPTER EIGHT

The bright, beguiling sunlight of the Belgian morning streaked through the parted drapes to awaken her. Like a purring kitten she stretched languorously; like an innocent maid who had just discovered the wonder of love she flicked shy lashes and reached a tentative hand across the covers to touch her new husband.

He wasn't there. Her eyes opened fully, and she smiled a sweet smile of contentment as she found him, sitting on a bedside chair, his strong fingers idly stroking his chin as he watched her. His dark hair was tousled, his broad chest incredibly sexy in its partial exposure at the loose V of his haphazardly belted robe.

But he didn't smile back, and Sloan's happily curved lips straightened tremulously. His look was as cold as ice, his piercing green eyes brutal in his tense, bronzed face.

Barely awake, Sloan blinked with confusion. It couldn't be Wesley staring at her that way! She opened her eyes again to find the glacial image still before her. She struggled inwardly to ease her bewilderment. What had happened to change the tender and gentle man she had married into this basilisk of condemnation? How could he possibly be staring at her with such venom after the night of passionate love they had just shared together?

"So you're awake."

His voice was low, pleasant, the tone almost silky. For the briefest moment, Sloan began to relax, convincing herself she was reading things into his pirate gaze that simply weren't there.

Then he began to speak again.

"It was . . . interesting? . . . my love, to see how you would handle the night. Very nice. I must say, darling, that when you sell out, you do go all the way with gusto."

A creeping cold chill of fear seeped rapidly through her

numbed senses. "What?" she whispered incredulously, moistening dry lips.

"The act is charming, Sloan, but no good." He flashed her a pearly smile with a rapier edge. "It's time for a little honesty."

Lord, she wondered desperately, what *had* happened? "I don't know what you're talking about!" she hedged, panicked. Forcing herself to keep a mask of calm on her features, she thought rapidly over the past events. He couldn't have any suspicions regarding her original motives for marriage; he would have certainly called off the wedding! He *couldn't* know anything harmful, she decided with a quaking bravado. Still, she clutched the covers protectively to her chin as she attempted a captivating grin and laughed gaily. "Really, darling, you should have warned me that you wake like a growling bear!"

Dark brows rose in an arch. "Should I have?" he inquired politely, the daggerlike smile still etched clearly into his taut profile. He stood and sauntered slowly to her while she watched him uneasily. She had the terrible, uncanny feeling that he was playing with her, as a great cat played with its prey before pouncing for the final kill. Her instinct was to run, but she was stubbornly insisting to herself that there was nothing that could be really wrong. Willpower alone kept her still, presenting a facade of guileless calm.

She felt his heat as he sat beside her, felt the tense, powerful coil of his thigh muscle against hers. She forced herself to meet his steel, green gaze unblinkingly, and when his fingers moved gently along her cheekbones and down to her throat, she silently prayed she would not flinch beneath the harsh rigidity that lurked, like a spiral about to spring, behind the tenderness of the gesture. Then she couldn't bear the tense, pregnant stillness any longer. "What is it, love?" she whispered.

"What is it . . . love," he repeated in a toneless, mocking murmur. Then the coil unleashed and the spring flew. His fingers clamped around her wrists like steel cuffs and he jerked her abruptly from the bed. She uttered a startled scream in protest, shocked by his sudden show of ill-controlled force, no longer uneasy or frightened but thoroughly terrified. She was well aware of the bricklike muscles that composed the frame of this man who was now a stranger, well aware that he could break her like so many match sticks if he so desired.

He was oblivious to her cries of protest as he ripped the protective sheet from her and pulled her into the bathroom where he positioned her firmly before the mirror, his hands on her shoulders but warningly near her neck, the breadth of his body behind her, holding her steady as she lowered her eyes and begged him to let her loose.

"Not just yet . . . wife. . . ." he spat, the iciness of his eyes losing nothing as he met the trembling liquid pools of hers in reflection. "We shall see what we have here, first. . . ."

"Wesley!" Sloan implored, stunned by his actions. Wesley Adams couldn't be doing this to her! Even the rough lover of the night before had been tender. . . .

"Now," he continued coldly, ignoring her outburst, his voice that of an informative teacher conducting a class, "What do we have? Do we see a woman approaching thirty, a mother of three, possibly fearful that she may be losing her looks, never again to be loved or cherished? Afraid that she shall not be accepted again by a new lover because of her children? No." One hand slid over her shoulder, cupped a breast, moved on over her rib cage to her flat stomach and harshly molded the jut of her hip. "No." he hissed again, emphatically. "This woman holds no fears. She is serenely confident of her femininity. No naive girl, this. She is a beautiful, bewitching woman, and she knows it. Like a black widow, she can easily lure a man into her web. She is a remarkable animal—breasts full and firm, seductively curved hips, a figure as slim as a debutante's. She doesn't even remember the definition of the word 'love.' "

"Wesley!" Sloan pleaded miserably, shaking with the unexpected vehemence of his mind-boggling attack. "Wesley, please, I beg you!"

"You beg me. Lovely." He laughed dryly, a harsh, bitter, and hollow sound. "Not yet, darling." His hands found her chin and forced her bowed head back to the mirror. "We haven't decided what we do have here, yet. But certainly not a woman clinging to a last line of hope! That I could have understood. Forgiven easily." Her chin jerked cruelly. "Open your eyes!" he commanded.

She obeyed and met orbs of such jade-green loathing that chills exploded violently in spasms throughout her. Still he showed no mercy.

"I have met street prostitutes with more scruples," he continued, his grip like a mechanical thing. "They sell openly, for a price. They make an honest bargain. They tell you what they want, and they tell you exactly what you get in return.

"But you . . . wife . . ." She gasped a choking sob as he spun her around to face him. "You were not honest one stinking step of the way. You lied, connived, cheated, and schemed. You sold yourself more callously than any common tramp. All for my money."

"No!" Sloan protested weakly in self-defense, slowly, sickly realizing he had been in the house at the beginning of her explanation to Cassie, hearing . . .

"Don't lie to me now, woman!" His raging growl bellowed through the room as he shook her so hard that her head lolled like a doll's and her hair fell in torrents over her shoulders. "God, don't try to play me for a fool any longer! Your little game is really up. I heard everything you had to say to your sister, my dear, and though I didn't want to believe it—a man's heart and his ego can be terribly sensitive at times—everything surely fit perfectly. One night you didn't want me crossing your doorstep, the next day you were welcoming me with open arms." He pushed her from him contemptuously. "And I fell for it all! All that false, wide-eyed innocence. I walked into your lair with starry eyes, wanting so desperately to believe in you, respecting your views on sex and marriage when all the while . . ." His voice broke off grimly as he tightly clenched his fist. The lines about his mouth were white with tension. Uttering a croak of disgust, he spun on his heel and stalked from the bathroom.

Sloan stood stock-still for a moment, scarcely breathing, unable to absorb the horror of the things he had said, unable to reconcile them with the man she had known so intimately just hours before. Then she followed him out, nervously grabbed the sheet from the bed to wrap herself in, and skittered into a corner of the room to watch him with dazed, fearful eyes. She had no conception of what he might do next. It was all too evident; the man she thought she knew, understood, the chivalrous wooer, the tenderly possessive lover, existed no more. And she should have never underestimated him. Her vague suspicions that he could be a dangerous man had proved all too true. A tiger, though tamed, was still in essence a wild beast, and Wesley, like that beast, had given up all pretense of civility. Raw instinct and basic fury were guiding him now. Reason and logic had lost all meaning. Like primitive man, he was the stronger, and he would call the shots.

Sloan watched, still too dazed to attempt the explanation he wouldn't believe as he began to pack his bags. Shrunken into her corner, she felt the tears which had formed in her eyes begin to trickle down her cheeks. Whatever happened she knew she deserved, yet how could she lose him now when she had just found him?

His glance fell her way as coolly as marble. "Don't bother with the tears. I'm not going to break your neck, though I should. Nor am I going to annul the marriage, though I should. The children are my responsibility now, too, and there is no reason they should be made to suffer because of their mother."

The tears fell anyway, despite his brutal statements. She couldn't believe the way he was treating her—not after the day and night they had spent happily in one another's arms! "Why? . . ." At first she didn't realize she had said the word aloud.

"What?" Wesley barked.

"Why? . . ." She shrank even further into her corner, unable to complete her question beneath the survey of his relentless anger.

In two seconds he reached her, pulled her to her feet, and swung her gracelessly into the middle of the room. "Why what?" he demanded, his eyes blazing a dancing flame of green fire. "Don't turn coward on top of everything else. You're not the least upset over what you did; selling out didn't mean a thing to you. You're only upset because you've been caught. What was the exact plan, anyway? How many months of blissful marriage was I going to be blessed with before you sued for divorce and a handsome settlement?"

Sloan's hair tumbled wildly over her face; her blue eyes peaked out in liquid sapphire pleading. "I wasn't—" she began with trembling lips.

307

For a fraction of a second it appeared as if Wesley might be softening. Then he emitted a sharp snort of disgust which effectively curtailed her words. "Spare me, Sloan. I've admitted you're a sensational actress, but you've already conned me once. Save it. I really don't want to hear any more. Ask your question."

Sloan bit through her bottom lip until it bled. All was lost. He hated her now. Her brief dream of happiness had been shattered by her own schemes, her own lies. Swallowing, she tilted her chin despite her trembling. She would hold on to her courage as he had suggested. Perhaps he could still admire her for something, even if it would sound like a futile lie to say she did love him now . . . had . . .

"Why did you go through with the wedding?" she asked quietly, her voice soft but thankfully steady. After a painful falter she added, "And why bother with yesterday?"

He shot her a glance with a shade less disdain as he continued packing, brushing by her as if she were an obstacle like a dresser or desk as he spoke.

"I'm not really sure," he admitted with a wry hint of humor. "Maybe I feel in the back of my mind that there is something I might be able to get out of this bargain myself. And, I did want you. Badly enough to marry you, since that was your price. Then yesterday . . ." He shrugged and neatly folded a stack of pressed shirts into the bag. "Yesterday, I wanted to see how thoroughly you planned to pay up while we were still going by your rules." He abruptly stopped his packing, arms crossed over his chest, and flicked his green eyes over her from head to toe with such formidable insolence that a crimson blush spread like a stain to her cheeks. "I must say, love," he spoke with the silky tone she had learned could be so cutting and dangerous, "you do pay up handsomely. I always knew, from watching the way that you moved, that you'd be dynamite in bed. Certain women are made for it. Even so, your veins must be filled with ice water for you to respond with such—talented ardor—to a man you don't love."

If he had slapped her soundly across the face, he couldn't have been more abusive. Sloan was still for a second, absorbing the shock, amazed that anyone could be so blind. Then her shock receded as anger, boiling like red-hot lava, raged through her system. She had been wrong, yes, but she didn't deserve the things he was saying. Fear, control, and all sense of reasonable logic fell from her like a cloak, and she flew at him with the speed and wrath of a whirling tornado. "You bastard!" she hissed, and she struck him cleanly with a fury-driven open hand that left him no time to ward off the blow.

It was his turn to stand dead still as the mark she had imprinted on his face quickly turned white, pink, and dark red. The sound of her slap seemed to reverberate through the room as he slowly rubbed his cheek, staring at her all the while. "My beloved wife," he drawled mockingly, "that was certainly uncalled-for. I've been desperately trying to remain nonviolent about this whole thing."

Sloan took a deep breath of trepidation. She wisely felt the time for courage ebbing. His features, so handsome and strongly formed, were twisted into hard, grim lines; his eyes, no longer icy, blazed with a fury more intense than that of a raging sea. She began to back away; once more frightened—she didn't like his expression one bit. His eyes suddenly flickered over her again, and she realized her unprecipitated blow had dislodged her improvised sheet tunic and that he was gazing upon the mound of one creamy, exposed breast. Flushed, she pulled the sheet more tightly around her, only to be rewarded for her efforts by a dry, mirthless chuckle from Wes.

"Rather late for you to turn modest, isn't it?" he demanded scornfully. The suitcase went to the floor, and he sat on the bed. "Come here," he ordered arrogantly.

She could see the rise and fall of his black-matted chest, read the desire that burned along with the anger in his eyes. Her gaze fell to his hands, large hands, wisped with coarse strands of the same black hair, hands with fingers neatly kept, strong hands, strong fingers, capable of holding her with infinite tenderness and arousing her to abandoned passion, capable of manipulating her forcefully and bending her to his will.

Her eyes slowly left the fascination of his hands and moved upward. A single pulse beat erratically in the fine blue line of a vein in his corded neck. She raised her eyes still further, saw the ragged, crooked smile set lazily into his sensuous lips, saw that the light in his eyes held no tenderness, no love. Just hard, cold fury and desire.

She shook her head softly, beseechingly, and whispered, "No."

"Come here." The devilish grin increased as he repeated his command. His tone was deceptively low and pleasant as he added, "Sloan, don't make me come to you."

Wincing, Sloan inched toward him, her eyes downcast, her thick lashes hiding the emotions that raged within them. A scuffle, she knew, would be worthless. She was probably lucky he hadn't decided to strike her back before . . . maybe, just maybe, she could talk to him. But she paused when she reached him, afraid to face him, finally lifting her lashes to meet his eyes with open pleading.

But he didn't glance into her eyes to read their message. He tugged at the sheet until it fell to the floor at her feet. The startling green gems of his eyes raked over her briefly with insolent satisfaction, then his arms came around her, and she was swept to the bed beside him. She tried to speak, but his lips claimed hers, and her words were muffled as his tongue sought her mouth with a unique mastery all its own. Then her mouth was deserted as his kisses roamed along the graceful arch of her throat and down to her breasts. But they were not gentle kisses, not even hinting at love or tenderness. They were rough and urgent; they demanded and violated. Salt tears formed in Sloan's eyes, and even as she felt a nipple harden beneath his mouth and inwardly admitted that a rousing fire was slowly coursing through her treacherous body, she protested, if somewhat breathlessly.

"Wesley—no!"

"No?" A single brow raised high as he lifted himself to challenge her scornfully. "And why not? You've got your ring and your money. I'm assuming this was my return offering. And, my darling," he hissed bitterly, "I haven't seen you suffering, yet."

Sloan blinked her eyes and winced, unable to move within the concrete prison of his arms. Bracing herself she began to speak. "Wesley, I will not let you make love to me like this—"

"Make love?" he interjected. "Sweet wife, it all has to be prettily wrapped and worded on the outside, huh? But you're not

310

going to play the hypocrite anymore. You enjoy my bed, darling; to deny that would be ludicrous. And more important, dear wife, *you made the bed,* and now *you will lie in it!*"

Dismissing anything else she might have to say as inconsequential, Wesley returned casually to his sure arousal of her body. His lips were searing her flesh like hot irons, and she knew she would eventually succumb. But she had to make him listen!

"Wesley . . . wait . . . you don't understand."

"So talk to me," he murmured, his words muffled by her flesh.

"You're angry," Sloan choked, forgetting the sense she was trying to make. "You're angry," she raspily repeated herself.

His lovemaking took an abrupt halt, and he raised his head. His eyes bored into hers like hot coals, and his lips twisted savagely. "Angry!" he roared. "That has to be the understatement of the year!"

His head lowered again, and Sloan could say no more. She was swept into the storm of his savage passion, capitulated to a high of blazing ecstasy by the undeniable fervency and ardor of the chemistry that linked them. Yet as he brought her to a shuddering crescendo, tears again filled her eyes. He did not hold her to him in their mutual satisfaction. He rolled away from her, and his weight lifted from the bed. Sloan pulled the covers over her still-burning body and buried her face in the pillow.

He must have stood staring at her for several minutes because she heard his voice, soft and very close, and sensed his presence.

"Play with fire, my love, and you do get burned."

Sloan didn't turn. There had been no mockery or cruelty to his words, but the pain in her was too fresh and intense to chance another wound. He moved away, and she heard the click of the bathroom door. With him safely out of earshot, she allowed her tears of shame to run freely into her pillow. He might not know it, but she was completely his creature. Even as her mind had rebelled against his forceful demands, her betraying body had succumbed with humiliating eagerness. If only he hadn't walked in without her knowing, allowing her words to damn her. And why didn't Wesley give her a chance to explain it?

Because, she knew, it had all rung too close to the truth because it had been the truth at one time! And she had been too sure of herself, too sure that she knew all the sides there were

311

to Wesley. But, she thought with belated remorse, she should have never made the deadly mistake of underestimating him. She had blissfully forgotten that danger could lurk in deep, quiet places.

Another click of the bathroom door informed her that Wesley was back in the room, and she dragged her head from the pillow. He was dressed, superbly handsome and cool in a baize linen jacket which emphasized the sleekness of his dark hair, the vivid green of his eyes, the bronze hue of his strongly chiseled features. He didn't bother to glance at her as he calmly hefted his suitcase to a chair and rifled his pockets for his wallet.

Sloan ran her tongue along her parched lips. "What are you doing?" she asked tonelessly.

His eyes darted to her with a flick of amusement. "That's rather obvious, isn't it? I'm leaving you to your independent bliss."

She had to moisten her lips again. "Where are you going?"

"Paris, probably," he replied with a negligent shrug. "I need a place to cool down for a while, and I do like the city."

Why wouldn't he say something substantial? she raged silently. He had taken his revenge, why didn't he help a little now? Why was he leaving this wreck of a situation entirely up to her?

Once more she forced herself to talk. "Do you want me to go home and try for an annulment? I may have to file divorce papers. I'm not really sure how it works—"

The amusement vanished from his face to be replaced by a grim, implacable anger. "There will be no divorce . . . now," he told her, tossing a wad of bills indifferently on the bed along with a blue vinyl checkbook. "My accountant will handle your monthly bills," he continued coldly. "All you will need to worry about will be your personal expenses."

Sloan stared at it with mortified amazement. She grabbed the checkbook and bills and threw them viciously back at him before covering her face with her hands. He wasn't a wonderful man at all; he was completely insensitive, domineering, and ruthless. He had purposely made a point of tossing the money on the bed with the full intent of twisting the knife further to underline his point. Payment in full. Money for services rendered. She was nothing better to him than an overpriced call girl. Less. Women of the trade, according to him, had a certain honesty.

Her action served to rekindle his amusement. "You do have problems, my love, calling a spade a spade. You want that sugar-coating on everything. But I can't handle this thing that way. You'll remain my wife for the time being, but believe me, love, you'll stay in line. And we'll keep things honest and on the level from here on out."

Sloan had to choke back jagged, sobbing laughter. The tricks of fate were so ironic! If only Wesley hadn't overheard the *wrong half* of her conversation with Cassie. She would have admitted one day that she had originally sought him out because of desperation, but she would have explained it properly and opened her heart to tell him how she had come to love him for his quiet goodness and strength and lovingly begged his forgiveness! They could have had a life of mutual respect and adoring happiness.

It would be futile to attempt any explanations now. He would never believe her. He would probably never believe another word that came out of her mouth.

"What do you want me to do?" she asked with heartless misery, her face still buried in her hands.

"I don't know, yet," he mused. "See Brussels for the next two weeks." She sensed his offhand shrug. "When you get home, say that I was delayed on business. I'll be getting in touch with you."

Sloan finally looked up, her face tearstained, her eyes reddened with abject despair. She was surprised to see that he still stood contemplatively in the doorway, watching her. His eyes were strangely soft for a moment, and although she knew he was feeling something for her, she didn't realize how completely she touched his heart. She was beautiful in her cocoon of sheets, her hair flared about her face in captivating disarray, her eyes wet and dazzling in their despondency. He walked back to her slowly and almost absently lifted a strand of her hair, marveling at the play of red, gold, and mahogany within its depths. A darkness filled his eyes which could have been taken for an agony as strident as Sloan's, an infinite yearning to take her in his arms and comfort and protect her.

She saw the tightening of his jaw and the moment of tender-ness vanished as completely as if it had never been. Suddenly,

Sloan couldn't take any more; she lashed out at him as coldly as he had her.

"I thought you were leaving."

His body stiffened perceptively, and she felt a mute satisfaction at wounding him after the terrible thrusts he had delivered to her. "Oh, I am going," Wesley said grimly. "This isn't exactly what I had in mind for a honeymoon either. Watch your step carefully, Sloan. I will be back."

"Why?" she demanded, rising haughtily to his threat. "You've made it rather clear what you think of me."

"True," Wesley countered sardonically. "But then, what difference does that make? You were willing to marry me while not loving me, why should it matter if I'm no longer enamored of you?"

"I never hated you," Sloan said bleakly.

Wes was still for a minute, then his finger hooked her chin to bring her face up to meet his. "I don't hate you," he said quietly. "In all honesty, I don't know what I feel. A lot of anger and humiliation at the moment, and that's why I'm leaving."

"Then go!" Sloan rasped icily. She wanted the words back as soon as they left her mouth, but once spoken, they couldn't be retrieved. He had spoken to her kindly; he had given her a golden opportunity to leave a salvageable thread in their marriage. But her own pain and confusion had registered only that he was leaving, walking out on her after showering her with verbal abuse and proving his physical mastery.

Words began to tumble from her mouth in a spew of unmeant venom. "I'm not so sure about you, Mr. Adams, either. You're not the man I thought you. You haven't a shred of compassion in your entire being, and you're about as kindly as a great white shark. You're ruthless, cruel, and vicious. Definitely not nice."

"That's enough!" Wes stated with frigid finality. The muscles were working in his jaw, and as Sloan stared up at him, she knew he was fighting a fierce battle for self-control. To his credit, he won.

"I never saw myself as walking benevolence," he told her, catching the sides of her hair and gripping them tautly to hold her face to his, "but then I do tend to be a fairly tolerant soul. You have to admit, Sloan, that the provocation has been great.

314

I probably am a nice man, darling, I'm just not the complete puppet you took me to be." His pull on her hair tightened for just a second and then released. He gazed at her for a moment longer, his mouth a grim, white line, and then turned for his suitcase and the door.

"Oh," he added, pausing with his hand on the knob. "Do us both a favor and remember one thing. You are married. Should you forget it, darling, after all the rest, I might be severely tempted to follow my first inclination and break that lovely little neck. And I will be back, hopefully civil by the time I reach Gettysburg." He raised his brows in a high arch of mocking speculation. "You do get my drift?"

Blue and green eyes locked in a cold stare. "I get your drift," she retorted defiantly.

"Good. It's one thing to be taken for a fool, love, but I promise I won't wear horns as well." His teeth ground together, and his tone became pained. "I don't ever want to subject myself to a repeat of today's performance." Then the pain and bitterness were harshly grated over; they might have been imagined. "I usually do discover things—as belated as it may be."

His eyes slid over her slowly in a last assessment; he didn't seem to expect any more answers—and she had none to give him. His gaze came back to hers in a final challenge.

Sloan's gaze fell from Wesley's, and sadly, she missed the gamut of torn emotions that raced through his eyes. In her stunned state of agonized confusion, it was doubtful she would have recognized them anyway.

Because he was split into more pieces than she.

As he stared at her, he was struck again with awe at her beauty. The sapphire eyes; the wild tangle of hair that held more colors than a rainbow—hair that could entangle a man and spin him helplessly into a drowning lair forever; the exquisite, supple body that was wiry, sweetly curved, unceasingly graceful . . . A dancer's form; an angel's face.

He had been in love with her his entire adult life—adulating her from afar, never finding peace or satisfaction because he knew she existed in the world and he was not close to her.

And then it had seemed that she was his.

He was a strong man; he had taken on life and received fame

315

and fortune. In return, he had paid his dues with decency and fairness. Knowing his own power, he had never willingly hurt another person. But he had never felt anything like the gut-wrenching pain of betrayal; the gnawing agony that seemed to eat away at his insides, bit by excruciating bit.

Betrayal by the woman he idolized over his own life.

And he had lashed out with full intent to wound. Not physically; he could snap her in half and he knew it, but because of his size, he had long since learned to control the forces of rage. No, he had gone after her with the strongest weapon known to man, words, calculated to rip and shred. . . .

But he had lost control of the words—gone further than he ever meant. He winced now at his own cruelty, but none of it could be undone. . . .

He had to come to terms with himself. She had used him and made a complete fool of him. But he still loved her, and the pain he had caused her was hurting him. Yet he couldn't go to her now—he couldn't erase any of what had happened.

And he couldn't forget that she had purposely seduced him into marriage for money.

But he couldn't give her up. Somewhere in the future . . .

Which was not now. His pride, ego, and heart were all wounded, raw and bleeding. If he stayed, her very beauty and his love for her would heighten his pain, and he would say more words that couldn't be taken back . . . that could never be forgiven.

She looked at him again, her crystal blue eyes brimming, but defiant, and hateful. As if a shutter had fallen over them, his own eyes gave nothing more away. "Good-bye, Sloan," he said softly.

And the door slammed coldly in her face.

She didn't cry again; she was numb with disbelief. For at least an hour she didn't even move, but remained lifelessly in the bed, staring straight ahead at the tapestried wall, unable to think and sort her whirling emotions. Then she finally obeyed the little voice that told her she had to do something, rose mechanically, and situated herself in the shower. Her hands began to steady as the hot water waved over them, and she finally forced herself to accept the situation.

A part of her hated Wesley for the things he had said and

done, for taking her and using her so brutally simply to prove that he knew her game and was changing the rules. She had sold out, and in his vengeance, he wanted her to know that she was now his and that when he said jump, her question should be, How high?

And a part of her hated herself. Color that was more than the force of the hot water filled her skin at the thought of her uninhibited response to him despite everything. Granted, the release of the anger Wesley had been harboring had created the passionate desire of the morning, and he would have taken her roughly in that bed no matter what her reaction. But Lord! she thought sickly, he had manhandled her, thrown her around, called her everything just short of tramp—albeit with a modicum of control—and she had protested but feebly and clung to him in wanton pleasure with gutteral whimperings in her throat that proved her to be an easily assailable toy. . . .

"Damn, I hate him!" she raged aloud to the cascading water. But she didn't. She still loved him, desperately, and a part of her even understood the violence of his reaction. He had loved her, really loved her, and as far as he could see, she had laughingly tossed that love aside.

There was still hope, she told herself, turning off the water. He had said he would come back. And when he did, his initial rage would be gone. She would talk to him. . . .

Her hands flew back to her face, and she shuddered. How could she talk to him if he continued to treat her as he did today? Her own temper would flare, and they would enter one disastrous argument after another.

No! she decided firmly. There would be no more repeats of today. Wesley was not a primitive caveman wielding a club, nor was she a helpless female at his mercy. Whether he ever decided to believe her or trust in her or not, they couldn't have any relationship without a semblance of dignity. She loved him, but she couldn't bear for this to go on . . . him nonchalantly pulling her about as if she were a puppet, there for his amusement and then cast aside at his whimsy.

Maybe it was best he didn't know how completely and thoroughly she loved him. He could wedge his knives so much

317

more deeply. Perhaps he should go on thinking her a cold, heartless schemer.

She was still trembling, shaking like a leaf blown high in winter. I've got to pull myself together! she wailed silently. But her dreams, so good, so wonderful . . . love, comfort . . . the security of being loved and cared for . . . had just been cruelly shattered in that same winter wind. She couldn't pull herself together; she couldn't even get out of the shower.

Sloan eventually did get out of the shower. She dressed; she even picked up the guide books Wes had left behind. A picture of Waterloo loomed before her . . . statues of Lord Nelson and Napoleon. Bruges . . . ancient walled city. Ostend.

Places and things they should have seen together. . . .

Sloan brushed the brochures to the floor. Tears flooded her eyes. She couldn't stay in Belgium . . . one brochure caught her attention. It was for the ferry that left the coast of Normandy for the fabled White Cliffs of Dover.

She would go to England, she decided dully.

But it was three days before she could even leave the room.

CHAPTER NINE

By the time Sloan returned to Gettysburg she had done a fair job of pulling herself together—or at least an acceptable job of creating a smooth shell to hide behind and a serene mask with which to face the world.

The mask was brittle, and beneath it she was a desolate and miserable wreck, but no one would ever know. To complicate matters, she had no idea what Wesley's next move might be, but since he had adamantly decreed that there would be no divorce, she was nervously determined to keep up appearances on the slender line of hope that something could be worked out.

She hadn't stayed in Belgium. After finally managing to emerge from her room, she found the memories of Brussels too haunting and beautifully ironic to bear. Besides, though of French descent, she had none of Wesley's gift for the language, and Flemish eluded her completely. She had moved across the English channel to Dover and on to London where she had forced herself to sightsee like crazy. For hours she had gazed upon the ancient tombs and history of Westminster Abbey, toured the endless halls of the Victoria and Albert, and strolled the shops of Piccadilly Circus and Carnaby Street. Her greatest pleasure, however, had been a day spent in the London Dungeon —a wax museum specializing in the rather barbaric practices of the various tribes and nationalities that combined to make the English people. With a spite she wasn't quite able to contain, she thought how nice it would be to contain Wes in a gibbet, boil him in oil, or set him to the rack. Her pleasure didn't last, however, because she knew she had no desire for real vengeance, only a yearning to go back in time and undo all the wrong between them and recapture the wonderfully golden moments when they had both been truly in love.

Nothing could be undone. She had to brace herself for the dubious future, steady frayed nerves that threatened to snap with the pressure of wondering when she would suddenly look up and discover Wes had returned.

With just the right amount of dejection Sloan informed Florence that Wes had been held up on business. She breathed a little more easily when Florence accepted her explanation without doubt—apparently Wes traveled frequently on business.

She didn't need to feign her happiness at her reunion with her children, nor stifle the delight that the children's pleasure over their foreign gifts gave her.

It was hardest to see Cassie. She didn't dare give away the slightest trauma—if Cassie were to discover that her trip of concern to her sister's house had been the catalyst to the destruction of her marriage, she would never forgive herself. Still, it was very, very difficult to listen to Cassie's sympathy for "poor Wes," working two weeks after his wedding away from his bride.

. . .

Sloan was extremely grateful for her own work, and she plunged her heart and soul into her classes. But as the weeks began to pass and no word was heard from Wes, her resolve to remain cool and collected despite the inner battle played beneath her shell became increasingly arduous. She kept up a strained smile when asked about Wes, always sighing and saying that he had called and was regrettably still delayed.

Finals for the students came and went, sending Sloan into mental chaos. She would have plenty of time to spend with the kids, but Florence had the house in complete control, and since the children loved their summer day school, she would have hours of nothing to do but chew her nails and worry and give vent to the tears that always lurked behind her eyes when no one was looking.

She was looking at the mess that was her attempted cleanup of her desk on the last day of classes, when an idea that had been vaguely forming at the back of her head rose to the surface with vehemence. Leaving papers and folders to flutter in her wake, she raced into Jim's office.

"Jim!" she exclaimed, interrupting his study of a thesis.

"Sloan!" he imitated her urgent tone with a chuckle. "What is it?"

Curling into the chair that faced his desk—an identical arrangement to her own office—she plunged right in before she could lose her nerve and determined impetus. "Have you thought any more about setting up your own school?"

Jim sighed and shrugged. "I've thought about it, but that's about all. I'm not really in shape yet to try my own wings."

"But I am!" Sloan whispered softly.

"What?"

"Think about it!" Sloan urged excitedly, planting her elbows on the desk as her dream took flight. "I can swing the financial end, you can handle administrative problems, and we both teach and eventually form a first-rate company. What do you think?"

"Sloan"—Jim shook his head—"you're not even going to be here—"

"Oh, I have a feeling it will be a long, long time before we make the actual move to Kentucky," she said dryly, wondering herself if she would ever be asked to accompany her husband to his home. "And besides," she added hastily, expecting his further objections, "it will be a business, a partnership. If I do leave, you hire another teacher, and since I know it would be a success, the investment would still be worthwhile."

Jim scratched his forehead thoughtfully, hesitating with his reply, but Sloan could see the light of anticipation dawning in his eyes. "Have you discussed this with Wes?" he asked.

"No," Sloan answered slowly. Then she bit down hard onto her jaw, remembering the taunting way he had tossed the money and cards on the bed in Belgium—payment for services rendered. "I'm sure Wes isn't going to care," she said, biting back the taste of bitterness the words cost her. "We'll be returning it all eventually."

"Sloan," Jim advised uncertainly, "you're talking I don't know how many thousands—"

"Don't worry about the money," she interrupted quickly. "I'll handle that end of it." She scribbled the names and addresses of Wesley's attorney and accountant on a scratch pad and pushed

321

it toward him. "Just be in the lawyer's office a week from Monday."

From that point on, Sloan gave little heed to the repercussions that might fall her way if Wes did return before she was set. He had been gone over a month without a single word, and though her heart often ached with a physical pain, she was hardening. Her ambition to set up her own school and dance company had her captured in a whirlpool she was powerless to stop or deny, and the whirlpool was swirling away with no hindrance.

Florence thought the idea wonderful; so did Wesley's attorney and his accountant—the latter telling Sloan that if all did fall apart, Wes could take a healthy tax break. She wasn't particularly fond of his lack of faith, but she didn't really care as long as he was helping her.

And thankfully, Wes had informed no one that he wasn't on the best of terms with his wife. She had feared at first that he might have put restrictions on her expenditures, but that was obviously not the case. The accountant didn't blink an eye when she held her breath and rattled off the sums she would need.

On the first day of fall her school was opened. As she and Jim had hoped, they were besieged by past and present students of the college who wanted to engage in more serious study.

"This is going to be a success," Jim said with awe as he looked over their records at the end of the day.

"Of course!" Sloan laughed teasingly. "We have to be the best this side of Philadelphia!"

"I hope so," Jim said fervently, "I just wish—"

Sloan cut him off, knowing his reference would be to Wes. She had become so accustomed to inventing phone calls and conversations with her husband that she didn't even think as the next reassuring lie slipped from her lips. "Oh, didn't I tell you? I talked to Wes last night, and he thinks the whole thing is marvelous! He still doesn't know when he'll be back, and this will keep me busy and off the streets."

She was kept busy. Another two weeks saw their venture in full swing. Although the work load didn't keep Sloan's mind from wondering achingly about her husband, it did keep her on an even keel. The studio was beautiful—she had grown increasingly ostentatious as she discovered the flow of her seemingly unlimited funds, and they offered every amenity to their classes. A smile that wasn't entirely happy but purely satisfied was on her lips when Jim ambled into their mutual, roomy, shag-rugged and leather-furnished office after his last tap class at five.

"Patty Smith is waiting for you down in the studio," he advised her with a tired but pleased grin. "I'll finish up in here while you get started with her. Then I'll be back down, and we can lock up together." He frowned slightly. "What's Patty doing here now anyway?"

"Private lesson," Sloan said with a wry smile. "She has an audition for the Solid Gold dancers on Monday, and we're going to work on the number she'll be doing—sprucing up at the last minute."

"Oh," Jim nodded sagely. "Hey," he asked as they both walked to the connecting door, "heard from Wes? Think he'll be impressed with the place?"

"Oh—ah, yes and yes," Sloan mumbled as she walked past him. "I, uh, talked to him last night, and he's still detained, but I'm sure he'll be quite surprised by our success." She lowered her head and winced as she hurried to the studio. Wes sure as hell was going to be surprised—if he ever returned. She was beginning to think the entire thing had been a fabulous dream that had turned to a painful nightmare at the end. But it wasn't a dream; the gold band and diamond cluster on her finger weighed heavily to remind her of reality.

Patty was a good dancer. Her instinctive grasp of dance was a natural talent, and Sloan had hopes that her student would succeed with her audition. She lost track of thought and time as she tutored her pupil. It was a fast, rugged piece, performed to a number by a popular rock group, indicative of the work she would be doing if she got her job.

"It's good, Patty, really good," Sloan told the anxious girl. "Just watch your timing. Let the music be your guide." She sighed as Patty stared at her blankly. "I'll run it through, Patty. Listen to the music while you watch."

Sloan set the stereo and moved into Patty's dance, allowing the beat of the music to permeate her limbs and guide her. Her concentration was entirely on the harmonious tempo of movement; she was heedless of anything around her. As the song neared its end, she rose in a high leap, one leg kicked before her, the other arched at her back, her toe touching her head.

It was then that she saw Wes, leaning nonchalantly in the doorway, his dark suit impeccably cut, hands in his pockets, his eyes glittering with a hard jade gleam as he watched her, that crooked smile that wasn't a smile at all set pleasantly into his features as he listened casually to whatever it was that an enthusiastic Jim was saying to him.

Sloan almost fell. She had a streaking vision of herself crumpled on the floor, her limbs twisted and broken.

But she didn't fall. She landed supplely and finished the piece for Patty, her thoughts whirling at a speed more intense than the rock music. She should have been prepared, but she wasn't. She was in shock.

Her eyes clenched tightly as she struggled to hold back tears of uncertainty. Had he finally come to call it quits? To tell her he had extracted whatever revenge he had required and that their best course now was a divorce?

Her heart was pounding tumultuously, and she knew it was more than the dance. She had learned painfully to live without Wes, but seeing him cut open every wound. He seemed to exude that overpowering masculinity which had first entrapped her senses as he stood there, so tall, so broad and yet achingly trim, the lines of his physique emphasized by the tailored cut of his suit. The profile, though hard, was still the one she had fallen in love with. . . . Her eyes flicked from the full sensual lips that could claim hers with such mastery to the hands that dealt pleasure even as they mocked. . . .

If only his eyes weren't so cold and hard . . . relentless, ruthless, and condemning now, contemptuous when they lit upon her.

She was shaking as the music ended, and she struggled for control. She loved him, and she wanted their marriage to work no matter how the odds appeared to be irrevocably against them. Now was her chance to at least show that she was willing. . . .

"Patty, keep working," she told the girl hastily, rushing to the

324

doorway. She forced herself to be calm even as she longed to throw herself into his arms, even as her eyes glimmered brilliantly with hope.

She stopped a foot away from Wes, halted by the chill in his eyes. She had no chance to take the initiative—he had already taken it and thankfully quelled her desire to throw herself at him before she made a fool of herself.

"Darling," he said coolly, brushing frigid lips against her forehead and encircling a cold arm of steel lightly around her waist. "Jim was just thanking me for sanctioning this little venture."

Sloan stiffened miserably within his grasp, knowing how he mocked her. She met his gaze with crystal defiance, miserably praying he wouldn't defrock her series of lies before Jim and that she wouldn't hit the end of her nerves and burst into the tears she was sure he would love. And still he had her hypnotized, trembling beneath her barrier of ice, wishing so desperately that she could forget everything and curl into his arms, satiate herself with the male power and light dizzying scent that radiated from him. . . .

"We are a success, as you can see," she said quickly, forcing a stiff smile. "Your investment will be made back in our first year."

"Will it?" Wes inquired politely.

"Yes, I really believe it will!" Jim said with innocent enthusiasm. He laughed as he realized neither Sloan nor Wes really paid attention to him. "This must be some surprise for you both. Sloan said you didn't think you'd be in for some time when you spoke to her last night!"

"Did you say that, darling?" Wes asked Sloan, his dagger gaze turning fully to her and his lips curling sardonically.

Sloan moistened her lips, hating him at that moment, ready to scream if he didn't clear things one way or another.

"Yes, I decided to surprise her," Wes continued in his pleasant tone with the iron edge. "And I certainly am surprised myself, darling. I never expected such professionalism when we, uh, *discussed,* your business." He brushed a damp strand of hair from Sloan's face. "That was quite a dance you were doing when I walked in, Sloan. "Cold As Ice," wasn't that the tune?" he inquired politely, his sardonic smile still nicely in place. He had missed his wife's expression of pleading when she saw him; she had carried off her reserve and dignity so well as she approached him that he had no idea that she was longing to see him, praying for his loving touch. All he saw was the woman who had admittedly married him for his money, who now appeared to be annoyed that he had come home to watch her spend it . . . the woman he had loved half his life . . . still loved. . . . "Cold As Ice," he repeated pleasantly, not waiting for her reply and murmuring his last comment as if he teased someone. "What is it, sweetheart, your theme song?"

Sloan grinned along with Jim's unknowing laughter, but she felt a shivering chill streak along her back. She knew he wasn't teasing, and she dreaded the confrontation coming between them when they were alone. She vowed as she forced that grin that she would never break to him; if he had pegged her as cold and mercenary and now despised her still, she would never let him know how the tables had turned and she pined for his love. "Yes," she teased as he had, but her eyes glared like blue ice into his, "my theme song."

"Lord," Jim jumped in, absurdly unaware of the tension that filled the air around them. "Here I am interrupting you two when you've already had a honeymoon interrupted. Sloan, Wes —go home, or wherever you two newlyweds want to be after a separation. I'll finish up with Patty and lock up."

"No," Sloan started to protest, fear of being with her husband alone suddenly gripping her fiercely. But Wesley overrode her protest.

"Thanks, Jim," he said, straightening and running a cold, taunting finger along Sloan's cheek, making her bite her lip to keep from flinching. "I would like to be alone with my, uh, wife." He dropped his hand from her face. "Get your things, Sloan." It was softly spoken, but undeniably a command.

Rigid with anger and the fear she couldn't quite squelch, Sloan lowered her eyes and opted for obedience. She had to face him sooner or later.

"I have my own car—" she started briskly as they left the school and Jim behind, "Cold As Ice" once more blaring from the stereo.

"Leave it," Wes said just as briskly. "We can get it tomorrow."

Sloan shrugged and walked along with him to the Lincoln, poker-faced as he opened her door and ushered her in. She was sure he was going to rail into her immediately, tearing her apart piece by piece for her actions during his absence. He was strangely silent instead, his attention on his driving, his hardened jaw and cold eyes rigid in the profile she glanced at covertly from the lowered shade of her lashes. It seemed to Sloan that the tension in the car mounted until it was thick and tangible and she was drowning in it. "Don't you think we should talk," she finally exploded, unable to bear the uncertainty a moment longer. "I really don't care to argue in front of the children," she added with cold hauteur.

His eyes slid from the road to her for a moment, searing her with disdainful ice. His hand shot across the car, and she flinched thinking he was coming for her, but he wasn't. He snapped the button on the glove compartment and the door fell open. With his eyes back on the road, he felt for a plump envelope, found it, tossed it on her lap, and slammed the door closed.

"I have no intention of arguing in front of the children," he said, "but neither am I in a mood to discuss anything with you while driving. Don't worry, the children are not at the house."

"What?" Sloan exclaimed, baffled by his words and the envelope lying in her lap. She glanced from it to Wes, afraid to touch it, unaware of what it might contain. "Where are the children?" she demanded.

"At a motel by Hershey Park by now, I would imagine," Wes replied briefly.

The import of his words sank slowly into Sloan's mind, and she was then struck by a fury that overwhelmed her in shattering waves. "*What?*" she shrieked, twisting to face him in the car. "How dare you send my children away, how dare you take it upon yourself—"

"They aren't your children anymore, Sloan; check the envelope on your lap. It's the final judgment. Legally, they are my children now, too." His gaze flicked to her steaming face with a quelling authority. "I didn't send them away, I sent them on a little vacation—with Cassie and George as well as Florence."

327

"A little vacation!" Sloan repeated incredulously, pushing the envelope from her lap to the floor with vengeance as she struggled against tears of anger and the impulse to fling herself at him and cause any bodily harm that she could. "You bastard!" she hissed. "You decide to waltz back in and just flick them aside—"

"You can stop now, Sloan!" Wesley's voice growled low with the sharp edge of deadly warning. "I'm not flicking anyone aside; I'm more aware of their welfare at the moment than you are. You want to hide behind them. I think it's going to be to their benefit not to be around while you and I settle the immediate future."

"I don't see where there is a future. Immediate or otherwise," Sloan hissed, grudgingly admitting to herself that the concern he was showing the children was sincere, but she wasn't about to say so. She was still seething with a rage that was in part a debilitating jealousy that she abhorred. Where had he been for all this time? . . . "Since you haven't bothered with a call for six weeks," she said aloud, "I hardly see any justice to your sweeping in like the north wind and thinking you can call the shots—"

"I will call the shots," he interrupted her curtly, "and that should be no surprise to you; I told you as much in Belgium. And if we're discussing justice, Mrs. Adams, let's bear in mind that you owe me."

"I don't owe you anything!" Sloan snapped. "You've already subjected me to payment in full."

Wes laughed, startling her with an honest twinge of amusement. "Payment in full? Taking a look at that school I so magnanimously funded makes you more in debt than ever."

Sloan crunched down on her lip uncomfortably. "You'll get your money back," she said with quiet conviction.

"I believe I will," Wes said indifferently. He raised a brow in her direction. "I don't remember ever accusing you of stupidity."

The car pulled into the house drive before Sloan could think of a reply to his double-edged statement. Sloan hopped out before he could come around and assist her and hurried for the front door, fumbling in her bag for her key. To her dismay it eluded her fingers and Wes was twisting the lock while she still fumbled. "Allow me," he mocked her, pushing open the door and ushering her in.

The house seemed empty and hostile with Florence and the children gone, fueling Sloan's fury that Wes should send the kids off without her approval. Deciding to ignore his dominating presence until she could rally from the shock of his sudden arrival, she dropped her things and stalked for the shower. Apparently, he didn't mind if the night was spent in slow torture. She might as well shower and be comfortable while she regathered her forces.

"What's for dinner?" he called after her, as if they returned home together every night of the week.

"How should I know?" Sloan shot back. "You're the one who sent the housekeeper away."

She was careful to bolt the shower door, but he made no attempt to come near. Emerging a half hour later with her skin pruned and her mind no closer to an answer on how to handle the impending evening, she found Wesley's travel things had all been neatly put away in her room. A rush of heated blood suffused her, but she wouldn't allow herself to remember the exotic pleasure of his arms. She'd be damned before she slept with a man who continued to treat her as Wes did. Belting a quilted housecoat securely around her waist, she took several deep breaths and headed out to meet her tiger.

Stripped of jacket and tie, the neck of his shirt open and his sleeves rolled up, Wes was reading the paper, annoyingly at home with his long legs stretched out on the coffee table, his socked feet crossed. He didn't look up as she entered the room, and for a moment she thought he didn't realize that she was there. But then he spoke, his eyes still on the paper.

"I repeat, what's for dinner?"

"And I repeat," Sloan grated with hostility, "how should I know?"

The paper landed on the coffee table with a whack, and Wes was on his feet. "Then let's find out together, shall we?" He wasn't really expecting an answer; his hand lit upon her elbow with determination and he propelled rather than escorted her into the kitchen.

Sloan spun ahead of him, tears burning behind her eyelids. She wasn't going to stand any more of the uncertainty, of the terrible fear that he was playing cat and mouse before pouncing with his demand for a divorce. Choking, she whirled on him, determined to have it out.

"Just get it over with, Wes!" she blurted angrily.

He stared at her with drawn brows and genuine confusion. "Get what over with?" he demanded impatiently.

"Tell me how you want to arrange the divorce, and then we can stop all this and you can go somewhere for dinner!" Sloan said quickly so as not to allow her voice to tremble.

He watched her for a moment and then turned to the refrigerator to rummage through it. "I don't want a divorce," he said blandly. "I want something to eat; I'm starving."

Relief made her shake all over again, but it was a nervous relief. She had no idea of where he had been for all that time, and he had yet to give her the slightest sign that he had decided he still cared for her in the least.

"Are you sure?" she asked.

Sloan instantly became convinced that he didn't really give a damn one way or another. His reply was not a joke; it was issued with exasperation.

"Of course I'm sure. I came in this morning and I haven't eaten since."

Gritting her teeth, her voice tight, Sloan asked again, "I mean, are you sure you don't want a divorce?"

"Dammit," he muttered, slamming the refrigerator door. "You spend money like water and there's nothing to eat in this house!" His eyes turned to her, the jade speculative and hooded. "At the moment, Mrs. Adams, I do not want a divorce." His gaze followed her form, and then he walked to the telephone, dialing as he added, *"I've decided there's something I just may be able to get out of this signed and sealed bargain of yours."*

Sloan felt as if she had been hit, sure his "bargain" referred to her. She willed away the wash of humiliation that assailed her and clenched down on her teeth. She knew Wes's temper; if she had expected mercy, she had been a fool. Still, she loved him, and she wanted her marriage to work and he wasn't demanding a divorce. She didn't intend to accept his dominating scorn, but she could make an effort at a little civility by swallowing her pride for the moment and attempting to put them on a level

330

where they could converse rationally. If they could only build up a friendship. . . .

"Who are you calling?" she asked huskily.

"Information," he replied. "Give me the name of any restaurant that delivers."

"Don't bother," she said, adding hastily at his frown, "I'm sure I can make omelettes or something."

Wes hung up the phone. "That would be fine," he said. "I think I did see a carton of eggs."

Walking around the kitchen as she prepared their meal, Sloan began to regret her offer. She could feel Wesley's keen jade gaze on her with every step and movement she made. Panic began to assail her in mammoth proportions. He said he didn't want a divorce—at the moment. But what good was having the legal contract that bound him to her—the contract she had strived so hard to achieve!—when nothing was right between them and she was constantly on tenterhooks wondering when his scorpion's sting would strike next? The cold ferocity of the anger he had shown her in Belgium had somewhat dissipated, but his comments tonight proved he didn't intend to forgive and forget. Was it because he still didn't believe she loved him, or had he lost all love and respect for her?

"You could be useful," she muttered irritably, thinking that if he stared at her any longer, she would throw the entire carton of eggs into the air and fly into a laughing tantrum as they fell. "I'd like a drink."

"Scotch?" he inquired politely.

"Please."

It was almost worse having him pad silently around her on his stocking feet. She was going to add that she'd like a double, but the portion he poured her while looking ironically into her eyes displayed his ability to read her like a book. "Thanks," she murmured, accepting the rock glass he offered her.

Cheese, ham, and peppers went into her omelettes. Wes continued to watch her, leaning over the counter, drinking his bourbon. She was feeling the terrible urge to do something erratic again—anything—to break the uncomfortable tension between them when Wes finally spoke.

"Sloan."

331

She glanced at him warily, but his expression was unreadable. "I'm sorry."

Her eyes fell quickly back to the eggs browning in the pan, tears stinging her lids again. Sorry about what? she wondered. His dry remarks tonight, the fiasco of a honeymoon, or the wedding itself?

"Would you like to say something, please?" he questioned, a tinge of annoyance seeping into his tone. "I said I'm sorry."

"About what?" Sloan forced herself to ask aloud.

"Belgium."

She remained silent, desolately thinking that things had changed much since then. Jealousy—the nightmares of him with a multitude of faceless women that had gnawed away at her during his absence—and the painful memory of his hard glare when they had met again kept her from accepting his words and perhaps setting things straight when her impulse was to fly to him and tell him how terribly sorry she was too. Her hand froze on the spatula as she began to realize her impulse might be the one thing to give her a chance at her marriage. But then the moment was gone.

"Dammit! Sloan! Say something," Wes grated.

"What do you want me to say?" she charged in retaliation. "That's it's all right? It isn't! You were terrible, and you haven't improved an iota."

She heard the sharp clink of his glass hitting the counter, but other than that, he controlled his temper. "I see," he said smoothly. "I was terrible—my actions were unforgiveable. But it's okay that Sloan decided she could live just fine with a man she could lead by a little rope just so long as that man was filthy rich."

"Go to hell," Sloan hissed, dropping the spatula on the eggs. "Prima's Pizza delivers, or you can finish this yourself. I'm going to bed."

"Oh, no, no, no, you're not, Mrs. Adams," Wes said grimly, his hand clamping on her wrist as she attempted to walk past him. "We have a lot to talk about tonight, and we havn't even begun to scratch the surface." He released her wrist and stalked to the stove to scoop the omelettes from the pan to a plate.

Inclining his head toward the kitchen table, he added, "Sit, please."

"May I fix myself another drink first?" Sloan asked with mock subservience, her eyes wide in sarcasm.

"Drink all you like, Sloan, but please do sit."

She poured herself another drink, stared at the glass, and heaped another portion of scotch into it. Maybe she could blur the razor edges of what was to come. . . .

"Do *you* want a divorce, Sloan?" Wesley plopped the food on the table and pulled out a chair for her as he asked the question.

She lowered her eyes as she slid into the chair, her fingers tightly gripped around the glass. She was caught off guard, expecting a further battle, not an almost indifferent query.

"Do you?" He sat down himself, and again she knew he stared at her, his seering jade gaze giving nothing but bluntly allowing her no quarter.

"No," she finally managed to whisper.

"Why not?" he demanded.

God, why was he doing this to her, she wondered. "What do you mean?"

"I mean, why do you want to stay married? Is the money worth living with a monster you can't forgive?"

Now was the time, she knew, to say something, to drop her pride . . . but she was so afraid he was setting her up. . . . "Yes," she said coolly. "I could say that I love you, but since you're not going to believe it, let's just leave it at cold cash. A signed and sealed bargain, as you say." Her voice suddenly cracked and broke. He had tried to apologize, and she had made a mess of it. "I'm sorry, Wes," she continued with a waver. "I do want to stay married, but God, not like this! Not like Belgium! Not with you gone for weeks at a time when I have no idea where you are or who you're. . . ." She stopped speaking and took a sip of the scotch she had stared at while she spoke.

"Did you care where I was?" Wes asked softly.

"Yes," she admitted to the amber liquid swimming before her.

"Did you really care, Sloan?" he persisted. "Or was your ego bruised? Never mind," he answered himself, adding with a trace of bitterness, "I wouldn't know whether to believe you or not."

333

He fell silent and Sloan chewed on her lower lip. "Wes?" she finally said quietly.

"Yes?"

"Could we try to be friends?" she asked tentatively.

His arm stretched across the table, he gripped her chin, firmly but gently, forcing her to look at him. "I didn't come back to argue with you, Sloan," he said gravely, and for the first time that night she sensed a thread of an emotion that hinted of tenderness in his eyes. "It doesn't change things, but I am very sorry for my behavior in Belgium. I can't promise I'm going to be a saint from here on out; I have an ego myself and believe me, it's very bruised. You have to expect a few snide remarks when you marry a man for his money, but yes, although I find it ironic to be discussing friendship with my wife, I should hope that we work toward that end since we both plan to keep the . . . bargain . . . going."

His touch upon her chin was wearing through the thin veneer that was left on her nerves. The callused gentleness of his hand brought back sweeping memories that combined with the nearness of him—the light but fully masculine scent that would forever be inbedded in her mind, the breadth of shoulder that was so enticing to lean against, the cleanly chiseled lines of his powerful profile—to nearly engulf her senses and bring her flying to him, promising anything, pleading, begging, anything to be back in his arms, held tenderly even if it was a mockery of love.

She couldn't allow herself to do that. They had to establish a wave of communication and respect first.

She stood, praying her blurring eyes and quivering voice would not betray her need. "Tomorrow," she said tentatively, "I'd like to tell you about the school."

"Fine," he replied.

"You don't mind about it, do you?" she said hesitantly.

"No, I don't. But I will be interested in seeing your books—I don't care what you spent, but perhaps I can be helpful on the business end."

"Thank you," Sloan murmured. She needed to get away from him, and he hadn't protested her rising. "I, umm, I think I pushed it a little with the scotch. I'm going to bed. I see that your things are in my room, so I'll just move out to the—"

"No, you *won't*!" Wes interrupted sharply, the cold, guarded glimmer slipping back over his eyes as he stared at her with full attention.

"Wes," Sloan said slowly, "I'm not talking about any permanant situation—"

"Forget it," he said curtly. "Permanent, temporary, or otherwise. In my book, a husband and wife share a room."

She was too tired and too frazzled to realize what she said next. "Terry would have—" Her voice broke off with abrupt dismay.

Wes stood. It seemed as if he did it very slowly, rising over her with a towering force that was chilling although they were several feet apart. His fingers were clenched tightly around a napkin, the knuckles white, the thin line of his grimly twisted lips just as devoid of color.

"I think we discussed this once," he said with soft danger. "I am not Terry. I do not sleep on couches, nor will you. *I am not Terry.*"

Sloan met his gaze, dismayed at the hard-core jade. He still intended to tell her just how high to jump. . . .

"No," she agreed scathingly. "You are not Terry. Terry was a nice man." She spun on him before he could retaliate and sought refuge in her bedroom, staring long at the lock on the door. She pushed it in, but then released it as his voice tauntingly followed her.

"Don't bother, Sloan. If you're in my—our—room, a lock isn't going to stop me from entering."

He didn't come to bed for a long, long time. Sloan lay in silent misery, her nerves and, yes, anticipation fighting sleep. Each time she heard a movement in the house, she jumped while her mind raced double-time. Damn! She did want him so badly, being near him and not touching him was like slow and torturous starvation. . . .

But all she really had now was a piece of paper and her pride. She couldn't allow herself to show how vulnerable she was. . . .

He entered the room in the dark, and she barely breathed, feigning deep sleep, hearing the sounds as he undressed as if each piece of clothing had fallen with the burst of an explosion. He crawled in beside her, and her entire body went stiff, her heart seemed to thunder, and her flesh was painfully aware of his heat as she waited. . . .

And waited.

He didn't touch her. He plumped his pillow, adjusted his position, stretched his body out comfortably. But didn't touch her.

Sloan lay in shocked confusion. And, she realized sinkingly, disappointment. Whatever she had been telling herself was a lie. She had been glad that he had insisted upon sleeping together; she had been wonderfully relieved that he was going to force her into his arms so that she would have an excuse to salve her pride.

But now she just ached, her disappointment becoming a physical agony.

She didn't know how long she lay there, her eyes open, staring blankly into the dark, when he shifted again, and his arm grazed her shoulder.

"What is the matter with you?" Wes demanded impatiently, obviously aware she had never been sleeping. "You're as cold and stiff as marble and shivering like a rabbit."

"I—I—" Sloan stammered.

She heard his soft chuckle; it was a gentle sound of amusement, and it caressed her warmth. "I see," he said, and although his voice was amused, it was tender. "You thought I was going to force you into keeping conjugal rights. No, my love, I'll not force you. I won't sleep in another room, but I won't force you."

"You . . . you don't want to make love?" Sloan said in a strangled voice.

She felt his hand on her cheek, the knuckles grazing her flesh, his whisper soft and gentle. "I didn't say that. But I want you to want to." He was silent for several seconds, his hand moving to smooth back her hair, to trail down her throat. Surely, Sloan thought, he must feel the terrible pounding of her heart in the erratic racing of her pulse.

"Do you want to make love, Sloan?"

His voice, threading through the night like deep velvet, was husky and wistful. It was the perfect touch to break her final grasp on control. Sloan lay still just seconds, her eyes closing, her

336

fingers clawing into fists at her side. Then she turned into him, her face burrowing into the dark hair on his chest, the tenseness of her body evaporating as she melded to him, her hands freed from their convulsive grasp to tremble as they rose to his shoulders, sweetly relishing the power play of muscles beneath them. "Yes," she whispered, barely audibly, "yes, please, Wes, make love to me. . . ."

"Oh, God." She heard his groan, deep and guttural within his throat. His hands raked through her hair, his kisses rained upon her face, covering her eyelids, devouring her mouth, falling with reverence over her breasts as he rolled over her with a need as urgent and demanding as she could have possibly desired. "Oh, dear God, wife," he murmured, divesting her gently of the silken sheath of nightgown that barely separated them, "I've missed you . . . wanted you, dreamed of you . . . making love to you . . .

Sloan's shivers of agonized thirst slowly abated as he filled her with his heat, making love to her with a gentle trembling thoroughness that proved the truth of his words. Beneath the assault of hands and lips that enticed and seduced while they commanded and took, she came alive as she had never been before, craving release from her consuming madness, but savoring each touch of hungry lips upon her, lips that bruised her breasts, her thighs, sending lightning streaks of electric excitement ever closer to the core of her need. Nor could she fill herself with the taste and touch of him, drowning deeper and deeper in sensation as he rumbled groans of the pleasure she gave him.

He burst within her and she was filled, so sweetly gratified that she was at peace, realizing only then how sorely empty she had been. And he whispered softly that he loved her, and she clung to the words because she wanted more than anything to believe them.

Wes did mean his ardent whispers, uttered with passion in the dark because he was afraid to face them by day. Her sighs of pleasure made him tremble. The darkness had hidden the shattering joy in his eyes when she had come to him . . . a humble joy . . . his wife was perfection . . . a potion that slipped into the blood and intoxicated for life.

There was so much he wanted to say to her. He wanted her

to know how sorry he really was, but it could never be explained, only felt.

And he couldn't explain anyway. She had taken him so easily once, cut him to the bone. She had the power to destroy him; he couldn't let her do it a second time. He couldn't talk to her as he wanted, until he could begin to believe, until time healed. They were wary opponents, ever circling . . .

He couldn't even assure himself that insecurity would keep him from striking out again . . . But now, as he held her close in the darkness, they had precious moments of mutual need . . . and caring. The battle tactics were out of the bedroom. Here he could love her.

And he did.

All through the night. He tooked what was his and cherished it, knowing morning could bring dissension and inevitably the light of day. Here, in the shadows, he could even accept her tentative whispers of love in return as the lazy comfort of satiation held them both in a spell and he cradled her to his form, softly stroking her hair.

"I do love you, Wes," she murmured softly against him, her voice so hesitant, so beseeching, that it hurt and he stiffened. Very, very faintly, he thought he heard a muffled sob.

"I love you," he said quietly. "But I don't trust you, Sloan."

"Then where do we go from here?" she murmured bleakly.

He was silent for a long time, but he continued to stroke her hair gently. "Trust is something that has to be earned," he said very softly, and fell back to silence.

Dawn was streaking through the windows, dispelling the guardian shadows of darkness, when they both slept, held together by the first tenuous thread of communication.

Wes was grateful that he held her in his arms against him, but his sleep was still not content or easy. He still had to wonder if she didn't wish that she slept with another man, a man she had also called husband and formed a relationship with that was her dream of near perfection. . . .

And he had to wonder if she really loved him, or if she still gave her love only to the ghost who remained in her dream.

She was a wonderful actress. He had learned that already. She could be protesting love for the mere convenience of saving the wealth she had plotted to obtain. . . .

Thank God she didn't know that any further acting was unnecessary. He loved and needed her so desperately that he would stay with her, give her anything in his power, no matter how she felt, just as long as he could be with her. . . .

CHAPTER TEN

"What in hell are you doing?"

Wesley's voice, rasping over her shoulder, startled Sloan so badly that the pill she had been about to take flew from her hand and sailed into the kitchen sink. Whirling to face her husband, she stated the obvious with confusion. "I'm taking a pill." He stared at her stonily for a moment, his arms crossed over the white terry of his robe, then brushed her aside to pick up the packet she had left on the table. Very deliberately, he punched each pill from its plastic socket and flung them down the drain, one by one.

"What in hell are *you* doing?" Sloan demanded, astounded by his behavior. She had left him peacefully sleeping, confidently believing that the ardent lover of the night would awaken in a decent, if not loving, frame of mind. But he didn't appear to be in a "decent" mood at all. The tension in his sinewed body that she was learning to read so well was all too apparent. She wasn't sure how, but she had seriously angered him. "Wesley," she repeated more softly, "what are you doing? I need those." Had the man gone mad?

The last pill swirled down the drain, and Wesley tossed the packet into the garbage bag beneath the sink. "Where's your purse?" he demanded.

"Why?"

"I want the rest of these."

"There aren't any 'rest.' I get them each month." Sloan planted her hands on her hips and added crossly, "Except now I'll have to run by today and replace what you just threw away. What in God's name did you think you were doing? Did you think they were some type of drug—"

"I knew exactly what they were," Wes said irritably. "And you have a hell of a nerve taking the damn things without first discussing it with me."

"*What?*" Sloan's exclamation of amazement was a shrill cry.

"You heard me," Wesley snapped. Sloan could do nothing but stare at him, working her jaw, but still unable to offer a suitably scathing comeback. He returned her stare with challenging eyes, then turned to the automatic percolator. "Have you made coffee?"

"I've made coffee," Sloan retorted blandly, energizing herself into action to tug on the sleeve of his robe. "Would you mind explaining your childish actions? What difference does it make to you whether or not I take pills? I would think you'd appreciate —"

"Well, I don't," he cut through her speech. "I told you last night I'd thought of something I could get out of our bargain." He poured coffee into a cup and began to sip it black, his eyes implacably on her.

Again, Sloan was stunned speechless. She blinked, swallowed, and sputtered before managing, "You want me to . . . to . . ."

"Conceive," Wesley supplied, calmly drinking his coffee. "Yes. That is the usual way to have a child."

"You want a child," Sloan echoed numbly.

"My, what astounding comprehension!" Wesley drawled mockingly. "Yes, I want a child. That, my love, is something I can get out of this, something I've always wanted. I told you last night that I had decided there was a benefit I might derive."

"I know you told me," Sloan mumbled, automatically reaching for the coffeepot to occupy her trembling hands, "but I thought . . . I thought . . . that you meant . . ."

"Let me help you with that," Wes said, amused by her confusion. He took the coffeepot from her hands and poured the steaming brew into a cup. He placed the cup firmly into her grip, then leaned nonchalantly back on the counter. "You thought that I had decided on your lovely person as sufficient payment for a . . . loveless . . . marriage." Sloan felt her skin begin to heat beneath his cool appraisal and choked as she sipped a burning gulp. Wes patted her on the back, laughing at her obvious dis-

341

comfiture. "Darling wife," he remarked with a small shake of his head, "you are so easy to read. That is exactly what you thought. Sorry—you were wrong." His cool green gaze raked her mirthfully from head to toe. "Not that I don't find your charms intricately pleasing, but in all honest reality, they are available elsewhere."

Sloan's hand rose automatically to slap his devilishly leering face and hopefully wipe the amused grin clean from it. But this time Wesley anticipated her action, catching her arm and salvaging her cup simultaneously. "Don't!" he warned imperiously, twisting her wrist until a small cry escaped her. His grip eased, but he continued to hold her wrist and his jaw was rigidly set. "Lady, you will learn to control those violent little impulses of yours. Lash out at me again and you'll be very sorry."

Sloan clamped her teeth together and glared into his eyes defiantly, tilting her head with regal pride. He wouldn't dare! Still . . . she might be wiser to learn to cut him with words as he did her. Her arm went limp within his grasp. "Perhaps, if you could learn to curb your tongue, Mr. Adams," she challenged coldly, "I could learn to control my violent impulses.

"And if you expect a child," she snapped, "you'd better start being a little nicer to its prospective mother."

Wesley's eyes flashed, and he dug his fingers into her shoulders to pull her against his heat-radiating length. "Is that a bribe or a threat?" he asked, but oddly, his voice held no menace. Something that belied his mockery was behind the question . . . tenderness?

Sloan's head fell as she shivered, and she buried it into his shoulder. "Neither," was her muffled reply. He had taken her by surprise at first, even appalled her with the suggestion of a child. But she suddenly wanted his baby very much. She loved children, and Wesley had already proved himself an excellent father with the sons and daughter of another man. He had every right in the world to a child of his own.

There was only one problem. The thought of two A.M. feedings again didn't bother her, nor did the idea of diapers or the demanding attention needed by an infant. The problem was Wesley. She loved him, ached for him with her entire being. Yet, how could she bear his child when she knew his love for her had died along with his trust and respect?

Trust had to be earned, he had told her, and it might be a long road to winning back his trust. But as he began to stroke her hair gently as her head lay against his chest, she knew she was willing to traverse that long road.

"Would you like a fourth child, Sloan?" Wes asked her softly.

She nodded, not trusting herself to speak.

"Be sure," he said carefully. "I wouldn't force you to have a child against your will. I'd rather you be honest with me than run behind my back and pick up another package of those pills."

"I am being honest," Sloan said, talking to his chest. "But would you . . ."

"Would I what?"

"Would you mind telling me where you've been for the past month?" Sloan intended her question to be bold and challenging, but fear of the possible answer added a note of pique.

Wesley laughed easily, annoying her to the core. "You mean who have I been with, don't you?"

"You know exactly what I mean!" Sloan snapped, pulling abruptly away from him to stomp across the kitchen. He had the exasperating habit of making her want to claw his eyes out, and she was desperately trying to avoid such useless behavior.

"I was in Paris for two weeks," Wes said, straightening and ambling slowly after her. "And since then I've been in Kentucky. In fact," he mused, planting hands on her shoulders while a rakish grin settled subtly into the corners of his mouth, "that's where I came up with my idea." He held her at arm's length and studied her with teasing appraisal. "One of my prize mares just produced her third colt, a magnificent animal, like the ones before him. The mare is a born breeder. Just like you, my sweet. I'm sure to get a healthy, beautiful child."

Sloan felt as if she were strangling. Blood suffused ringingly into her head with fury. "A brood mare!" she hissed, shaking his hands from her shoulders. "A brood mare!" her voice rose shrilly. "That's what you think of me!" Her wrath was causing her teeth to shatter. "That's just marvelous, Wes. Just marvelous! Suppose we have this child? What happens then?"

"Then we see," he said softly.

343

He wasn't fast enough to catch her hand when it flew across his face that time, and she had whirled away from him while the stinging sensation still seeped into his stunned cheek. "Go back to Paris, Wes!" she called over her shoulder as she stalked down the hall. Aware that he had made a mess of the whole thing and willing to apologize, to try to explain . . . "Sloan!" he called again, more sharply.

She made no reply, and he heard the lock click in the bedroom.

"Dammit!" he roared, his apology dying in his throat as she ignored him. He followed her down the hall. "Sloan, I'm talking to you! Open the damned door!"

He didn't ask a second time; the door gave with a single lunge of his shoulder, and Sloan, seated on the bed in a dejected huddle, straightened with wide eyes as she met the thunder of his face, features as harsh and stormy as if he were about to meet the defensive line of the Green Bay Packers.

"Get away from me!" she hissed, startled and frightened. She hadn't ignored him on purpose; she had been so preoccupied with her inner dilemma that she had really closed out everything. She jumped as he approached her, attempting to elude him but failing.

"Sloan," Wes tried to begin, clasping her upper arms.

She had no conception that he was still trying to apologize; she was sure from his face that his intent was dangerous, and she flailed against him heedlessly. "Sloan—" he tried once more, but at that moment her flying fingers raked against his chest, the nails clawing, creating rising welts.

They both stood stock-still, Sloan with horror, Wes closing his eyes and clamping down hard on his jaw, shaking as he tried to breathe easily and leash the steam rising within him.

"Oh, Lord, Wes, I'm sorry!" Sloan cried.

"Damn, you have a vile temper!" he muttered, opening his eyes. She was gazing up at him with eyes of liquid sapphire, naked and beautiful with remorse. The hands that held her drew her into him, and he smelled the sweet scent of her wild hair. He brushed her forehead with a kiss, lifted her chin with a finger, and kissed her lips with a hungry intensity.

"What are you doing," she asked breathlessly as they broke,

and he lifted her into his arms, cradling her to warm, sinewed muscles.

"Well," he murmured, "my first impulse was to wring your lovely little neck. I could do that. Or I could make love to you . . ."

"You're crazy. . . ."

"Yes."

It was a tempest, a reckless soaring into foaming rapids, riding crest after crest, twirling, whirling, crashing, rebounding.

Yet temper brought no ruthlessness. Wes harbored her, cherished her, swept her into the glory of his wild winds.

She should have denied him.

He had made his opinion of her so very clear.

But she held on to her love, clinging to the belief that no man could be so gentle and tender against such odds if there wasn't truth to his love.

It was a matter of truth. . . .

And learning. . . .

And if loving was part of that trust, then she was right to love. But did any reasoning matter? He touched her, and it didn't matter. But it should matter. . . . She should have the strength to insist that they have more than the consuming physical need. . . .

She didn't have the strength . . . only the need. Only the desire to believe the cherishing, bend to the storm . . . be there as he was with her when they soared over the fall, gently guiding her to the still waters beneath. . . .

Where she turned from him and curled into a little ball of solitude, bewildered and confused.

She couldn't understand her own behavior, much less begin to comprehend his. They could reach the borderline of friendship, and then all was lost with a reckless word or deed. Then they were mortal combatants, then the most tender and passionate of lovers.

But when it was over, they were on the defensive again. And it would be hard to go back and see just what had triggered what. . . .

* * *

"Sloan."

A quality in his tone compelled her to look his way, but she stubbornly denied herself. With obstinate willpower she kept her head in her pillow.

"What?"

"Look at me," he persisted with firm patience.

She turned slowly, wincing as she realized that countless muscles were sore. If his mood were similiar to the one that had precipitated the broken door, she reasoned with herself, it would be plain old stupid to disobey his soft-spoken order.

His head rested in his hands, and his eyes were on the ceiling, seeming strangely to reflect her own emotions. As she watched him, his gaze riveted sideways to her.

"I never mean to hurt you," he said quietly.

"You didn't hurt me." She frowned, adding bitterly, "You know you didn't." She winced at the sight of the scratches she had inflicted. "I hurt you."

He grunted impatiently and leaned over on his elbow to face her. "That's not what I mean. I acted without thinking—or discussing, rather. I said things in haste, and although I was teasing you about the mare bit, I'll admit I was crude." He smiled ruefully. "I was scared."

"What?" Sloan whispered incredulously.

"You might have turned me down," he said flatly.

"Oh!" Sloan murmured, shocked that it meant so much to him.

"I goad you a lot, Sloan, and I'm usually quickly sorry," Wes continued, "but still too late. We all say things in anger, and the problem is that they can't be taken back. If I could undo half the pain I caused you in Belgium, I gladly would. But I was hurt, Sloan, and that hurt was like a knife wound in the back that made me angrier than I've ever been in my life. You can't imagine how I felt to reach your house and find you telling your sister how you had planned to marry me for my money. It was crippling, I had never felt so used and betrayed. . . . I planned to surprise you with a kiss and instead I got the surprise. I slammed the door because I couldn't stand to to hear any more of it. . . . Damn, Sloan," he muttered fiercely, running a knuckle down the length of her arm, "I really wanted to throttle you that night.

I had to leave . . . and then, I still had to have you, but I had to let you know too that I was well aware of your motives."

"Oh, God, Wes," Sloan moaned, longing to reach out and touch his cheek with its slightly rough edge of overnight shadow, but rubbing her own temple instead. "I'd give anything to take back that night—you only heard half a conversation. It was true, but it wasn't true . . . and I can't take any of it back or undo it. . . ." she trailed miserably.

He was silent for a minute, then shifted so that he was sitting to draw her head against his side and take on the task of rubbing her forehead himself. When he spoke again, it was with the thread of silk she loved.

"I don't want to spend my days in constant battle. We have major problems, but I don't want a divorce. I don't believe that you do either—especially not while you're still financing that new dance school of yours."

"Wes . . ." Sloan implored.

"Sorry, I was doing it again." Wes grinned ruefully. "But we are going to set down a few ground rules. Legitimate deals. I promise no more wisecracks, and you promise to control your temper—no more slaps. I won't go anywhere without your knowing exactly where I am—and we both make a pact to say what we really mean instead of striking out below the belt when we're bothered. And please, no more businesses that I know nothing about! How about it?" His soothing fingers moved from her temples to tug gently at the ends of her hair.

Sloan nodded slowly. "Wesley," she said, biting down on her lip. "You *didn't* hear the whole conversation. I told Cassie that night that I did love you . . . had loved you. . . ." Taking a deep breath, Sloan tried to explain the whole thing. "Cassie came over that night because she didn't want me marrying you because she was afraid it would be a disaster. She knew I wasn't crazy about seeing you in the first place, and then things moved so fast. . . . She is my sister, but she thinks the world of you. . . ." Sloan lamely sought the right words. "I was trying to tell her the truth—that yes, at first the money had been the draw, but only at the *very* first. I had no idea that you had heard any of the conversation, but when you left, I really didn't need to explain any further to her! She knew that I loved you, really loved you. . . ." Again, her voice trailed away feebly. "I won't suggest that you just ask Cassie," she started again with quiet dignity. "I realize that she is still *my* sister—and that you could well imagine I've had plenty of time to warn her that you heard what we were saying. . . . I can understand that . . . but, God, Wes, it is the truth! I did love you, and I did tell her that night. . . . I wish you would believe that!"

"It should be very easy to try," Wes said softly in sincere promise, "because I want to."

It was a qualifying statement, but a start. Sloan buried her face into his shoulder. They had been ripping one another apart when they were really after the same things. "Wes?" She could let matters lie, maybe should let matters lie . . .

But then she couldn't . . . she had to ask. . . .

"I spent two rotten weeks in Paris by myself," he said, anticipating her question, "and since then, I was in Kentucky. Alone." His touch was gentle as he smoothed her wild hair. "I haven't been near another woman since the night I first walked into your house. Does that answer your question?"

She nodded mutely against his chest.

"And do you believe me?"

"I—I think," she faltered, thrown by the question. "I want to believe you—"

"Don't you see?" Wes queried lightly. "That's the point." His voice became passionate and intense as he groaned, "I want to believe you. I want to trust you more than anything in the world. . . ."

"But I do love you, Wes," Sloan choked, burying deeper into his side. "I did need money, everything was going so badly, but I never meant to be . . . mercenary. Your love was like a dream come true, and then I knew that I loved you, too. Then, and, I do love you now, Wes!"

"That is what I want most to believe," Wes said, his voice a soft whisper again. "And I am trying to. It just takes time for wounds to heal. We need that time."

They both fell silent, but it was a comfortable, restful silence. For the first time, they were totally at peace in one another's company.

It was Sloan, who, growing drowsy, finally broke the bond of quiet. Resting her chin on his chest, she looked into his eyes, determined to take a further step on the new road to open honesty.

"I do want your baby, Wes," she told him wistfully.

His arms tightened around her, and his reply was one of the most tender she had ever heard. "Thank you."

CHAPTER ELEVEN

Things should have worked out simply from that point, Sloan thought; they were capable of talking, capable of breaking across the barriers of mistrust.

But talking didn't necessarily mean that the past could be erased, and although their relationship had become pleasant and cordial in the week of Wesley's return, she knew that they both still held back, both clung to a measure of reserve.

They had hurt each other, and she supposed it only natural that they both still wear armor when treading upon the soft ground of one another's feelings.

It was therefore with a little unease the following Friday night after the children had long been asleep and Florence too had retired that Sloan sought Wes out in the den that he had turned into a pseudo-office.

She had had visions of the scene, played it a million ways. And in all her visions, it had been beautiful. She had teased and tormented him, smiling while promising him a secret. She had played the feminine role to the hilt, insisting upon an elegant dinner out before allowing her secret to leave her lips. And Wes . . . well, of course, he had responded with all the joyous enthusiasm and tender care she could have desired. . . .

But when it came down to it, she was frightened. She could give him news that should surprise and elate him—news he wanted to hear. News that had thrilled her. But despite all of her happiness she was also filled with a heavy feeling of anxiety, almost a sadness. *We should have had more time,* she kept thinking. They should have had the time to keep talking, to break down the guards and barriers, to learn how to live and love together. . . .

But they didn't have the time. She had verified a slow dawning suspicion this morning, and although she could have waited to tell him, she didn't deem it fair. She had begun all that was wrong between them with a lie—withholding this information would seem to be as great a lie as the one she had used to play with his emotions in a time that now seemed interminably long ago.

Besides, she couldn't have held back any longer. Despite the shaky foundation of their marriage, she was hesitantly glowing. Deep inside she was thrilled and smug with herself—already madly in love with and protective of his child. She had to share the baby's existence. . . .

And yet it didn't go a bit as she had envisioned in her daydreams—hindsight would tell her it was her own fault, but as she approached Wes that night, she wasn't privy to hindsight. She was nervous, and afraid. From this point on, she would never really know if Wes had forgiven her completely, or if he was merely satisfied with his end of the bargain.

Her voice was consequently sharp when she stood in the doorway, her throat constricting as she watched his dark head bent over his papers, his attention fully on his work. "Wes."

He glanced up at her, his eyes registering both surprise and annoyance at her tone. "Yes?" He didn't snap at her; he was polite but aloof. That was about all that could be said for the week, Sloan thought dryly—polite and aloof. He was determined not to argue with her, determined not to bring up the past. They communicated just fine in the bedroom at night with the lights off, but in the morning the wary remoteness was back. Sloan began to wish he would yell or scream or argue—anything to dislodge that invisible shield that still kept them apart.

"I have to talk to you," she announced, once more wincing at her own tone. She wanted so badly to be natural, to share the enthusiasm she was feeling. . . .

"Come in." He pushed back from the desk and indicated the wingback chair a few feet across from it. "What is it?"

Settling into the chair, Sloan knew her chance to change the cool tide of the conversation had come. All she had to do was put warmth into her abrupt tone, let her feelings show. . . .

But it was as if she had lost voluntary control of her actions.

She didn't tease, she didn't torment, she didn't leave the chair and force herself into his lap, curling her arms around his neck, as she longed to do. She blurted her information almost brusquely.

"You're getting your part of the bargain, Wes. I'm pregnant."

A barrage of emotions flashed through his eyes in less than seconds—then they were guarded, opaque. His dark lashes swept over them, and Sloan suddenly felt as if she were facing a stranger.

"Are you sure?" His brows were knitting into a frown. "I didn't think it was possible to know so quickly—"

"It isn't quickly," Sloan interrupted, feeling a flush steal over her face. Absurd that she could still blush in front of him, after all they had shared. But what she had to say went back to Belgium, a time when she would have doubted they could have even come to this strange, touching-but-not-touching existence. Her own lashes fell over her eyes. "I conceived on our . . . honeymoon." She didn't mean it to sound bitter, she really didn't —but it did.

Wes was silent for a long time. So long that she began to think he didn't care anymore, that his request of a week ago had merely been another way to taunt her. . . . But no, she didn't believe that; Wes had been too sincere when they did speak. He was honest with her. He did love her; she knew that and clung to it—even as she knew through his admission that it would take time for him to trust her.

She couldn't know that he was silent because he was busy berating himself. A child, their child, and she was offering the wonderful information as part of a "bargain." Because of him. Because he had come back so determined to keep her, and weld her to him, that he had forced her to do so. What a damned idiot he had been—it was almost as if fate laughed at him. If he had said nothing . . . if he hadn't come upon her like a bear . . . she might be coming to him differently now. She might have come into the room full of the joy and enthusiasm . . . He never needed to force her into a bargain . . . she had been pregnant with his child at the time. . . .

"Are you sure?" he asked huskily.

"Positive," she answered, still afraid to risk a meeting with those opaque eyes again. But he was going to force the issue.

"Sloan, look at me."

She did so finally, hands clasped tightly on her lap, her posture rigid with tension.

"Are you happy?" he asked softly.

Her nod was jerky; she could feel tears hovering behind her eyes and bit down hard on her inner lip to prevent them. "Are you?" she managed to ask.

He stood with an easy movement and made his way around the desk, his eyes never leaving hers. And then the opaqueness was gone; he was kneeling down beside her, taking her quivering hands into his. She glanced at him, suddenly feeling the tears drip down her face as he finally replied, "I'm not happy, my love, I'm ecstatic. That is, if you are."

Sloan nodded as he touched her cheeks, brushing away the dampness with a gentle finger.

"Why are you crying?" he demanded gently.

Sloan shook her head; she couldn't explain. "Because I'm pregnant, I guess," she told him, star sapphires seeming to gleam in eyes that were wide and liquid. She didn't realize that she now looked to him with ardent appeal—and an aching need. "Women are supposed to be highly emotional at this time, didn't you know?"

He chuckled. "So I've heard." His voice went very low in answer to her appeal. "I don't mind 'emotional' at all, just as long as you are happy beneath it. I love you, Sloan."

Suddenly she felt as if the barriers were gone—she hadn't erased mistrust, but she was comfortable in the belief that Wes was trying, that his love was great enough to eradicate the mistakes they had both made in the past.

"I love you, Wes," she echoed, eyes beseeching that he believe her. She was always so afraid to say those three little words.

He didn't dispute her. Very tenderly he kissed her hands, then her forehead, then abruptly and with far less tenderness, he plucked her from the chair and into his arms, laughing at the startled expression that replaced her tears.

"My darling," he explained, heading through the den door, "you came in like a prisoner of war to give me the most marvelous news of my life. Then you start weeping all over me! This, Mrs. Adams, is a time for celebration. We've a bottle of Asti Spumanti in the back of the fridge, and we're going to toast one another to death. Hmmmmm . . . maybe I'll do the majority of the toasting. . . . I don't believe you should be drinking too much. . . ."

Sloan's tears were changing to giddy laughter. "I can certainly have a glass of champagne!" she protested. "You forget, I'm an old hand at this."

"Well, I'm not," Wes protested, "And so you are going to follow all the rules. You don't smoke, that's good, and we can hire a teacher to work with Jim—"

"Hey!" Sloan protested, laughing as she was deposited on the kitchen counter while he prodded through the refrigerator. "I'm not going to stop dancing—I don't have to, Wesley, really. I danced professionally until I was five months along with both Jamie and Laura."

Wes stopped his prowling for a moment to gaze her way with stern eyes. "I don't like it, Sloan. You're ten pounds slimmer than you should be to begin with; you've been taking pills—" He halted abruptly; his stare seeming to narrow and bore into her. "Sloan," he said tensely, "why were you taking those pills so long?"

"Because I didn't know, Wesley," she explained quickly. Oh God, she thought mournfully, could he really believe that she would try to lose his child? "I'm afraid I've never known for quite some time." She was blushing again; how ridiculous. "I didn't even suspect until Monday morning, and probably only then because we had been talking. . . ." How lame she sounded. "But it's all right, Wes, really it is. Many women take pills accidentally, and, and, nothing happens."

His gaze softened. "You really do want this baby?"

"Yes." She kept her eyes level with his. "I told you that I did, and I mean that, Wes." She didn't tell him how good it felt, how wonderful to cherish and nourish his child within her.

"All right," he said gruffly, "you can keep teaching then—for a while—but we won't stretch it too far. And you can have one glass of Asti Spumanti." His eyes had taken on a twinkle, and she felt like crying again with relief. Things were going to be all right.

Then she was in his arms again, laughing as he stuffed the cold bottle and two crystal glasses into her hands so that he could carry her.

"What about your work?" she demanded as he booted open the door to their bedroom.

"It won't go anywhere," he promised gravely. And then the door was being slammed behind them, and she was laughing while he undressed her. She still attempted to hold the champagne and glasses and feel the inevitable warmth and sensual stimulation steal over her with his commanding touch. . . .

Things *were* going to be all right.

And they were all right. Wes started coming into the studio with her, telling her he was looking at books, but she was sure he was watching over her.

She didn't mind the feeling.

In fact, the only spur in her existence was an uneasy feeling in the back of her mind which she usually managed to ignore. Wes had been back in Gettysburg for two full weeks, and he hadn't mentioned a thing about Kentucky. She knew he hadn't decided to remain in the north indefinitely—his business holdings outside of Louisville were too vast for him to suddenly forget them. She also knew that he loved his home, his work, and the prestigious empire he and his brother had created together. She was aware that he would have to be going back—but he made no reference to her going with him. She should bring it up, she told herself, but she was loath to do so. She didn't dare do a thing to mar the happiness the announcement of the child had brought them both. As long as things were moving along so very comfortably, she couldn't dare make a change that might be disastrous. She was also still afraid of answers she might receive if she questioned too closely. She didn't want to take a chance on hearing that their marriage was still on a trial basis—not complete until she had actually delivered the child Wes craved.

In that respect, she wasn't frightened. She had three beautiful children—even Terry, born early in the midst of grief and shock, had clung tenaciously to life and health.

They were becoming a rounded family, and Sloan loved becoming that family in all the simple ways. Sharing dinners, watching television, planning their time. The money that Sloan had once longed for now meant so little. Her pleasure was in the man—watching him help Jamie with projects, chastising Laura while still treating her like a little princess, taking Terry with his toddling precociousness beneath his own wing. As it had always been with him, what was hers was his. No blood brother could have been better to Cassie, more companionable to George.

If only she didn't carry that edge of nervousness over his refusal to bring up his own life, and the home far away.
. . .

It was two and half weeks after his return that the bomb dropped. It was late, near midnight, and she was comfortably curled to Wes's side as they both read paperbacks, when the phone rang. Their mutually curious expressions as Wes picked up the phone signified a loss at who could be calling so late.

Curious, Sloan's raised brows knit into a frown. After Wes's initial "Hello," he went silent, listening, as seemingly countless seconds ticked by. Then his reply was a brief "Hold on a minute." Handing the receiver to Sloan, he slipped from the bed and into his robe. "Hang that up for me, will you please? I'm going to take it in the den."

Not waiting for her acknowledgment, he exited the room. Sloan was glad he didn't turn around—he would have seen her jaw drop and her eyes widen with startled pain. He had just dismissed her as nothing more than a personal secretary—not trusting her, and not caring that she was worried. . . .

But then Wes had the sure capability of turning from ardent lover to cold stranger—hard stranger—in a matter of seconds.

Staring bleakly after him, Sloan eyed the receiver she held. Temptation was overwhelming, because her pride had been wounded. She had a right to know what was going on in her home at midnight. She was, after all, Wesley's wife. . . .

Sloan brought the receiver to her ear just in time to hear Wes pick up downstairs. She intended to announce herself, but he began to speak immediately. "Okay, Dave, I'm here. I can get there immediately; I picked up a little jet the other day. In the meantime, call Doc Jennings—I don't care what you have to do to find him or what you have to take him away from. If our entire stock is down—" Wes's voice didn't fade away; it stopped abruptly. She was startled by his tone becoming as curt and precise as an icicle, although, because of his brother's hearing of his words miles away, he did couch his request politely. "Sloan— I have it down here, thank you. You may hang up now."

"Hey, Sloan," Dave cut in cheerfully. "Didn't know you were there. How are you?"

"Fine, thanks, Dave," Sloan murmured quickly, feeling as if her face had gone afire. She mumbled a good-bye and set the receiver hastily into its cradle, wondering with bleak but increasing anger how Wes could have managed to be so curt, so icy cold, to her. And then she realized that he had left the room purposely so that she would not hear his plans—his full intention had been to shut her out. . . .

Alternating between the despairing realization that nothing had really changed—Wes trusted her less than one of his well-nurtured horses and had no intention of sharing his life with her, even if he did humor her and join into hers—and the infuriating proof that he would continue to do what he pleased with no regard to her feelings, Sloan sank into the bed, her limbs also torn between racing heat and numbness.

He was leaving; he was going to Kentucky. And he was leaving in a plane he had purchased—and neglected to mention to her.

And on top of all that, he would shortly come stalking back up to the room to coldly denounce her as an eavesdropper, condemning her with that oceanic stare that was like a razor's edge. . . .

The hell he will, she decided grimly, slipping from the bed in his wake. For a moment her body protested her movement; her stomach, always a little queasy in her first months of pregnancy, wavered out a warning signal. Sloan ignored it; she was never truly nauseated, and her decision was taking precedence. She was going to challenge Wes with all the wrath she could muster before he hit her with his icy disdain.

Donning her robe and sliding into her slippers, she followed his trail to the den with equal determination. When she entered, he was just hanging up the phone, appearing ridiculously dignified and coolly authoritative for a man with tousled black hair clad in a velour robe. His eyes, in fact, chilled her; they brought her back in time to a cool morning in Belgium when she learned she had indeed pulled upon a tiger's tail. . . .

"Ahhh, my wife," he murmured, "the eavesdropper."

Sloan flushed but refused to be intimidated. "Sometimes eavesdroppers hear what they should have been told in the first place."

His shrug seemed to be another dismissal. "Obviously, you would have been told. I'm leaving tonight. I did assume that you would notice when I packed." Why was he snapping at her? Wes wondered. He knew the answer; he didn't like to admit it to himself. He was afraid that she wouldn't notice, not really notice. She responded to him, she professed to love him, she was charming, she was his—everything he had loved all those years— everything he had planned on having—prayed to have—since that day he had watched her. He didn't covet her as another man's wife; he had only come to that when he knew she was alone and yearned to alleviate her pain.

And now he wondered if he had ever come to do so. She wanted the baby—badly—he believed. But Sloan loved children. And the baby had been conceived long ago. . . .

He wasn't prone to insecurity, but he was uncontrollably insecure now. He didn't believe that she intended to leave him, but he still wondered if she didn't close her eyes at night and envision him as another man. . . .

Wes watched now as stunned hurt filled her eyes before she could shade them, and he was ready to kick himself. "I'm sorry," he apologized gruffly. "But I don't appreciate your listening in on a private conversation. I wanted the facts first so that I could tell you how long I would be gone."

"How long will you be gone?" she asked hollowly. Did she care, Wes asked himself desperately. As long as she was left with provisions and memories, did she really care. He heard hauntings of her soft voice telling him she loved him, but he had heard it before when it had been false.

"About two weeks," he replied curtly.

"You're flying yourself out?" Again, her voice had that hollowed sound, curiously strained.

"Yes," he replied impatiently. "If I were to keep driving all the time, I'd spend half the time on the road."

"Wes"—was there a note of anguish in her voice?—"you didn't tell me you had purchased a plane. You never even told me that you were a pilot."

"I'm not a pilot. I have my pilot's license."

"Wes"—her voice was definitely rising shrilly—"don't you think we should have discussed it?"

Stupidly, he didn't realize what she was getting at. "I can afford the plane, I assure you. I don't remember you discussing the setup of an entire business with me."

He heard the sharp intake of her breath; something sizzled into her sapphire eyes. "Wes, you seem to have forgotten I've lost one husband in those little planes." She turned away from him suddenly. "But suit yourself."

God, she could sound cold. He wanted to tell her that he was sorry, but he felt the terrible chill of her demeanor. "Cheer up," he heard himself saying. "Since you're planning my demise, I'll remind you that you'll be a very rich widow this time." He saw the heave of her shoulders and suddenly hated himself with a black passion. Belatedly, words of apology came to his lips, and his strides were eating the distance between them. "Sloan," she tried to shake off the restraining hands on her shoulders and look away, but he wouldn't allow her. Fighting back tears, she met his eyes rebelliously. "Sloan," he persisted softly, "I'm sorry. Yes, Terry died in a plane crash. But millions have died on the highways. I'm a very good pilot. I'll be safer in the sky than I would be in a car."

He could feel her shaking; she knew it. It would be impossible for him not to feel her trembling as he held her. But somehow, she couldn't reply to him. "Sloan," he insisted tensely, "answer me."

Bleak, liquid eyes lifted to his; the indifferent tone was back in her voice. "What do I say?" she asked. "You're flying out tonight; you'll be gone two weeks. It's settled."

Yes, it was settled. Her opinion didn't matter. He had apologized, but he hadn't changed a thing. Even his apology, she was sure, had been issued because he had seen her wince with the sudden tension in her lower back. It was frightfully apparent that

359

he didn't want her upset. But then that, of course, was because of the baby. And it didn't seem to occur to him that she could tolerate the plane—even happily board it—if only he wanted her with him. . . .

He exhaled a long sigh. "Go on back to bed, Sloan; you're shivering, and you need to get to sleep. I have a few things to get together down here, and I won't need to pack much, so I shouldn't disturb you."

That was it—a dismissal. He was leaving. Sloan nodded dispiritedly and turned away as he released her. "Sloan." She heard a slight catch in his voice and turned back. "It might be nice if you kissed me good-bye."

He took her in his arms before she could have a chance to refuse him, and his mouth claimed hers with a bittersweet combination of persuasiveness and demand. Unable to resist him, Sloan felt herself melt to his touch, knowing it would be denied her for what would seem an eternity. She arched herself against the warm strength of his frame, hungrily met his thrusting tongue with her own. And then she felt the salt of tears on her cheek and disentangled herself, turning away before he could see them. Saying nothing else, she quit the room.

The encounter had left her absurdly weak. Returning to the bedroom with her thoughts in a turmoil, she at first ignored the pain in her back that was proving to be persistent. Wesley didn't want her in his home. He was leaving for two weeks, but she had no guarantee that he meant to return at that time. He could leave, and find himself busy, and not care if he hurried back to a wife he didn't trust.

Of course, he would be back eventually. He wanted to see his child. . . .

The next stab of pain she felt was so shocking that it ripped her cruelly from her mental dilemma and sent her staggering to the bedpost for support. Stunned, she held on as the pain continued to rack through her. In disbelief she thought she had felt nothing so horrendously unbearable since Terry's birth.

It was then that she started to scream Wesley's name in a long low wail of agony and terror.

Her cry jolted him with panic as nothing ever had before in

his life. Wes bolted from the den and made it to the bedroom as if jet-propelled. At first he couldn't ferret out what had happened. Sloan was doubled over on the floor, her slender hands losing their grip on the bedpost. He took a step nearer, and it felt as if his heart sank cleanly from him; he held his breath. She was saturated in blood. So much blood. How could it possibly have come from such a wraithlike figure? How could she possibly have any left to pulse through her veins, to keep her heart beating . . . ?

He was galvanized into desperate action, knowing even as he shook as if palsied that he had to move quickly. He was shouting as he scooped her into his arms, loud enough to raise even Florence, and then he was issuing curt commands to the frightened but alert housekeeper. She was dialing the hospital even as he was slipping Sloan into the car, loath to take a chance on wasting the precious minutes to wait for the ambulance. She opened her eyes once; a weak, pained smile touched just the corners of her lips. "Wesley," she whispered, and then her sapphire eyes closed once again, and all color was gone from her ashen face.

My wife, he thought desperately. No, my life, my existence. . . .

And then he was careening toward the hospital, her cheek resting against his knee. . . .

In actuality, he wasn't shut out long. But every second was an eternity. He paced the empty, sterile halls, praying.

And his mind would return to the nightmare. The grim look of her obstetrician—the man who had delivered not only her three children, but Sloan herself. A man who had made it to the hospital after Florence's call almost as quickly as he.

An older man, but obviously competent, obviously deeply caring for his pale, lifeless patient. A man who had assured Wes he wouldn't let her die as he wheeled her away.

But he had been worried. Wes had known he was worried. The sharp old eyes had taken in all the blood.

And so Wes kept pacing, a caged tiger stalking the relentless prison of his heart, fighting fear, cruelly cutting into himself with blame. There was the possibility that he might lose her—and it would be his fault. No, he hadn't been cruel to her, he hadn't misused her. He had even been what some might term a good husband since his return. But he knew what she had known—he had held back. He had denied her the security and faith that she had needed from him. . . . He had forced her to have the child . . . no, she had wanted the child . . . no, he derided himself fiercely, he had forced her; he could remember with stabbing clarity the way he had taken her in Belgium, the time the child very likely had been conceived . . . and even that had been all so unnecessary. He had known she didn't love him, but he had also known that she intended to remain his wife, to offer what she could.

But like a fool he had been insanely jealous of a ghost. If she made it, he swore, he wouldn't care. He would simply cherish her, be there, take care of her as he had longed to do since he first set eyes upon her gamin face and sapphire eyes.

No. He stopped his pacing and raised his eyes heavenward in a solemn vow, a strange figure, a virile giant in a bloodstained velour robe silently beseeching God.

I'll release her. I'll see that she never has another worry, another care, but I'll let her resume her life alone.

That was the state Cassie and George found him in. Cassie, already worried by Florence's call, saw the blood on Wesley's clothing and burst into frantic tears as she raced toward him.

Wes took one look at the panic and anguish on his sister-in-law's face and was suddenly sure that she knew something he didn't. He felt his breath leave him, his heartbeat waver. His world became the swirling mist of miserable gray he knew it would be without Sloan.

With an agonized cry that would rip apart the heart of anyone within hearing range, the virile giant crashed to the floor.

Consciousness came back to him with sharp severity which he strove to fight off. He didn't want to come back. But then he heard Cassie's voice, felt her touch.

"Wes, she's okay, she wants to see you. Wes!"

He opened his eyes. He hadn't been out long—he was still on the floor, his head dragged onto his sister-in-law's lap. Hovering above him were the faces of George and the doctor—both filled with relief, a relief that was slowly dawning to amusement.

"Your wife is going to be fine, Mr. Adams," the doctor was assuring him. His voice lowered. "You know, of course, that she has lost the baby, but she will be fine."

"Oh, God." His hands were shaking convulsively as he buried his face into them, oblivious, uncaring that his tears of relief and joy were damp on his cheeks.

"Wes," Cassie reminded him softly, "she wants to see you."

He stood up, her empathetic eyes still on him, and he found his strength within them. Squeezing her arm, he turned to rush down the corridor.

"Wait." George caught his arm and stuffed Wes a large paper bag into his arms, his head inclined toward Wes's robe. "Florence told us you ran down here in your robe. I'm not so sure it would be good for her to see you looking like that."

Wes nodded his thanks with a brief, rueful smile, then directed his hasty steps for the bathroom to change. "We'll be here," Cassie called after him softly. "Tell her we'll see her as soon as we can in the morning."

"Five minutes only, Mr. Adams," the obstetrician called. "She needs rest now."

Wes nodded to them all, still dizzy with gratitude to the deity who had allowed her to live.

She was still under sedation, and the world was misty. But even while disbelief assailed her, the misery of truth was there. The tiny life that had been within her was gone. The baby was dead. Doc Ricter had tried to tell her that it wasn't her fault, that miscarriages were often a mystery, an act of God. But Sloan couldn't believe him. She had killed her own baby, she had been oblivious, she hadn't taken care. She had insisted on dancing. . . .

And it wasn't just her baby she had killed; it was Wes's. The baby he wanted so badly . . . the baby who had held them together, offered them hope . . .

She had asked for Wes because she had needed him. She hadn't been able to control her plea with the sedative making her weak. But as the seconds ticked by in her world of white, she knew she could no longer ask him to stay. Doc had severely warned her against trying again for quite some time. . . .

363

She had nothing left to offer him.

But suddenly he was standing in the doorway, paused for a second, and then he was at her side.

Her hand was enveloped within his large ones; he was on his knees. She could vaguely feel a dampness as he brought her fingers tenderly to his cheeks, and then to his lips.

"Wes," she whispered, trying to get the words out without choking on the ever-present tears, "I've lost the baby."

"I know, my love, I'm so sorry, so very sorry."

It was like Wes, she thought vaguely. Always so concerned for others first. She had to keep trying, she had to make him understand. "Wes, we . . . I may not be able to have another."

"Hush," he murmured, his fingers moving to brush back her damp hair. "It doesn't matter. Nothing matters. You're going to be all right and I'll never ask anything of you again; I'll see that you never want for anything. . . ."

Oh Lord, she thought sinkingly, he did want to be rid of her; he would care for her, pay her anything, to be free of her. . . .

"I . . . I don't want anything, Wes," she murmured miserably. "I'm going to release you so that you can have your child for sure. . . ." She simply hadn't the strength to prevent them. In anguished silence the tears began to cascade down her face.

"Child?" he was awash with confusion, not daring to believe what was staring him in the face. "Oh, dear God, Sloan! I don't care if I ever father a child; you gave me three of them already. . . ." She was still dazed, he knew; she might not be understanding all he was saying, but his words were coming in a torrent. "Sloan, I wanted the baby because I wanted to tie you to me any way that I could. I loved you since the day I met you, and that never, never changed. My pride was wounded in Belgium—and so I struck out at you, but while I was away, I knew that somehow I had to keep you. Yet even having you I wasn't sure. I've been so afraid that you were still in love with Terry. . . . I was there, you see, the day that you buried him. I knew that I had to give you time. . . . I never had to come to Gettysburg; I made business here. . . ." His voice trailed away softly. "All I ever meant to do was care for you, Sloan, to make you happy, to take some of your burden from you. . . . If you want me, my wife, my sweet, sweet wife, I'll be with you."

Into her gray swirl of misery was rising a gleaming ray of incredible hope. "Terry," she murmured blankly, fighting the mind-robbing sedation. "Oh, Wes, I did love Terry, I'll never deny that. But I don't think I ever even felt for him what I do for you. I thought you weren't sure because you never seemed to plan to take me to Kentucky. . . . You were leaving alone. . . ."

"Oh, Sloan, I have been afraid, but because of you. Your life was here. I was afraid that if I took you away, you would eventually leave me. . . ."

She tried to pull him up by threading her fingers through his hair, but her strength wasn't sufficient. "Wes." He finally looked at her, moved to sit beside her on the bed. "Wes," she repeated softly, "my life is with you—wherever that is."

They stared at one another for moments of excruciating happiness, all barriers gone. They would still mourn for the child they had lost, but they would mourn together. Wes finally broke the contact, his eyes closing as he lowered his head to touch his lips against hers, lightly, gently, reverently. There was still so much to be said, but it was all inconsequential when compared to the silent love and security they had now discovered.

A throat was suddenly and very gruffly cleared from the doorway. "I'm sorry, Mr. Adams," Doc Ricter advised quietly, "but your wife absolutely has to get some rest."

"Yes, she does." Wes released her hand and stood immediately. Doc Ricter tactfully disappeared, and Wes bent to touch her lips one last time. "I'll be here first thing in the morning," he whispered against her mouth. "I love you."

Sloan savored the taste of lips that knew passion and tenderness. "I love you," she whispered back, knowing that he believed her, knowing that they would both say the words over and over during their lifetime together, and both be fully aware of the depth of the emotion that lay behind them.

Sloan closed her eyes while still feeling his touch. She was sinking into a haze, losing herself to the sleep of sedation, but his touch lingered. The pain of loss and sadness was still with her, but so much less now that it was shared. Her husband had given her rest. He had given her love; he had accepted love.

One day her sister would tell her how her giant of a man had fallen into oblivion with the fear of her loss, and she would smile with tender adoration.

But that was in the future. Now she slept with the memory of his gentle, sustaining lips against hers.

EPILOGUE

As she swirled and floated with grace, with beauty, she was mercury; she was the wind, so fluid and light that she was ethereal, a goddess of the clouds upon which she appeared to hover. As always with her, she was a creature of the music, a dancer by instinct, a woman of regal beauty which the passage of time merely served to enhance.

To most who watched her, she was untouchable magic. An illusion of splendor to view, but never to capture.

And yet she had been captured, by one man in the audience.

He too was ageless. His presence would always be noted; till the day he died he would be petitioned for autographs, advice, appearances, and opinions.

It was also his name that blazed outside on the marquee. It was the prestigious Adams Dance Company that the audience had come to view, although the audience was not necessarily aware that the Adams who would be remembered as a football hero was the same who owned the dance company.

It didn't really matter.

At the performance's end, he cordially signed autographs, but his mind was not with his automatic action. He was anxious to get backstage.

She had teasingly promised him a surprise, and he had been about to go crazy even while seduced by the performance.

Backstage, she was quickly changing into street clothes, a secret smile on her lips—her mind also absent as she replied to others. She was eager to see her husband; she had marvelous news for him. Intimate, wonderful news.

Wes tapped lightly on his wife's door, then stuck his head inside. She was just brushing out her hair; her eyes met his in the mirror and she smiled. "Come in for a second," she said, dropping her brush and swirling in a circle to display the soft folds of the beige silk skirt she wore. "Like it?" she inquired.

"Umm, very much," he assured her, brows raising as she finished her twirl in his arms, planting both hands on his chest and giving him a mysterious, tantalizing smile. He caught her wrists. "Okay, minx," he charged. "I love the outfit, but why so dressy? And what's this secret? I've been going nuts the entire show."

Sloan laughed, unperturbed by his determined demand.

"I'm 'dressy,'" she informed him, "because you're taking me somewhere elegant for a late supper. And"—she ran her fingers lightly over his lapel—"after you've suitably wined and dined your hardworking wife, you'll be in on the secret."

"Un-unh," Wes shook his head. "Now."

"I'll compromise." Sloan chuckled. "As soon as you've ordered the champagne, I'll tell you."

Sloan let out a startled gasp as she felt a vise clamp on her wrist—and her feet suddenly fly across the room. "Hey!" she protested laughingly.

"I'm compromising," Wes explained patiently, "but let's get there."

With stern patience, he did wait for the champagne. Then, when the waiter had moved on, he leaned his frame over the table and his eyes challenged hers. His patience was at an end. "Okay, Sloan, out with it."

She didn't hedge a minute longer. "I'm pregnant."

She saw the frown creep into his brow, the worry and concern wrinkle his forehead. She loved him for it.

"Sloan," he began carefully, taking her fingers into his. "I'm happy, of course; you know what this means to me, but not enough to take any risks. We have three children; we've discussed this before—"

"Wes!" Sloan pressed a finger against his lips. "Don't worry, please don't worry." In a hurry to assure him, she began to trip over her words. "I've known for some time. . . . I waited to tell you to make sure. . . . Wes, I'm past the real danger point, and I had ultrasound today. Everything is fine. I promise."

He caught her hand, kissing the palm, then each finger. His

eyes met hers; the love and joy she saw in their green depths were all that she would need to sustain her for a lifetime, come what may.

"When," he asked, his voice absurdly shaky.

"April." She smiled.

"Oh, Sloan," he murmured, clasping her hand to his cheek. "You have to be so very careful. I don't think I could bear the thought of losing you again—"

"I intend to be very careful," she said softly, the fingers she held moving against his cheek. Was it possible that he could love her so very much? That all their trials had come to this magnificent result? The past—the time they had spent crossing in the night but never touching—was now so worthwhile. It made their lives so infinitely more precious; it made them both realize how important it was to always value the love that they had learned to share.

Suddenly stern, Wes lowered his voice, still holding her hand, but clasping it firmly. "I don't think I've ever been happier in my life, Sloan, but this will be it—I want your promise. A son or a daughter will be wonderful—but then we will have four. No more risks, promise."

Sloan twisted her lips into a wry smile. "I'd like to promise, Wes, but—"

"No 'buts,' " he said sternly.

"Wes!" she chuckled, eyes wide. "I'm not trying to dispute you, but I can't change what already is."

"What are you talking about?"

Sloan took a moment to refill their champagne glasses. "I think you're going to need a drink," she told him sagely.

He accepted his glass from her fingers, his green gaze wary upon her face. "I have my drink."

"Well . . ." Sloan took a sip of her own champagne. "I told you I had been to the doctor . . . or did I? I'm not sure. By my own choice, not his—he says I'm as healthy as ever—I've decided to curtail the dancing for a while. Tonight was the last performance I'll be doing with the company until next summer—"

"Sloan," Wes interrupted, "I approve, I'm glad to hear all this, but why do I need the drink?"

"Because we are going to have five children," she explained

369

with a guileless smile. Laughing at his stunned confusion, she lightly tapped his cheek. "Twins, Wes. We're having twins."

"Twins." He repeated the word.

"Twins." She agreed.

"Wow," he said blankly.

"Aren't you happy?"

The slight edge of nervousness in her voice spurred him out of his shock. Oblivious to any other patrons in the restaurant, he inched around the booth and enveloped her into his embrace, claiming her lips fully with both tenderness and passion, love and desire. Sloan had no objection. Her lips parted beneath his as they always would, savoring his love afresh each time.

At long last he broke away. He lifted a champagne glass to be shared between them. "To our twins," he murmured, his eyes caressing her with his love, "to our family of five," he continued, his voice lowering to the husky sound of velvet she would always thrill to, "but most of all, my darling, to you. A dream of a lifetime come true."

Wes started to sip the champagne, but Sloan held him back. "Wait a minute," she murmured, lashes lowering as she lifted the glass to him. "To you, Wes." Her eyes raised back to his. "To knights in white armor who do come along!"

"To us!" Drawing her into the firm shelter of his arm, he was finally able to sip his champagne.